What the Cats of Kakislane Know

A Tale of the Seven World Dominion

Eileen R Hickman

Shadowed Word Press

To Lizzie and Spencer
With All My Love
These Cats are for you.

And in Memory of Sir Ivanhoe and Topaz
Who taught me what it means to love and be loved by a cat friend.

ENJOY MORE OF EILEEN R HICKMAN'S STORIES

To get updates on new stories in the Seven World Dominion, sign up for Eileen's monthly newsletter at www.eileenrhickman.com. As a thankyou gift, you'll receive the free story, *Dragon Light*, which introduces you to the first world in the Dominion, Sek-Nar, and to the dragons who rule there.

Next, get your first glimpse of the second and third worlds, Luxera and Exalton, with the novella, *At the Boundary Between Daylight and Shadow*. In the novella, a resistance fighter on Exalton must battle the Dark Spinner government to free the recruits it is her duty to protect.

In the same volume with *At the Boundary Between Daylight and Shadow*, you'll also find the short story, *Tendrils of Shadow*. This story finds a Light Spinner on Luxera in a desperate struggle to resist the shadow. Can she find a reason to hold onto the light, or will she succumb to the darkness threatening to envelop her?

Contents

KAKISLANE INTERIOR

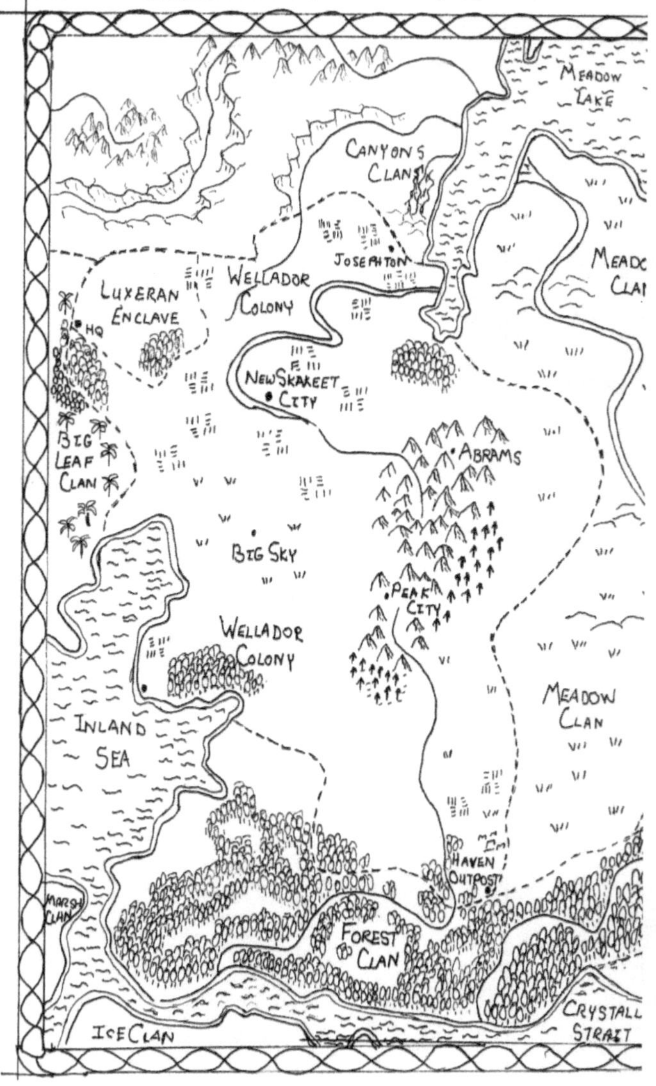

CAT CLANS AND WELLADOR COLONY

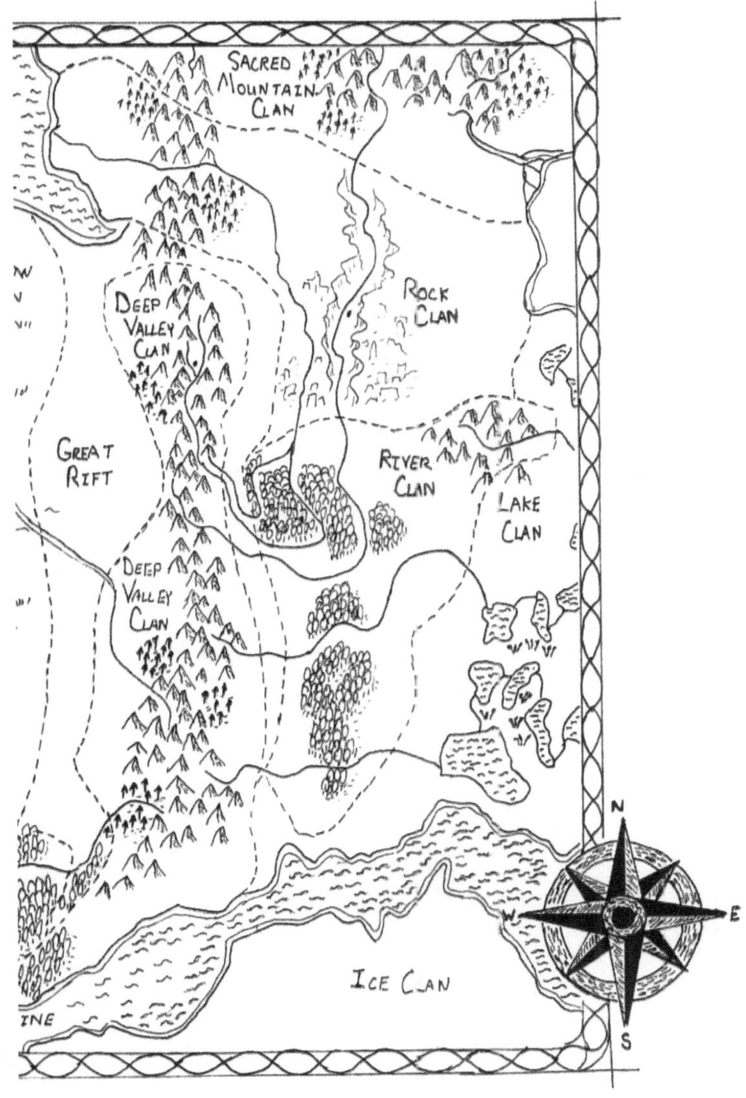

1

TRAYLE

From the void of space, Kakislane gleamed in the light of its sun, green and beige and aloof, a world that did not give up its secrets easily. Fajora surged toward it, as if to grasp it and wring those secrets from it forcibly.

She knew Kakislane, as much as any outsider knew this world of enigmatic cats and owls and almost equally reticent humans. Here she had spent years of service—happy years, most of them—and here she had experienced her greatest calamity.

Fajora perceived the splashes of color that indicated Kakislane's mountains, valleys, meadows, and forests as she searched for the Wellador Colony, and, more specifically, for the Luxeran enclave in a tiny corner of colony territory. She perceived, but did not see, not precisely. Traveling in the form of spinning light, she had no eyes with which to see.

No eyes to shed tears, either. No heart to accelerate, no stomach to flutter, no arms and legs to grow weak and tremble. This form, in which her physical characteristics dissolved into the pure energy of light, blunted her and allowed her to hold grief and anger at bay.

She did not know if she could maintain this control when she landed and resumed her solid physical form. Would she remain calm, or would the memory of the turmoil during her last days here with Jayzam overwhelm her? She would find out soon, for the orb of the world grew large and the land rushed up to meet her, the enclave clear now in her perception.

Fajora avoided the well-groomed, level landing space near the cottages and training dormitory. Most agents landed here, but doing so would subject her to immediate attention, both from her contact agent and from any other agents who loitered in the area, giving her no privacy to gather her wits and assess her emotions.

She knew of an alternate landing site, a small, uneven, overgrown area below the escarpment. Too near the boundary with Big Leaf Clan for comfort, it had been abandoned by the time Fajora and Jayzam left Kak-islane two years ago, but the official records still listed it as a recognized landing pad. Fajora had been sure to check before she left Luxera.

She headed for this lower site. The junior agents assigned to meet her expected her at the upper, well-maintained landing area. Even if they saw her light as she zoomed through the atmosphere and detected her aura as soon as she coalesced, they would need a few minutes to reach her down below. Minutes she required to establish emotional composure.

She found the site without difficulty and slowed her spin, coming down easily. As soon as she touched the ground, she began reforming her physical shape, feet first and with slow, deliberate care. The red boundary marker stuck up from the tall grass only a meter and a half in front of her. If a cat watched near the border, she didn't want to startle it or provoke aggressive behavior.

She let her eyes and ears finish forming while her arms and legs, though mostly solid, continued to tingle with light so she could translate back for a quick escape if necessary. A hint of darkness touched her mind; she recognized this touch as the aura of a Dark Spinner. Pausing the process of coalescence, she strained for a clear sense of the dark aura, for its location and a sense of personality, but it dissipated before she could get a fix on it.

Shaking off the unease left by this brief touch, Fajora scanned the thick vegetation along the boundary, her gaze snagging on a pair of unblinking yellow eyes. Cat's eyes. Above the eyes, above a white and orange forehead with black markings, a pair of black-tipped ears twitched as the cat watched her. The rest of the creature's body remained hidden behind a screen of shrubbery, leaving Fajora to guess its size and gender.

No sounds came from within the shrubbery. No growls, no rustling indicating the cat was shifting into attack position. For the moment, it seemed content to watch her. Continuing to solidify her body, Fajora held her light ready until she was confident the cat would not attack. All the while, her mind raced. She had spoken to a Big Leaf Clan cat once before, in an official capacity, when a Dark Spinner had landed in their territory. This was different. She had no business with the clan now, but a chance to speak to a cat was not to be missed. If only she knew how to begin.

As soon as she completed coalescence, she spoke, keeping her voice low and calm. "Greetings and honor to Big Leaf Clan."

The cat blinked once. Did it acknowledge her greeting or warn of attack? It emitted no accompanying growl, a promising sign. Strict adherence to the treaty prevented the cats from crossing the boundary for any reason, but with deadly teeth and claws involved, Fajora preferred not to count on such restraint. She tried to calm her pounding heart, hoping her eye flecks did not swirl in a dizzying pattern that might alarm her visitor.

The cat did not attack, but it also did not answer her greeting. It remained motionless, without blinking again, but its ears twitched. She had its attention. But what did it see as it watched her? An intruder? A tool to rid its world of Dark Spinners? A curiosity of no real significance?

Whatever the cat thought about her, Fajora felt they shared a moment of acknowledgment. She wanted to build on that connection, but she couldn't think of anything else to say that might elicit a response.

Movement up on the escarpment at Fajora's back warned her of an approaching Luxeran agent. She felt the agent's aura first, before she heard the rustle of footsteps moving toward the pathway down to the landing site.

She leaned forward, wet her lips, blurted the first thing that came to her mind. "Please relay my greetings to your leaders. I've just returned to Kakislane after a long absence. I hope we'll meet again."

Still no response. Of course not. She hadn't said anything worth responding to. But the cat's ears twitched. It was listening.

The Luxeran aura drew near.

"Agent Fajora?"

"Yes." Fajora turned away from the boundary.

The agent scrambled down the path, arms flailing to either side, transiting to a half-spin as the way became treacherous. She regained her solid form at the bottom and flashed an impish grin. She wore the uniform of a full agent, but her flushed face, her bronze-red curly hair escaping its braid, her boyish figure, all suggested a girl barely into her twenties.

"I'm Agent Trayle. Welcome to Kakislane. I'm to show you to your quarters." The agent might be young, but her voice and her posture bristled with confidence. Her amber eye flecks, swirling in a lazy, controlled pattern, confirmed her poise.

"Thank you. I'll be right with you."

Fajora turned back toward the boundary. The leafy screen swayed unbroken in the breeze. In the way of the cats, the watcher had vanished without a sound. A bird landed on a nearby bush and trilled a song, a sure sign the cat was gone and not merely concealed by the vegetation. Wanting to be certain, Fajora stood motionless, focused on the foliage, until Agent Trayle touched her shoulder.

"Agent Fajora, if you please. What are you staring at? You're too close to the boundary. Come with me, this way."

"A Big Leaf cat was here." Fajora let the wonder of it flood her awareness. One saw the cats only if the cats allowed it. She did not accept this gift lightly.

"A cat? Where?"

"It's gone now."

"It probably wanted to warn you away from the boundary. Come up above, now, please."

"Yes, yes." Fajora straightened her spine and lifted her chin. "Agent Trayle, right? Tell me, Agent Trayle, did you notice a dark aura while on your way to the landing site?"

Trayle's eye flecks swirled with increased speed, but she showed no other sign of surprise. "No. Why do you ask?"

"I felt something as I coalesced. It was fleeting, but I'm sure it was a dark aura." She wasn't entirely sure, but if she wanted the incident to be taken seriously, she must not voice uncertainty.

"Well, I didn't notice anything." Agent Trayle repeated, "but I'll report it for you. Maybe send word to the colony. Their sensors might have picked up something."

"Yes, why don't you do that right away, please."

"As soon as I get you checked in. But come now. We're too close to the boundary."

"We're fine. If we're not across, we're not too close. But I would like to get settled."

Without waiting for Trayle to guide her, Fajora climbed the steep path to the top of the escarpment. She waited while Trayle scrambled up behind her. The girl resorted to a half-spin again, to manage the ascent, and Fajora looked away, rolling her eyes.

Someone had let physical training protocols slide. She couldn't imagine any justification for the lapse. Inadequate physical training resulted in injury or, in extreme situations, death, especially for inexperienced agents. Senior agents had a responsibility to ensure the youngsters had the tools they needed to succeed. She must make a point to investigate this once she settled into her new job. After she resolved her more pressing business.

Trayle led her to one of the private cottages on the edge of the enclave compound. Fajora deliberately averted her gaze from the larger cottages farther on as she looked at her new abode. At ten meters by eight, divided into two rooms plus a tiny washroom, it was half the size of the cottage she and Jayzam had shared. Alone now, she had no need for so much space, and at her rank she did not have to share.

Trayle went through the inventory check with exaggerated efficiency. She bustled through the rooms, speaking too loudly and remembering only occasionally to keep her words deferential. As she stepped back out onto the small entrance porch, a fresh breeze blew into the corners of the house, and Fajora drew a deep, cleansing breath along with her cottage. She didn't plan to invite this girl for a visit any time soon.

On the way to the door, Fajora paused to shift a rocking chair to a more casual angle and make a swift appraisal of the room. Satisfied, she joined Trayle outside.

The young agent stood at the edge of the porch with one foot on the first step. "I'm sure you'll find everything to your liking. I personally attended to your refuel basket to make sure it had that special welcoming splash." She glanced back toward the interior of the cottage with a grin and took another step down, as if planning a quick getaway. "I'm pretty sure I thought of everything, but look me up if there's anything else you need. Agent Fazok must like you. He's given me leave to procure anything you want."

"More lamps. At least two. Three, if you can manage it."

"What do you need more—"

"And whom do I approach to arrange a special assignment? Head Agent Fazok, or is someone else handling such things now?" She normally wouldn't ask this type of question of a junior agent. There were more appropriate channels for inquiry. But sometimes stepping around the protocols provided information without drawing the notice of the wrong people.

Trayle's brow furrowed. "Agent Kinovic, usually, but I don't think he'd be too receptive to that with a new agent. He only allows agents with council status or above to make requests."

"And I hold special advisor status. Last I checked, that qualifies."

"Ooh." The girl's eyes widened, and she leaned close to ask in a conspiratorial whisper, "How'd you manage that? Agent Jiselle's been trying for over a year to move up to council status, and here you are, just arrived, and you get the special advisor slot. Jiselle's going to be spinning wild for days when she hears this."

Fajora pursed her lips and stifled a sharp retort, opting for a more measured response. "Experience, my dear. I've earned this position. I started my first rotation here on Kakislane before you were born. When I left two years ago, I held Kinovic's job. He reported to me, and I controlled duty rosters and special assignments."

"Wow!" Agent Trayle's grin widened. "You don't look old enough for all that. You're so fit. And no gray yet in that lovely blue hair. But why did you leave if you had such a splendid position?"

Fajora almost laughed out loud. Unconventional and without inhibitions, unafraid of flattery, this girl tempted Fajora to respond to the compliment about her age and appearance. She resisted the temptation, knowing this child-agent not only deserved, but probably also needed, a reprimand for her impertinence. Any adequately trained junior agent should know better than to offer such personal comments and questions to a superior officer. Perhaps the enclave needed a refresher course in chain of command protocols along with the enhanced physical training.

Trayle still grinned, but her eyes held a hint of uncertainty. The amber flecks swirled erratically, which suggested she recognized she'd overstepped. Fajora offered a calculated smile, cordial but not too warm, and patted Trayle's hand, which rested on the railing.

"A word of advice. Unless you know otherwise, always assume any agent you meet is older and wiser than they appear, and has more authority than you expect. That way, you'll treat everyone with an appropriate measure of respect and not get yourself into trouble. As for my reasons for leaving, they are personal, not open to discussion. That's all. You may go."

Dismissing Trayle rather than letting her wander away on her own volition started the retraining process. Or so Fajora hoped.

The young agent raised her hand as if to protest, but then dropped it. "Yes, ma'am. Let me know if you find anything missing from your cottage."

"Thank you, Agent Trayle. I will."

She watched the young woman's progress down the hill toward the group of buildings that comprised the enclave headquarters. Trayle walked lightly, with flair, as if she might at any moment begin to dance rather than merely walk. Fajora's lips twitched in a suppressed smile. She looked forward to more encounters with this young agent. They would tangle, she decided, especially if Fajora implemented the training she had been making mental notes about. They would tangle, and Trayle would grin the whole time. Fajora must deal with this young woman with a firm hand before she got out of control.

Fajora's smile faded as she eyed the headquarters buildings. Trayle's behavior might be an aberration, a consequence of an unquenchable personality, or it might be the first indication of trouble in the enclave. Would she find, after two years, that the corruption infiltrating service headquarters on Luxera was sneaking in here as well?

She must investigate, cautiously, but she could take time to settle in first.

With Trayle out of the way, Fajora turned back to her cottage door. Time to unpack. She stumbled and caught herself on the doorframe. Her limbs trembled, reminding her of how depleted her energy was after her long spin through the void. She sucked in a deep, stabilizing breath and made straight for the table where her refuel basket waited, the one Trayle had attended to personally. Beside the basket stood a pitcher of fresh water with a glass, already filled, beside it. Odd that Trayle had poured the water for her, as if expecting her to be too weak to do it for herself.

After a sip of the delicious, citrus-laced water, Fajora ate her way through a pile of fresh honey wafers with nut butter and consumed a tangy fruit salad. She sampled a plate of sliced fruit drizzled with cream, and a dish of honey-dipped nuts. Finally, as energy returned to her limbs with a pleasing surge, she turned to the last dish, a collection of sliced vegetables slathered with a cheesy spread. She remembered this dish. The enclave cook, who had been here for most of Fajora's previous assignment, had developed this spread as one of her specialties. Fajora's mouth watered.

She lifted a spear of squash and took a huge bite. It tasted exquisite, but in the next instant, fire seared her mouth. She half-expected to see flames flickering from her tongue as she dropped the squash and grabbed the waiting water glass. She emptied the glass and poured a second, downing that as well before the liquid tamed the fire in her mouth and down her throat.

Trayle's grin and her surreptitious glance through the cottage door as she told Fajora she had arranged for the refuel basket to have a special welcoming splash took on new meaning. Somehow, she had gotten into Cook's special concoction and spiced it up. No wonder Trayle had left the glass of water standing ready; she knew Fajora would need it.

The youthful agent needed to be shown her place. Her actions were so out of line, Fajora wasn't sure what her response should be. Was this typical behavior, and was Head Agent Fazok aware of it? She needed to have a talk with him. But she smiled in spite of herself as she envisioned Trayle's irrepressible grin. She would be sure to have her talk away from Kinovic's hearing. Trayle needed to have her jokester tendency checked, but she didn't need the grim response Kinovic was sure to give. She needed training, not breaking.

2

——— ● ———

A REQUEST

Refueled and energized, Fajora turned to her unpacking. Her duffle bag sat near the front door where she'd left it when Trayle showed her in. Emptying it was the work of minutes. She had learned, after numerous off-Luxera assignments, to pack light and avoid the drain of spinning from world to world with heavy luggage. She preferred to be bright and energetic when she arrived on a new world.

She had only a few articles of clothing, old favorites for relaxation in her off hours. The enclave supplied fresh uniforms, and she could supplement her off-duty clothing in one of the human shopping districts in New Skakeet City. Several shops carried clothing designed for the taller Luxeran form. Besides the clothing, and a few personal toiletry items, she carried three books, Luxeran classics not available in the humans' electronic libraries. These she placed on a table near a comfortable chair.

Finally, she pulled several framed likenesses from the bottom of her bag. Two were light-etchings by masters on Luxera. The first featured her and Jayzam on the day of their joining; the other, larger one, included their three children, their spouses, and the grandchildren. These two light-etchings went on the mantle above the fireplace.

The final frame held a photograph of Jayzam in full color. He gazed at her from the frame, a slight smile on his lips, as if he shared the room with her. No light-etching captured such startling realism. Only human technology could achieve this. Fajora was grateful for the time on

Kakislane that had allowed Jayzam to have this picture done. He would be forever with her. She gave the frame a tender caress as she placed it on the bedside table.

"I'll finish what you started, dearest. I promise."

He stared back at her, unanswering. That didn't matter. She had given him the same promise before he died. It had taken longer to get back here than she'd expected, but she was here now and ready for action. The threat to Kakislane couldn't be neutralized until someone exposed it. She had made this her mission—to convince the authorities, starting with Fazok, of the true situation here.

She secured the cottage and headed down the same path Trayle had followed earlier. Time to check in with Fazok and find Kinovic. Delaying would not make him any easier to deal with.

She paused on the path to take in the administrative complex below her. The late afternoon sun cast a warm glow over the stone and timber buildings, making them appear homey rather than efficient. She thought of the Big Leaf Clan cat she had seen at the landing site. If it stood beside her now, what would its impression be?

Not homey, certainly, for the cat's idea of home would be very different. What then? Settled? A fixed entity, here to stay whether the cat wished it or not? Possessing an air of self-satisfied certainty?

Fajora saw all these things as she gazed at the complex and pictured the man she was about to confront, and a wave of uneasiness passed through her. Had the Luxerans forgotten they were here by invitation because they provided a service to this world. The Luxeran Anti-Shadow Service and its Light Spinner agents existed as penance for the darkness they has loosed on the Dominion.

Even I think I belong here. Feel it is my right. But what would the cat say?

Fajora shook herself out of her reverie. She would think about this more and try to develop a more measured ideology concerning this world and her own presence here, but right now she had business to attend to. She continued down the path, and the imaginary cat faded into the recesses of her mind.

She passed under a stone arch into the inner courtyard and hesitated near the door to Fazok's office, trying to plan this first meeting after such a long furlough. Should she make it a personal greeting time, with inquiries about Fazok's family and the usual chit-chat? Or should she go over Kinovic's head and present Fazok with her mission request?

That would be certain to offend Kinovic. But as head of the enclave, Fazok had the power to grant her request, and he would regard it as a natural step, since they had worked so closely together during her last posting here.

Before she decided, a door opened across the courtyard—the door to her old office, now Kinovic's office—and both Fazok and Kinovic appeared. They headed straight toward Fajora.

"Fajora." Fazok took her hands and squeezed them in a fatherly manner. His hands were cold, his grip weak, but before Fajora could question him, he dropped her hands and rushed on with his greeting. "Glad you made it. Expected you'd be busy getting settled in and what-not. Yes, hmm. But here you are. Coming to see me, are you?"

"I longed for a glimpse of your face after all this time."

Fazok beamed. "Of course. I'm delighted. Come on in. You, too, Kinovic. We can talk about Fajora's duty assignment after we catch up a bit. Get that done while we're here, hmm?"

He reached for the door handle. His hand shook. As he steadied it, he gave Fajora a surreptitious glance. She returned his glance with careful scrutiny, noticing things she should have seen at once—the pallor of his skin, pale even for a Luxeran and sagging around his jowls, his stooped posture, his slow movements.

He had the door open and motioned for her to enter. "Come in, hmm. So good to have you back, my dear. And how are the children?

Surprised you wanted to leave them again after they lost their father and all."

Fajora stared. What an odd, muddled thing for Fazok to say. He knew all about Fajora's family, knew the children had lived many years in the loving care of relatives while Jayzam and Fajora had come and gone between various off-world assignments. They had thrived under these conditions and needed Fajora even less now that they were no longer children.

"The children are grown up and have children of their own," she told him. "They'll hardly miss me." Fajora sat on the edge of the chair Fazok waved her into and gave his office a swift appraisal.

Nothing had changed in the two years since she last sat in this chair. The light etching of his family from a hundred years ago still held a place of prominence on his desk. On the wall opposite the window, the photograph of his wife, taken by a human artist before her last illness, held the place of honor. Familiar, well-worn books filled the bookcase, blanketed by a layer of dust. The same woven carpet covered the floor, in excellent condition except for the worn spot by the window. Fazok must spend a fair number of hours standing there for it to have become so threadbare in only two years.

"Right." Fazok moved to the window and pushed it open. As a cool breeze wafted in, he pulled a handkerchief from his pocket and wiped his forehead. "Well, we're glad to have you back. The question is, what are we going to do with you?"

Kinovic took a seat in the third chair across from the desk, leaving one chair empty between himself and Fajora. He spoke before Fajora could answer, his cold voice matching his stiff posture.

"You don't need to concern yourself with that, sir. It's my job to assign duties to the enclave agents. Agent Fajora is no different. I'll find tasks for her that will be appropriate for the settling-in period. No need to worry about her being overwhelmed with work."

"Hmm." Fazok's gaze did not leave the view out the window, but his hunched shoulders straightened and he raised his chin. "Not exactly what I had in mind. I think I'll take Fajora in hand myself. Still a thing or two she should learn from me before we turn her loose."

Fajora blinked and gave a tiny headshake, struck again by how odd Fazok's conversation was. When she left two years ago, she was fully trained to step into Fazok's job. Now he suggested she needed more training.

"Are you undermining me, sir?" Kinovic's voice held a cold threat in its tones.

Fazok's shoulders slumped, and he walked with a slow step toward the desk. When he reached it, he grasped its edge and felt for the chair, sinking into it with a sigh.

"What do you think, Fajora?" Fazok pulled a writing tablet forward, though he didn't reach for a pen. "You hold equal rank with Kinovic, but this enclave is too small for two positions at that rank. Where shall we assign you?"

Fajora felt Kinovic's gaze on her face, a gaze as hot as his voice was cold. Did his expression contain a warning? A threat? If Fajora asked for Kinovic's job, Fazok would give it to her, earning both of them Kinovic's undying enmity. But she didn't want Kinovic's job. Not yet, anyway.

She would have preferred to make her request to Fazok first, without Kinovic listening in, but Fazok did not leave her that option.

"I'm hoping for a special assignment, sir."

"What assignment?" Kinovic's voice was sharp.

"Investigation of claims that the cat clans, Rock Clan and River Clan in particular, are harboring Dark Spinners. Are, perhaps, even ruled by them. And that humans are there, under DS rule as well. Some of them against their will."

Fazok lifted a hand, as if preparing to speak, but again Kinovic forestalled him.

"What claims? No one has come to me with such a wild story. Have you heard any such crazy tales, sir?"

"Well, hmm. Ah, no. Not recently, that is."

"This claim is two years old," Fajora said, "and to my knowledge, it has yet to receive adequate attention."

"Two years!" Kinovic's eyes widened. "You don't mean Jayzam's ravings after he returned from his *unauthorized* foray into clan territory?"

"That's precisely what I'm referring to."

"He was injured. Dying. Delirious. You surely didn't believe him?"

"Of course, I did. He was not delirious." Fajora leaned toward Fazok, gripping the arms of the chair as she fought a dizzying wave of grief and anger. No time for that now. "Sir, you spoke with him. You can attest to his lucidity. And I know no one followed up on his debriefing, or made any genuine attempt to verify it. I've seen the reports."

"Those reports are classified," Kinovic said. "What breach of security allowed you to see them?"

"No breach. As the plaintiff, Jayzam had a right to receive the reports. So, I know that you, Kinovic, shut down any suggestion of an investigation. I've been wondering why for two years. Perhaps you'd like to explain."

"Yes, explain." Fazok's voice was faint. His pale skin shaded toward gray. He lifted his handkerchief with a trembling hand and wiped his forehead, but his eye flecks marched in a determined pattern.

"I didn't think it necessary to include all my conversations with Light Spinners and humans in my report," Kinovic answered. "No Light Spinners had any corroborating evidence, not even a sense of unidentified auras. And the humans are an untrustworthy, irrational people. But I assured myself that all their citizens were accounted for. No recent reports of anyone gone missing. No complaints by distraught relatives or neighbors. Jayzam's story had no foundation. He, like you, Fajora, had a dangerous fascination with the cat clans. He trespassed in clan territory and made up a story about Dark Spinners and humans to justify the transgression, no doubt embellished in his delirium. No sane Luxeran believed his tale. The authorities on Luxera least of all."

Fajora glared at Kinovic. "Jayzam expected you to say that. It doesn't negate what he saw, and it doesn't change my responsibility. I promised Jayzam I'd follow up for him. I'm sure he didn't imagine the humans. He knew what he saw. Sir, you know I'm right about my husband."

Fajora turned toward Fazok in time to see him lean over in his chair and begin a slow topple toward the floor. She translated into a spin so fast she made herself dizzy, reaching him just in time to pull him into her light before he hit the floor.

She coalesced back to physical form much more slowly, depositing Fazok back in his chair as she did so and steadying both him and herself, as she fought to regain her equilibrium and calm her swirling stomach. Fazok's eyes were dull, his eye flecks swirling in a sluggish pattern. Sweat beaded on his forehead.

"Is Agent Paltoz still the medic here?" Fajora asked Kinovic.

"Yes."

"Go get him. Now."

When Paltoz arrived, Fazok roused a little. He endured Paltoz's examination with evident impatience while Kinovic hovered in the background.

"I don't know what's wrong," Paltoz said. "A virus, maybe. I still don't understand the pathogens on this world."

"Which is why I will go to the hospital in New Skakeet City tomorrow," Fazok announced. "The doctors there do understand and will have a treatment."

"You'll trust your life to those human doctors?" Kinovic asked. "They're as likely to kill you as to heal you."

"No, I don't think so," Paltoz said. "I believe it's the best course of action."

"Sir, I protest," Kinovic said.

"Which is why you won't be accompanying me." Fazok raised his head to stare at Kinovic. "As of now, I'm transferring Fajora into my personal service. She'll take me to the hospital tomorrow. Agent Trayle will join us to run errands and ferry correspondence. Now go. I'm sure you have work to do, hmm? Paltoz, Fajora, help me to my cottage. I need to rest."

Fajora leaned down to take Fazok's arm, trying to ignore Kinovic's glare. She and Paltoz helped Fazok to his feet while Kinovic stood back, watching but not offering to help. As Paltoz mopped the perspiration from Fazok's forehead, Kinovic leaned close to Fajora's ear.

"I think it best if you supervise the junior agents for a while. After all your experience, you must possess a great deal of wisdom to pass along to them. When you return from the hospital tomorrow, I'll have the documents ready for your signature. You'll start right away. And no more talk of missions into clan territory or I'll report you as unfit to headquarters on Luxera."

"You wouldn't dare. You can't. I'm working directly for Fazok now." Fajora sputtered the words through the white-hot haze that clouded her vision for a moment. Her free hand swirled with light, a short step away from spinning a weapon.

"I can and I will. Things have changed in the two years since you left. On paper, Fazok's head of this enclave, but I'm the one in charge. I make the decisions and send the reports. You don't want to challenge me. I'll take great delight in bringing you down." Kinovic smirked, spun on his heel, and strode through the door.

Fajora stared after him until Fazok's shambling attempt to walk reclaimed her attention. Kinovic was right about one thing. Fazok was in no condition to lead the enclave. And countermanding Kinovic's orders without the older man's support would be difficult. Damaging to her career, or worse.

"We'll have to spin him to his cottage," Paltoz said. "Can you take him while I swing around to my office for additional supplies?"

"Yes." Fajora pulled Fazok into a spin. As she carried him toward his cottage, she sensed his aura's determination wavering in the face of unrelenting exhaustion and knew she couldn't expect help from him, even if he wanted to support her, which was by no means certain. Whatever she did she would have to do on her own, regardless of the consequences. And try to discover, in the process, what drove Kinovic to oppose her.

At Fazok's spacious cottage, she settled him in a comfortable chair and removed his boots. Noting that he was sweating again, she opened a window to let in a fresh breeze, then found a blanket to cover him, to prevent a chill. A few minutes later, Paltoz arrived at the door, his arms full of bags and bottles. As he arranged his supplies on the table, Trayle also arrived, a covered tray in her hands.

"I heard about Fazok's collapse," she explained. "I thought food might strengthen him. I brought enough for all of you. For dinner."

"Nothing spicy, I hope." Fajora kept her voice neutral, but couldn't help being pleased at the blush that crept into the girl's face.

"No, ma'am. Just broth and honey cakes with nut butter. And fresh fruit and vegetables. No splash." Her blush faded, and her eye flecks swirled with irrepressible mirth.

Fajora watched her, nonplussed. How would she keep this agent under control?

Fazok, gaining awareness, motioned toward Trayle. "Thank you, Trayle. I'll try to eat in a while. Meanwhile, go to your quarters and pack. You'll go to New Skakeet City in the morning with Agent Fajora and myself. The hospital."

"Hospital?" Trayle's eyes flicked between Fazok and Fajora, and then to Paltoz. "It's that bad, sir?"

"I'm afraid so," Fazok said. "Or at least, I hope not, hmm, but taking no chances. Don't want to throw you and Fajora to the cats any sooner than necessary."

"I understand, sir. I'll be ready. Send for me if you need anything tonight." She paused with her hand on the doorknob and glanced at Fajora. "I hope the lamps work out for you." With an impish grin, she pranced out the door.

After Trayle left, Fajora pulled a chair close to Fazok, balancing a tray of broth, honey cakes, and vegetables on her knees. As she dug into her food, hungry despite her large snack earlier, she asked, "Sir, why Agent Trayle? She's a jokester. Can she understand anything serious or take appropriate action when needed? You might be seriously ill. Perhaps someone more senior should go."

Fazok gave her a weak smile. "Got you, did she, hmm?"

"Sir?"

"Was it a toad in your washbowl? Or the wrong linens on your bed? But no, you haven't been to bed yet, so it couldn't be that, hmm."

"Hot spices in cook's cheese sauce. Turned my throat inside out. But if you know about this tendency, why do you put up with it? Why do you want her on your team tomorrow?"

Fazok swallowed a spoonful of the medicine Paltoz offered him, then patted Fajora's hand with a fond smile. "Don't make the mistake of assessing her on those outward things. A model agent can be rotten on the inside. You've been on Luxera for what? Two years? Dealing with Headquarters? You know that."

Fajora started. How could he know what she had put up with, the corruption she had discovered as she worked to get this assignment? Unless he did know. He had been in the service a lot longer than she had and knew its inner workings. She suddenly recalled the letters, written on official letterhead but marked for his eyes only, delivered to him weekly during most of Fajora's previous posting here.

"Meanwhile," Fazok continued, "a saucy attitude, maybe even a touch of rebellion against protocols, can hide a heart of utmost loyalty."

"Agent Trayle?"

"Yes. Agent Trayle. Besides, she puts Kinovic off-balance. What better reason? And she understands what she's doing. I suggest you take lessons from her. There's more than one way to accomplish a mission, especially when you need to keep it quiet."

Fajora stared at him, startled, but with growing comprehension. She ate in silence, trying to imagine ways Trayle's irreverence might be useful.

Paltoz drew near with another tray and helped Fazok eat. When the dishes were empty, Paltoz caught Fajora's attention and pointed toward the door. "I gave him something to help him sleep. I'll need to get him to bed before it takes effect. Go get some rest. You'll need plenty of energy to spin him to New Skakeet City tomorrow. He won't be able to do it on his own."

"I shouldn't leave him tonight."

"I'll stay with him. He'll be fine."

"And if he isn't?"

"I promise I'll send word."

Fazok patted Fajora's hand again and waved her toward the door. As she left, Paltoz brought night clothes to Fazok's chair and lifted him up to remove his uniform. Fajora closed the door to give him privacy and strode up the path to her own cottage in the growing dusk.

Fajora stepped into the dark cottage and snapped on the overhead light, grateful for the technology on this world. Luxerans had nothing like it. Didn't want it, in truth. And Fajora accepted that, but she enjoyed the conveniences while on Kakislane. Only the Wellador had power so readily available and groomed for so many uses, so that one could flip a switch and have instant light.

She gasped as she looked around her sitting area. Besides the one lamp that had been in this room when she left, there were now—how many? Four, five, she counted. No, another one on the floor beside the rocking chair. And there, in the corner behind the table, yet another. Seven lamps. A note lay on the table, a few words scrawled across its top: *Hope these are adequate. Let me know if you need more. Agent T.*

With trepidation she crossed the floor, brushing against lampshades as she went, and peeked through the door to the bedroom. Ah. Only the original one lamp in here. She made her way back to the rocking chair, where she sat looking at the lamps.

One had a base of curved metal with streaks of bright greens and yellows along each side. Hideous. Another, a frilly affair, white with pink flowers painted on its base, included a pink shade, frothy with lace. Next to it, a purple and turquoise stone lamp created a jarring contrast. Instinct told her Trayle might actually like that one. The longer Fajora examined it, the more her lips twitched in amusement. Finally, she gave in and laughed out loud, a great, cleansing, belly laugh. Fazok was right. If this girl acted the trickster toward Kinovic with half the glee she directed toward Fajora, she would be worth all the aggravation she caused.

And a closer perusal of the lamps revealed several that were usable, even beautiful. One of cast iron, tall enough to stand on the floor by her chair. Another of such simple design, it could go anywhere and provide light without calling attention to itself. And one with a base carved in the shape of an owl. She got up for a detailed inspection. She had seen a Kakislane owl only once, and it had been a brief glimpse, but the vision had stayed with her in every detail. This lamp reproduced that vision with precision and with extraordinary workmanship.

She arranged her three chosen lamps, giving the owl lamp a place of honor, where anyone entering the room could see and admire it, herself most of all. The other four lamps she shoved into the corner for Trayle to remove when they returned from the city. Perhaps she would offer the purple one to the girl in thanks for her astute choices. For she suspected

Trayle knew which lamps she would choose. The others comprised a statement.

Fatigue after her long journey through the void and the awareness that she must rise early sent Fajora scurrying to bed once she had the lamps sorted. Concern for Fazok surfaced as she lay down, but she forced it aside. She could do nothing for him tonight, and the doctors in New Skakeet City had far more skill than Luxeran physicians. She didn't need to worry yet. She found a distraction from her concern by exploring a myriad of ideas for using Trayle to confound Kinovic. The ideas swirled through her thoughts and invaded her dreams. She even forgot to cry herself to sleep this first night on Kakislane without Jayzam.

3

A STEP CLOSER

The façade of the hospital gleamed with steel and glass, its smooth surfaces reflecting the similar structure of the Colony Government Building across the street. The splashing water in a blue tiled fountain and the wind whispering through the trees clustered around the buildings broke up any harshness in the city center but could not disguise the attitude of nonchalant assurance with which these structures stood their ground.

The hospital's interior was as sleek as the outside, with an antiseptic smell that brought back memories of Fajora's last few days on Kakislane two years ago. She had been here with Jayzam until the doctors admitted defeat and sent him home to Luxera to die.

The human doctors cured many illnesses and injuries, though anything related to the light spinning abilities of the Luxerans puzzled them. Since Fazok's illness didn't appear to have any relation to spinning, Fajora turned him over the medical staff with confidence.

They put him on a floating cart and took him to a lift to transport him up to their examining rooms. At his insistence, they invited Fajora and Trayle to join them.

"Does the governor know you've admitted me?" Fazok asked as the lift doors opened on the upper floor.

"He's being informed as we speak," the orderly assured him. "He'll send a representative over soon, I'm sure."

"Good. My assistant, Agent Fajora, will have questions. I'd appreciate it if she could be given time and access to government officials while she's here. She's pursuing a line of inquiry not related to my illness, hmm. With my authorization, of course."

"I'll relay your message," the orderly said.

Fazok turned his gaze toward Fajora. His eye flecks, though sluggish, swirled in a pattern of amusement. "There are many ways to foil Kinovic, my dear. Always remember that."

The orderly moved Fazok onto an examination table and began hooking him up to various machines by way of needles, tubes, and wires. Watching, Fajora felt as gray as Fazok looked. Human medical practices were not natural, but they were more effective than Luxeran medical practices. She folded her arms over her chest, trying to stifle the urge to pull the tubes and wires away from Fazok.

A woman with a physician's badge bustled in. She took one look at Fajora and motioned her toward the door. "We have a lounge across the hall where you can wait if you prefer. It might be easier on you."

"Thank you. But I don't want to miss the governor's representative."

"We'll make sure they find you. I'll send someone to help you order refreshments. I'm guessing you need to refuel after your spin down from the enclave."

"Thank you for remembering."

"So fascinating, your Light Spinner physiology. I'm Silviann Bloch. Let me know if you need anything else."

Fajora waited a while for someone to come to the lounge. When her hunger became insistent, she walked to the shiny black wall she knew contained a control panel and touched it. It blinked into life, with lights and buttons and cryptic words flashing across its surface. Now, how to order food? It had been too long, and she had barely understood it when she was here before. Trayle probably knew how it worked, but the junior agent had not come with her to the lounge.

She still stood there, afraid to touch anything, ten minutes later when a man with a familiar, bearded face hurried into the room. The beard always struck her as odd, humorous even, but now it felt comforting in its familiarity.

"Agent Fajora? Dannel Crowner here. We met before, a few years back, at a barbeque down at the ranch. Do you remember? So good to see you again."

"I remember. Lieutenant Governor, isn't it?"

"Yes, well, not that it matters. Now, I'm guessing you want food. Yes? What will it be? Sorry I can't whip up something fresh for you. Room's not equipped with a cooking surface, but let's see. A vegetable au gratin, or a veggie wrap, or a salad. Shall we start with the au gratin?"

As she nodded, Dannel began punching buttons on the control panel. A few minutes later he placed a steaming dish in front of her and poured two glasses of the russet payo nectar Fajora remembered with great delight. She grabbed the fork as her stomach rumbled.

"Now, what's this I hear about a line of inquiry not related to Fazok's illness?" Dannel asked.

Fajora laid her fork back down on her plate. "It's a follow-up on my husband Jayzam's last mission here."

"No, don't rush." Dannel motioned toward her fork. "Eat up, but tell me when you're ready."

Dannel must know the story. He had been lieutenant governor when Jayzam embarked on his fateful mission and would have received briefings both before and after Jayzam infiltrated cat territory. He might even know more than Fajora did. But he sat patiently, watching her and waiting for her to speak.

So, between bites, Fajora recounted the story. She told it all. The disappearance of a young woman, a student from one of the boundary villages in the north part of the Wellador Colony. The unconfirmed scans by human techs suggesting Dark Spinners had spun into Rock Clan territory. The vocal dismissal of these claims by several senior enclave officials. Governor Dario asking Jayzam to look into it, quietly to avoid alerting the dissenters in the enclave. Jayzam's slow infiltration into clan territory, one short spin at a time as he tried to avoid notice. The warnings of Deep Valley Clan leaders. How Jayzam had ignored the warnings for one last spin into Rock Clan's domain. The young woman there, tied to a post, surrounded by cats. Too many cats for Jayzam to get close. His shock when he saw other humans roaming free among the cats. His greater shock when Dark Spinners arrived and the cats welcomed them with deferential treatment.

"He tried to get a closer look, but he wasn't careful enough," Fajora said. "The cats detected him and attacked. Their claws tore at his face, his chest, his arms. He managed a spin and got away, but he didn't have anything but an emergency medical kit and he'd already used up his food supplies. He couldn't hunt for natural foods with the cats on his trail, and he lost a fair amount of blood. So, he spun on lower and lower energy, until he exhausted his light just before he got out of clan territory. He staggered across the boundary near a village, where colonists found him barely alive. They brought him here and your doctors treated his wounds, but they couldn't do anything about his light. He couldn't spin, and when a Light Spinner can't spin, well . . . ." Fajora swallowed hard and blinked away tears.

"I remember the day you left to take him back to Luxera." Dannel's voice was gentle. "We all hoped he'd recover there, but he didn't, did he? Word came later that he had died."

Fajora nodded, not trusting herself to speak.

"And now you're back."

"I promised myself I'd investigate and prove him right when everyone else labeled him delusional. He warned me not to. Told me to stay away from Rock Clan. To avoid dealings with Deep Valley Clan as well. He had contact with them, and they warned him to go home, but he wouldn't tell me anything more. Only that I should stay away. I think he didn't want to feel responsible for pushing me into danger, but I'm a trained agent. Danger is part of my calling. So I promised what he never asked of me."

They sat in silence for a while after she finished. Fajora had emptied her dish. Now she noticed how all the talking had dried out her throat, and she drained her glass of nectar. Dannel rose and disposed of her dish, refilled both glasses, and brought two plates of a dark, rich-looking dessert to the table. He placed one in front of her.

"I remember all this, of course," he said as he resumed his seat. "Or most of it. I hadn't heard about the Dark Spinners being welcomed in Rock Clan. That's disturbing. But the girl, yes. Clarise Howard. One of our most brilliant engineering students. Equally gifted in medicine, with some interesting ideas. Doctor Pellar and the head of the engineering school nearly came to blows when she reached recruiting age." Dannel chuckled at the memory.

"Which did she choose? Engineering or medicine?"

"It seemed even for a while. Her propulsion theories promised to let us move as fast through the void as a Light Spinner." He held up his hand to forestall a question. "Not that we're traveling through the void. Not at all. But if we'd wanted to, she'd have figured out the speed part.

"But she also worked with natural medicine. We have records from Exalton of the remedies the Sashosans concocted with herbal substances and certain minerals. Clarise studied them extensively, hoping to find similar solutions using plants and minerals indigenous to Kakislane. The doctors founded a school of natural medicine in her name a short while after she disappeared. Some believe she wandered too far collecting plant specimens and ended up across the border. But she didn't live that close to the border, so not a plausible explanation. Not sure what happened."

Dannel fell silent, staring out the window, lost in his own musings. Fajora had to prompt him to get him talking again.

"Sir? What did Clarise decide?"

"Oh, yes." He brought his gaze back to his guest. "She accepted a fellowship with the engineering school. Such excitement over there. They hadn't had a student with so much potential in fifty years. A sweet girl, too. I'd love to see her again."

"Do you believe she's alive?"

"Interesting question." Dannel rubbed at his ear, then picked up his glass and sipped his nectar. "Aren't you going to try your cake?"

Fajora picked up her fork and stabbed at the cake. It crumbled, but she managed to get a chunk into her mouth and was rewarded by a decadently rich flavor. Dannel laughed as she hurried to cut another bite. He filled his own fork, but sat staring at it without eating. "Interesting question, indeed," he said as if there had been no interruption in their conversation. "Why an engineer? Or an astrophysicist?"

"What?"

"Sebastian Tornbar. Astrophysicist extraordinaire, stationed down at Haven Outpost. They reported him missing two weeks ago. Colleagues say he walked along the boundary most days, and they worried he'd cross. They think the cats got him."

"What do you think, sir?"

"Oh, they're probably right."

"I didn't think the cats came across the boundary for any reason."

"No, they don't."

"Then he would have been the one to cross."

Dannel gave Fajora a bleak smile. "That's right. Question is, why? He knew the rules as well as anyone. And what happened after that?"

"What are the possibilities?"

"There are several. He's a prisoner of one of the clans. Or a prisoner of Dark Spinners, although our scans didn't detect any DS activity near the time of his disappearance. But scans don't show everything. If it's

DS, they may even have taken him off-world. Or he's wandering around, wounded and disoriented. Or he's already become cat food."

"Sir!" Fajora's stomach lurched. "You don't believe they ate him? They're sentient. One sentient species doesn't eat another. I'll never believe that."

"You might be right. Not sure how we can find out, though." Dannel stroked his beard and gave Fajora a speculative look.

She stared at him, and then down at her cake. Was he offering her the chance she sought? And if so, did she have the courage to carry it through? It had been easy to defy Kinovic while sitting in a comfortable office discussing assignments. But now, if Dannel implied what she guessed, she moved a step closer to setting foot in clan territory. Forbidden territory, where she risked not only teeth and claws, but three hundred years of uneasy peace between species on this world.

"Sir, let me go in and find out what happened. To both of them." Fajora's voice trembled, and she steadied it. "Let me track down the Dark Spinners and find out why the cats are tolerating them. Or worse."

She caught Dannel's brief smile as she looked up, but his eyes remained somber.

"I can't ask you to do that. Not after what happened to Jayzam. You've been through too much already. Maybe a team from the enclave should go. You think?"

"That's a great idea, but it will never happen, especially with Fazok sick and Kinovic in charge. Kinovic covered up Jayzam's report. He tried to keep me from discussing it with Fazok. It took me more than a year to convince the service to send me back here. They were concerned I'd do something rash in my grief. That's how they put it. Tried to convince me Kinovic had everything under control here."

She dropped her fork onto her plate and twisted her hands together. How much should she tell Dannel about the situation on Luxera, about the dysfunction in the service? She didn't want to arouse his distrust unnecessarily. But if she wanted his help, she'd have to give him something.

She lifted her eyes and found his steady gaze regarding her. She had difficulty gauging his frame of mind accurately, since he had no eye flecks. This lack made human expression harder to read, but she thought she saw kindness there, along with the detachment needed for a thoughtful appraisal. She decided to trust him.

"I spent a year making appointments with every official I thought might know something or have influence in the service. But every one of them avoided giving any direct answers. Some hid things from me. I'm pretty sure others were afraid to be too forthcoming. The official memo said Kinovic had investigated and found no reason for concern, and the matter was closed."

Dannel laid down his own fork, a bite of cake untouched. "There's isn't anyone you can trust at your service headquarters? Who can dig into the matter for us?"

"No. Well, yes, one or two that I trust. I'll send a message and hope it's not intercepted. But they aren't in the inner circles. They'll likely hit the same walls I have. Kinovic seems to have anyone with real power eating out of his hand."

"And you've talked to Kinovic already since you returned? What exactly did he have to say?"

"He claims to have followed up two years ago. Said he checked with the colony and assured himself that no one was missing. But you've just confirmed Clarise's disappearance prompted your governor to send Jayzam into the territories. Did the governor hide that from Kinovic, and did Fazok know and keep it from him as well? Or did Kinovic know of Clarise's disappearance and doesn't want to admit it?"

"I can't answer that. I wasn't privy to conversations between Governor Dario and anyone in the enclave. Dario informed me about his intention of sending Jayzam in, but he may have deemed it none of

Kinovic's business. Kinovic held a less exalted position in the enclave at that time. I'll ask Dario when I see him. We shouldn't proceed too far until I have a chance to talk to him. But in my experience, Fazok has always been reasonable. Might he overrule Kinovic and send in a team? He has that ability, if I understand your enclave structure."

"If he was healthy, perhaps. I'm not sure. He hinted yesterday that he has some concerns about Kinovic. I'm not sure what's going on with that. But now he's physically weak. Exhausted." Fajora paused before voicing something she'd hardly dared suggest even to herself. "I'm not sure how clearly he's thinking. Mostly sharp, but then a bit muddled at times. Saying some odd things. Or, at least," she paused, working out a new idea, "he wants people to think he's muddled."

"People, meaning Kinovic," Dannel asked.

"Yes." Fajora thought of Trayle, a foil to Kinovic. "Yes, possibly. But, either way, I don't see him overruling Kinovic."

"Too bad. I'll have to talk with Fazok, get a line on his mental state if I can. Always good to know what we're dealing with." Dannel stroked his chin, smoothing his beard, while his brow furrowed in thought. "So, we're at an impasse. I can't ask you to go alone into clan territory. Kinovic won't let a team go in. And we humans aren't allowed in by terms of our treaty with the cats. But I'd surely like to know what's going on. It's a blank screen out there beyond our borders. Our scans only show so much. I've told the techs to boost scanner signals, but we can't hope for much more than we already have."

"But sir, you don't have to ask me to go in. I'm volunteering. You're right. We have to know what the Dark Spinners' business is with the cats. And what has happened to the humans involved."

Dannel studied her, still stroking his beard. His piercing gaze seemed to see beyond the surface of her words, into her soul.

"I don't suppose you'd mind vindicating your Jayzam either, am I right?" He smiled as heat coursed up Fajora's neck into her face. "Well, can't say I blame you. And since you're volunteering, as you say, maybe we can work something out. You Light Spinners do have more leeway than we humans. You're allowed in to retrieve Dark Spinners. Might be able to work with that."

"I can say I'm scouting to confirm Dark Spinners in Rock or River Clan. It might get me past the other clans, at least."

Dannel gathered up the dirty dishes and carried them to the control panel. At the touch of a button, a bin slid out below the panel. He dumped the dishes into the bin and stood staring at them.

"Yes, indeed. Good idea," he said after a moment. He closed the dish bin with another touch of the panel and returned to his chair near Fajora.

"We've got a tech here in the hospital who's a good friend of Sebastian's," he said. "Sonja Benjamin. I think I'll send her to the outpost to look through his things, see if she can figure out why he wandered off. Why don't you go with her, see what she knows, go from there?"

"Do you need to talk to the governor about this?"

He dismissed the question with a wave of his hand. "Dario's heading for retirement coming up pretty soon. Hardly works anymore. Lets me do whatever I want. Any messes I make will be mine to fix once he's done, anyway. I'll fill him in, of course, and ask a few questions, but I guess we can proceed. At least as far as sending you to the outpost. I'll send word if he has any serious objections."

"What will you tell the Luxeran enclave? Kinovic will be furious."

"We've got the head of your enclave right here. We'll check on his condition in a bit. If he's lucid, we'll get his permission. From what Silviann told me, we'll need to keep him for a few days, if not longer. Need to get Doctor Jerrod Pellar up to take a look. He's our best." He paused with a thoughtful nod. "Coming from the outpost, as a matter of fact. Should be here by evening. We'll have a quick chat with him, after which you and Sonja will take the transport down to Haven in the morning."

"And from there into clan territory?"

"Well, then. Perhaps, but let's take it one step at a time."

Good advice, but Fajora read Dannel's eyes clearly this time. He knew as well as she did, she would cross the boundary and risk the teeth and claws. Her promise to Jayzam, to herself, compelled her.

4

— · —

REASONS

"Poison! Are you sure?"

Fajora stood at the end of Fazok's bed, staring around in disbelief at the faces of the medical staff. "Who would do such a thing?"

Fazok lifted a feeble hand, catching her attention, then let it drop back onto the bed. "We know who. Or a good guess, anyway, hmm?"

"Yes." Fajora fought the urge to form a sword and go charging back to the enclave to challenge Kinovic. If Fazok guessed correctly, this had progressed from mere obstruction to attempted murder. Kinovic had made it clear he wanted to run the enclave, but Fajora had not imagined he would go this far to get control. Unfortunately, she had no proof, which made it impossible to press accusations against Kinovic. She curled her hands into fists and tamped down her light, turning to the doctors with a burning question instead. "You have the cure, right?"

Doctor Jerrod Pellar, to whom Dannel had just introduced her, cleared his throat. "We hope so. We're having trouble identifying the poison, and we can't be sure of an antidote until we are certain what it is. In the meantime, we'll administer a broad-spectrum antidote designed to combat a variety of toxic substances. That may do the trick even if we don't get a specific identification."

"May? What if it doesn't?"

The doctor shrugged. "He's stable for now. We have time. We'll keep the lab techs working until we get the answers we need. Don't worry. But I do suggest, if there's any business you need to take care of with Agent Fazok, you do it now. Some of the stuff we'll be shooting into him will knock him out, or at least make him dazed and confused."

"Well, then, perhaps you doctors will give us a few minutes alone with your patient," Dannel said from where he leaned against the door frame. "And give me a digital voice recorder, if you have one on hand. Or more than one, in case Fazok has instructions for his enclave while he's incapacitated."

With these few words, Dannel cleared the room. Even Trayle, who had been hovering around the head of Fazok's bed, sensed she was not wanted and followed the medical staff out. Dannel pulled a chair close to the bed and gave Fazok a summary of the plan he and Fajora had come up with.

"I knew there had to be more to things than Kinovic reported," Fazok said, "but I didn't have anyone I could send to investigate. No one I trusted, hmm. Or who was up to infiltrating clan territory. There's just one worry with sending you in."

"Only one?" Dannel chuckled. "The more I think on it, the more objections I come up with." He raised a hand to stop Fajora's protest. "Nothing to make me backtrack on the plan. Not yet, unless I get riled by Fazok's worry."

"Well, I don't know as I'd go that far," Fazok countered. "Might come to nothing. But the mail from recent couriers is full of news about a young agent gone rogue. One of our best, and now he's spinning shadow. Came through here on training about a year and a half ago. Syjaz by name. Do you know him, Fajora?"

"No. Is he coming this way?"

"Indications suggest he is, but we don't know for sure. We're to look out for him, but I can't trust Kinovic to keep him out of your way.

Especially since Kinovic won't know where you are. Could complicate things, hmm?"

"I'd say." Dannel adjusted his chair, frowning, then turned his scrutinizing gaze on Fajora. "Maybe we'd better call the whole thing off. Yes?"

"No, I'm still in. I've been alerted, so I'll know to watch out for him. It will be fine." Fajora put more confidence than she felt into her answer. She wouldn't have her plans disrupted now. She had promised Jayzam, and the lives of at least two people were at stake. Even more so, perhaps, if a rogue spinner prowled clan territory.

"Good. Just be careful." Fazok winked at Fajora. "We won't inform the rest of the enclave of this. Not right away, at any rate. Let them think you're here, attending me, shall we? Trayle will help me maintain the fiction. I'll fill her in when we're done here. She'll know what to do."

Dannel turned on one of the voice recorders, and Fazok recorded an official commission of assignment for Fajora. Then Dannel left them alone while Fazok made additional recordings of instructions for Kinovic and other agents in the enclave. Normally, they conducted enclave business on paper, or occasionally parchment here on Kakislane, where animal skins were plentiful, but the hospital had neither parchment nor paper, so Fajora fumbled with the foreign equipment until she got it to work.

When the orders for the enclave were complete, Fajora turned on a third recorder, and they composed a message for Service headquarters on Luxera concerning Fazok's condition and the doctors' findings.

"Without any evidence pointing to a perpetrator, this is unlikely to prompt more than a cursory investigation, but at least it will be on file," Fazok commented. "Maybe someone will get hold of it who cares about justice, if any such person holds power in the service."

"I'll pursue it further when I get back," Fajora promised. She grabbed the recorders as Fazok's hands dropped weakly onto the blankets. He wet his lips to speak, then shook his head.

"Rest now," Fajora said. "I'll look in on you in the morning before I leave."

When he slipped into an exhausted doze, she left him and went in search of Dannel, who promised to have his assistant transcribe the recordings and hand them off to Trayle. She would see that they reached the appropriate destination, either the enclave by the local courier, or Luxera by one of the service's world-to-world couriers.

Dannel settled Fajora into one of the hospital's guest rooms. She found Trayle in the room next door and brought her up to date. Then she went to her bed, where she slept fitfully, anxious for morning and action.

In the morning, she made a quick check on Fazok, but he was too heavily medicated to talk. Trayle sat by his side reading on one of the colony's electronic devices. She said she'd spoken with Fazok earlier. He had spoken to her of Fajora's upcoming absence.

"I understand you'll be helping the colony analyze their files on the prophecies," Trayle said with a wink. "A perfect assignment for you, given your specialization in prophecy during your final few training modules at the academy. And a study furlough on Sek-Nar to confer with the dragons."

Fazok, the wily old agent. Why hadn't Fajora thought of that? To be sure, she'd only specialized in prophecy because Jayzam dabbled in prophecy as a hobby. His green-flecked amber eyes and rakish smile had mesmerized her, and she had done anything she could to catch his attention. Same with the study furlough. Jayzam's first assignment was to Sek-Nar, but the service assigned Fajora to Merdoma. Not willing to risk the relationship in its infancy, she'd applied for the study grant as a long shot, the only thing she could come up with. As an indifferent student of prophecy, she'd been surprised when it had been approved.

That had been over fifty years ago, and Fajora had forgotten most of what she'd known about the prophecies. Her clearest memories of the study furlough involved that high ridge, a favorite spot, where she often sat with Jayzam's arm around her while they searched the skies for soaring dragons, wings glowing in the blazing sun. The prophecies had sparked little passion in her, but she remembered enough to use that specialization as a cover now.

She pulled herself back from the memories, aware of Trayle watching her, curiosity evident in her dancing eye flecks.

"That's right." Fajora forced brightness into her tone, as if she were quite aware of her ostensible mission. "Agent Kinovic doesn't need me at the enclave in the immediate future, and Agent Fazok is eager to build stronger ties with the Wellador Colony. I don't know how long I'll be down there."

"Of course. Do you want me to pack a lunch for you?" Trayle asked with a smirk.

"No, thank you." Fajora hid her own smile. "Just keep Kinovic off my back and take care of Fazok."

"Yes, ma'am." Trayle's voice turned uncharacteristically sober and respectful. Then the grin flashed out. "I know what Kinovic likes. He's about to have adventures he never imagined."

Fajora rolled her eyes, eliciting laughter from Trayle.

Satisfied that things at the hospital were as settled as possible, Fajora slipped out of Fazok's room and across to the lounge, where Dannel and Sonja Benjamin waited for her.

Sonja's wide smile put Fajora at ease immediately. Her eyes were bright in her dark face, shining with the anticipation of adventure. At her feet lay a small animal, short, with perky ears and reddish coloring like the small foxes that roamed the Luxeran countryside. It sported a white stripe down its forehead, and other white patches marked its red coat. Its open, panting mouth appeared to be smiling.

Fajora had encountered humans who kept animals as pets during her previous stay on Kakislane, so the animal's presence didn't puzzle her, and the practice amused her. She had observed that the dogs and other small pets had a clear understanding of the characters of their humans. This ability was not on the order of the sentient cats' ability to discern truth, but a faint echo of that ability. If an animal accepted and relaxed in the presence of a human, that human could be trusted to be a person of good character. This animal's relaxed attitude with Sonja reassured Fajora.

She reached down now and let the animal sniff her fingers and stroked its fur a couple of times before giving Sonja a questioning look.

"Your dog, I presume?"

"Yes." Sonja's smile widened. "This is Bessie. She came with me when I moved to the city. My father insisted, thinking I would be lonely otherwise." She bent and stroked Bessie, and the animal leaned into her hand. "He was right, too. She's made all the difference. She likes going with me to Haven Outpost. She has more chances to run, though I do have to watch her carefully to make sure she doesn't get too close to the boundary."

Sonja attached a leash to Bessie's collar and retrieved the duffle bag from the floor beside her. "We'll catch the transport in about half an hour," she said. "I'm all packed. Do you have your things?"

"Yes."

Fajora had only a small pack with two spare uniforms. She considered offering to spin Sonja and Bessie to the outpost. But humans often experienced extreme discomfort when carried in a spin. Besides, Fajora was curious to try the transport, so she kept quiet and followed Sonja to the station.

The transport was a gleaming vehicle designed to fly at any altitude from a meter above the ground to high cloud level. It had seats for twenty passengers in addition to the pilot, but today only two others boarded, choosing seats near the front. Sonja led Fajora to the back of the vehicle and explained how to fasten in. Bessie curled up on the seat beside Sonja as if she did this every day.

Once they were in the air, flying just above the city roofs, Sonja leaned toward Fajora with a serious expression.

"Dannel says you're going to find Sebastian."

"Your friend, I understand. But you're not an astrophysicist, are you?"

"No. We know each other through the Society of Letters. We're both interested in the old prophecies."

"Prophecies? Ah, I see." Now Fajora understood why Fazok had used her training specialty as a cover. She searched her memory for something intelligent to say based on her old studies. "A lot of people are fascinated by anything that comes from the dragons." A generic statement, but one that caused Sonja to frown. What had she said wrong? The dragons were involved with the prophecies, hence the study furlough on Sek-Nar.

"Well, of course." Sonja nodded. "But the prophecies don't come from the dragons. The dragons only interpret and explain. The prophecies, most of them, originate on our home world, Exalton. Mostly from before the war, although I've heard an enticing rumor about new ones leaking out of Exalton." Sonja's eyes danced, then she sighed. "It's only a rumor, of course. I don't know of anyone who has contact with Exalton. I'm not sure where the rumor started, or, if it's true, how new material would get smuggled out. It's intriguing to think about, though. But for now, what we have is from the war or earlier."

"And your people brought them along when they came to Kakislane?"

"Exactly. We still study them. What survived, that is. The first colonists had equipment malfunctions and lost some of the writings. We only saved fragments of those. That's what interested Seb. He studied the fragments and tried to piece together what they meant."

"Do you think any of them have something to do with his disappearance?"

"I don't know. Here. I brought copies of the stuff he told me he was working on last time we talked."

Sonja pulled a pair of handheld devices out of her pocket and brought up some documents on them. The two women spent the rest of the flight with their heads together, reading over the fragments and looking for clues as to why Sebastian crossed the boundary into clan territory.

But they were no closer to an answer when the transport descended to the landing pad at Haven Outpost.

"I don't see any reason for him to cross over." Sonja turned off the devices and stowed them back in her pocket.

"We're authorized to look through his quarters," Fajora reminded her. "Maybe you'll find something there."

She looked out the transport window to get her first glimpse of the outpost. She had visited several human settlements during her previous assignments on Kakislane but had never been here. The outpost sprawled in a large meadow with forest on three sides, much like the Luxeran enclave compound.

Unlike the enclave compound, this collection of buildings did not try to blend into its surroundings, but proudly proclaimed what it was—a highly technical research station. The northwest corner bristled with towers and dish-like structures. Near these stood a domed building. Fajora presumed this housed the outpost's famous telescope. Perhaps she would ask for a peek through its lens while she was here.

Close to the forest on the west side, a row of greenhouses glowed with artificial light. Beyond these, on the southwest corner of the outpost, loomed a large building of shiny metal, its function a mystery to Fajora. Another research facility of some sort? It contributed to the air of remote busyness. This was a community where serious scholars came for work and contemplation.

As she had done when viewing the enclave, Fajora imagined what the cats thought of this settlement. Even though this collection of structures was clearly more alien to this world, Fajora found less to object to here. The place gave the impression that it was minding its own business and letting its neighbors do the same.

On the fourth side, a little way apart from the outpost, rocky formations rose from a bed of stone, most of them fifteen meters high by Fajora's estimate. The largest spread its flat top at least as wide as it was high.

"The Council Rock," Sonja said in answer to Fajora's query. "Neutral territory, sort of. Meadow Clan cats meet with our leaders there sometimes."

"How does one set up a meeting?" This could be useful. Why hadn't Dannel suggested it?

"We don't. Can't. The cats don't come at our bidding."

"But I bet we come at theirs. Yes?"

"Yes." Sonja grinned. "If a cat wanted a meeting, wouldn't you go?"

"Absolutely. But why does it only work one way?"

"We're on their world and barely tolerated. They have too much disdain for us to come when we call. We, on the other hand, are trying to promote peace and goodwill. And I don't know of a single human who feels disdain toward the cats. Dislike or resentment, sometimes. But not disdain."

Fajora scanned the rock, searching for movement, a feline shape, a signal of some sort, but the top appeared deserted. Deflated, Fajora followed Sonja toward the collection of low buildings circling two larger central structures of gleaming metal. They checked in at the nearest large structure, the administration building, where they received guest room assignments and picked up key codes for Sebastian's apartment.

After dropping their packs in their quarters, they took Bessie for a run in the open area beyond the compound. Fajora, ambling behind her new friend, scanned the nearby woodland for signs of cat watchers. Sonja had told her the cats patrolled this boundary more than any other, since the outpost sat so close to the line, but the wall of trees across the boundary line was blank.

"Do you suppose there are any cats nearby?" Fajora called ahead.

"Forest Clan cats are black," Sonja said over her shoulder. "There could be several watching us right now, but they blend into the shadows of the trees so well, you'll never see them."

As she spoke, a rustling among the trees brought Fajora to a standstill. She peered into the shadowed forest with total concentration, but saw nothing. The sound came again, higher up than she had expected. Not a cat, unless one was up a tree."

"Do the cats here climb trees?" she called softly. "I hear something up high."

Sonja put the leash on Bessie and walked back to Fajora. She focused on the spot Fajora indicated.

"Forest Clan does climb, but not usually that high. Wait, look."

A shape flitted through the trees, gliding as no cat could do.

"An owl," Sonja breathed. "It's gone now. Too bad. I've only had a few sightings. I wish I'd seen this one." She turned an inquisitive gaze toward Fajora. "Have you ever heard the owling?"

"Yes, once, when I visited a small village near the enclave. Can we hear it here?"

"Yes. We'll come back out at dusk. Let's go check out Sebastian's apartment now. Time to get to work."

The walls of Sebastian's apartment, in one of the low buildings, reminded Fajora of the control center at service headquarters on Luxera, crammed with information. The wall of the kitchen nook showed the shiny blank face of a dormant panel, something Luxeran control did not have, but the other walls were covered with maps and charts just as at control. But unlike Luxeran control, this room exuded an air of thoughtful scholarship, with an undercurrent of excitement, as if some important discovery was waiting to happen within these information laden walls.

A desk against one wall held data devices in several sizes, surrounded by piles of papers with handwritten annotations and mathematical calculations. Another, smaller table held piles of documents and rolls of paper. More maps?

Sonja examined the maps on the walls, rotating to take them all in.

"I haven't been here for a while," she said, still turning. "Most of these are new. He said he'd uncovered new information he wanted to share with me. Then he disappeared."

"What do you make of it?" Fajora lifted the top paper off one pile on the desk and skimmed it, but it looked like gibberish, even though the language was Standard. Notations referred to other documents, but without knowledge of those documents, she had no frame of reference. She put down the paper and chose one from another pile. Same result.

Standing by the small table, Sonja plucked a note off the wall near a large map that showed all of Kakislane, with clan territories marked out.

"What is it?" Fajora peered over Sonja's shoulder to read the scrawled note.

Clans rising into the void—Chelton commentary refers to tribes of Arabah. But why the Arabah? Only called clans twice in lit. What about the cat clans?

"What does that mean?"

"I'm not sure." Sonja tacked the note back up on the wall. "It's in a fragment I'd forgotten about. But I haven't studied it. I don't remember what the whole fragment says. And I don't understand why Seb thinks it refers to the cats. They'll never rise into the void."

"Would the tribes of Arabah? I've never heard of them."

"The Arabah is on Exalton. It's impenetrable to technology. I don't see them rising into the void either, I guess. Unless they make an alliance with someone on Exalton who retained void-faring capabilities. Or has them again. Unfortunately, Exalton itself seems impenetrable. We've had no reliable word from there since we arrived here three hundred years ago. Except . . . ."

"Except what?"

"Oh, that rumor about a prophecy. But that's all it is. A rumor."

"So this isn't helping us any."

"No."

Sonja leaned toward the table and picked up a sheaf of documents with a passage highlighted in yellow on the top page. She scanned it, then lifted her eyes to study the large map of Kakislane. She placed a finger on the map near its top edge and traced a line down toward the middle. Her finger stopped at a large red X, and she stood still for a long time.

"No," she murmured at last. "Is that possible?"

"What? Is what possible?"

Without answering, Sonja hurried to the desk and riffled through the piles of papers. She muttered to herself as she searched. Fajora only caught a word here or there, not enough to figure out what the other woman was looking for.

"Aha! Here." Sonja grabbed a sheaf of papers from the bottom of a pile and flipped through them, nodding. When she lifted her gaze toward Fajora, her eyes were wide and her mouth threatened a smile. "I wish Seb had told me."

"What?"

"When our ancestors came here from Exalton, one of the void ships went down in clan territory. A malfunction shut down their engines, and they couldn't get them restarted in time to avoid a landing. The cats quickly surrounded the site, but two smaller ships got in and rescued most of the people. They lost nine adults and two children. They confirmed two of the adults dead on impact. The others probably died fighting the cats or trying to traverse mountainous terrain to find the colonists.

"One other man almost missed the rescue ship as he frantically downloaded computer files. With the cats closing in, he had to leave before he finished. We've always known we have only half of one document, so he could have downloaded more. And that half is a duplicate of one of the files fragmented in the colony's early malfunctions."

Sonja paused, flipping through her pages again.

"So what did Seb find?" Fajora pressed. "Did he discover the full document? And why would that drive him to cross into cat territory?"

"Not the full document. But another file embedded in the partial file, with a list of the documents the man left behind. Some we have in our files, or at least we have fragments of them, and some I don't recognize at all."

"But I still don't see . . . ."

Sonja held up a hand to stop Fajora. "Not just a list of documents, but a notation of coordinates." She paused to scan the papers again, both the highlighted set and the set she had found on the desk. "It's the location of the crash site. It has to be. The survivor noted the coordinates and scribbled, *Go back when the cats are used to us.*"

"So, Sebastian saw this and decided to go? But that notation was made three hundred years ago. Those files wouldn't be good. On this humid planet, everything would be rotted and ruined by now."

Sonja shook her head emphatically. "No. It depends on the condition of the wrecked ship. If some compartments remained sealed, they could be in working condition, waiting for someone with the right knowledge to come along and power them back up."

"But Sebastian's an astrophysicist, not an engineer."

"Doesn't matter. We're all trained in the basics of engineering and computers. Besides, in Seb's line of work, skill with computers is crucial.

If he could get power, he could get the computer working. That is, if the cats don't get to him first."

Fajora went to the map and put her finger on the red X. "Whose territory is this? And what are the coordinates?"

Sonja came to stand beside Fajora and read off a list of numbers, then peered at the map. "That's in Deep Valley Clan territory. Will you go there and find Seb?"

"Deep Valley! Jayzam had contact with that clan. He refused to tell me any details. I've been wondering what he saw that made him so close-mouthed. Now this has me wondering even more."

Sonja moved away from the map and returned the papers to the desk, her face crinkling into a frown. "Maybe he found the wreckage. I wish someone from the Society of Letters had been able to talk to him."

"I doubt he would have told them anything. He wouldn't even talk with me about Deep Valley Clan, except to warn me away from them. Told me not to go there, or anywhere near. He was emphatic about it. No explanation. Just stay away and leave them alone."

"So, what do you do? This is where you need to go to look for Seb."

"Jayzam wanted to protect me from something. I'll have to go there to find out what. And to look for Seb. First, though, I have to find out if there are Dark Spinners in Rock or River Clan. And if Clarise is still there. Jayzam saw her in Rock Clan two years ago. And Dark Spinners, as well. That's where I'll have to start." She kept her voice neutral, trying not to focus on the enormity of the mission she had set for herself.

Sonja pulled out the desk chair and sat down, her face solemn. "Those clans are the worst. Especially Rock Clan. We'll have to clear this with Dannel. Your enclave, too, I imagine."

"Of course. Dannel and I already talked about it, but I'm sure he'll want to know what you found. How do we contact him from here?"

"I'll go to the admin building and send a message before I go to my quarters later. Dannel will get back to us by morning."

"Good. Thank you." Fajora watched Sonja as she sorted through more of Sebastian's papers, then turned back to study the maps. She needed as much information as she could get to orient her spins through the wild. She would let Sonja go through the motions of getting permission. No reason for both of them to get in trouble. But Fajora knew by the time Dannel replied to the request, she would already be deep in clan territory.

5

— · —

CHANCE ENCOUNTERS

Toward dusk Sonja led Fajora to a hillside overlooking the territory of Forest Clan to the south. They sat on the grass with Bessie snuggled between them as daylight faded. Fajora strained her eyes, looking for movement among the trees, but nothing suggested life there until the first long call of an owl drifted across the shadowed landscape.

The mysterious, alien call hinted at meaning, but not a meaning Fajora could discern. A second call answered the first, followed by a third, in a lower tone that harmonized with the first two calls. Fajora strained to catch anything that indicated words or recognizable patterns of language. But though the utterings implied deliberate composition, with long and short calls and rising and falling tones, the meaning remained a mystery, a wild music that suggested the heart of the creatures that uttered it but gave nothing more. It kept itself apart from the outpost—near but making it clear one had nothing to do with the other.

More owls joined the canticle, their calls wafting back and forth across the forest and lifting to the sky. For a few minutes, the evening resounded with owl song before the calls slowly died away. A shape, barely visible against the darkness of the forest, detached from a low branch and drifted in front of the trees, propelled by a few strong beats of long wings spread wide. A second shape followed close behind, angled away from the trees, and swept over the west side of Haven Outpost, its dark shape boldly defined for a moment against a clear sky that still held a hint of the day's sunlight.

Fajora hugged herself, watching and listening, as silence fell over the evening. So many voices, so many individuals. Any other winged creatures, gathered in such numbers, created a flurry of sound and movement as they dispersed, but not the owls. They simply disappeared, silent and elusive.

Fajora breathed deeply of the evening air with its earthy scent of wood and humus and the flowering jasmine vines that flourished along the edge of the forest. Though her memories of Kakislane were colored by the last few terrible days before she took Jayzam home to die, this beautiful world now worked its enchantment on her. She stroked Bessie's coat absently as she strained to see Sonja's expression. Sonja, her dark face hidden by shadows, remained silent even after the owling faded away and the night creatures took up their ordinary noises.

"I wish I knew what they were singing," Fajora said at last, hoping to prod Sonja into conversation. "It sounded like language and not, at the same time. Do you understand any of it?"

Sonja turned her face toward Fajora with a little shake of her head. "No one does. No humans, at least. It's rumored the cats do. That they talk with the owls and are friendly, even cooperate. Some of them, anyway."

"I've never heard that. All the years I've been on this world and no one has ever mentioned cooperation between the native species. How do you know this? Did the cats tell you?"

"No. The cats say little to us. Only what is necessary when there's a treaty question or Dark Spinners that need to be removed. But the rumor persists. It grew out of an old tale written by one of the first human settlers here. How she came by this information I've no idea, but according to the story, Rock Clan and River Clan attacked a nesting during fledging season. The owlets couldn't fly yet and were in grave danger. Then some of the other clans came to the rescue. They drove off the attackers and helped the owls to get their young to safety. Owls apparently have long memories and still feel they have a debt to pay. Especially when Rock or River Clan threaten one of the other clans."

Sonja reattached Bessie's leash and got to her feet. "Are you ready to go in? I'm tired, and we have a lot of work to do tomorrow, sorting through Sebastian's things. Hopefully we'll find some more useful information."

"Yes." Fajora rose and walked beside Sonja toward the residential buildings. "Which cat clans have the most interaction with the owls? Do you know?"

"Yes, and that's something that gives credence to the old rumor. The old story says Deep Valley Clan helped rescue the owlets. And that clan supposedly has the most interaction now, along with their close neighbors, Meadow and Forest Clans."

Fajora's heart sped up. If she found Sebastian in Deep Valley Clan, perhaps she'd find owls as well and have a chance for real contact, or at least a closer view.

"In what ways do the cats and owls cooperate?" she asked as they reached their building.

"I'm not sure, but some say the owls act as spies." Sonja grinned, her teeth flashing white in the dim light of the lamp above the door. "And maybe as messengers. The latter seems more realistic. I don't see how they could do anything physical. The cats don't need help hunting, or anything."

"Do they fight together?"

"Hmm. That's an interesting idea. I don't know much about clan wars or what a fight between clans might look like. I'll check the database and see if there's any information about that."

Fajora thought about that early the next morning, as she prepared to leave her guest quarters. Slipping out secretly meant she wouldn't find out what Sonja learned. If she got caught in a clan war, she'd have to adjust in the moment without proper briefing and trust her training and experience to get her through any difficulties.

She reflected on the blessing of a kitchen that never closed as she nibbled on honey wafers and stuffed less perishable food supplies into her pack. She had no idea where the food came from. If real people prepared it, they were fast and never slept. Fajora had only to manipulate the touch buttons on the control panel in her apartment, as Sonja had instructed her, and food appeared, no questions asked.

When her pack was full of supplies, she ordered up a dish of mixed grains and vegetables to go with her wafers, even though she no longer felt hungry. She must fuel up as much as possible. When she had forced the last bit down, she tested her access to light. It came in a strong surge. She formed her sword and examined its spin for speed and tightness. Good. If she needed it, it was ready. Not that she expected to need it. She held fast to the stricture that forbade killing except for self-defense or the defense of the helpless in her care. But when it became necessary, she wielded her blade with conviction. She could do no less for her cause. For Jayzam.

The merest glimmer of morning light showed above the Council Rock when she left her quarters. She shivered in the morning chill and pulled her jacket tighter over her uniform tunic. She kept a sharp eye for humans wandering through the compound who might question her about her business at this early hour, but she saw no one.

An owl called in the distance; an answer came from much closer. Fajora scanned the trees at the edge of the compound. All seemed still, and she was about to turn away, when a dark object launched itself off a branch high in a tree to the right of her line of sight, the sudden movement drawing her gaze. The large bird, perhaps one she had heard sing the evening before, soared along the edge of the trees, banked into the forest, and disappeared. A shiver ran down Fajora's spine. She stood motionless for several minutes, a quiet acknowledgment of Ya-Lohim's varied creation, a sort of morning vespers.

Awareness of the pale blush in the eastern sky, precursor to dawn, set her feet moving again. She walked to the base of the Council Rock and stared up at the steep, crumbling stairway leading to the top. Shaking her head in disgust at her own laziness, she translated to light and spun to the broad surface of the rock. No cats lounged here, keeping watch, as she had both hoped and feared. She hadn't expected any, but she had wanted to be sure before heading into their territory.

From this vantage point, in the growing light, she viewed the entire compound, the patches of fields and forest to the north that were part of Wellador territory, and the thick woods to the south and open prairie to the east that were clan territory. Forest Clan and Meadow Clan, if she'd read the maps in Sebastian's apartment correctly. She'd start in Forest Clan territory, where she hoped the trees would conceal her a little, though she wasn't sure one could hide from the cats. Nonetheless, it seemed wiser to at least try to hide than to walk or spin in the open country of the meadows to the east.

She spun only a short distance into the forest before resuming her solid form. She was too far from the enclave for any Light Spinners to notice the slight change in her aura's location, from compound to forest, but the humans had tracking technology. They would notice someone crossing the boundary if the tech finishing up the night shift was awake and alert.

She walked for a while, vigilant for signs of cats. As she penetrated deeper into the forest, the air became damp and chill, without movement, smelling of moss and decaying leaves. A trill of birdsong was followed by a flutter of wings, high and to Fajora's left. She shied away from it, then laughed softly at her skittishness.

The forest remained otherwise quiet. No animals crossed her path or rustled in the undergrowth. The creatures of the woods must be hiding from her as she lumbered through their home. Or perhaps they hid from a large predator. Or more than one. Her skin prickled as she imagined dozens of cats' eyes watching her.

The feeling of being watched increased. Fajora reached for light, intending to spin away, but a low growl from a dense clump of bushes on her right side stopped her. The leaves of the shrubs were dark green, almost black, the perfect spot for a black cat who wished to remain hidden. But though she could not see the cat, Fajora heard it clearly when it spoke to her. It forced the words through vocal apparatus not designed for Standard speech, yet it spoke clearly, and Fajora had no trouble understanding it.

"Light Spinner, what are you doing here?"

The voice, neither friendly nor threatening, demanded an answer.

"I'm on a mission. I believe Dark Spinners are among the clans." A truthful answer as far as it went. The cat, with its ability to detect truth, should have no problem with it.

"There are no dark ones in Forest Clan," the cat said. "You should not be here."

"I'm only passing through."

"Where do you think these dark ones are?"

"Rock Clan. Or perhaps River Clan."

During the following silence, Fajora held light ready but carefully under control, not letting a single spark escape. And she kept equally tight control on her emotions, so her eye flecks would not swirl erratically and betray nervousness. She wasn't nervous, anyway, she told herself. Of course not.

"Go home," the cat said at last. "It is currently unsafe for you in the territories."

"But the Dark Spinners."

"The dark ones can wait. If they remain in the clans, you can retrieve them another time."

"Why will later be better? How much later?"

"War is imminent among the clans. I give you this warning, as honor demands, to keep you and your kind from getting involved where you have no business. If you are also honorable, you will heed my words." Another growl rumbled from the cat's throat.

Fajora swallowed hard but did not back down. "Yes, I am honorable, which is why I must complete my mission."

The bushes swayed and swished, giving Fajora a glimpse of the cat's glossy black fur as it turned. It growled again. "Complete it then. Quickly if you must do it today. Or wait until a more suitable time."

It turned again, away from her this time. She caught sight of the tail waving briefly above the bushes, black with a tip of gray a hand-span long. The bushes swayed a moment longer and were still.

Fajora waited, watching the shrubs, which moved with the breeze, but nothing more. The cat was gone. Or nearby, watching without allowing Fajora to know its location. She let the quiet of the forest saturate her senses as she thought through the cat's words.

War among the clans. Instinct told her Rock Clan would be involved. She had chosen a bad time to infiltrate the territories. But if Clarise lived, languishing as a prisoner in Rock Clan, life would become even more precarious for her, trapped in the middle of a war. Sebastian, if he also lived, would be in grave danger as well, in Deep Valley territory or wherever he had ended up.

Going back to the enclave to gather help was not an option. If Kinovic had been set against infiltration before, how much more now with a clan war to work around? Especially with the war just starting. Or about to start. It might be swiftly over, but wars had a habit of perpetuating themselves, making a rescue unsafe for months, or even years, by which time it could be too late. Much too late.

Which meant Fajora must continue with her plans now, despite the increased danger. She had no time to waste, but must take advantage of this moment while the clans hovered on the brink of war but had not yet plunged over the edge. And if Dark Spinners had any part in fomenting war, foiling them might stop the conflict before it started.

Fajora translated to light but did not return to the colony as the Forest Clan cat had advised. Instead, she zoomed through the forest, finally coalescing in a more open area. Widely spaced trees lined ridges above slopes covered in rockfall. With fewer places to hide, she worried less about being watched, though cats easily blended into the rocks when they remained still. She wouldn't see one unless it chose to show itself.

Fajora had a good head for coordinates. By her best estimate, she now walked in the Great Rift—the unclaimed land between Forest Clan's territory and Deep Valley Clan's holdings. She altered course, veering north, hoping to stay in neutral territory for as long as possible. Farther north, Deep Valley Clan's territory narrowed to a thin strip of land. If she spun across at that spot, heading to another strip of neutral territory farther east, she could eat and regroup there before entering River Clan's domain, or perhaps continue north in the neutral land until she reached Rock Clan's border. Better not to test Deep Valley Clan's acceptance of her yet, especially since she didn't know how much time she had to find Clarise and assess conditions in Rock Clan.

She continued north, watching the sun as it climbed toward its zenith and using its angle to estimate her location. The forest on her left gave way to grassy hills. Meadow Clan's land began a little to the west. She translated to a spin, taking advantage of the open space to cover a lot of ground quickly without losing her bearings.

When she coalesced, the sound of rushing water greeted her, near but out of sight. A dozen steps brought her to the edge of a cliff. Far below, a frothing torrent of water rushed through a steep-sided canyon. She stared at it in confusion. The maps portrayed the Great Rift as barren, with only one river large enough to mark down. It spread across flat land, flowing in a sluggish path into Meadow Clan before emptying into a lake to the north. This could not be it, this turbulent flume cascading through so deep a gorge. Steep cliffs jutted up on her left and mountains rose to majestic heights beyond the canyon. Turning around, she saw that she stood far above the open, rolling land to the west—the Great Rift, with Meadow Clan beyond.

She searched her memory for a precise image of Sebastian's map. She recalled as many as seven major rivers starting in Deep Valley's high mountain ranges. Most flowed east toward River Clan. Of the two that flowed west, one headed into Forest Clan. She could not possibly be far enough south to have encountered that river.

The second became the slow, wide channel that betook itself into Meadow Clan before turning north toward Meadow Lake. After a moment of uncertainty, she decided she had already spun north of that river as well. That left only the eastward flowing rivers, all starting in the mountain ranges within Deep Valley territory. Did any of them curve west into the Great Rift, or did all of them remain contained within Deep Valley's holdings?

She squinted, trying to make her remembered map conform to her wishes, but without success. The longer she thought about it, the more convinced she became that none of the northern rivers strayed west outside Deep Valley boundaries and into the Great Rift. She had come too far northeast, into Deep Valley Clan territory.

Her senses sharpened. She rotated, looking and listening for signs of cats as she tried to realign her inner compass. She would spin away as soon as she determined where she needed to go. It would be easiest to spin high and get an overview, but she didn't want human technology to detect her. Dannel might be willing to let her go, but if too many people learned where she was, he might not have that option.

Treaty agreements dictated that humans never cross the boundaries, so they wouldn't bring a transport to haul her back to the colony, but they could inform the Luxeran enclave. The last thing Fajora needed to see was Kinovic coalescing in front of her with a glare and a spun weapon.

No, spinning low was her best option. She had her coordinates now, or close enough. She reached for light.

A low growl rumbled a warning, and she dropped her nascent spin.

Movement drew her attention to the base of the nearest cliff. A dark splotch she had taken for a variation in rock coloration detached itself and resolved into the shape of a cat. Its dark coat shimmered to a lighter brown when it walked into a patch of sunlight, giving the appearance of burnished bronze. Its tufted ears stood high above its dark eyes, twitching with every slight sound carried on the breeze. It snuffled, sampling her scent, turning its head into the breeze and snuffling again to catch the scents in the air.

Acutely attuned to the environment, it missed nothing, and though it was only of medium size for a cat, standing less than waist high on Fajora, its fur rippled with muscle. One false move on Fajora's part would bring swift contact with heavy, weaponized paws and powerful jaws. She readied herself for a spin, poised for a fast transition if the cat pounced. Then she waited, balancing readiness with patience in the hope of gaining valuable information from this encounter.

The cat padded to within ten paces, then sat on its haunches and watched her. It was too close for her to spin cleanly away if it chose to prevent her. She might escape, but not without injury. Remembering Jayzam's bloodied body after his encounters with Rock Clan, she shuddered.

The cat's ears twitched. Fajora held herself still. No more reminiscing. She must keep her attention on this moment and remain calm and confident. She stared at the cat's unblinking eyes, trying to read something from its expression, but it was too foreign to her.

The cat shifted, letting its gaze rove over the landscape before coming back to her face. It rose and came closer, walking around her, sniffing at her clothing, at her hands, her feet. Then it sat, a mere five paces away, and regarded her again.

"Light Spinner, what are you doing in Deep Valley Clan's territory?" It spoke as clearly as the Forest Clan cat, though its tone was more formal. "There are no dark ones here for you to retrieve. I know of no business that could bring you here."

"My business is not with Deep Valley Clan. Not today, at least." Fajora's voice trembled. And what must her eye flecks be doing? If they swirled as wildly as her heart pounded, the cat would be sure to notice. She had been calm with the Forest Clan cat, hadn't she? Why was she nervous now?

She steadied her voice as she continued. "I didn't intend to land in your territory. My business today is with River and Rock Clans. However, I do have some matters I wish to speak with leaders of Deep Valley Clan about, if possible, while I'm here."

"I ask again, what is your business?"

"I have questions about my husband, Jayzam. He had dealings with your clan. Two years ago, now."

The cat lifted its chin, and a low rumble rose from its chest. Fajora's heart beat faster, but she held her ground. "Do you remember him?"

"This was many seasons ago. This Jayzam promised not to speak of us. We believed him to be a creature of honor who would hold true to his word. I see we were mistaken."

"No. He told me nothing, except to stay away from you."

The cat cocked its head and its gaze pinned Fajora, boring into her as it sniffed for her scent. "Yes. You speak truth. So, it is you who have no honor, that you disregard the word of your mate."

"No, it is honor that brings me here. His honor. After his return, as he was dying, our own people dishonored him. I seek information that will vindicate him."

"You will not find it here. Go back home to your people. You have no business here."

"I do have business, as I said before, with River and Rock Clans. I believe they are consorting with Dark Spinners, perhaps also holding humans against their will. We are pledged to seek out these Dark Spinners before they cause trouble among the clans. I am here as a scout in advance of a Dark Spinner retrieval team."

This last stretched the truth. A retrieval team depended on Fazok's ability to command the enclave, uncertain at best. And Fajora's reasons for believing the Dark Spinners were there were badly outdated. But she wasn't about to reveal to this cat how thin her evidence was, how shaky the grounds for her mission.

As if sensing her partial deception, the cat rose and walked around her again, sniffing at even greater length this time. When it sat once more, it lifted its head and pointed its ears toward the sky, which made it appear taller than it was, and more intimidating.

"This is my word, the word of Bardu, first-level member of Deep Valley Clan's male council. My word will stand before the elders. It is not good for you to be here. You must leave our lands at once."

"I intend to. I'll spin over your land to neutral territory and cross into River Clan."

"No. The neutral territory is contested. We beat back incursions of Rock and River Clan almost daily. Soon we will be at war. You put yourself in danger there and interfere with conflicts that are not your own."

"Very well. I'll spin straight to River Clan's uncontested domain."

Bardu growled, deep in his throat. "You misunderstand. You must return to the human lands. Agreements sanction your assistance in dealing with the dark ones only when an immediate presence is identified. I detect a partial truth in your scent. You have no word of any dark ones there now. Therefore, you have no business in clan territory."

"I have no direct word, it's true. But I have reason to suspect ongoing relations between the Dark Spinners and the clans. And they have a human prisoner who is a victim, innocent of wrongdoing. I'm honor bound to free her."

Bardu thrust his head forward, his paws working the ground, scratching at it with extended claws. "You are foolish. Humans who cross into clan territory are not innocent. They have broken treaty provisions and forfeit their freedom. If this one you speak of yet lives, she will receive the penalty for trespassing."

"But that's not right." Fajora leaned toward Bardu, prompting him to pull back a little. Fajora's fear washed out of her. It no longer mattered that this cat could kill her. She wouldn't leave Clarise in danger, or Sebastian either, because these haughty creatures were more concerned about treaties and boundaries than about decency and kindness. If Deep Valley held Sebastian, she'd have to deal with its members once she was done with Rock Clan. She hoped she'd find someone easier to work with than this overbearing individual, if such a cat existed, but it wouldn't hurt to lay some groundwork now.

"She hasn't hurt anyone. Why should she suffer?"

Bardu rose with a snarl. "Has she not hurt anyone? Are you so sure? If humans are allowed to come and go as they please, we will soon be as beset by human incursions as by Rock Clan incursions. We will lose our privacy, and after that our autonomy. The damage from these humans is far greater than you know."

"That's no reason to mistreat them, perhaps even torture them," Fajora shot back. "My honor requires me to help them. I'll leave Deep Valley Clan, if you wish, but I must look for human prisoners in Rock Clan."

But Bardu, circling her now with lethal grace, did not appear impressed by the honor inherent in Fajora's mission. "You do not understand the danger, or the viciousness of our enemies. It is not your place to engage them, and these prisoners are no longer your concern. It is a matter between clans. Go home and stay out of clan territory until it is time to come and claim Dark Spinners."

A growl punctuated his last word, and he crouched a few paces away, his tail sweeping the ground behind him. He was prepared to spring.

6

— · —

AKACHI

Fajora knew better than to test Bardu's patience further.

"I'm going." She translated to a spin and shot away toward the open plains of the neutral territory behind her.

But she didn't go far. As soon as she deemed her light beyond Bardu's range of vision, she swerved northeast, skimming across Deep Valley Clan territory toward the contested land on the far side.

She traveled farther than she thought necessary, wanting to be sure to land well beyond Deep Valley Clan's domain. She coalesced on the side of a mountain, with a broad valley spread before her. Deep scree blanketed the slope where she stood. One foot slipped, then the other, and she was sliding, kicking up showers of stones as she traveled downhill, gaining speed. She grabbed for light, pulling herself into a spin and flying to the valley floor.

She watched from a safe distance as an avalanche of small stones crashed to the bottom of the slope. The roar of the rockfall belied the small size of the stones. Any cats in the vicinity were now aware of her presence. And despite her effort to travel beyond Deep Valley Clan's territory, she was still in the mountains. She had not gone far enough.

Having had two inauspicious confrontations with cats already today, she could ill afford another. Bardu had told her to leave Deep Valley Clan territory. Any encounter with a clan member now increased the possibility of ill-will between the cats and the humanoid species who shared this world. In that case, Fajora's foray into cat territory was not likely to end well, even if she found the human prisoners. She must be more careful going forward.

A low gap between the mountains ahead of her beckoned. She pulled a pouch of nuts from her pack and munched on them as she walked toward the pass. When they were gone, she took a drink from the water flask she carried, then dug out more food. She might as well refuel while she walked.

Fajora consumed as much food as she dared. She didn't know how long her supplies had to last, so she closed her pack before she was satisfied. What she had eaten provided for her immediate energy needs. As new strength coursed through her limbs, she picked up her pace. She gauged the energy needed to scramble up the boulder-strewn path to the pass and decided to spin to the top. With the sun beginning to slant toward the west, she coalesced at the pass, looked beyond, and uttered a deep sigh of relief.

She had not been so far off in her calculations. A broad plain spread before her. She knew from Sebastian's maps that this must be unclaimed territory—contested land, Bardu had called it—a barren jumble of rocks and sand. Why would anyone fight for this space? They must want it for its strategic importance rather than for any intrinsic merit. No worthwhile prey could live there, nor would it be an attractive place for birthing dens or community gathering spots.

Fajora calculated the expenditure of energy needed to cross on foot, as well as the danger of an accident or an attack. Either seemed likely in the forbidding terrain—a disaster waiting to happen. She decided to spin across.

To the south, she detected the sparkle of water—one of the rivers that flowed into River Clan's domain from the mountains of Deep Valley Clan. A line of trees on the east side of the contested land identified the path of the river as it turned north. Those trees also marked the boundary of River Clan territory.

As she stood assessing the landscape and planning her spin trajectory, Fajora noticed movement to her right on the edge of her vision. Heart thumping, she turned her head toward the motion.

A cat wended its way down the nearest slope. It resembled Bardu in its coloring, brown shimmering to bronze in the sunlight, but it was smaller and moved with a quickness that spoke more of exuberance than caution. A young one, then?

Where a kit wandered, an adult must stalk nearby, especially this close to contested territory. Fajora scanned the nearby slopes. She detected no other cats, though she knew one or more must be there, somewhere. Her spine tingled with a suppressed shiver. She hated being watched when she couldn't see the watchers.

The young cat drew near, circling, drawing nearer with each circle. It stretched its neck out and sniffed, then sat on its haunches examining her with black eyes. It was not as small as she had first estimated. Young, yes, and not quite grown, but not a kit either. It held itself with the confidence of youth, reminding Fajora, incongruously, of Agent Trayle.

The comparison made her smile, and the cat's tufted ears twitched. It leaned forward for one last sniff before speaking.

"Are you human? You do not appear quite as other humans appear."

Fajora's smile broadened. This individual did not recognize her as Luxeran—might never have seen one. It did seem to have experience with humans, but not enough to tell the difference between the two species. The cat's ignorance might give her leverage and a chance to control the conversation.

"No," she answered. "I'm Luxeran. A Light Spinner. My name is Fajora."

"Oh." The cat pulled back a little. "Are you aware, Light Spinner, that you are trespassing in Deep Valley Clan territory?"

"Yes." Not intentionally, but this youngster didn't need to know that. Not yet, at least.

"What is your business here?"

"I'm just on my way through."

The cat thought about this for a moment. "Most odd. Where are you going?"

"Across. There." Fajora pointed to the trees hiding the sparkle of the river.

"Oh." The cat stood and drew back a few paces before sitting again. "You are a spy. I did not know Light Spinners spied for River Clan. Only the dark ones."

Fajora tried to quiet her pounding heart as she leaned into her question. "Are Dark Spinners in River Clan territory?"

The cat thought longer this time, then lifted its head as if delighted with its own superiority. "That is a silly question. As their spy, you should know the answer."

"I'm not their spy."

A low growl rumbled in the cat's chest and Fajora reminded herself that, young or not, this creature could still kill her, or at least inflict a serious injury. It approached and sniffed at her then sat back, its head at an inquisitive angle.

"You seem truthful," it said. "But why else would you be here?"

"I'm hunting for Dark Spinners and humans. River Clan or Rock Clan have them. I plan to rescue the humans and find out what the Dark Spinners are doing there."

The cat's tail switched back and forth. It lowered its head to lick the fur on its chest. After several good licks, it lifted its head, though its tongue continued to work, cleaning its muzzle. Fajora's muscles tightened, an unconscious preparation for flight.

The cat gave one last lick and yawned, showing its teeth, fully as large as those of any adult, and razor sharp. Why did cats insist on showing their teeth and reminding one of how lethally armed they were? This one closed its mouth with a snap and lifted its head in an arrogant pose, with its tufted ears angled toward Fajora. She tilted her own chin up a fraction as she tried to relax her jaw and the muscles in her shoulders.

"I do not think there are any humans in River Clan," the cat said.

Fajora sucked in a quick breath. The cat's ears twitched, affirming it had heard, but it remained otherwise still.

"How do you know this?" Fajora asked.

"Recon."

"What?"

"Re-con-nais-sance." The cat pronounced each syllable carefully, with a slight lisp, but clearly understandable.

"You've been into River Clan territory?" Fajora tried unsuccessfully to keep the surprised squeak out of her voice. So much for her dominant position and leverage.

"Yes."

"Then you're the one who's a spy."

"Scout."

"What is your name and status in your clan? Aren't you young for such a dangerous assignment?"

The fur around the cat's neck bristled, and the tail gave a sharp twitch. "I am Akachi, fully initiated member of the male council. Top candidate in my denning. Evaluated first in stealth and stalking. I am well qualified."

So. A young male. Fajora hadn't been able to guess at gender to this point. A male, full of spunk, with a still-vulnerable sense of pride.

"So, you've been to River Clan. Impressive. But what about Rock Clan? Rock Clan's probably too far away for such a young scout."

Another low growl emanated from Akachi's chest. "You were not listening, Light Spinner. I am fully qualified."

"Of course." Fajora gave the cat her best instructor's voice, mollifying while conceding nothing. "But you must prove yourself with lesser assignments before receiving such a dangerous mission. Yes?"

Akachi stood and paced around her, his tail twitching, his low growls expressing his displeasure. Fajora had hit close to the truth, and he didn't like it. She guessed he had been tempted to go into Rock Clan despite his orders. But had he acted on the temptation? This was the crucial question. If she could get him to own to an unauthorized incursion, he might be less likely to report her equally unauthorized presence within his own clan's domain.

Akachi showed no inclination to confess but continued to circle her. Either he hadn't been to Rock Clan territory, or he needed more prodding.

"Even if you'd infiltrated Rock Clan, you might not know if they are holding humans prisoner. They would be in the most heavily guarded area. Hardest to penetrate."

"Argg." The cat's evident irritation brought him to a standstill in front of her. Sitting about five paces away, he bared his teeth and licked his muzzle before speaking. "I know more than you imagine, Light Spinner. You have little knowledge of our ways."

"What do you know?" she asked in a low, conspiratorial tone.

He studied her with unblinking eyes, then yawned. "They have humans." His tone was casual. "I do not think they are prisoners. They might not want to be rescued, even if you could rescue so many by yourself. You should take more Light Spinners if you want success."

Fajora stared at him, trying to make sense of this. Jayzam had mentioned an unspecified number of humans roaming unhindered through the Rock Clan settlement. She had reported the observation to Dannel, but even she had not believed this part of Jayzam's story. Apparently, she should have.

"How many?" she managed at last.

"Difficult to count, with much coming and going. At least one hundred individuals in one settlement. As you say, I am young. I have not had time to discover all their settlements."

Fajora held Akachi's gaze while her mind reeled. Jayzam hadn't even hinted at such a large number. And Dannel had said nothing about so many people going missing from the colony. He worried about Clarise after two years, so surely he would have at least mentioned other disappearances. But if these people were not from the colony, where did they come from?

As Akachi said, it seemed unlikely they were all prisoners. Some other mystery accounted for their presence in Rock Clan. But that didn't mean the clan had no human prisoners at all.

"I do not seek any humans who live there willingly," she told Akachi. "But I believe one or two are being held against their will. Perhaps tied up, or otherwise restrained and mistreated. Is that something your clan sanctions?"

"No." Akachi perked his ears higher. "It would be shameful to allow the mortal enemy of Deep Valley Clan to behave in such a way. If it is so, the clan must be informed. Honor requires action."

"But first, we need information," Fajora said. "Recon. We need to know for sure if they have prisoners, and where they are."

"I will find out."

Without another word, Akachi stalked away from her, heading toward the contested land.

"Wait." Fajora started after him.

He stopped and looked over his shoulder, his chin lifted in a gesture of tolerance rather than welcome.

"You shouldn't do this by yourself." She saw the sudden arching of his back, the bristling around the shoulders. His was a tender pride, needing to prove itself. Wounded pride often led to foolish risks, for which she would be responsible. She spoke quickly, to placate him. "My people are also honor-bound to help these prisoners. It's part of my mission. Will you take me with you? Show me the way to the settlement with humans?"

Akachi sniffed. "If you follow me, it is nothing to me. It will save me hunting for you when I have the information you seek."

He stalked away again, turning north before he reached the bottom of the slope. With a sidelong glance toward Fajora, he loped away across the lower slopes of the mountains. He traversed with ease a jumbled terrain of rock and brush Fajora knew would take her hours to navigate.

But she was not about to lose him while she had hope he might lead her to Clarise and Sebastian. Or Dark Spinners. Taking a quick siting of his trajectory, she translated to a spin and zoomed forward.

7

———·———

INTO RIVER CLAN TERRITORY

Fajora didn't have to wait long to confirm she had sited correctly. She barely had time to regain her physical form and get her bearings before Akachi appeared, sailing over a large boulder and bounding toward her with casual grace. He stopped when he reached her and sniffed with his head held high.

"An interesting way to follow," he said.

"Which way next?"

"There is a place farther on where the hills curve out into the disputed land. I will stop there, but if you miss it or do not keep up, I will not wait."

"Understood."

The distance was longer this time, and Fajora arrived before Akachi. He took so long to appear, she wondered if she had misunderstood him and traveled to the wrong spot. To distract herself, she dug more food out of her pack. She consumed it in haste, washing it down with several gulps of water from her flask. And still the cat did not arrive.

Fajora climbed to a higher ledge to get a good view of the surrounding area, hoping to see Akachi, though she knew the cat's coat would blend in with the terrain. A scan of the rocky slopes nearby revealed nothing, but farther out, on the disputed plain, movement caught her eye.

Would Akachi traverse the disputed territory? To make faster time, perhaps? But no. More than one shape moved on the plain, heading south rather than north, and darker than Fajora's young friend. These were other cats, but from which clan?

She shaded her eyes with her hand, trying to get a better look, then started to feel her way, one cautious step at a time, down the slope.

"Stop. Remain still. They will see you. It would be better if you were not so tall or so bright."

Fajora jerked toward the voice. Akachi crouched a short way behind her, up the slope. He kept his head low, and his tail twitched, sweeping the ground behind him. From below, he would not be visible. Fajora, on the other hand, stood out like a beacon with her tall, green-clad form.

She crouched down and scooted toward the shelter of a large boulder. Here she was visible to her guide but not to the cats below. She peeked around her boulder for another look. The darker cats had moved farther south, diminishing into indistinct moving blobs against the lighter-colored sand.

"Who are they? Not Deep Valley Clan, I'm guessing."

"No. River Clan. Scouts."

"Do you need to warn your own clan?"

"No. The River Clan scouts are heading straight for a patrol crew. They will be intercepted."

"And what will you do?"

"Wait. Be silent now."

Fajora settled herself more comfortably, scooting over enough to get a good view of the receding cats while remaining concealed. When the River Clan cats were out of sight, she turned toward Akachi, expecting him to start again toward his destination, but he remained motionless. Suppressing a sigh, Fajora turned back to watching the plain.

Her attention wavered and her eyelids grew heavy as the late afternoon sun warmed her back. The boulder in front of her presented a convenient place to lean her head. She was about to give in to temptation when a low rumble from Akachi's chest snapped her back to alertness. She scanned the plain, which remained empty, desolate. But as she moved her gaze farther out, she caught movement.

Two cats paced in front of the trees marking the border of River Clan's territory. Their brown coats blended with the shadowy foliage. Even with her keen vision, Fajora would have missed them had they remained still.

They focused their attention south, in the direction the other cats, the scouts, had taken. They stopped for a moment, their bodies straining toward something beyond Fajora's view. One stepped out into the barren plain and bounded onto a tall boulder. It remained there for an instant before jumping down and racing to the south. Its companion followed in a shower of sand and dust.

As soon as they were out of sight, Akachi rose from his crouch. "Now we go. Keep as low as you can."

Fajora couldn't guess where Akachi might head next, and he didn't give her a chance to ask. He took off at a fast walk, keeping low and silent. Knowing she couldn't crouch low enough to remain concealed, Fajora translated to a spin and followed Akachi, hovering a half meter above the ground and sliding along behind boulders to shield her light from River Clan territory.

This type of controlled spinning, low and slow, was more difficult and draining than speeding high above the atmosphere or through the void. Akachi stalked ahead of Fajora with apparently boundless energy until the sun dipped behind the mountains to their left. When he finally stopped, Fajora coalesced and collapsed into a huddle. She yanked her pack off her back and dug into it for a honey nut bar and a piece of fruit.

"What are you doing?" Akachi's tone was more accusing than curious.

"Refueling. Spinning light takes a lot of energy. If I keep spinning and don't eat, eventually I won't be able to spin."

Akachi paced in a circle around Fajora, sniffing, sometimes leaning toward her as he sniffed. When he had completed the circle, he sat in front of her, observing her as she ate.

"Very well," he said. "You speak truth. This is a most curious way of being. Are you flesh or are you light?"

"Both. Flesh first. Flesh last. But in between, light is as natural to us as flesh. But only if we have sufficient fuel. So, I must eat."

Apparently satisfied with this explanation, Akachi sank down into a crouch and stared across the plain, waiting with no sign of impatience. Fajora took advantage of this to eat more than she had planned. They were getting closer to River and Rock Clans' territories. Not knowing when she'd have a chance to refuel again, she ate until sated, drank from her flask, and used a little water to clean her hands and mouth. The cats were sensitive to smells, and she didn't want to be any more conspicuous than necessary.

When Fajora had stowed her supplies and secured her pack, Akachi rose and pointed with ears and nose toward the plain below them and to the trees of River Clan beyond.

"Now the light is low enough for us to cross into River Clan. I will go first. It will take me about one sunprowl to get across. Come then, a little beyond the first group of trees. There is a small river. We will meet on its bank. Go high into the sky if you can, so the light you become is not seen crossing the plain."

"I understand. Yes, I can do that. But wait." Fajora's words stopped Akachi, who was picking his way down the slope. Now his posture hinted at impatience. "How long is a sunprowl? We have no such measure of time in my world."

"I do not know how to tell you. It is something I have always known. I do not usually need to describe it."

"How many sun prowls are there during the daylight?"

"From sunup to sundown there are fourteen this time of year. In the winter there are fewer. One must consider the season when telling prowls."

"Fourteen now. So it's close to the humans' hour here on Kakislane. A little longer, but not too much. Without a timepiece, I won't be exact, but I'll do my best."

"Very well."

Fajora watched his progress down the slope until the gathering dusk hid him. Her training included an understanding of time calculations, but she was less adept at this than at spatial determinations, and even that ability had failed her today. Besides, she had been up and traveling all day after a short, restless night. She longed for sleep. Just a little nap. She wished she had brought one of the human handheld devices with her. They could be set to alert their holder at a specified time. Without such a device, she dared not sleep, unless she wanted to be right here when the sun rose again in the morning.

So, she struggled against the desire to close her eyes. Yet, despite her efforts, she slipped into a light doze.

A sound jerked her awake. She sat motionless, barely breathing, listening, expecting to be discovered at any moment. A long call, deep and soft, floated across the valley, sending shivers along Fajora's arms and constricting her chest. Had the owl's call awakened her? If so, she was grateful to it.

She strained her eyes, searching for a flying shape in the dusky sky. But the owl did not show itself, and Fajora detected no further sound beyond that of the wind moaning through the rocks. She shook herself, focusing her mind on her mission. She was late now, judging by the absence of light. Past time to go.

She stuffed her pockets with packets of nuts, dried fruit, and grain wafers before she shrugged into her pack and translated to light. She spun in a high arc over the plain below, aware the Wellador Colony's sensors might detect her, giving them her location. But she didn't have a viable choice. Akachi guided her now. With him, she had her best chance of finding what she sought. So she followed his instructions and hoped for a sleepy or distracted sensor tech.

From above, she discerned a ribbon of silver glinting with moonlight among the trees. Akachi's river, she assumed, and arched toward it. She coalesced on its bank and peered around, trying to see in the dark as her eyes adjusted. She detected no sign of Akachi. He could be anywhere along the river, in either direction. Or he might have given up on her and continued with his scouting mission.

She opened her mouth to call for him, then snapped it shut. If the flash of light as she landed here had not attracted the notice of River Clan cats, calling aloud surely would.

Fajora moved away from the river bank, scanning for tracks as she did so. Nothing. In the dark, she might simply be missing them, or there might be none to see.

The shadows shifted as she moved, giving her imagination ample material with which to concoct every shape of danger. A small shadow trembled; she drew breath to cry out, but stifled the cry as she realized she saw the trembling of a low-hanging tree branch. Larger shadows became other cats, older scouts and warriors, River Clan cats, Rock Clan cats, and the orange-and-black-striped Big Leaf Clan cats, though they lived far from this river. No cats, other than those from Big Leaf and Sacred Mountain Clans, stood tall enough to make that shadow on the far side of the stream. She had never seen a member of Sacred Mountain Clan, so her subconscious mind reasoned the cat must be from Big Leaf Clan. Until a breeze shook the shadow and it became a large shrub.

A shadow ghosted through the air above her head. Prepared to laugh at herself for her vivid imaginings, Fajora realized an instant later this shadow was an actual creature, another sentient being. She saw wide-spread wings moving with silent strength as only owls' wings can do, gone before she thought to call out or voice a question, the answer to which she would not have understood, anyway.

She waited for a time, ten to fifteen minutes, she judged, but Akachi did not appear. How long should she wait? He must be across the plain by now. Deciding she had waited long enough, that she had come too late and he had moved on, she started northeast, picking her way across the rocks along the river to avoid the deep brush farther out.

Stealth had not been part of her training; no matter how hard she tried to be silent, she made constant noises. Her boot scraping a rock. The swish of a branch as she brushed against it. A tiny splash as her foot struck a puddle in the hollow of a stepping stone. Small noises, but cats, with their sharp hearing, would notice them. One was bound to find her soon—Akachi, she hoped, and not a River Clan cat.

A wild scream, followed by angry snarls, brought her to a stop. A chill shivered down her spine. More snarls and yowls and hissing reverberated through the forest, though how near and from which direction eluded Fajora. She stood frozen, unsure which way to run, or even if she should run at all. She reached for light, held herself ready to spin, then waited, muscles tense, for a signal telling her what to do.

The yowling and snarling continued for several minutes, followed by a piercing cry. Fajora shivered. She wanted to translate to light, but she forced herself to wait.

A feline form rushed out of the shrubbery west of the river. Fajora gasped, then bit down hard on the yelp that tried to escape her lips. The cat reached her before she could spin. She stumbled backwards.

"You are late," a familiar feline voice said in a low grumble. "River Clan knows we are here. Follow me and do not fall behind."

Fajora let out her breath in a gasp. She started to shake, an unexpected reaction. She was trained to react in a cool, decisive manner, but her body apparently didn't realize that.

Akachi's dim form disappeared among the dark vegetation. She dashed after him.

He stopped short of the river bank, sniffing at the ground before he approached the water's edge. Here he hesitated again, and a shiver ran the length of his back, accompanied by a low growl. He dipped a paw into the water, testing it, then plunged in, holding his tail high.

The shallow water came halfway up his legs. It sloshed over the top of Fajora's short boots as she followed him in. Warm and slow-moving, its current tugged gently at her legs. The river bottom, smooth, with more sand than rock, made for easy walking.

She eyed the far bank, looking for an easy place to climb up out of the riverbed, but Akachi didn't head that way. Instead, he turned and sloshed downstream, lifting his paws high. His whole body proclaimed his disgust, but Fajora gladly remained in the riverbed, thankful for the open space it provided, where she could see her guide clearly. If he came up out of the river and started through the thick vegetation, she would have trouble seeing him to follow.

They stayed in the river until they came to a wide pebble beach. Here, Akachi led Fajora out of the water. They followed the beach for a time until the forest opened up and the underbrush thinned. Akachi stalked up the low bank and into the pathless forest, padding over a thick layer of mulch and leaf mold.

Fajora tried to ignore the squishing of her boots and be grateful for the easy walking this open woodland afforded, but she remained tense. It was effortless walking, but too open. Any cat in the area would see them long before they saw it. But Akachi stepped along with no sign of concern.

The only concession he made to possible danger was to stop often and sniff the air, but if he detected other cats nearby, he didn't tell Fajora. She could only guess at what information the air brought him. When he increased their pace, did it mean cats were behind them? When he plunged into denser underbrush, was it because River Clan cats converged on the open area? When he broke into a fast trot, did he think they'd been seen?

She could not mistake what Akachi detected when he stopped, sniffed, flicked his ears toward the path behind Fajora, and hissed at her.

"Run." His command ended in a low growl.

8

PUSUIT

Akachi shot away, weaving through the brush on paws that scarcely touched the ground. Fajora struggled to keep him in sight, hampered by the darkness that allowed her to discern him only as a flitting shadow. Her height was a liability, making it difficult to evade branches the cat slunk beneath. They slapped at her, scratching her hands and face, and stole her attention when she needed to focus on the rough ground beneath her feet.

She pushed a tree branch out of her way, and it rebounded, slapping her on the back as her foot struck a rock in the path. She stumbled, keeping her feet by grasping at the next tree branch ahead of her. Her breath came hard and gasping. She was creating a trail of sound and disturbed vegetation no cat could fail to notice.

Akachi led her out of the dense brush and into a narrow space between two soaring boulders. Relief surged as Fajora got her feet more firmly under her, then ebbed away as the space between the boulders dwindled. Akachi slunk through the narrow slot without a sound, without touching its walls. But Fajora's shoulders scraped the boulders, and when she angled her body to avoid this, her pack scraped loudly against the stone.

She paused to slip one arm out of its strap, which allowed her to hold the pack toward the opposite shoulder. She moved more easily after that until the unevenly distributed weight of the pack fatigued her. But as her steps lagged, a yowl behind her sent prickles down her spine, and a rush of adrenaline gave her renewed energy. She saw the sharp line of sky ahead, brightened by moonlight and contrasting with the deep dark of the boulders, as they gave way to open space. A little farther and she would win free of this tight space, ready to run again, or turn and fight.

The boulders pulled together before the opening, making an even tighter space. Fajora squeezed through without diminishing her speed, but jerked to a stop as her pack flipped sideways and stuck. As she tugged on it, she scanned the open area in front of her. The flat, smooth stone disappeared into black nothingness in about twenty paces. A gulf, too wide for her to see the other side in the dark, opened abruptly with no clue as to what lay beyond.

Akachi was not far ahead of her. He slowed his pace long enough to cast a quick glance back at Fajora and toss his head to urge her forward. Then he sped up, bunched his muscles, and sailed over the yawning gulf. Fajora heard his scrabble for firm footing and a deep growl followed by a hiss. After that, silence.

An attack on the far side would have been accompanied by additional growls and the scuffling of combat. Akachi's vocalizations must be his way of calling her to follow. If that wasn't enough to move her, the sounds of snarling approaching behind her gave her all the motivation she needed. But she could not free her pack. For a moment, she considered leaving it behind. But if she didn't have her pack, she didn't eat. And if she didn't eat, she would soon be stumbling homeward, hoping to reach safety before her light gave out, a second Jayzam, emaciated, weak, perhaps even dying.

Then her mind cleared and she reached for light, enveloping her pack, tightening her spin. In a flash, she cleared the gulf, guessing the distance by sound, and coalescing beside Akachi. She caught the gleam of his dark eyes as he turned away from her.

"Come." His movement muted the snap in his voice. He wasted no time checking to see if she followed as he broke into a swift trot.

Fajora snugged her pack over both shoulders and hurried after him. As she followed Akachi into the dense undergrowth of a new swatch of forest, she glanced back toward the abyss but could see nothing in the dark. The yowls and snarls from that direction left no doubt, however, that the River Clan cats had emerged from between the two boulders across the gorge. Had they glimpsed her before the trees concealed her? Cats had great night vision, but even if they didn't see her, she left an unmistakable trail of scent along her route.

Akachi kept a fast pace, so fast that even with her long legs, Fajora had difficulty keeping up with him. She lost sight of him and considered translating to light, but then, unaccountably, he paused and she caught up to him. He sniffed at a plant growing in a patch of filtered moonlight. When Fajora skidded to a halt beside him, he batted the plant with his paw.

"Bring a branch of this," he said. "Do not make it obvious you have harvested it."

With that, he took off again. Puzzled, Fajora broke a stem from the back of the plant where the break didn't show. Securing it in her fist, she chased after Akachi again, the earthy fragrance of the plant's leaves refreshing her as she ran.

Now, Akachi traveled at an easy lope that allowed him more time to sniff the air and identify the plants along the way. Three times more, he paused and indicated a branch for Fajora to harvest. Though the scent of the plants differed, they all exuded a strong fragrance, pleasant at first but overwhelming to Fajora's senses by the time the odor of the fourth branch mingled with the others.

They came to a wide, shallow stream. Akachi paused, flicked at the water with one paw, and, with a shudder, waded in and followed the flow downstream. Fajora hesitated as well. Her boots were beginning to dry, and she didn't want to soak them again. But there was no better way to throw their pursuers off their trail than by hiding their scent in moving water. River Clan cats might not have Akachi's reluctance to get their feet wet, but they would have to divide their numbers to check both upstream and downstream, and would have slow going as they tried to determine their prey's exit point.

Akachi showed no inclination to leave the water, and they waded for nearly an hour by Fajora's uncertain estimate. The stream grew narrower and deeper, and Fajora felt, more than saw, the banks rising higher on either side. Akachi slowed, sniffing loudly, looking for something. Another plant? But why? The usefulness of those Fajora already carried eluded her. What use was one more?

Sniffing hard with her inferior smelling apparatus, Fajora caught a familiar scent. It matched one of the plants she carried, and it grew stronger as they waded closer to the right bank. The bank loomed high above them, thick with vegetation. Akachi stopped and sniffed, then rose up on his hind legs, front paws resting on the high bank, which loomed tall enough now to make even Fajora feel short.

Akachi lowered himself back onto all four paws and turned toward Fajora.

"Cave. Do you see it? Can you get into it without making light?"

Fajora edged close to the bank and felt around until she found an opening a little under shoulder high. She patted the edges with her hands and brushed hanging vines aside as she explored its width and height. It was large enough to hold herself and Akachi, if it went back far enough.

She tried lifting herself up, reached for light, let it go. She understood Akachi's warning against making light. Her pack and the branches in her hand made her awkward. She shifted the pack off her shoulders and laid it inside the opening against the left side, keeping one strap out, ready t0 grab if she needed to run before she could get into the cave. She laid her fragrant branches on top of the pack, and, with a small jump to get high enough for leverage, she hoisted herself into the opening.

The inside of the cave was deeply dark, but, from a kneeling position, Fajora reached back to test the size of the space. Her hand bumped against a rough back wall. A meter, she guessed. Maybe a little more. And about as wide. A mere grotto.

As she turned around, squirming into a sitting position, a shadow flew at her from outside, followed by a thump and a spray of water. She gasped and a low hiss answered her. Fur, wet in places but as soft as the first coat of a baby chezok, rubbed her arm as Akachi turned and settled with his face near the cave opening. Fajora caught his scent, faint but alive and clean. She breathed deeply, resisting the urge to bury her face in his coat. She pulled back instead, making herself as small as possible as he leaned his head forward, his ears erect and his nose working.

When he was satisfied, Akachi turned toward her. "The plants. Do you have them?" His voice came to her as a low rumble, barely audible above the music of the stream below them.

"Yes," she whispered. "What do I do with them?"

"Lay two of them beside me and rub yourself with the leaves of the others. All over. It will disguise your own scent."

"Which do you want?"

"Any two."

Fajora fumbled with the plants as she gathered them from atop her pack, and their scent pervaded the small space. She laid two of the branches on the floor of the grotto. Akachi scooched his hindquarters closer to the back wall and rubbed his head and neck across the leaves. He turned and twisted onto his back with his paws in the air, rolling a little to expose both sides to the oils in the plants.

Fajora watched, forgetting her own leaves, enchanted by the supple agility of his body. His movements had the appearance of play, though his purpose was deadly serious. As he completed one turn, his head came up, and he fixed his gaze on her, sniffing. He uttered a low growl as he commenced a second roll on the branches.

Taking his warning to heart, Fajora bunched the leaves of her own plants into one hand and rubbed her skin briskly with them. The odors, pleasant in themselves, minty and earthy, overwhelmed her senses. She felt a sneeze coming and buried her face in her sleeve to stifle it.

She started rubbing again, working with slow methodical motions to keep the fragrance to a bearable level. Akachi finished rolling on his leaves and pulled back to the deepest part of the grotto. His paw touched Fajora's elbow, motioning her back as well. She scooted back until his barely audible hiss warned her to stop. Lifting eyes to the rim of the grotto, she caught motion as a tail swished down from above, once, twice, three times.

A River Clan cat sat above them on top of the stream bank.

9

WHAT RIVER CLAN FOUND

Fajora held her hand still, the branch pressed tight against her skin, and worried that the fragrance of the freshly crushed leaves was too strong. The cat above must detect the scent. Fajora huddled against Akachi's soft fur, waiting for the River Clan cat to leap down and discover her. She imagined its eyes, intent and unblinking, as it called to its fellows, and its sharp teeth and claws ripping into her flesh.

And what would happen to Akachi? She had heard of cats adopting the young of another clan into their own community, but Akachi was too old for that. A trained warrior of Deep Valley Clan, he would not be dissuaded from his loyalty. They might hold him as a hostage, or, more likely, kill him on the spot if he could not fight his way clear.

Fajora gave herself a mental shake. Why such dire thoughts, when she needed only to spin herself and her guide into light and flit away from the enemies all around? She reached for light, but at the first glimmer swirling around her fingers, sharp teeth gripped her sleeve, pressing into her skin. She turned her head to find Akachi's dark eyes glittering in the faint spark of light, their glare warning her, commanding her, even.

She dropped her spin and pressed closer against him, ready for light but willing to wait. River Clan had not discovered them yet. The grotto that concealed them and Akachi's subterfuge with the scented leaves might be adequate to hide them. When the others cats moved on, Fajora and her companion could emerge and continue their quest for the captives.

She leaned back, taking deep, controlled breaths.

Akachi showed his approval by turning away from her. With silent movement, he stretched out his front legs and laid his head on his paws, appearing to be at rest, though he held his ears erect and his nose sniffed in a ceaseless test of the scents on the air.

Time slid away. The tip of the tail hanging in front of the grotto entrance curled up, then flicked out of view. Fajora held her breath and leaned forward, listening, but heard no sound except the croak of a frog a little way upstream. If Akachi, with his sensitive nose, knew whether the cat still sat above them with its tail curled around its body, or had moved on, he gave Fajora no sign.

The longer she sat, cramped in the small space with no idea what was going on outside, the more Fajora's fear gave way to impatience and curiosity. What were the River Clan cats doing? Did they have any idea where she and Akachi were? If they gave up on the stream, where would they go next? She didn't believe they would give up on trying to find intruders in their territory. With war in the offing, she expected patrols to be even more aggressive than usual, regarding any intruder as a threat to be neutralized.

Ever so slowly and quietly, Fajora scooted forward toward the grotto opening, trying to catch any sound of movement outside, trying to get a better view. Akachi glanced her way but didn't stop her. The first glimmers of daylight created a world of flitting shadows as the trees and shrubs danced in the breeze and the stream skittered along below them. A cat could be in the vegetation, camouflaged by the shift of light and shadow, and she would never see it. But it would see her if she stuck her head out too far.

Even so, her curiosity prompted her to lean out farther. Still Akachi gave no sign. When she could no longer tamp down her impatience, she leaned close to his ear and spoke in a low whisper.

"Are they still there, outside? Or can we move on?"

Akachi lifted his head and turned his face toward her. "I do not smell them. They have gone. But how far? It is too soon for us to move. We wait."

He put his head back on his paws and closed his eyes. Unless Fajora wanted to spin away and continue without him, she had no choice but to wait until he was ready. She slipped a packet of mixed nuts and fruit out of her pack and munched on them, then pushed the pack into the back corner of the grotto to make more room for her legs. As comfortable as she could get in the small space, she leaned her head against the back wall and closed her eyes.

She had been up all night, and had started early the previous morning, so, as soon as she let herself relax, she fell asleep. She slept until a soft paw patted her cheek. Opening her eyes, she squinted against the bright light filling the grotto opening. A furry face sniffed her own, and a wet, cold nose nudged her. It took her a confused moment to remember where she was, who Akachi was.

As she opened her eyes wider, Akachi pulled away and sat on his haunches.

"We go now," he said.

"Is it safe?"

"As safe as it will be. You must go first. Down into the water. The near side is rocky. Jump to the far side where there is flat sand on the bottom."

He pushed at Fajora with his nose, urging her to the opening. The sun blazed above the edge of the trees and beat at her face as she pulled herself to the lip of the grotto and prepared to jump. She sat at the edge, letting her feet dangle, then pushed off with her arms, propelling herself to the far side of the stream. She landed with a splash but found good footing at once, and, after a little wobble, she got her balance. A moment later, Akachi landed beside her. The splash of his landing wet his coat, and he shook the water away with a low growl.

Fajora suppressed a giggle as she followed him downstream. He lifted his feet high with each step and held his tail high, proclaiming his disdain for this wet trail with every step. But despite his dislike of the water, he kept to the stream for several hours, until the sun reached its zenith. Finally, when the bank had fallen to only a slight rise on the right-hand side and a broad, gravel shingle opened out on the left-hand side, he led Fajora out of the water.

She wanted to take off her boots and wring out her socks, but Akachi didn't stop until they were well away from the stream. He waited until he found a secluded opening encircled by tall shrubs and warmed by the early afternoon sun.

Here he sat on his haunches and worked on his coat, licking with an industry that amused and charmed Fajora. He gave his paws special attention, working around each toe and licking until it seemed they would be as wet from his tongue as from the stream.

Watching him reminded Fajora of her own wet feet. She tugged her boots off and turned them upside down to drain. Then she pulled off her socks and wrung them hard. Water poured from them. When she couldn't wring another drop from them, she laid them on the grass beside her and spread her feet out in front of her, wiggling her toes and letting them dry in the sun.

She knew she should put everything back on at once in case she had to run from an attack of River Clan cats, but Akachi showed no concern as he worked on his coat, so she risked the luxury of letting the socks dry as well. As she settled more comfortably to wait on Akachi's grooming, her stomach rumbled. Except for her quick snack in the grotto, it had been hours since she had eaten. It wouldn't do to get too low on energy.

Even walking required energy, but that was nothing to what spinning required. She had to be ready.

So, time to eat. She reached around for her pack, but didn't find it. She jumped to her feet and turned in a circle, scanning the clearing while her heart rate accelerated and the rush of adrenaline weakened her legs.

"Akachi, my pack. Where is it?"

Akachi lifted his head from his work on his chest and stared at her with unblinking eyes. He made a quick scan of the area.

"It is not here. Did you leave it in the cave?"

Fajora thought back. She had shoved the pack into the corner to make more room. And when it came time to leave, her focus had been on getting out of the grotto and across the stream for a safe landing. With never a thought for retrieving the pack.

"Yes. I have to go back for it."

"Why? Does it not encumber you needlessly?"

"No. I mean, it is easier walking without it, but it has my food. I need it. I can't go too long without eating."

"It is an axiom of mission training that one must sometimes operate on short rations, and go hungry if the conditions demand such."

"No, you don't understand." Panic made Fajora's voice crack. She took a deep breath to steady it. "If I don't eat, if I don't keep my energy high, I won't be able to spin when I need to. It requires extreme energy always at the ready."

Taking several more deep breaths to push away the panic, Fajora looked around the clearing carefully. Were there native sources of food she could substitute for the supplies in her pack? A glow of red on one of the shrubs warranted closer inspection.

A shiny berry hung, tantalizing, on a low branch. Fajora didn't recognize it from her studies of native foods. She plucked it, sniffed its bright red skin, and held it toward Akachi.

"Is this safe to eat?"

"Spring berry," he said. "Useful to give kits when they eat something they should not. Makes them vomit. Your system is different, so you might be able to eat it. I do not think it will kill you."

Fajora shook her head. "I can't afford to make myself sick. Are there any fruits or nuts, or even roots, nearby that are safe?"

Off-world training for new agents included a course in edible wild foods on each world. Agents must review the lists every year and pass identification tests. Fajora knew of several possibilities growing in River Clan territory, though most were low on the energy index. But nothing in this clearing looked familiar.

"Cats do not eat many plants," Akachi answered. "I know of some succulent grasses near my home in Deep Valley territory, but I am unfamiliar with plants in River Clan."

"I'll find some things, if I have time to forage."

"We cannot linger. River Clan cats will find us if we stay here too long."

"Right. I've got to get my pack." Fajora sat and pulled on her socks, then reached for her boots.

"That, too, is dangerous," Akachi said. "River Clan scouts will be watching the area. You will walk into an ambush."

"I'll spin there and back." She pulled on her second boot and stood. "It won't take long. They won't be able to follow me. Wait here."

Without giving him opportunity for further protest, Fajora translated to a spin and headed back to the grotto. It took only a moment to reach the stream. She slowed, becoming a hovering light only a little brighter than the sunlight sifting down through the foliage of the trees except that, unlike sunlight, she was not stationary, but drifted upstream. She didn't remember how far they had walked and she didn't want to zoom past the grotto, missing it altogether.

Her slow pace was fortuitous, for she became aware of a commotion around the little cave before she reached it. Though without physical eyes while spinning light, she was aware of things around her in a more nebulous way. She perceived that several cats paced along the bank above the grotto opening and two cats stood in the stream below.

Fajora veered away from the stream and hid her light in a tree on the far bank, a little removed from the cats but still within view. Identifying a branch strong enough to hold her weight, she settled above it and partially coalesced. She checked to be sure the foliage protected her from discovery before bringing herself almost into full physical form. She held onto a shimmer of light so she could translate and spin away in an instant if the cats detected her.

As she settled on her branch, she scanned the surrounding trees. She knew cats climbed trees, and she didn't need any surprise companions. Her gaze roved from left to right, checking the trees across the river as well as those nearby on her side. As her survey reached the tree closest to her on the right, a dark shape came into her line of vision. Startled, she teetered and flung an arm out to restore her balance. She grasped a branch over her head and froze, with breath held, hoping none of the cats below noticed the sudden movement. After a quick, reassuring glance down, she lifted her eyes to stare at the shape on a branch a little higher than her own.

An owl roosted there. About as tall as Fajora's forearm was long, with ear tufts that added to the appearance of height, it had delicate facial markings and bolder patterns of brown, gray, and white on its chest and wings. Its eyes were closed, making the long, yellow beak the prominent feature in its facial disc.

Fajora had never seen an owl at such close quarters. A shadow in the dark, a flash of wings in muted colors, the glow of eyes quickly shuttered. These things she had seen, or thought she had seen. But nothing compared to this owl, complete in its majesty and its indifference. She marveled at how self-sufficient the beings of this world were, the cats and owls, who, sharing sentience with her own people, the Luxerans, and with the humans, yet seemed to regard them as unnecessary beings, intruders in their world.

Fajora recalled little from her youthful foray into prophecy, but one idea stuck, an idea most scholars agreed upon. All sentient species would share in the final struggle against the shadow of the Dark Immortals and their subordinates. As she gazed at this magnificent creature, she wondered at this prophecy. Though the owl must be aware of her arrival so near its roost and could rip her apart with its sharp beak and clutching talons, it ignored her, giving the appearance of unconcerned slumber. What event, what threat, could wake this creature to its brotherhood with the other sentient beings of the Dominion?

For the moment, Fajora preferred the bird not notice her. This allowed her to deal with her business down below without more than a niggling of fear. If the owl opened its eyes or moved, she must be alert, ready to quit its neighborhood at a moment's notice.

With one last, careful inspection of the owl, who did not move or show any awareness of her, Fajora turned her attention back to the river and the cats. She could see the opening into the grotto. She had a clear path to spin in, envelop her pack within her light and flash out again. Unless . . . . Movement caught her eye. Was that a tail hanging over the rim of the opening? She leaned forward to get a better view into the dark, shadowed cave.

A large cat came to the opening. Fajora bit her lip so hard she broke the skin. The bitter taste of blood echoed her bitterness of spirit. With cats in the cave, she had little chance of retrieving her pack.

If she moved with boldness, she might spin in, twisting around the cats, snatch her pack, and spin away again. The cats wouldn't be able to follow her light. But during that brief time in the cave, as she decreased the speed of her spin to absorb the pack into her light, too much could go wrong. Even the slightest wavering of her concentration could slow her spin too much and expose her flesh, giving a cat something to dig its claws into. And if that happened, she would likely lose her spin altogether and be at the mercy of the River Clan cats.

Even worse, Akachi might decide to come looking for her and step into an ambush. Even now, the longer she waited, the higher the chance he would wonder what kept her and come, assuming she was in trouble. She couldn't wait, and a return to the cave later would further sap her diminishing reserves, perhaps with no better result.

She probed at her logic, checking for a hole, for whatever she had overlooked that would let her snag her pack. And came up with nothing. She needed to go back, taking a direct route and conserving her energy.

Such a careless mistake, one that would have merited a stiff punishment had it been made by a trainee or junior agent. Well, she would receive punishment enough, she feared. She felt her mission slipping away, and the final blow came like an insult when the cat in the cave pushed something to the edge. Fajora identified it as her pack as the cat rolled it over the rim and sent it hurtling into the stream below.

The two cats in the stream pounced on it, snarling, and dragged it to the bank opposite the cave. The largest, a sleek brown individual with white markings down its back and tail, swiped at it with unsheathed claws, creating a great rent down one side. Packages of food spilled out. The cat sniffed at them and tore several of them open before pushing them aside. The other cat pawed at them, its snarling loud enough to reach Fajora's tree branch.

They examined each package, clawing at it until they rendered it unusable. Even if Fajora managed to salvage some of the food, it would be difficult to carry with the packaging ruined and the pack itself slashed open. But the chance of retrieving something kept her clinging to her tree, watching the cats with a mixture of horror and curiosity.

Turning from the scattered food with nose twitching and indistinct snarls, the two cats pulled Fajora's spare clothing from the ruined pack. A tunic held their attention, and one of them called to the other cats who watched from the grotto and the upper bank. The large cat in the grotto answered.

Fajora didn't understand their speech. It consisted of hisses, yowls, and growls, a language better suited to their vocal apparatus than Standard. The meaning of the conversation became clear, however, when the other cats jumped into the stream and waded across, showing none of the hesitation or disgust Akachi had exhibited at getting his feet wet. The cats congregated around the tunic, sniffing and pawing at it, then pulled a pair of underdrawers from the pack and treated it to a similar examination.

Fajora cringed at this display of her undergarments, though modesty was the least of her worries. When two of the cats grasped these garments in their mouths and loped away with them, she understood their intention. Soon every member of the clan, or at least every member with a part in her pursuit, would have learned her scent. They need not come back to the trail to hunt for her. Any place she went within their territory, guards and scouts would be on the lookout for her. And there could be only so many ways to hide her scent. Even Akachi would run out of strategies.

She pressed her lips hard to hold at bay the tears that threatened despite her careful training and long years of experience with every kind of setback. Though she had handled worse defeats, more serious setbacks, they had been in the line of duty and impersonal. This was personal. The failure of this mission meant the failure to keep her promise, her last word to Jayzam.

As she shifted on her branch, preparing to leave her hiding place, she glanced one last time at the owl. Its round eyes were open, the yellow orbs staring at her with an unblinking, penetrating scrutiny. The knowledge, the sentience of the creature shone through its gaze. Fajora stared back, mute, caught by the deep assurance of truth and justice she read there, an assurance requiring no response.

The owl blinked and closed its eyes again, releasing Fajora.

10

UNEXPECTED IN ROCK CLAN

Fajora translated into light and headed back to Akachi, adopting a moderate, relaxed spin to conserve as much energy as possible. She coalesced in the middle of the tiny clearing to find the young cat pacing around its edge and growling. He stopped and sat on his haunches, watching her with unblinking eyes as she finished taking on physical form.

"You do not have your pack?" The inflection of his voice made this as much a question as a statement.

She told him what she had seen and her conclusions about why the cats took her clothing.

"Yes," Akachi agreed. "River Clan has your scent. But we are near their border. Soon we will cross into Rock Clan territory. I do not think River Clan will follow us there."

Finally, some good news, if Fajora could believe it. She didn't expect the cats she had seen at the cave would give up easily. And it wouldn't matter much if they did. She could not go far without food. She told Akachi this.

"I have only a few packets of food in my pockets. I will eat those and have the energy to go a little farther, or to go home, but not much more."

Akachi sat regarding her for a long moment, unblinking. Finally, he twitched and bent his head to give his chest a few licks. His actions gave Fajora the sense of a shrug.

"I see," he said when he finished with his brief grooming session. "As my denning master often said, one must determine the balance between safety and boldness. At times it is necessary to take great risks, but at other times, one can leave a mission and regroup to try again when there is better hope of success. Wisdom suggests this is one such time."

Fajora sat down hard and pulled her knees close to her chest. "I'm not sure you understand. If I go back now, I won't get another chance. I have enemies at home who will make sure I don't come back. Might even make sure I get sent home to my own world."

"And your mission? It is so important you would be willing to take bold risks to achieve success?"

"Yes." Fajora pushed fallen leaves around with one hand, trying to think of a way to make this cat, from a foreign culture, understand. What values could she appeal to that would resonate with him? She knew of only one.

She lifted her head and met his gaze. "It's about honor, you see."

His ears pricked up. Good. She had his full attention now.

"First, it's about my husband's honor. My mate. Jayzam. The humans asked him to come and find a woman who had disappeared. Clarise. He found her in Rock Clan. He had a duty to rescue her, but too many enemies came against him, and he failed. People back home didn't believe him when he claimed Rock Clan held Clarise prisoner. They laughed at him and dishonored him."

"Why is he not here to restore his own honor?"

"He died." Saying it bluntly was easier than making long explanations. "So I came to finish his mission and restore his honor."

"That is well. Any clan member would do the same. The whole clan is dishonored when one member is dishonored."

Fajora flashed a brief smile. "Good. You understand one reason I'm here. But my people also dishonor themselves by allowing Clarise to remain a prisoner. Rock Clan mistreated her and Jayzam saw Dark Spinners involved. A retrieval mission should have been organized at once, to remove the Dark Spinners and rescue Clarise. But no one would do anything. So, I'm here to restore Jayzam's honor and the honor of my whole people. How can I give up and go home?"

"Ah." Akachi flicked his tail and paced in a circle around Fajora. He sniffed at her from time to time, but she suspected he was less interested in investigating her truthfulness than in buying himself time to form a response.

After making several circles around her, Akachi stopped in front of Fajora and sat on his haunches, his gaze steady, his ears perked to their most erect position. He spoke to her in formal tones.

"Light Spinner, I honor your mission. When we met, I did not know you came on a mission of honor, but by taking it upon myself to guide you, I now share in your mission. Your honor is my own. To abandon you now would dishonor myself and my clan. In addition, my enemy, Rock Clan, must be held accountable for their dishonorable actions, if they are mistreating humans. Come. If you wish to continue, to find this human and restore your mate's honor, I will find food for you, but not until we are in Rock Clan territory. We must go now and reach the border before River Clan picks up your scent."

He trotted off into the brush without giving her a chance to answer. Fajora stared after him, feeling a new surge of hope. She scrambled to her feet and followed him, pushing through the same brush, hoping she hadn't already lost him.

She found him a short way ahead, sitting on his haunches and waiting for her. As soon as he saw her, he stood and walked on again, not giving her a chance to catch up.

Akachi's route took them down a long slope and into a rocky ravine. After a short scramble up the other side of the ravine, they entered a more barren area filled with rocky formations. At first, these rose shoulder high on Fajora, but as she and her guide wended their way among the structures, the formations grew taller.

"Here we enter Rock Clan territory," Akachi said over his shoulder. He did not wait for Fajora to comment, but turned back to sniffing out the trail ahead.

When the tallest formation towered far over Fajora's head, they came to a small, slow stream. It wound through a mini-oasis, where a dam of stones and rubble created a wide pool. Fajora longed to stop in the shade of the one sizable tree flourishing there, but Akachi did not slow down. Fajora paused, letting him get farther ahead while she scanned the vegetation around the pool for anything edible. But she saw nothing, other than a few more of the shiny spring berries. After letting her eyes linger a moment longer on the green of the oasis, Fajora hurried to catch up with Akachi, following him along a trail that quickly gained in elevation.

He stopped at a smaller pool, high enough above the oasis that Fajora looked down on the larger pool. No vegetation grew in the rocky ground nearby, but the pool held deep, clear water. Fajora sank down and scooped the water in her cupped hand, letting the cool liquid slide down her throat and wash away the dust of the trail. Akachi, too, came near and lapped at the water, though his ears twitched and he lifted his head often to look around.

When they had slaked their thirst, Fajora leaned against one of the rock formations, taking advantage of the shade created by its bulk. Akachi performed a quick clean-up after his drink, then stood, sniffing.

"You wait here," he said in commanding tones, "but keep a sharp lookout. I will hunt."

Before Fajora could respond, he bounded away, as silent and swift as a flicker of spun light, leaving Fajora alone. She suppressed a grunt of exasperation. If junior agents under her supervision took this much initiative without even discussing options with her, they would be in for strict discipline. Not because she wished to stifle and control them, but because her experience equipped her to understand dangers and risks better than they.

But Akachi didn't appear to consider himself under her supervision. Despite his youth, he took charge as if he were the leader of the mission. And Fajora didn't like it.

She mused on this for a while, stretching out her legs and leaning against a stone pillar in a comfortable position for thinking. It had been a long time since she had experienced this preemptive assumption of command from the underside. Was this how younger agents felt when she gave orders?

Of course, they were expected to follow the chain of command as appropriate for their rank in the service, but might a little more leeway elicit a higher level of performance from them than a slavish adherence to command structures? A picture of Trayle formed in Fajora's mind. Yes, she must give more thought and experimentation to this when she returned to her duties in the enclave.

While she waited for Akachi to return, she soaked in the warm sunlight, letting it bolster her lagging energies. Soothed by the light's warmth but needing to stay alert, she set herself a series of mental exercises to calm and prepare herself for whatever she faced next. She completed them just as Akachi trotted into view, a mangled, bloody animal hanging from his mouth.

He dropped the creature at his feet and sat on his haunches, regarding her with an expectant gaze.

"What is that?" Fajora suppressed a shudder. Similar to the rabbits of her native Luxera, the animal was bigger and leaner, with leathery paws and huge ears. Blood soaked its sand-colored fur.

"It is a Rothfur. A little tough, but good for energy."

"I don't have any way to skin it. I don't have a knife. And I can't eat the fur."

Akachi blinked, then moved forward and caught at the animal with his teeth, holding it while his unsheathed claws ripped the fur away.

"There," he said. "It is ready for you."

"Umm. I'll need wood to make a fire."

"A fire! What do you want that for?"

"I need to cook the Rothfur before I eat it." The sight of the bloody meat made Fajora's stomach churn. Luxerans did not normally eat meat, though agents were trained to do so when necessary. She had eaten roasted goat on Sek-Nar, and pan-fried fish on Merdoma. She had never eaten raw meat.

"What foolishness. The meat is good. It will help you do this spinning you do whether or not it is cooked, yes?"

"Yes. If I can eat it. But I'm not sure I can." Fajora looked again at the bloody flesh and shuddered.

"You must try. You cannot have a fire in Rock Clan territory. Even I know this, young as I am." Akachi turned his dark gaze on her and bared his teeth. "Too young you think I am, but I know better than you in this. I have hunted for you. Eat."

With trembling hands, Fajora reached out and touched the meat. It was warm and sickly moist, with a strong smell of blood. Holding her breath, she leaned closer as she picked it up, bringing it up to her mouth. She bit into it and gagged. She pulled away, taking deep, slow breaths, trying to calm her stomach, and tried again.

This time, she forced herself to bite into it, tearing off a small piece with her teeth. She swallowed without chewing and tore off another bite, trying to get it down before the first bite came back up.

Her stomach heaved. Swallowing hard, she gulped her second bite down. Ignoring her churning stomach, she tore off a third bite. This time it sat in her mouth too long and she tasted the blood. With a choking cough, all three pieces hurled out of her mouth and across the sandy ground.

Akachi sprang back, snarling. Fajora glanced up at him, her eyes smarting as she tried to control her stomach. She scooted to the pool, plunged her hands into the cool water, then rinsed her mouth and took a long drink.

Cupping her hands, she gathered water and poured it over the meat. A little of the blood washed away. Better, but not good enough. Several more times, she poured water over the meat, not willing to contaminate the pool by dipping the meat into the water.

As she prepared to try again, she steeled herself by repeating the names *Clarise* and *Sebastian* over and over in her mind to remind herself of why she did this, of why she could not give up on her mission, though she wanted to in that moment with all her heart. With their names on her lips, she took another bite and swallowed quickly, not trusting herself to chew. She followed the bite with a sip of water, and this time the meat stayed down.

In the end, she kept down more than half of Akachi's kill before her churning stomach warned her to stop. When she turned away and refused to eat any more, Akachi grabbed it and tore into it, cleaning the bones in a few minutes. When he had finished and busied himself with his cleaning, Fajora took a packet of nuts from her jacket pocket and chewed on them, to clear her pallet as much as for the energy.

She had a few more small packets of nuts and wafers in her pockets. Not enough for a good meal, and she decided to save them. The nuts and the meat she had kept down had given her the energy to continue for a while. She had no doubt she could continue to walk, even if she had no other food. She would not try to spin except in an emergency. She lifted a silent prayer to Ya-Lohim that she would have adequate energy when the need arose.

And she fervently hoped Akachi did not decide to hunt for her again. She had already offended him by her attitude toward his age. Then she had compounded the insult by her treatment of his gift of food. Further offense might put her life in danger, and worse, his as well, depending on how he reacted.

When Akachi indicated they should move on, she got up and followed him without protest. She concentrated on the path in front of her, finding the easiest way among the boulders and conserving her energy as much as possible. It wasn't much of a savings, but every bit helped.

Akachi led Fajora on a winding route through a landscape of strange, wind-twisted monoliths. At lower elevations the monoliths towered overhead, three or four times Fajora's height. A brisk breeze chased them from one formation to the next.

Fajora and Akachi were short on sleep and Akachi worried about running into a Rock Clan hunting party after dark, so as the sun slanted low in the west, they sought a safe place to rest. A small stream offered an opportunity for a drink and to confuse anyone who might pick up their trail. They waded downstream until they came to an area of arches and jumbled boulders. A geologic upheaval in the past had left this area a maze, with nooks and sheltered areas, like rooms in the ruins of a large house.

Akachi left the stream and led Fajora to one of the smallest of these enclosed spaces, not exactly a cave, but close, with a small arch overhead. The front afforded a view of the stream. A single opening at the back, large enough for Fajora to squeeze through, offered a way of escape if Rock Clan cats found them.

Several small shrubs struggled to survive along the edge of the stream. Fajora recognized in one of them a promising source of food, as both its blue berries and the bark were safe and packed with energy. Though late in the season for berries, enough lingered on the bush for two small handfuls. She plucked and ate them eagerly. She offered some to Akachi, but he declined, and she didn't ask twice. They were filled with tart goodness and settled easily into her stomach.

She had more difficulty with the bark. To strip it from the pith, she needed a knife, something she did not have. She made a mental note: if she survived this mission, she would buy a good knife in New Skakeet City and devise a way to carry it, perhaps in her boot, where it would always be at hand as a tool for scavenging or as a backup weapon. For now, with no knife, she had to be satisfied with chewing on several twigs and stripping the bark with her teeth.

They slept for five or six hours. Small noises woke Fajora several times, and she stared into the dark, straining to hear whatever had awakened her. Once, Akachi also stirred, and she heard him sniffing. On the other occasions, he gave no sign of wakefulness. Each time, Fajora slipped back into sleep, but her dreams were filled with pursuit by nameless, shapeless creatures, vague representations of Dark Spinners trying to form themselves into the shapes of cats or owls.

Finally, Fajora awoke and could not get to sleep again. She sat, leaning against a boulder, trying not to shift her cramped legs and disturb Akachi. She soon discovered she need not have been so careful. When she finally changed positions, Akachi's voice came to her clearly, with no sleepiness in its tones.

"Are you awake, Light Spinner?"

"Yes."

"Good. We can go. But we must move slowly, and as quietly as possible, to avoid meeting up with hunters."

Fajora knew Akachi aimed the comment about moving quietly at her, for he always moved with natural stealth. Concentrating, aided by their slower pace, Fajora managed to tone down the noise of her passing. Her footfalls were not silent, but she did avoid crunching the gravel under her feet or splashing in the stream.

They walked for several hours, until the sun was well up and making them hot. They left their little stream, but when they found another one,

Akachi left Fajora to drink and wash while he hunted. He was gone long enough to alarm her and finally returned without game.

"It is barren land," he said. "We could have walked all night without meeting a hunting party."

They walked through Rock Clan's austere landscape for two more days, sometimes climbing down into a canyon, where they had relief from the sun, and sometimes traversing high ridges dotted with strange rock formations. Fajora foraged for roots and berries along the trail, careful to hide the disturbance in the ground when she pulled a root. Rock Clan cats would detect her scent if they happened on these spots, but she needn't make it easy for them. The findings were scarce, too scant to keep Fajora well fueled.

Nonetheless, she resisted the temptation to consume her remaining snacks. She would save them as long as possible. In a moment of dire need, they might mean the difference between survival or death.

Akachi hunted, with enough success to keep them on their feet, and Fajora learned to eat his offerings without choking or getting sick. She found it easier if she didn't look at or think about what she ate. Even though she found the meat unappetizing, she was grateful to Akachi. He put himself at risk, stalking game in another clan's territory, and Fajora knew he did it for her. He could have continued much longer than she without eating.

She thought often about how much time they took to cover territory she could have spun over in a matter of minutes. She reminded herself of the drawbacks of spinning, even if she had adequate energy. No one had sanctioned this venture. Fazok and Dannel had sent her off with Sonja to the outpost, but from that point, her authorization became nebulous. To ensure no one recalled her, she must keep her location secret, keep the Wellador scanners from detecting her, keep Light Spinners in the enclave from sensing her aura. So she trudged behind Akachi until her motions became automatic and the idea of actually getting somewhere receded.

About midday on the third day after Fajora lost her pack, as they began a gradual ascent, the breeze quickened and the monoliths grew shorter and more squat, less twisted. As the formations became straighter, the gouges scoured by the wind grew deeper, revealing layers of color from deep rust-reds to rich browns fading to soft grays.

The wind gusted and swirled through the stone formations, loosening Fajora's hair from its tie and whipping it about her face. It picked up loose sand and flung it at her, stinging her eyes. She arranged one arm over her face to shield her eyes, stumbling as she tried to see and keep up with Akachi. He crouched low, and his ears lay flat against his head. The wind would prevent him from hearing anyone approach and make determining their location by scent difficult. But any Rock Clan cats scouting the area would have the same difficulties. Fajora and Akachi, and the scouts would only see each other if they stumbled upon one another by accident.

Akachi led Fajora into a thicker group of monoliths, which gave a little shelter from the wind, and right up to the edge of a cliff.

"Get down," he said, as he crouched in the shadow of the tallest formation.

Fajora sank to her knees and crept closer to the edge. Leaning forward, keeping low, she peered into a deep valley below the cliff, then leaned farther, squinting, trying to make sense of what she saw.

A river wound through the valley. It bent in a wide curve where the valley broadened out, creating a swath of verdant ground. Here trees and shrubs flourished, along with plots of cultivated vegetation and a wide, grassy area fenced to contain thirty-five or forty shaggy grazing animals.

The agrarian areas shared ground with a scattering of monoliths and other rocky formations. Some of these had cavities at their base—cat dens, Fajora surmised. In the cliff base on the far side of the valley, to both the east and the west, where the valley narrowed, she saw caves she presumed were also homes to the Rock Clan cats.

But among the vegetation, almost at the river's edge, sat forty or fifty free-standing structures—buildings of stone and wood, such as only humans or Luxerans built. Cats had neither the physical capability nor the cultural need for such structures. And against the cliff wall at the widest part of the valley, a much larger structure hulked. It sprawled wide and towered high against the cliff wall, sloping down from its tallest point to its front edge, which sagged to little more than the height of a tall human.

This last dimension became clear as a human man emerged from an opening near the left side of the front wall. Though Fajora had been hoping to find humans here, and indeed, had been expecting to after Akachi's account of a settlement of one hundred or more, the sight still gave her a shock. She stifled a gasp and forced herself to focus on her surveillance.

She followed the man's progress through the settlement until he passed behind one of the smaller structures. When he emerged a moment later, two other men and a cat accompanied him. They walked to yet another structure and disappeared inside.

Turning her gaze to other parts of the settlement, Fajora now noticed other activity. Two women worked in one of the cultivated plots. Another woman carried a pot from one of the buildings to the riverbank. A man and a cat sat in the shade of a monolith conversing. The man gesticulated wildly with his arms, and the cat rose to its feet and paced, its tail held low. Several children played in the shadow cast by a group of closely clustered houses.

Fajora leaned away from the cliff's edge trying to process the scene below. No holding spot for colonists who had wandered into cat territory by mistake, this was an established community, with houses, gardens, families. A community in which cats and humans lived side by side, something she had been led to believe the cats would never tolerate.

Who controlled this village? Were the humans descended from earlier generations of prisoners and held in subjugation? Or had they conquered the cats and forced them to accept the human occupation?

She leaned forward again, watching for a sign of dominance in one species or the other. Cats emerged from the caves and dens and moved about the settlement. Two groups, one comprised of four individuals, the other of six, headed out toward the west, to hunt or on patrol. Another group arrived from the same direction a few minutes later. They headed into a long, low shed near the large building and emerged with something in their mouths. Meat, Fajora decided. The cats drove off a woman trying to approach the shed. She waited a short distance away until the cats had all come out and headed toward the dens before entering. She came out a moment later with her hands full, and Fajora was certain she carried meat.

So, the cats shared the bounty of the hunt with the humans, but only after they had taken what they wanted. The woman had to wait, which suggested the cats were in charge.

Children were called in from play, and, for the first time, Fajora noticed kits among them. The kits moved toward the dens and caves when the children went into the buildings. Other than the woman standing aside at the meat shed, Fajora discerned no clear sign of dominance by either species.

She leaned toward Akachi. "Who are they?" she asked in a whisper.

"Rock Clan cats. Humans."

"Yes, but where did the humans come from? So many of them. And with children."

"I do not know," Akachi answered. "They have been here many generations. Others, those older than I who have scouted in the past, have known of them. The elders in the council of Deep Valley Clan have stories of them from long ago. They rarely fight with Rock Clan in the clan wars, but our warriors have seen them near the battle sites. Perhaps the elders can tell you more. We can return to Deep Valley territories and ask them for their wisdom."

"No." Fajora reached out and touched Akachi's shoulder. "Wait. Look."

She pointed to a group of humans emerging from the large building: three men and a young woman. The woman's hands were bound and one of the men held onto her arm. When she tried to step away from him, he jerked hard on her arm and slapped her face.

Fajora had never seen Clarise, and she could not see the woman's face, but she felt a shiver thrill through her. Had she found the missing woman? Alive, but a prisoner and handled roughly, exactly as Jayzam had said?

Akachi growled deep in his chest. "They are dishonorable humans, to treat one of their own in such a way. Deep Valley Clan must correct this behavior, since Rock Clan will not. We must return to Deep Valley and get help from the clan elders."

"That may be Clarise. I can't go anywhere until I'm sure."

Fajora had not told Akachi of her meeting with Bardu, first-level council member of Deep Valley Clan, who had warned her to leave the clan territories. She would not be welcome before the elders and could not expect them to help her now. Even if Akachi went back, she would stay and work on a way to free the young woman. But if she could convince him to lead her closer, that would be even better.

"We need to get down there. We need more accurate information to convince the elders. You need to show you've done thorough recon, no half-measures."

Akachi regarded her with gleaming eyes. "I am fully qualified. And you are correct, Light Spinner. It would be better if the information we present to the council is accurate and detailed. We will try to get closer and see where this prisoner is being held. Come."

11

ATTACK

Akachi's tail twitched, and he again scanned the settlement below, his ears erect and his nose working. Then he scooted back from the edge and stood.

"There are a few ways down. We will choose the one least likely to be guarded, but you must be ready."

Ready for what? But Fajora didn't ask. She could guess. Ready to run. Ready to fight. Ready to envelop Akachi in her light and spin away. She might have little time to decide which action to take if they met members of Rock Clan on the way down. She and Akachi were only two, while any cats they met would have ready reinforcements. She must make the right decision the first time. There would be no room for error.

If they met humans along the way, that was another matter. Fajora intended to speak to them if they gave her a chance. To find out more of who they were and why they were here. To see if they knew anything of Clarise or Sebastian.

Akachi led her well away from the cliff's edge, keeping among the thickest monoliths to avoid being seen from below. The wind died down, and the crunch of Fajora's boots on the sand-strewn ground sounded loud in her ears. Every cat in the settlement below must know they were coming.

They hiked east, well beyond sight of the settlement, before working their way down toward the valley floor. Akachi found a path of sorts, full of jutting rocks and dotted with clumps of vegetation. Though these obstacles made the climb down more difficult, Fajora found them reassuring. This path did not get much use.

Twice, Fajora stumbled and nearly crashed down onto her guide. After the second instance, Akachi turned, scenting her as his eyes probed her. When he started again, he set a slower pace. Fajora brushed a weary hand across her forehead. Did she look as spent as she felt, that he detected her distress? She slipped a grain wafer from her jacket pocket and munched on it as she walked.

She revived a little and considered consuming her remaining meager supply of snacks, but she knew she might need them more later, so she forced herself to leave them alone. She kept her gaze roaming over the landscape, searching for edibles, but the plants along this path were tough, prickly specimens, two of which she identified as poisonous. She saw nothing usable.

Fajora tested her energies by starting a small spin of light in one hand. She allowed only a slight sparkle, but it reassured her. Light was still her ally, her weapon, her fail-safe.

They reached the valley floor without incident. The river wound near the place where the path flattened out. The damp ground supported thick vegetation. Tall shrubs supported blooming vines, while smaller shrubs, grasses, and moss lined the way to the muddy river bank. Staying close to the cliff base where the vegetation hid them from view, Akachi led the way west, toward the village.

Though grateful for the cover, Fajora knew they would have to leave the shelter of the shrubs and enter the more open settlement to find Clarise. The sun already slanted westward, and dusk would come sooner here in this deep valley than up above. Perhaps they should wait for darkness to conceal them before getting too close.

She hurried to catch up with Akachi to suggest this course of action. She found him nosing around a thick clump of shrubs surrounding a hollow in the cliff base. Not a cave. Not nearly deep enough. But with the branches of the shrubs pressing close overhead, the little cavity created a place to hide until darkness fell.

Fajora settled into the hollow with her legs stretched out in front of her, hidden under the shrubbery. Akachi curled next to her, his body pressed up against her thigh. Her hand touched his fur and again she marveled at its softness. She longed to stroke him, to revel in the wonder of his silken coat, but she dared not. It would be an affront to his dignity. With his head held high and his ears erect, he carried as much dignity as any adult cat she had seen. He was neither a pet nor a child, and she could not treat him as such.

She let her eyes close. It wasn't fair to Akachi to let him watch while she slept, but Fajora's energies had run down and she had no other way to replenish them. She must be ready for anything once they moved again toward the settlement.

Akachi's low growl roused her a while later. He no longer pressed against her, but crouched with his rump against the back of the hollow. The tip of his tail beat against Fajora's leg as it twitched in an angry rhythm. His ears, perked forward, swiveled to catch every minute sound. The low growl rumbled deep in his chest again.

An owl called, not far away. It was not a long, drifting call such as Fajora had heard before, but rather a series of short verbalizations, varied in length and tone, ringing with purpose. Akachi listened, ears twitching. Did he understand the language of the owls, and was the bird's message friendly or hostile? Fajora could not discern the intent behind the calls, but she felt adrenaline rushing through her body, preparing her for confrontation, and her senses sharpened.

The owl fell silent. A remnant of daylight filtered into the valley, but Fajora saw only the shadows of foliage swaying in the slight breeze. She strained to hear, listening for signs of movement. Cats made little sound at the best of times, so she didn't expect to hear footfalls or rustling vegetation, but surely some sound or shift in the shadows would signal where the danger lay.

She waited, holding light ready, centered in her right hand—her sword hand--but reining in the urge to form her weapon. Even the tiniest glimmer of light could give her away in these dusky conditions. Careful not to brush against the shrubs or scrape her boots in the sand, she got her legs under her and knelt on one knee, ready to spring into action.

Agonizing moments passed. The silence pressed on Fajora, suffocating in its uncertainty.

Furious snarls broke the quiet. Akachi wiggled his hindquarters, getting his muscles coiled under him. A cat's head, gray with white markings, pushed through the foliage. Its snarl turned into a yowl, echoed by more snarls from beyond the shrubbery.

Akachi sprang. His bronze fur blended with the gray of the other cat, and Fajora could not make out either individual distinctly or even tell how many cats were in the fray. For more cats had thrown themselves into the tangle. The Rock Clan cats were larger than adult Deep Valley cats, and Akachi was not full-grown. He compensated for his size deficit with a surplus of energy and ferocity, but he fought alone against at least three.

Fajora stood and let her sword form in one hand, while she fashioned a pair of light-spun throwing discs in her off hand. The fight had moved beyond the hollow, and she followed it. Beyond the deep shadows of the foliage, her vision improved. She saw the fighting cats, a roiling mass as they twisted and lunged, striking toward one another with unsheathed claws and bared teeth, and squirming away from the attacks of their opponents.

Dread mingled with awe as Fajora watched Akachi fend off three cats. He could not keep this up indefinitely. One unfortunate strike of a barbed paw would rob him of his edge. She must help him.

She edged closer, looking for an opening for either her sword or her discs, but the cats moved too quickly. Any strike she made might as easily hit Akachi as one of his opponents. She couldn't risk it.

She would have to spin him away. Light still came at her bidding, despite her low energy reserves. She must time this carefully, to conserve what strength remained to her and get herself and Akachi well away from here.

But again, the entanglement of cats foiled her. She would have to take all four cats, or none, but four was too much of a burden and would only keep Akachi beyond the reach of their claws and teeth while she held the spin. The moment she coalesced and they all took on flesh again, they could resume their struggle. She didn't have the energy resources to take them as far as a Deep Valley Clan settlement to get help, even if she knew where to find one.

The deepening dark made it harder to see, but a hiss ending in a snarl warned Fajora of another cat approaching from the direction of the settlement. She stepped forward to block its approach, her sword ready. The approaching cat saw her and backed off, the growl rumbling through its chest warning her of its anger. It moved toward the river, trying to circle around her, but again she cut it off.

Shifting her stance, Fajora prepared her discs. She didn't want to kill her opponent, only take it out of the fight. A disc could incapacitate the cat without dealing a fatal wound. She drew back her arm for the throw.

As she released the first disc, she heard a murmur from her left, from the cliff base. Movement? A growl? Her throw was off. The spinning projectile hit her target with a glancing blow. The cat yowled, and she palmed the second disc, getting it ready.

But the murmur again, from the left. A streak of gray in the waning light.

Fajora rotated, swinging her sword toward the sound. A cat hurling itself toward her swerved to avoid the shining blade, but though its attack went astray, it distracted her, leaving an opening for the first cat, the one she had been blocking. Now nothing prevented it from joining the melee around Akachi, but instead, it came for her.

She sensed its movement, but didn't adjust fast enough. She felt the searing pain of razor-sharp cat's claws as the cat's paw struck her right thigh, digging deep, pulling hard against skin, muscle, even bone. Her vision clouded and she staggered, trying to keep her sword up and spinning to fend off a further attack.

For a while, she held the two cats at bay, pivoting with her sword ready in front of her, while the cats circled. She tried to ignore the blood soaking her trouser leg, refused to acknowledge the pain.

But the wound sapped her already lagging energies. She struggled to hold the light, to keep it spinning. She let the throwing disc dissipate first. It was a small thing and not so useful at close quarters. Next, she shortened her sword, but she had to fight to keep it spinning, and it drained her energies further.

Fajora's chest tightened as the reality of her situation became clear. She could not help Akachi. She could not even help herself. If she had the strength, she must turn to light and spin out of here now before she completely lost the capacity to protect herself.

She reached for a spin as her sword dissipated. She almost succeeded. If she hadn't been distracted, she might have achieved translation, enough, perhaps, to spin in short bursts until she reached the Wellador Colony, just as Jayzam had done.

But the cats didn't leave her the leisure to translate slowly, as she must do now. As soon as her sword shank away into shadow, they rushed her from two sides. One bowled into her legs, knocking her off her feet, and the other pounced, landing on her torso. The shock of her landing on the hard ground broke her concentration, and she lost the beginnings of her spin.

The cat that had pounced on her rolled her over onto her back and straddled her, a continuous growl rumbling in its chest. Staring up into its face, seeing the lips curled back to reveal dagger-like teeth, Fajora waited for the final blow. Would it come from teeth or claws?

She tried not to think as she waited. Tried not to imagine the pain when the cat tore her throat open, the instant of agony before death released her. Reached instead for thoughts of Jayzam, whom she would join in the Immortal worlds. And of the Malechem, the Immortal servant of Ya-Lohim, who would come for her and deprive the cats of their prize.

She waited, but the final blow did not come. Why did the cat wait? Perhaps it did not want her dead? Not yet. Maybe she had a chance. She thrashed, trying to dislodge the individual on top of her, though her movements were weak and ineffective. The second individual, who had been prowling back and forth near her head, stopped and swatted at her. Its paw landed heavy against the left side of her head. Though the cat kept its claws sheathed and did not inflict the deep scratches and flowing blood she expected, the blow was heavy and jarring.

For the second time, her vision blurred, but this time it did not clear as it had after the first shock of her leg wound. Fajora struggled to keep her eyes open, struggled to see in a dark deeper, blacker than the dark of night. Feeling herself sinking into the darkness, she reached for comforting light, but her energies were spent and the light eluded her.

As she sank further into the blackness, she heard the noise of movement around her, and sensed noses snuffling at her. Had more cats arrived, or were these the cats who had been fighting Akachi? And what had happened to him? Was he dead? Or had he fled, as she had been prepared to do, when he saw he could do nothing more to protect her? She prayed to Ya-Lohim to make it so, her last thought before she sank into the abyss of darkness.

12

— · —

IN THE DARK

When Fajora came to, the darkness persisted, but she saw moving shapes, and she perceived it was merely the dark of night obscuring her vision now. A cat grasped the shoulder of her jacket, dragging her along the ground at an awkward angle. Her head lolled forward or bobbed to bang the cat's nose, causing it to snuffle and growl. One shoulder and arm rode high, jostling against the cat's flank. The other shoulder and arm scraped along the rocks.

As soon as she realized how her arm dragged, she also noticed the sting of multiple cuts and bruises. Her wounded thigh throbbed with each forward pull, and the warmth of flowing blood spread down her leg.

Weak though she was, Fajora struggled, lifting her dragging arm to swing it at the cat's head. The cat dropped her with a hiss. Taking advantage of her relative freedom, she rolled over and pushed herself to her knees. The effort sent a wave of nausea through her, and she swallowed hard against the bile that rose in her throat. Her stomach was empty, a small mercy. She remained on her knees, supporting herself on her hands, head hanging, until a cat bumped against her with a rough nudge.

She ignored the first bump, but when it nudged her again, more insistently, she raised her head. Four cats clustered around her, snuffling and circling in a restless, demanding motion.

So, they wanted her to move, did they? Tired of dragging her along the ground? And where was the fifth individual? Had Akachi dispatched one before he either succumbed or fled?

Well, she guessed four were sufficient to enforce their demands, and she resented being dragged along the ground. Moving on her own would be more dignified and less painful.

Or so she thought until she tried to stand. With a stab of pain, Fajora's right leg gave out as soon as she put weight on it. She lay face down, breathing hard, conscious only of the daggers of fire piercing her thigh. But when the pain eased a little, she noticed the cats nudging her again, and felt one of them nosing around her jacket, felt its teeth against her neck as it sought a hold on the fabric.

No. The fabric was too fragile, and besides, she would not be dragged. She preferred to crawl. She jerked away from the cat, who rewarded her with another hiss, followed by a menacing growl. Ignoring it, she lifted herself up on her arms, then raised her hips until her knees were under her. The pain made her dizzy, and she reached her right hand out to steady herself on the nearest cat.

The cat shifted, its skin twitching at her touch. Then it stood still, waiting. When she moved her legs in a stilted crawl forward, it moved with her. Growing bolder, she took her weight off her left arm and straightened, wrapping her right arm over the cat's back and leaning harder. The cat bore the weight without protest, and she took another crawling pace forward.

Her knees scraped against the rough ground, but her thigh tolerated the weight and movement better than when she had tried to stand. She moved again and tried to get a rhythm started but made extremely slow progress. She couldn't guess how far they had to go, how far they were from the settlement, since she had no idea how far the cats had dragged her while she was unconscious. But at this pace she would either pass out again or collapse, drained of energy, long before they reached their destination.

The cat she leaned on gave no sign of impatience, but the other three cats circled them in a restless dance, snuffling at her, growling low in their throats, blowing their hot breath against her legs. Their desire to push her faster beat at her like a live thing, a pressure, which Fajora understood without words. But she could not go faster no matter how much they pressured her. If that meant they took further action against her, either to pull her again, or to dispatch her and be done with her, she had no way to prevent it.

She continued to shuffle forward, her mind sinking into a growing haze of pain and weakness, each crawling movement a lesson in torture. She paid less and less attention to the surrounding cats. Only the one she leaned on seemed real to her. Its fur, soft and warm beneath her hand, and its slow, steady movement reassured her even though she knew this cat had no more desire for her good than any of the others.

Sounds from ahead trickled into her awareness. A murmur of voices, the slap of feet against the sandy rock. A harsh exclamation in a human voice.

Another cat greeted her four in the language of cats. The one she leaned on stopped, then moved away, causing her to crash back down to the ground. She caught herself with her arms, bracing them to keep from slamming onto the rocky ground. She swayed on hands and knees, fighting against collapse, fighting to get a glimpse of the people surrounding her.

There were humans here. Fajora's vision was hazy, but she could smell them, a smell of the earth mixed with the odor of sweat and urine. She had a sudden, incongruous appreciation for the clean scent of the cats, and she tried to hold on to this thought. It seemed important, though she knew of no reason this should be so.

One of the humans stooped and touched her thigh. Fajora screamed but the human ignored her wordless protest and moved her leg, lifting it for a moment before letting it drop. She felt something tighten around her thigh above the wound. A tourniquet? Again, her mind marked this as important, though her thoughts were too confused to understand why.

One of the humans put something against her mouth. She felt liquid trickle down her chin and she opened her mouth, instinct prompting her to accept the water before her mind could make sense of what was happening. She drank the warm, sour tasting water eagerly, and moaned when the container was taken away before her thirst was quenched.

A human grabbed her under her arms, lifting her to her feet. She cried out as pain shot through her thigh and her right leg gave out under her. But the human kept a tight grip on her and lifted her higher. She glimpsed male features and shaggy hair before she closed her eyes. Moaning, she concentrated on enduring the pain.

She felt movement on her left side, smelled the approach of another human. Someone shifted her body so two humans supported her, one on either side. They spoke to the cats and to several other humans nearby. Their speech sounded like Standard, but her ears buzzed with the sound of her own blood pumping through her aching head, and the words made no sense.

Speak slower, speak louder, so I can understand. But she couldn't articulate this thought, and they jabbered on among themselves, the cats answering from time to time. She understood the cats' speech, when they resorted to Standard, more easily than the humans,' and she gathered they were recounting the fight. She tried to pay attention, hoping to find out what had happened to Akachi, but though she understood some of the words, her murky mind refused to piece together the story they told.

When the cats finished, one of the humans holding her, the male who had first raised her up, grunted a reply and moved forward. Fajora tried to get her legs to move, to keep rhythm with them and walk, but the pain and her weakness hampered her, and they moved much too quickly for her.

They paid no attention to this, and soon they were dragging her, while she fought a losing battle against the pain jolting through her thigh at each step. Dizziness increased with each jolt. She felt consciousness slipping away, but this time she welcomed the darkness when it came.

When Fajora regained consciousness, she was aware, first, of light filtering through the lashes of heavy-lidded eyes. Dim light, but growing stronger, with the promise of morning. She felt limp and her thigh throbbed, but she lived. For the moment. But for how much longer?

She pushed the question aside and opened her eyes wide enough to examine her surroundings. Her captors had dumped her on the ground in a large, circular space, bare of any vegetation and surrounded by structures such as she had seen from above the day before. This closer view revealed stone construction, with wood in the framing of doors and windows. Skins covered these openings—skins scraped thin to allow light to pass through and to drape loosely or fold back with a tie. Fajora saw no one among the structures. Only the spiraling smudges of smoke drifting from several chimneys above thatched roofs gave evidence of life.

The massive, slant-roofed building—a shingle roof rather than thatch—which Fajora had seen from above, filled one side of the circle and extended deep into the wall of the canyon. Cliffs hugged it on either side, soaring above it despite its great height. A platform squatted in front of the structure, leaving the building's entrance unblocked on the left side. Though supporting boulders raised it to about the height of Fajora's waist, the platform itself consisted of wood planks, flat and smooth, clearly the work of the humans in the settlement.

Lifting herself up and supporting herself on her elbow, Fajora gasped at the stab of fire shooting through her right leg. Reaching down, she touched her thigh with her fingertips, surprised to feel a bandage wrapped around it. She tried sitting up to get a better look. The effort left her shaking and sweating. She leaned her head on the knee of her good leg and took shallow breaths, trying to gather strength, drained from lack of food and loss of blood.

Fajora ignored her leg for the moment, needing to know the worst. Focusing her remaining energy, she reached for light. She waited for the telltale tingle, for the warmth and well-being spreading through her body as she translated.

But there was nothing. Only a dull ache in her stomach and the constricted throat that attested to her rising panic.

Something less strenuous then, for starters. Surely it would be possible to turn her fingers into light. She held her left hand out in front of her and concentrated harder. She had done this as a child recently turned five, the first thing she had ever done with light. She remembered her delight, her laughter welling up and bubbling out. The cheers and congratulations of her parents and older brother.

But now, though she focused on her hand and thought about light, trying with every ounce of strength she possessed to translate her fingers, just the tips of her fingers, nothing happened. Not even a spark.

She pulled the knee of her good leg up to her chin, wrapping her arms around it, and fought to breathe, fought the ringing in her ears. If she swallowed, she would be able to breathe again. But she couldn't swallow. And she was pretty sure she was going to pass out in a minute. An outcome she would welcome. Unconscious, she wouldn't notice the absence of light. She could wait peacefully for the cats to come and finish her.

Let it be soon. She saw no point in staying alive if she couldn't spin. If spinning to safety wasn't even a possibility. If she couldn't even comfort herself with a stray spark flicking off her fingertips. A Light Spinner without access to light had no future. It was just a matter of getting to the last breath as quickly as possible.

She would not save Clarice and Sebastian. Would never know where they were, or even if they lived. Would never know if Jayzam's stories had been true or, as Kinovic suggested, the ravings of an overwrought mind. Would never find out if the Wellador doctors identified the antidote for the poison killing Fazok. Would never sort out the training practices of the enclave and get the junior agents back into peak condition. Would never see her children and grandchildren again.

So many things to regret.

She stifled a sob and waited, eyes closed, for the relief of unconsciousness sure to come at any second. Wondered, as she waited, where the cats and humans were who had brought her here. Wondered what tortures they had planned for her death. And knew it didn't matter. They had stolen her light. They could do nothing worse to her.

13

ROCK CLAN DELIBERATIONS

A wave of dizziness swept through Fajora, warning of another blackout. But a moment later, the dizziness passed, and she still sat upright, one knee hugged close to her chest while the other leg sprawled on the ground in front of her. She sat, waiting, until a cramp in her left calf forced her to stretch out her leg and wiggle her foot to gain relief. Then the right leg begged for another position as well, one that might offer a modicum of relief from the pain.

She stretched both legs in front of her. Time to inspect her wound before she lost consciousness. She already knew the worst, her loss of light, but an agent should always have as complete a picture of her situation as possible.

Someone had wrapped her thigh in a long strip of beige cloth, now soaked through with blood. The stain darkened, drying, and Fajora didn't think any fresh blood was seeping through. She wanted to know how the wound looked—how deep it was and whether it was clean or taking on infection. But without water and salve and a fresh bandage, without knowing when her captors might return, she didn't dare peel back the bandage and risk ruining it or restarting the bleeding.

She might, however, try to stand, testing whether the leg would hold her weight. She shifted, getting her knees under her, then her left foot. She looked for something to brace herself on, to pull herself up, but the nearest structure was at least fifteen paces away. So, with jaw clamped tight, she pushed off with her hands and her good leg and stood on the left leg with the right one dragging to the side.

Intense pain shot through her thigh, though not as severe as on the previous night. Sweat poured down her face and slicked her hands, but her head remained clear. She concentrated on the platform ahead of her, studying it to provide the distraction she needed.

Was the platform for storytelling? Or maybe the leaders of the clan ruled on disputes from this greater height, giving their authority more force. She puzzled over this while letting the muscles of her thigh contract to draw her right leg in line with her left, forcing herself to ignore the pain.

Fajora knew too little of cat culture to do more than guess the reason for the platform. And the presence of humans here complicated any ideas she came up with. But her questions served their purpose. Glancing down to check her position, she found she now stood on both legs, though she had yet to put as much weight on the right as on the left. The wounded thigh throbbed, but the pain was manageable. Slowly, she equalized the weight, and felt a surge of triumph as she pulled herself tall with both feet firmly planted.

She stood, testing her balance, and stuck her hands in her jacket pockets. Her fingers found packets of nuts and grain wafers—from the shape, she determined she had two of the wafers and one of the nuts. They had come, largely undamaged by the feel of them, through the fight and the dragging and the slow crawl across uneven ground. And neither humans nor cats had searched her and confiscated them. Hunger, hard and sharp, forced itself on her awareness, and she pulled one of the wafer packets out of the pocket.

But even all three packets of food would be insufficient to restore her light. If she ate these now, they would provide only a slight boost in her energy levels, a waste of resources. If she saved them, there might come a time, if she survived long enough, when a burst of energy would make all the difference.

She let her fingers open and dropped the food packet back into her pocket. With a sigh, she turned her attention back to her injured leg. She had proved she could stand on it and keep her weight on it. The next question was, could she walk on it? It took her a long moment to work herself up to the effort. Her legs trembled, whether from weakness or apprehension, she did not know. Keeping her left leg planted, she lifted her right foot and moved it forward, setting it down a half-pace ahead. Then she leaned forward and shifted the weight from her left leg.

Toppling forward, she landed hard on her hands, feeling the jolt up her arms and into her torso and head. Fire shot through her thigh again, and she collapsed to the ground, curling into a ball and whimpering.

It wasn't fair. Jayzam had suffered similar wounds, but he had been able both to walk and to spin. He made it home, though his wounds proved fatal in the end. But she, with a wound not much different from his, could neither walk nor spin. She would die here, helpless to complete her mission or even to report what she had learned.

It was her own fault, of course. Jayzam had kept possession of his pack. Even though he ran out of food, he had other supplies. He was able to clean and bandage his wounds soon after he received them, stemming the flow of blood and the hemorrhage of his energy.

If Fajora hadn't been so careless as to leave her pack with her food and other supplies behind, she could have spun herself and Akachi away last night. And once she lost her pack, she should have aborted the mission and returned to the colony, while she still had sufficient fuel. Her actions resembled those of an inexperienced and headstrong junior agent. But knowing where to place the blame made her situation more bitter, not less. She had failed Jayzam. She had failed Clarise and Sebastian. Kinovic had won without lifting a finger against her.

She curled tighter, wrapping her arms around herself and shivering, even though the morning sun now cast a blanket of warmth across the open ground. She buried her head in her arms, shutting out the soothing sunlight. It wasn't right the sun shone so cheerfully when she was so miserable. Her life was ending—and did she hear a bird? She tried to burrow her head deeper, to cover her ears and muffle sound as well as sight, but she could not block out the sound of a cat's voice, alarmingly near her head.

"What a noble sight." The enunciation was remarkably clear for a cat and carried a timbre of mocking. "A brave agent of the Light Spinners, curled into a posture of anguish. Perhaps she is trying to deceive the brave cats of Rock Clan into thinking they have defeated her, so they will not be prepared for her lofty deeds yet to come."

Startled, and more than a little vexed at the cat's tone, Fajora uncovered her eyes to get a glimpse of gray fur with black markings. The cat paced toward her, and she squeezed her eyes shut and pretended not to notice it.

But she could not shut out the creature's warm breath when it bent close and snuffled at her head and around her hands. A heavy paw rested on her forearm, and she braced herself for the blazing pain of tearing claws, until she realized the paw kept its weapons sheathed.

The cat withdrew a few paces. "Hmm." Its voice was quiet, meant for her ears alone, but no more respectful than before. "I might have been mistaken in my estimate of her prowess. Weak and afraid. She is worthy prey for the proud and mighty warriors of Rock Clan."

Fajora couldn't mistake the mocking in its voice. Against her better judgment, she opened her eyes to get a better look at this individual. Deep gray fur with streaks of glistening black down its sides and back clothed the heavy, well-muscled body. The cheeks each had a black streak starting at the inside corner of the eye and slanting down to the jowl. Markings above the eyes mirrored these streaks, starting above the nose and shooting up nearly to the ears. These distinctive facial markings resulted in a rakish appearance.

Male, Fajora thought. Too heavy and deep-jowled to be female

He watched her, his steady gaze making it clear he knew she studied him as well.

Stifling a groan, preferring not to give him clear evidence of her agony, she rose up on one arm and rolled into a sitting position. "Who are you, that you stand over me and mock me?"

"I mock you? What an idea. I must have your head for such an accusation." He marked his words with a huge yawn, displaying a full set of very sharp teeth. Fajora tried to ignore the teeth—especially the long, pointed canines—and the strong snap of the jaw as he closed his mouth.

"Why are you here?" she asked, pretending a calm she didn't feel. "What is your position in this clan?"

"I am Jelok, a cat with no position in this clan. Or perhaps I have every position." He yawned again and licked a paw. "No, I think you will find the elders grant me no position. And yet they are not here, and do not even know their prisoner is awake and alert. How awkward for them."

He paced around her again. "It is well I am here. Otherwise, you might stand and walk out of the camp, depriving them of their prize. I, Jelok, will guard you for them until they rise from their deep slumber." He made a rumbling sound deep in his throat.

Fajora stared at him, puzzled until she realized he was laughing. If that was possible. Did cats laugh? She had never imagined such a thing, but it seemed to be what he was doing. She didn't see anything funny in the situation. Her hand clenched into a fist, but she restrained the impulse to strike out at him. Any blow she landed would be weak and ineffectual, and might serve only to provoke him to use his weapons.

The sound of human voices came from beyond the buildings behind Fajora. Movement caught her eye to the left of the large structure. A cat appeared. Then another. And then many, strolling out from the dens in a silent promenade. A moment later, the first human arrived, followed by a flow of others advancing into the circle with the murmur of chatter.

Two large cats, taller and heavier than Jelok, paced toward the platform. Before they reached it, several human males rounded a nearby building, walking with hurried steps. They watched the two large cats and quickened their steps to reach the platform first. One, a man with bushy gray hair and beard, stopped at its base and motioned to the other two with a gesture that commanded them to ascend. They bounded up steps on the platform's right side, hidden from Fajora's view.

This stopped the two cats momentarily, then the larger of the two leaped to the platform, moving with unhurried grace and power. Though the two humans advanced to the center of the platform at once, when the cat approached them, they gave way, moving several steps back.

The cat, a light gray individual with striking white markings across his shoulders and one white paw, sat on his haunches surveying the growing crowd below him. He gave the white paw several licks, then set it down with deliberation, a signal even Fajora understood. The cat had command of the situation and could wait, all day, if necessary, for others to recognize his superiority. Only his ears moved, twitching to catch sounds from various angles.

His gaze, meanwhile, found Fajora and remained fixed on her. She glared back at him, though with growing uneasiness. Under his scrutiny, she remembered the pain of sharp claws and noticed anew the trembling of her limbs and her overall weakness.

The gathered crowd quieted and lifted their heads to observe those on the platform, as if the cat there had a magical aura that drew their attention. The humans gave Fajora surreptitious glances, but the cats ignored her, except for two, a male and female she judged by their build and body weight. These two approached and took up positions behind her, one on either side.

When everyone in the crowd had found a place and become quiet, the cat spoke, its voice clear and precise. It spoke Standard rather than the feline language of snarls and hisses Fajora had heard in River Clan's territory. This surprised her, but she was gratified to be able to understand.

"I, Groknor, honored by the elders of the council, speak on their behalf. The dark ones will come soon. Today, or early tomorrow, for it is the time they set at their last appearance. We must make plans to ensure we gain our due recompense for our new prisoners."

One of the humans on the platform, a man with long, stringy red hair and stained leather tunic and trousers, stepped forward to the cat's side.

"The man is ours. You promised us this. He's our only leverage with the woman. Honor demands you keep your word. What say you?" He spoke in a strange accent, harsh and choppy, not as clear as the cat's, though he had the more appropriate vocal apparatus. Fajora, struggling to understand him, caught her breath as she took in his words. A man and a woman prisoner?

Jelok, who had not moved from his position near Fajora during this exchange, gave her a sideways glance and rose to his feet. He paced toward the platform, taking a circuitous route and sniffing at various individuals, both feline and human, as he wended his way among them.

Groknor shifted his gaze away from Fajora to watch Jelok, after a quick, disdainful glance toward the unkempt man at his side. His voice was icy as he answered the man.

"Though you speak without permission, Brunean, the man is, as you say, yours. You have never known this circle of elders to dishonor our word. It will not happen now, although . . . ." He paused. The man leaned forward, towering over the cat. Groknor's tail thumped. Once. Twice. And he yawned, showing his teeth. His white paw, fully armed, kneaded the wood of the platform. The man jumped back a step and motioned for his companion to come closer. The other man sidled closer to the stairs instead, apparently unwilling to support his bolder comrade.

"Although," Groknor repeated, "you have not made good use of him. He has not helped you with your navigation, nor has he encouraged the woman to do as you wish. She is no closer to repairing your technology than the day she arrived. We expect better success soon or you will turn both the man and the woman over to the elders for the good of the clan. Our patience grows small. Tell your leader this. Or is he here, skulking nearby and listening, too cowardly to come forward?"

"No, he's . . . ."

"You have seven days. Such is the word of the elders. If you do not show progress by that time, we will give them to the war council. They will find use for them in the disputes with Deep Valley Clan and Sacred Mountain Clan. Or, perhaps, on a future meeting with the dark ones, we will offer these humans for their use."

"No!" Brunean burst out. As Groknor's tail thumped again, Brunean backed another step and continued more quietly. "Please, the dark ones don't understand. They'll waste the woman. And the man, too. These two know how to make things work. We need them."

"Then the elders suggest you find new methods. Perhaps you are too gentle with them."

"Oh yes, just the thing," a voice said from the crowd. Fajora shifted, trying to see who spoke, though the familiar voice gave her a clue. To the left of the platform, the clustered humans shifted and Jelok came slinking from among them. "Where beatings and rape fail, killing will succeed. They will return from the Immortal lands to fix your poor little machines. Their sojourn in those eternal realms will teach them the wisdom of such benevolence."

"Silence!" Groknor punctuated his command with a menacing growl. "The elders have not given you permission to speak."

"Oh dear," Jelok said, putting a little whine into his words, though his posture as he paced toward the platform showed no sign of dismay. "They never want me to speak. So afraid, they are, that my words might show the true shape of their wisdom. But, oh dear, it is so difficult to obey." His voice took on loftier tones. "I do so love to speak. To hear my well-modulated voice in the company of such inelegant speech. What is it the humans say? If you want something done right, you must do it yourself. So, you see, I cannot, with honor, keep silent."

Jelok turned away from the platform and walked back through the crowd, his head held high, his tail even higher. Both the clusters of humans and the groups of cats made way for him. He headed for Fajora, but before he reached her, he veered away and she lost sight of him in the crowd.

Groknor swished his tail in sharp, quick motions, and Brunean stepped farther away. Groknor turned to the man and hissed, and Brunean stumbled down the stairs, pushing his companion ahead of him. When they were well away, hidden among the crowd, Groknor turned his face back toward the center of his audience. His tail slowed and became still. He raised his paw, not the white one this time, and licked it several times before speaking.

"It is not to discuss these human prisoners that the elders have called this gathering. We have a new prisoner, a rare prize, taken through the prowess of our warriors, whom we must take council about."

His gaze returned to Fajora, and every head in the circle swiveled toward her. A low murmur passed through the crowd. Groknor waited until the sounds hushed, waited a moment longer, until everyone returned their attention to him and only him.

"It is true, as Brunean suggests. Honor and wisdom demand we keep the human prisoners, the man and the woman, here within Rock Clan territory. Though they have not yet proved useful, they have knowledge we need. We will work harder with Brunean and his team to extract this knowledge, so our greatness and honor may be known throughout our world, among the clans, and even beyond, in the realm of the stars."

Now what was that about? Cultural studies revealed the cats' desire for honor among the clans, each clan always seeking to gain preeminence over the other clans. Not that they usually tried to conquer another clan's territory, but merely sought praise and recognition for their prowess, often staging raids against other clans to prove their superiority. Rock Clan, if they truly aspired to control all the clans, increased the normal level of conflict exponentially.

However, despite the glory-seeking nature of this society and the aspirations of Rock Clan, cultural studies, affirmed by conventional wisdom among the Wellador colonists, had never suggested the clans knew or cared what went on beyond their own world. Their only concession to outside events, their acceptance of the Wellador on their world and the subsequent treaty agreement, had been brokered, forced even, by the Lochemeri and Malekemi, Ya-Lohim's Immortal servants. That the clans had acquiesced to the Immortals came as no surprise. The Lochemeri, peerless warriors of the Dominion, mighty and radiant, wielding weapons of alchemized steel, would impress even the warrior cats. Of course, the cats had acceded.

They had been careful, very careful, in the three hundred years the Wellador had been on Kakislane, to limit any additional association with the non-feline universe. Or so everyone had thought. But these cats lived with humans, though the humans appeared to be under the cats' rule. Now their elder speaker expressed the ambition to be known in the larger Dominion. What had brought about such an extraordinary change?

Or was it a change at all? Had the rest of the Dominion been wrong about the cats' knowledge and aspirations all along?

Groknor's voice broke into Fajora's thoughts. She jerked her attention back to his speech. She could puzzle over the clan's behavior later, if she lived. Right now, she needed to discover what they intended to do with her. She caught Groknor's voice mid-sentence.

"... but this new prisoner, the Light Spinner woman, who attempted a raid on our encampment last night, thinking we would not notice or apprehend her, she is a different matter. We have already awarded honor to those who fought valiantly against her accursed light and earned a glorious victory. Rock Clan has nothing more to prove against her. We may now use her as will best benefit the clan."

Groknor paused, letting his gaze roam over the crowd, assessing their mood, and coming back to rest on Fajora. She felt its coldness, even from a distance. He or the elder council had already decided her fate.

"It has been long," Groknor intoned, resuming his oratory, "since we have had a suitable gift for the dark ones. They grow displeased with our lack of progress on our noble project, and we will have nothing more to report when they arrive for this next visit." Groknor glared in the direction Brunean had gone, though the man had hidden himself well at the back of the crowd where the force of Groknor's ire would have less impact.

Groknor turned back to the center of his audience. Many of the humans leaned toward the platform now, as if eager to hear what he proposed, and the cats sat tall on their haunches with ears perked forward. He had their full attention.

"So now, I propose, by the will of the elders, that we offer this captive Light Spinner to the dark ones when they come. They will be pleased by such a gift and will show more patience in other matters. The full council will make a final ruling at the sixth sunprowl. Until then, think on this matter, but know the will of the elders stands. I, Groknor, have spoken."

A collective sigh ran through the crowd, and many individuals turned their heads to stare at Fajora again. She ignored them as she fought a wave of nausea. She would not give in to it in the sight of the entirety of Rock

Clan. As the wave passed, she began to shiver. The sun seemed to give no warmth.

And how could it? Only cold and darkness awaited her as she went, helpless and weak, into the domain of Dark Spinners. She would rather the cats dig their claws into her flesh and tear at her throat with their teeth than face the swirling darkness with which the Dark Spinners would absorb her, to carry her through the void to Exalton, or to one of their enclaves on another world.

When they questioned her, with the threat of that shadowy energy, that non-light always as their weapon, would she keep her courage, or would she tell them all she knew about the fight against darkness, about the strategies of the service, about the movements of its agents?

14

SEBASTIAN AND CLARISE

The crowd stirred, and some turned away and headed out of the circle. But a disturbance among the people closest to the platform turned most of them back to search for its source. Jelok emerged from the largest cluster of humans and bounded up onto the platform, his movements lithe and powerful.

He circled Groknor twice and then crouched low to one side. Groknor sat taller and turned his head away, showing his disdain for Jelok.

Jelok wriggled closer to the elder and spoke in ingratiating tones that carried to the edges of the circle.

"Oh, my gracious lord from the dark realms. How awesome are your shadowy tendrils. I subject myself to you. Please, allow me to give you a valuable gift, that I might gain your favor?" Jelok inched closer yet, and looked up at Groknor with his ears pinned back and his tail low and tight to his body. "Oh, most worshipful, please take this prisoner. We are so honored." Jelok paused, then repeated with greater emphasis, "We are so *honored*, yes, and it gives our great Rock Clan such glory to serve you and prostrate ourselves to you."

As he said this, Jelok rolled over on his back and let all four paws wave in the air, leaving his belly open and vulnerable. He wiggled on his back, and his tail swished back and forth, while he chanted in a high-pitched whine, "Oh most gracious dark one, oh my master, oh most gracious dark one, oh my master forever."

Groknor hissed at him, but several humans in the crowd chuckled or hid grins behind their hands. From among the cats came indistinct sounds which might be growls or that unanticipated and marvelous laughter.

Jelok rolled back to his feet and strolled in a circle around Groknor.

"You are insolent and insubordinate," Groknor said in a tone bordering on a growl. "Your behavior is unbecoming a member of this honorable clan. You must desist and be gone from here."

"Oh, I am a mess, I know." Jelok gave a little bounce on all four feet as he started another circuit around the elder. "But my words are true. The dark ones come and the elders prostrate themselves. The entire council and all the people follow their example, and the entire proud and honorable Rock Clan is groveling before these invaders from another world who dare to come and make demands of us."

Groknor turned away, lifting his nose with a sniff. Jelok danced around him until they stood nose to nose. Groknor turned the other way, and Jelok danced again, to his other side. Groknor turned again, and Jelok pranced around him again. And again. Until Groknor seemed to realize he was being made to look ridiculous and stared forward over the crowd.

"What would you have us do?" Groknor's words were hard to hear from Fajora's position at the back of the assembly. "We have welcomed the dark ones as honored guests and made agreements with them. To show disdain for them now would be dishonorable."

"Hmm." Jelok sat down beside Groknor and stared out over the crowd, imitating the elder. He spoke as if in conversation with Groknor, but he clearly addressed his words to every member of the clan. "Yes, we have made agreements. Perhaps the wisdom of the clan has been lacking in recent years, that we welcome outsiders so easily. It is true we cannot, with honor, turn our guests away when they come.

"But," and his voice turned hard, "our agreements do not demand we fawn on them and turn over to them any prisoner we take. Our prisoners are our own. Why give one away to win the favor of the dark ones? Why do we need their favor? They come to us with fearful shadow and subtle words, but they are powerless. Their shadow swords are no match for tooth and claw and the agile strength of a warrior cat. Their shadow is weak here, unless we feast them, taking food from the mouths of our own young to give them the fuel they need. They give us nothing in return."

"No, I say. No." His voice had turned harsh, supported underneath by the rumble of a low growl. Both humans and cats near the platform moved back a collective step. "No," he said, more quietly. "We must keep our prisoner. A Light Spinner is a prize we must not waste. We must give her to the dark ones only when they give us something valuable in return. Only then is our vaunted honor served." He tilted his head higher and let a moment of silence fall over the crowd. Before they became restless, he added, in a voice so quiet that everyone, Fajora included, leaned forward to catch his words, "I, Jelok, who hold the Sanctum and tend it, as did Dordan, my sire, have spoken. I speak for myself. Let my words be known."

He sat poised, clothed in dignity, his tail wrapped around him, letting spectators see the tip of it twitch, the only part of him that moved. Then he jumped smoothly down from the platform and wended his way toward Fajora. The members of Rock Clan, both feline and human, were still for a moment, watching Jelok, and also Groknor, who still sat on the platform. When Groknor did not speak or call Jelok back, they moved with a murmur and began to disperse.

When Jelok reached Fajora, he ignored her, addressing the two cats who stood guard behind her.

"House her with the other prisoner, the man. Have the humans take her. The woman may come and care for her wounds, and the young one will bring her rations, as she does for the man."

Jelok gave a quick twist toward a woman sidling past with a girl in tow. "You, Marita. Come here."

The woman stepped closer, but left a good ten paces between herself and Jelok. She had a hard face, and she stared at Jelok with expressionless eyes. She kept the child close to her side, partially hidden in her skirts, so that Fajora saw only a slim form in a ragged dress and a mop of dirty hair hanging low over the eyes, hiding them.

"You will provide food for this prisoner as you do for the others. Her rations must be strictly limited. You will be compensated as you are for the others. Your girl will bring the food to the house where the man stays. Do you understand?"

"Yes." The woman's voice was as hard as her face, but when she glanced at Fajora and met her eyes, something else flickered in her gaze. Compassion, perhaps? Fajora leaned forward a little, hoping to form a connection, however brief, with this woman, but the woman quickly averted her eyes and hurried away, pulling the girl with her.

Jelok gave Fajora one sidelong glance before loping away, disappearing among the buildings behind her. One of the guard cats left as well, but returned shortly, followed by two human men. One of the men leered at Fajora and ran his eyes up and down her body with a speculative grin as he grabbed her under one arm. His companion frowned at him as he jerked on Fajora's other arm, helping pull her to her feet. The men smelled of onions and sweat and were none too clean.

Fajora's thigh came alive with shooting pain as they lifted her, but she gritted her teeth and didn't make a sound. Never, in front of these abhorrent creatures, would she divulge the depth of her agony. At least the pain took her mind off the stench of these men.

She tried to get her feet under her, but the men were in a hurry and dragged her across the circle without giving her a chance to walk. They lugged her past several buildings—homes from which came the smell of cooking food.

Hunger, pushed to the background for a time by pain and other pressing concerns, assaulted Fajora again, leaving her light-headed. Forgetting about her inability to put weight on her wounded leg, she tried to pull out of her captors' grasps to dash into one of the homes, hoping to grab whatever food came to hand. She squirmed and jerked, but her feeble effort only caused the men to tighten their hold on her.

They continued until they reached the outer perimeter of the circle of clustered homes comprising the settlement. One last building sat close to the bank of the river. Too close, for when the men dragged Fajora along the path to the door, the ground squished under her feet. The song of the river as it flowed over boulders and rushed on down into a canyon beyond the settlement enticed the ear, but it would have taken only one or two high water events for the residents to abandon it as unusable.

The clan apparently found it adequate for housing prisoners. One man lifted the ragged hide hanging from the doorway, and the other shoved Fajora inside. She glimpsed a hide-covered window, which let in a few stray beams of light and left the single room otherwise in shadow. She stumbled, unable to catch her weight on her wounded leg, and sprawled across the middle of the dirt floor, managing to get an arm under her to soften the jolt to her head. The men's rough laughter rang in her ears as they dropped the hide and walked away.

She lay still, cushioning her head on her arm. The floor was damp, though not so much so as the path outside, and the room had the sour smell of human waste. She didn't bother lifting her head to look around. She didn't expect she'd see anything worth looking at, even if the light had been better. She preferred the muffled darkness of her arm.

A gentle cough warned her she was not alone. She jerked her head up and peered around the dim room. A shadowy form in one corner took on the shape of a man. She caught the glint of his eyes as he spoke.

"I've been wondering what the fuss was about out there," he said in the plain, clear accent of the Wellador Colony. "Too far away and closed-in here to catch more than a word here or there. Sounded like Jelok, up to his tricks, at one point, but I had no idea why. It never occurred to me they might have another prisoner." He chuckled, an abrupt sound holding more censure than humor. "I was pretty sure only one of us would be stupid enough to cross the boundary this season, or this year, even."

"Who are you? What are you doing here?" Fajora struggled to a sitting position, groaning as she flexed her thigh, then scuttled to the opposite corner, ignoring pain as she tried to put distance between herself and this possible new threat.

"Oh, sorry." He chuckled again, this time sounding more like he meant it. "Never have been good with manners. Suppose I'm even worse now. Not much use here, manners."

"No, you're excused, but who are you? You didn't answer."

"Sorry. Again. I'm Sebastian. Sebastian Tornbar, that is. Astrophysicist and sometime Antiquarian. Of the Wellador Colony."

"Sebastian? I wondered. But what are you doing here? Sonja said you were headed to Deep Valley Clan."

"Oh, figured that out, did she? I meant to go there. Thought I was headed the right way, too. But I got turned around and Rock Clan found me before I could straighten myself out."

"Good. No, not good, but I mean, I came to find you. Partly, that is."

"What? Hmm. I didn't expect that. No one ever goes after the duffers who cross the boundary markers. Treaty forbids it. No humans can cross over no matter what. You are human, aren't you? The light's not too good. I can't see you well, but what else could you be?"

"Light Spinner."

"Really? But that's brilliant. So, you're going to spin me out of here. Will it make me sick? What are we waiting for? But no, wait. We have to find Clarey first. We can't leave her . . . ."

"No."

"What?"

"I can't spin you out of here. It's been a couple of days since I've had food. I'm wounded, and the loss of blood has weakened me even more. I have no light. I can't even make a spark, let alone spin out of here, with a passenger no less."

"Two passengers. I won't leave unless we take Clarey."

"Doesn't matter. We're not going anywhere."

Sebastian stood and charged the few steps across the floor to tower over her, his pale face and flaming red hair coming into sharp focus. "Why did you even bother? I thought we were saved, and now you say you can't spin. What kind of rescue is this?"

"Not a very good one, I admit," Fajora answered. "It hasn't turned out like . . . ."

Movement at the door stopped her words. A hand reached around and lifted the hide covering and a slim young woman stepped in, carrying a basin and a small bundle. The sudden brightness from outside cast her into shadow, making her features hard to discern. She dropped the hide and Fajora blinked, trying to get a clear view of her.

The woman, barely out of girlhood, was so thin no womanly curves showed beneath her loose garb. She wore a dress of supple leather that fell just below the knee, its bottom edge scuffed and uneven. Her feet were bare. When she stepped closer, her thin face and large eyes came into focus for Fajora. Her face, several shades darker than Sebastian's and framed by waist length, tangled hair, was marked by an odd mottling.

The woman set the bowl down beside Fajora, sloshing water over the edge as she did so. She laid her bundle on the floor next to the bowl and unrolled it, revealing several strips of cloth and two covered jars. As she arranged her supplies, Fajora flinched, imagining the coming pain when the woman tore the blood-encrusted bandage away from her wounded thigh.

Sebastian stepped over to the window. "Do you need more light, Clarey?"

The woman nodded, and Sebastian lifted the hide and tucked it up to let light stream in across the floor. Blinking against the brightness, Fajora got a better look at this young woman, Clarey. Bruising caused the strange mottling, she realized, with more on both arms below the short sleeves of her dress.

What were these people doing to her? These were not the marks of a cat's weapons. Only humans could do this. It appeared Jelok's comment about beatings and rape had not been merely embellishment for the sake of argument.

Fajora looked back at Clarey's face, meeting her gaze for an instant before Clarey lowered her eyes. Fajora stared at her, willing her to look up again, but the young woman kept her focus on Fajora's leg as she loosened the stiff wrapping and unwound it. The blood-encrusted fabric resisted her gentle tugs. She gave a harder jerk and it came away, revealing four deep vertical claw marks across the middle of the thigh.

Fajora yelped and bit hard on her lip to keep from whimpering. Blood welled up from the gashes. Someone, perhaps Clarey, had cut away part of Fajora's trouser when applying the first bandage, removing enough to treat the wound without destroying too much of the garment. But blood stained the ragged edges of the trouser leg a deep rust and now soaked them again.

Clarey dipped a clean rag in her bowl of water, wrung it out, and dabbed at the wounds, cleaning the blood away. Fajora squeezed her eyes shut, concentrating on stifling the moans of protest she wanted to make until Clarey finished touching her leg. Gathering her courage, she screwed her eyes open to examine the wounds.

They looked clean, showing none of the redness or swelling indicating infection. She drew a deep, relieved breath. Cat-inflicted wounds were notorious for causing infections that challenged even the best doctors in the colony. Fortunately, neither humans nor Light Spinners tangled with cats often enough for this to be a big problem.

But enclave records did tell of a Light Spinner who had gone into Big Leaf Clan territory to expel Dark Spinners and had come back with several scratches much like Fajora's. Within a week doctors had to amputate first one leg and then the other, and within two weeks the spinner died. It was an instructive tale and the reason all Light Spinners carried medical supplies, including the Wellador doctors' magical antibiotics, whenever they ventured into clan territory. Supplies Fajora had lost. She must depend on this young woman, Clarey, and whatever medicines she had managed to concoct in this isolated community.

"I'm surprised they're letting her treat my wounds," Fajora commented to Sebastian. "I expected they'd let me get infected and die."

"No, not their way." He left the window and came close, squatting beside Clarey to watch her work. "The humans might do so, if the cats allowed it. But the cats find such behavior dishonorable. Even if you're an enemy and they want you dead, they grant you the honor of a clean kill. They must want you alive, to bother with bringing you here. And if they want you alive, they'll want you healed. Less trouble and drain on resources. They can't put you to work if you're lying here crippled."

"Well, I'm grateful."

Fajora looked at Clarey again, in time to see the young woman's hand coming toward her with a jar, now uncovered and emitting a foul odor. Before she could ask what was in the jar, Clarey upended it, pouring a steady stream of liquid over the wounds.

Questions fled, and Fajora screamed. Pain, like sharp, hot needles, shot up and down her leg and into her belly. She gasped, unable to get a breath, and for the third time in less than twenty-four hours, she felt the darkness coming. As she fought to retain consciousness, she met Clarey's gaze. Those eyes, blurred though they were by Fajora's faltering vision, hinted at important knowledge Fajora needed. She tried to form a question, but the sense of what she needed to ask slipped away as she lost consciousness.

She wasn't out long. When she came to, Clarey had the other jar in her hand and plastered the wounds with a soothing salve. Fajora could breathe normally again, and she knew the question she needed to ask.

"Are you Clarise Howard?"

Clarey lifted startled eyes to her face. Her quick reaction confirmed Fajora's suspicions. Clarey stared at her for a moment, then gave a slight nod and lowered her eyes to the wounds again.

Sebastian leaned closer to the two women. "Clarise Howard? I remember that name. I should have known. But it's been a while."

"Two years," Fajora said.

"Yes. I remember hearing about it and reading the notices in the news feeds. I lived down south, and the disappearance seemed remote to me, happening in the north. Right on the border of Canyons Clan. That surprised me because no one has ever seen one of the Canyons Clan cats. They don't patrol the boundary the way the other clans do that share a border with the colony. Not close enough to take someone who only strayed a little past the markers. You must have gone a long way into their territory." He addressed this last remark to Clarise.

She didn't look at him, but she gave an emphatic shake of her head.

"No?" Sebastian stood and paced the few steps to the window and back. "Did you cross at all?"

Again, the negative head shake.

"And the cats came across and took you?" This time, Clarise gave a nod, though she kept her head down, not looking at either Sebastian or Fajora.

"The cats violated the treaty? And nobody in the colony knows this. Someone needs to know. The cats are such sticklers for compliance on our part, and then they come across. What did Canyons Clan want with you? Why did they do it?"

Clarise set the jar of salve aside and reached for a clean strip of cloth to wrap around Fajora's leg. Then she paused and glanced up at Sebastian with pursed lips. Her head shake was almost imperceptible.

"No? No what?" Sebastian paced again, back and forth two times, before stopping again near Clarise. "It wasn't Canyons Clan at all, was it? It was Rock Clan all along. They crossed neutral territory, skirting around the north side of Deep Valley Clan. No, that would take them through Meadow Clan and the colony. Too dangerous. They must have gone through the edge of Sacred Mountain Clan along the shore of Meadow Lake, then crossed between the lakes at the stone bridge. Then down through Canyons Clan's territory, and finally into Colony lands. And they came for you. No one else. Just you. Do I have it right?"

Not looking up, Clarise nodded again. She shuddered and began wrapping Fajora's leg. The pain had eased, leaving a slight throbbing, quite bearable. Though hunger and weakness clouded Fajora's mind, she forced herself to work through Sebastian's statement until she grasped the meaning that had escaped her before.

"They wanted Clarise for something, badly enough to violate their honor by breaking the treaty with humans and trespassing on other clans' lands. What did they want? What do they still want? Does it have something to do with this noble project they talked about at the gathering this morning? And what is that, anyway?"

"That's easy," Sebastian answered. "I've heard of nothing else since I arrived here. They want her to fix their void ship for them."

15

CLARISE'S REFUSAL

Fajora stared at Sebastian, too astonished to speak while Clarise finished the bandaging. She found her voice again as Clarise gathered her supplies.

"Did you say void ship? Like you came in, I mean your ancestors came in, when they came from Exalton however many years ago?"

"Three hundred. Yes."

"That's why there are humans here. Did they come on a colony ship?"

"No."

"No? So they came separately? Was that after the colonists came, or before?"

"It must have been before. Our sensor scans have never detected a ship landing here. And you should see the ship. What's left of it. It's an old hulk. I'm familiar with the design and technology of colony ships. This is much more primitive. I mean, for a void ship. Their replication system is rudimentary, and the weapons don't look very powerful. Though it's hard to tell for sure, since none of it works."

Clarise picked up the bundle she had made from her supplies, and the bowl with the now bloody water, and carried them to the door. She gave Fajora and Sebastian one last glance, her eyes expressing a silent plea, and then pushed through the hide covering and disappeared.

Sebastian sighed and returned to the corner where he had been sitting when Fajora first arrived. She wanted to question him further, but a moment later a much younger and dirtier girl entered--the same who had been with the human woman, Mariza. She carried a jug and two plates, each covered with a large leaf to protect the food, a natural napkin. The smell of food drove all other thoughts from Fajora's mind.

The girl put the plates on the floor, then stood staring at Fajora, apparently waiting to watch her eat. Despite her voracious hunger, Fajora hesitated, unnerved. The child's stare was predatory. She wanted something from Fajora, but not the food. Some sign, some concession, some connection. Or, perhaps a tidbit of information to use as currency in the community's ring of gossip. Whatever it was, Fajora did not feel inclined to accommodate her.

"You can go, now," she said in a brusque voice.

The girl spoke a long, hurried stream of gibberish. The only words Fajora understood were "need" and "plate."

"Does she usually wait for the plate?" Fajora asked Sebastian. He had not retrieved his food yet either.

"No. I leave it outside the door. Someone gets it later."

"Go." Fajora shooed the girl away with her hand. "Go away."

The girl stared a moment longer. Then she dashed toward Fajora, who was too startled to react, except to throw her hand up in front of her face to ward off a blow. But the girl did not strike at her. Her dirt-streaked hand snaked out and grabbed a handful of Fajora's hair. She held it a moment, then ran her fingers through it. Flashing a smile that revealed a gap between her front teeth, she let go of the hair and patted it. Whirling around, she dashed out of the house, leaving the door cover flapping behind her.

Sebastian got up and came to claim his plate. He stopped to study Fajora before returning to his corner.

"That's something I haven't seen before," he said, "but I haven't seen blue hair before, either." He settled with his back against the wall and ate, shoveling the food into his mouth with his fingers.

"Why did she do that?" Fajora asked, but she didn't wait for an answer. Sebastian was intent on his eating, and her plate waited.

The food was plain and there was not nearly enough of it. A square of corn bread with minimal seasoning and lacking any kind of spread, a soggy pile of overcooked greens, and a strip of meat, roasted and poorly seasoned like the bread.

Fajora ate fast, devouring the greens and the bread, hardly taking the time to chew. She hesitated at the meat. It looked tough and greasy. Her stomach turned over at the smell as she brought it to her mouth. But at least it was cooked, and she couldn't afford to be choosy.

She finished eating and scanned the room, hoping she'd missed something—another plate of food, perhaps. What she had eaten might keep her alive, but it would not fuel a spin. She couldn't touch light now, but sufficient fuel might restore it. She had to find a way to get more food, even if it meant sneaking out at night and stealing it. However, her leg needed to heal before she made the attempt.

Sebastian carried the plates to the entrance and slipped them outside. A few minutes later, a hand appeared, just visible in the space below the door cover, and carried them away. Sebastian went to the window and stood looking out. Fajora, her stomach still rumbling, leaned against her piece of wall and tried to make a plan, though she had no clue where to start, since she knew nothing about the operations of the clan. She had no idea when and where there would be scouts, where the humans stored their food, which parts of the settlement were occupied at different times of day. Or when Dark Spinners might arrive.

She yawned and tried to keep her eyes open. No use. She had been through too much, lost too much blood, and was too short on sleep and fuel. Strategizing would be easier if she rested first. She lay down on the damp floor and tried to get comfortable. Turning over, she saw Sebastian standing over her with something in his hands.

"Here." He dropped a bundle beside her that turned out to be a furry hide. It was soft and smelled only of earth and dampness. "Take this. If we're lucky, they'll bring us another one before night, but either way, you need it more than I do. You'd better drink this, too. You're probably dehydrated." He offered her the jug the girl had brought.

"Thank you." She took the jug and found it two thirds full of water. It tasted clean. She gulped half of it, then set it aside with a nod to Sebastian. She felt a twinge of guilt at taking his bedding, but she couldn't bring herself to refuse. The kindness, even more than the relative comfort offered by the hide, prompted her to accept.

The door flap opened and a man stepped in. Fajora recognized him as the third member of Brunean's group earlier, the one who had pushed Brunean and his companion onto the platform. Like all the humans, he wore dirty ragged clothing, and he had a scraggly graying beard that gave him a bestial appearance. Fajora smelled his unwashed body from across the room. He was tall and muscular, not someone to disregard. Fajora steeled herself, ready to be dragged about the community again.

But he only glanced at her before motioning for Sebastian.

"You. Come. You're wanted at the ship. You need to encourage the girl. Move smart, now." He pushed Sebastian out the door and made to follow him, but turned back to scrutinize Fajora. "You stay here. Can't have you about when the dark ones come."

He went out, leaving Fajora alone. But not as alone as she could wish, she soon realized. Movement beyond the hide-covered doorway, and a gray fuzzy tail swishing in and out beneath the hide, which didn't quite reach the floor, told her a cat guarded the doorway. Even when the tail disappeared, she had to assume the guard had simply moved away from the wet ground near the front of the door. She required a clever plan if she hoped to outwit the watchfulness of cats. She'd work on it right after she had a nap.

The need to relieve herself woke her hours later. She found a shallow trough along the wall in the corner opposite Sebastian's corner. From the smell, she identified it as a makeshift latrine. She shuddered, but she had no option. With her stiff and aching leg, she made awkward work of her business, hoping no one, cat or human, walked in on her. She made a mental note to ask for other arrangements. If she could get them to take her to a secluded place outside, it would also give her a chance to appraise the settlement.

As she prepared for another nap, she felt the first Dark Spinner arrive. She sat up, alert, probing her sense of this aura. She had not expected to recognize her dark counterparts, but this aura carried the distinct smoky undertones of anger she associated with Kinovic. It came to her in a strong flash of understanding before more incoming auras smothered it. She felt the next three as well-defined individuals, all strangers, as she had expected. After that, they lost their distinctness. She thought they numbered between six and eight, including Kinovic.

She understood now why Kinovic had been so set against her. Any information she discovered here in Rock Clan could jeopardize his position—a Dark Spinner posing as a Light Spinning agent. She examined this revelation with growing consternation. If a Dark Spinner could operate in a prominent position in an enclave, right under the noses of experienced agents, where else might they be? How many of Kinovic's contacts at Headquarters on Luxera were also Dark Spinners, or sympathizers?

After a while, it occurred to Fajora that if she recognized Kinovic, he might also identify her. He probably noticed her aura, even if he didn't have time to confirm who she was. The others might notice it as well, if other matters didn't distract them. Would the cats be able to withstand the dark ones when they asked questions and made demands?

She spent the rest of the day huddled in Sebastian's bedding, trying to pull in and stifle her aura as much as possible. No Luxerans could entirely dampen their auras, of course, but all agents learned to make it less palpable by keeping the mind and spirit quiescent. She must not fret but must disengage her mind from anything that might interest and enliven it, and must tamp down desires and emotions. Even anger. Especially anger.

When Sebastian came in at dusk, she explained briefly, after which she avoided conversation with him. She noticed numerous small cuts on his arms and legs but did not dare ask about them. She couldn't risk rousing her anger and attracting the attention of the Dark Spinners. Kinovic knew her aura in anger and would identify her beyond doubt.

She ate her evening dinner as a duty, paying little attention to what she ate or how it tasted. She restrained her worry about how inadequate the portions were, forcing her mind away from these issues, shielding her despair from detection by the Dark Spinners nearby.

The same girl who had brought food in the morning came again and stood watching while Fajora ate. This time Fajora did not wait, did not send the girl away, and did not pull away when the girl again came and patted and stroked her hair. Emboldened, the girl fingered the sleeve of Fajora's tunic and leaned down to run her hand over the toe of Fajora's boot. She waited until Fajora and Sebastian finished their meal, then took their plates away, giving them both a shy, secret smile as she left.

Fajora tucked this behavior away in a compartment in the back of her mind for perusal once the Dark Spinners had gone, if she survived that long. This girl might hold the key to understanding these people, at least the humans among them. Exhaustion had kept her from recognizing this in the morning, but now she saw the possibilities.

Clarise came later to check Fajora's wounds and change the bandage. She brought a second furry hide for bedding along with her medicinal supplies. Her attention went first to Sebastian, as she cleaned and applied salve to his cuts. When it was her turn, Fajora endured the pain of the procedure in stoic silence. Maintaining a mental distance from what went on around her helped with this, as did her genuine thankfulness when she saw the wounds were healing cleanly with no sign of infection.

"Thank you," she said as Clarise leaned close to fasten the new wrapping.

Clarise looked up, meeting her eyes for the first time that evening. She nodded her response before lowering her eyes again. The bandage secure, she gathered up her supplies and left without speaking.

A little later, when the languor of the Dark Spinner auras suggested they were sleeping, Fajora questioned Sebastian, who lay wrapped in his hide on the far side of the room but stirred restlessly.

"What about Clarise?"

He stopped tossing, and silence fell over the room. Fajora thought he wouldn't answer, but at last he asked, "What about her?"

"I haven't heard her say a word either time she has come. Do you know why? Can't she speak?"

Another silence.

And a deep sigh.

"I suspect she could if she chose. She did when she first came, as far as I can tell from what her handlers say. But they took everything from her and gave her nothing in return but abuse. How else could she fight back but to refuse to cooperate, including not speaking to them? I keep thinking she'll speak to me, but I'm not sure she can bring herself to break her silence, it's gone on so long."

"How badly have they abused her? I saw the bruises."

"I don't know. She can't tell me, and no one else sees it as abuse. Or they don't care. Probably that. But it's bad. All the usual things, I'd guess."

"Would they quit if she gave them what they want?"

"Maybe." He turned over onto his side with a groan. "I don't know if they can think of her any other way, other than an object to use and abuse, at this point. Besides, she won't give them what they want. She'll die first. I see that much in her eyes."

"And what they want? For her to fix their ship? Could she?"

"I don't know how much she can do with the old hulk. But I remember the news feeds from when she disappeared, and even before. The colony hailed her as the greatest engineer in the 300-year history of the Wellador Colony. Propulsion. Aerodynamics. Replicator systems. Guidance and sensor systems. Lasers. She excelled at it all. And more. Even at her young age she bested most of her teachers. So, yes. She could fix it."

"And if she did, what then?"

"Then these dirty, ignorant, evil people would launch themselves into the void along with their feline overseers." Sebastian's voice was harsh. "And if they didn't burn out in the void, there's no telling what mischief they'd make."

"You think they would have enough power for that?"

"It's not just power. It's chance, happenstance. I've studied the old documents. History. Philosophy. Prophecy. Sometimes people of great power do things that change the world. But sometimes, it's people with little power, who are in the right place at the right time, whose malice does the greatest harm. Keeping these people grounded is incredibly important. Clarise holds great power for good in her slim hands, just by resisting them. If she can hold out. I know I never could have this long. I worry what I'll do to keep them from abusing her anymore."

He fell silent for a moment. When he spoke again, his voice was lower, hesitant, confessional. "I've already examined their astronomical charts for them, when they threatened her." He gave a short laugh. "Fortunately, they are so out of date, even I can't help them. I've no way to make the precise mathematical calculations to get them back on track with the primitive tools they have here. Or I could, I suppose, but it would take months. I hope I'm not here long enough to give in and do the work.

I'm sorry your rescue didn't work out. We could have used a rescue right about now."

He rolled to his other side, his back to Fajora, letting her know the conversation was over. Fajora, for all her weariness, lay awake for a long time, thinking over what he'd said and searching for the solution that eluded her.

16

ROCK CLAN STRATEGY

The next day, Sebastian shared Fajora's imprisonment. He had the grace to turn his back when she used the latrine trench, and she did the same for him. The stench grew unbearable, and Sebastian kept the window covering tucked open, though the slight breezes wafting in gave only minimal relief.

"Last time Dark Spinners came, they stayed for four days, coming and going. Probably spying on the colony. They didn't leave until Light Spinners from the enclave started this way."

Fajora groaned. Four days of this mental fog as she fought to keep her aura as neutral as possible would drain her even more than her wounds and loss of blood had done. She wasn't getting enough fuel to sustain the effort, to say nothing of regaining her light.

But at midday, she felt the first Dark Spinner leave. Most of the others followed soon thereafter. Two lingered. Kinovic's aura reached out, questing, probing. Fajora held herself, physically, mentally, and spiritually, as still as she could. Did he sense her and recognize her?

At last, he departed, but one more aura remained in the settlement. Fajora didn't recognize this one, had not even distinguished it among the others as they arrived. It came to her strongly now, and its distinct arrogance and primal maleness confused her. Personal traits usually remained inconspicuous in an aura except to a spinner in direct contact or very close, or in the case of a personal acquaintance.

The aura persisted vividly for a few moments and then dissipated but didn't entirely disappear. It lingered on the edge of Fajora's awareness, and she suspected this individual, though nearby, was outside the settlement, drawing in his aura as she had been doing. The humans and cats had no way to detect a Luxeran's aura, so his attempt to avoid notice suggested an awareness of Fajora's presence.

If he thought Fajora could not detect him, she wasn't going to do anything to enlighten him. She let her own aura expand with a great sigh of relief. By doing so, she signaled to him that she believed all the Dark Spinners had gone. Perhaps, by pretending to be unaware of him, she might entice him to unintentionally reveal something useful. Who said only Dark Spinners could be devious and deceptive?

Soon after this, the man who had taken Sebastian the previous day came again. He motioned for Sebastian.

"Come." He turned to Fajora. "You come too."

He didn't wait or help her. Sebastian gave her a hand to help her up. She found her right leg supported her weight now, though it flamed in protest. She hobbled outside, clutching Sebastian's arm. As soon as the man saw them emerge from the house, he started off through the settlement, pausing only to motion them on. He scowled at their slow pace, but didn't show any inclination to help.

"Hurry up," he said once, when Fajora pulled to a stop to wait out a spell of dizziness.

"Tornton, she can hardly walk," Sebastian shot back. "We're coming as fast as we can. You could help."

"I can't be bothered. You keep on helping her, but don't dawdle. There's work to do."

Fajora was glad Tornton didn't relent and come back to help. Support on both sides would have allowed her to move faster, but she cringed at the thought of that man touching her, or of having to smell him up close. Sebastian was pungent too, but not like their guide. She supposed she would smell ripe soon, if she went too much longer without bathing. But for now, her body odor and Sebastian's were subdued enough she could enjoy the clean scent of rock and sand and the evergreen-laced wind blowing down from the far cliff top, where bushes and a stand of scraggly trees were visible.

Tornton led them through the settlement to the large structure and held the door open, waiting for them. It was dim inside after the bright sunlight. Light shone from the left, and Tornton directed them there. Several artificial lamps hung suspended from the ceiling high overhead. They cast a garish light over a row of four bulky machines, two of them glowing with red and green bulbs. In the shadows, a huge metal shape hulked, receding into the back of the structure, giving only a hint of its true size.

This was technology such as Fajora had come to identify with the Wellador Colony. However, it lacked the sleek appearance of the colony's machines. The shadowed ship had an air of dilapidation, the colored lights blinked erratically, and one of the overhead lights flickered. Tornton gave it a sharp blow, and the flickering stopped.

He walked around the larger of the two unlit machines and grabbed someone from the shadows. Fajora recognized Clarise as her face came into the light. Her left eye was swollen and purple, and she stumbled and caught herself on the nearest machine. Her captor slapped her, but she did not cry out.

He pulled a metal stool in front of one of the machines and thumped Clarise down onto it.

"There. Now work. Fix the replicator. The boys have the power cells hooked up, but there's a problem with the connection somewhere. Shouldn't be hard for you to figure out."

Clarise put her hands into her lap and stared straight ahead. Tornton grabbed her hair and yanked her head back.

"Do you want to do like yesterday? I've got two of them this time. They can take turns." He dropped her head and pulled a knife from a leather sheath at his back. "Don't got the fancy weapons yet. We'll work on them another day. Don't need them for this work."

He started toward Sebastian, testing his knife's edge with a dirty finger. A drop of blood welled up from his thumb, and he grinned. Sebastian took a step away from him.

"No. Not again. You're stupid to do this. It won't change anything. She'll never help you. Clarey, don't pay any attention. Don't do what they ask."

Fajora stirred, ready to help Sebastian overcome this man. Two of them could best one man, surely. But as she shuffled toward them, she saw movement in the shadows.

Two men closed in behind Sebastian, and two or three others lurked behind Fajora. Too many for Fajora and Sebastian to overcome. One man plunked down two more metal stools and forced Fajora and Sebastian to sit. He left Fajora alone after that, but tied Sebastian's legs to the stool while his partner held his arms back. The first man stood and grabbed one of Sebastian's arms from his partner. He motioned toward Tornton with a grin.

"Got him ready for ya."

Tornton glanced at Clarise. "You can stop this, ya know. Jest get to work and I'll hold off on your friend, much as I like doing him over. I'm willin' to sacrifice my own pleasures, ya know, to get them replicators workin'."

Clarise did not respond. She gave no indication she even heard him. Tornton shrugged and advanced on Sebastian. Fajora felt his fear, almost as strongly as she felt the auras of other Luxerans. But he made no sound, his only response to Tornton's approach a defiant glare.

Tornton grabbed Sebastian's arm and examined it, then brought the dirty knife to bear right along the edge of one of the previous day's cuts.

Sebastian sucked in a draught of air, then bit down hard on his lower lip. Blood welled up on his arm and started a slow crawl toward his hand. A second cut produced another slow trickle of blood and still Sebastian made no sound.

Tornton grunted and sliced deeper the third time before dropping the arm in disgust.

"You want me to quit, you need to cry out, groan, scream, something. She won't be convinced to help if she don't hear you. If she won't look at you bleedin' and you won't scream, how's she to know what's goin' on? How's she to understand she needs to work to make it stop?"

Sebastian's stare remained defiant. Clarise kept her head turned away, refusing to acknowledge Tornton's blackmail. This was, Fajora supposed, the new method Groknor had charged the humans to find in order to advance their project. It might have worked with lesser people. But these two had steel in them, steel that reinforced their determination.

"She understands," Fajora said, drawing Tornton's attention away from his victim. "But she's tougher than you realize, with a purpose greater than yours. She's not going to help you."

"She used to." Tornton turned away from Sebastian to study Fajora, his finger absently testing the edge of his knife. "When she first came here, we used to work together, and she told me things she learned in that fancy school she went to. Had us some sweet conversations. And this baby . . . ." He gestured over his shoulder at the shadowy void ship. "She was right taken with it. Wanted to make it fly again as much as me. Could have done it by now, too, if she hadn't quit on me."

Tornton turned and glanced at Clarise. His eyes softened for a moment as he observed her unmoving form. His voice became quieter, pensive. "I planned on taking her with me when we finally went up to the void. Would have been a fittin' reward for her help and I fancy her company. Can't take her, though, if she won't help." He dropped his knife hand to his side while his other hand reached out toward her. When he noticed what he was doing, he brought his knife hand up and used his free hand to test the weapon's edge again. "Too bad. The dark ones will probably get her in the end. Probably get you all."

Fajora ignored this last statement. Better not to think about it. But she wasn't done with Tornton. He showed a spark of human feeling, along with a confused intelligence. Maybe she could open his mind a little.

"Things might have turned out differently if Clarise had been treated better. She probably lost interest in helping when she learned your true character. Yours and your community's. She realized she mustn't help you get to the void, that the Dominion must be protected from you."

Tornton rounded on Fajora. In the instant between her words and the open-handed smack he delivered to her left cheek, she thought she saw a glimmer of understanding in his expression. It flickered out before she could be sure. She reeled from the blow that sent pain jolting through her head and neck and blurred her vision. She started to topple, but the man standing behind her caught her arm and settled her roughly back on her stool.

"What you say such things for?" Tornton narrowed his eyes and gripped his knife hard. Fajora steeled herself to endure whatever pain he delivered next. But Tornton held back from any further physical abuse, his mind apparently more taken with justifying himself. "Why shouldn't we have as much right as any to travel the void? Our people came from there, back awhile, in this very ship. Came from another place. A whole different world. Had a problem with the ship, otherwise we wouldn't be here now. We'd be back in our place, and that's where we're going, soon as we get this baby up and running. Would have it working, too, even without her help, if the books and manuals were written better, so's we could make more sense of them. Who are you to say otherwise?"

Several retorts rose to Fajora's lips, but she suppressed them and kept silent. She had probably already harmed her situation more than helped. Better not to raise Tornton's ire farther.

As if to assert his right to fly a void ship into the vast reaches of the Dominion, Tornton turned away from his captives and produced a large book from a shelf near the replicator machines. He thumped it on a small table, thumbed through it until he found what he sought, and bent over, studying it. From time to time, he called out to his men, directing them as they tinkered with the machines. Fajora knew too little of technology to know if anything he said made sense, and neither Sebastian nor Clarise gave any clue from their expressions.

His study of the manual gave his captives a short reprieve, but it didn't last. When none of his instructions produced the results he desired, he returned to harassing Clarise and Sebastian, though he avoided Fajora, not even looking at her.

The afternoon dragged along interminably. Fajora lost count of how many times Tornton and his henchmen cut Sebastian's arms and legs, or punched him in the stomach, how many times he turned and rained his abuse on Clarise with slaps and blows.

He did not touch Fajora, only made her watch. But that tormented her more than physical pain and humiliation would have done. If she made so much as a twitch suggesting movement toward either Sebastian or Clarise, men blocked her way. They finally tied her legs to her stool the way they had done with Sebastian, and she thought her turn had come, but they left her alone to watch, assured she could not interfere.

At the end of the day, as the men untied Fajora and Sebastian, and one of them held the door open to take them back to their house, Tornton finally spoke to Fajora again.

"Think you're so smart, don't ya? If you were as smart as you think, you'd see how to stop what goes on here. Surely would try, if you cared about these ones at all. Light Spinner and all, they'll listen to you. Talk sense into them and it will all be good."

Fajora squared her shoulders and walked out without answering. Anger boiled up inside, rivaling anything she had ever felt toward Kinovic. She would have jumped in front of the knife to save Sebastian. She would have taken the blows for Clarise. But she would not help these men get what they wanted.

Tornton's curses, rough and crude, rang in her ears as she limped from the hangar. The settlement bustled with activity as Fajora and Sebastian made their slow way back to their house. Humans and cats hurried to finish up work for the day or started out as part of night-time patrols and hunting parties. Many inhabitants stopped their activity to stare at Fajora and Sebastian. Fajora ignored them all, even the murmurs of pity she heard from several women who were close enough to see Sebastian's bleeding cuts. She feared if she tried to respond, she would say things that would do more harm than good. Sebastian's wounds spoke more eloquently than words.

Their escort delivered them into the care of a cat guard at their doorway. Sebastian headed inside, but Fajora hesitated. When the cat, a young, medium-sized male, lifted its head and sniffed at her, questioning but not hostile, Fajora was encouraged to speak.

"I request that you, and other guards, take us somewhere on the edge of the settlement, or to a designated latrine area, to relieve ourselves. I can't do it inside anymore. The smell is making me sick."

The cat sniffed again. "I have no orders regarding such matters. I cannot allow you to leave this structure without orders."

"Ask someone. Please, it's important."

"I am not accustomed to questioning my superiors, or the counsel. Go inside."

"No. Wait," she added, as the cat unsheathed its claws. "They haven't realized what my needs are. I can't . . . ."

"What is causing this commotion?" a new voice asked. A familiar voice.

Fajora had not seen Jelok since the morning of her arrival. She wasn't sure if she wanted him here or not. But the guard cat sat up tall and sheathed his claws, so she decided it was worth pursuing the matter.

"I've made a reasonable request, but this individual is reluctant to entertain it, for fear he'll get in trouble with the council."

"And the request?" Jelok's voice was clear, sober, without the hidden laughter much of his speech had hinted at in their first encounter. However, the glint in his eyes suggested he found the situation amusing.

"I asked to be allowed to take my latrine business to a different location, rather than having to do it in the corner of the house and live with the smell. Myself and Sebastian both. It's unhealthy, to say nothing of unpleasant."

"Ahh."

Jelok regarded her and her guard, the tip of his tail twitching. He sniffed. After a moment, he nosed through the hide door covering and disappeared inside. He dashed back out an instant later, his tail low and thrashing, his whiskers laid flat, and his ears rotated back. He crouched low and emitted a rumbling growl.

Seeing Fajora and the guard cat watching him, he shook himself and rose out of his crouch as his ears rotated forward.

"Well," he said. "I see why you have made your request. The odor inside is foul. No one, not even a human, should be expected to exist in those circumstances." He took a few steps farther from the doorway before addressing the young guard. "You must take her and the man to a place where these smells will not contaminate our community, a place where the wind will carry them away from the dens. The edge of the settlement, if they can be guarded adequately. If the human homes are compromised, well, that is of less concern. They should have acted on this before, but did not. Extra guards will be assigned from now on to make this possible. I will inform the council."

"Thank you," Fajora said. "I'm deeply grateful."

"Humph. Kit-sitting. That is what I will be doing next. You wanted to know my position in this clan. It appears I am the one designated to fix the mistakes of all the fools in this place." He sniffed loudly and stalked away.

The guard nosed Fajora toward the door. "When a second guard arrives, you may go out. Remain inside until then."

Sebastian, waiting inside, plied Fajora with questions.

"What was that about? That cat is a menace. I thought he was coming to eat me or something."

Fajora explained.

"I asked for the same thing," Sebastian exclaimed, "and got stares and snarls. That strange cat . . . ."

"Jelok."

"Yes, Jelok. He must like you. I'm not even sure I believe you. We'll see what happens. He's a menace to the whole settlement. Upends everything anyone else wants to do. Plays tricks on everyone, and seems to run the whole place, even though I can't figure out what his position is."

"He claims to have no position." Fajora paused, smiling. "Kit-sitting, he thinks, will be next. Or is it every position?"

"I don't get him. But if you ever come up with a plan to get out of here, you'd better take him into consideration. He's bound to mess up any idea you have."

17

SUNSHINE AND SHADOW

The next day, the third of Fajora's captivity, Tornton again came for both Sebastian and Fajora. Fajora saw her own dread reflected on Sebastian's face, but by unspoken agreement, neither said a word nor made any protest.

Sebastian again supported Fajora as they walked, though her wounded leg continued to gain strength and steadiness. As they progressed slowly through the settlement, Fajora detected a sudden, strong flicker of shadow and foreboding. A Dark Spinner aura hovered nearby. Slowing her pace even more, exaggerating her limp to hide her true purpose, Fajora scanned the houses as she passed, paying close attention to the shadows cast by the morning sun. There would be deeper shadows wherever the Dark Spinner hid, tendrils of them winding unnaturally about a roof or window or low shrub.

She stared, concentrating, but she saw nothing but the shade the houses cast. The Dark Spinner, if he watched her, as Fajora was certain he did, kept himself well hidden. She slowed almost to a stop, and Tornton barked a command at her. Scowling at him and picking up her pace, she felt the world right itself as the awareness of the dark aura dissipated.

The ephemeral encounter unnerved Fajora, and she followed Tornton numbly into the void ship hangar. Inside, the four replicator machines sat dark and silent, and only one of the hanging lights glowed. But light emanated from the hulking metal shape that lay further back in the building. Fajora's mind refocused clearly on the present moment as she realized where Tornton was heading.

She couldn't shake a twinge of amazement as they went up a narrow ramp into the void ship itself. In this metal contraption, a group of humans had done what only Luxerans had been created to do. They had left Exalton and traversed the void, a place they were never meant to be, carrying their exploration at least as far as Kakislane. If Sebastian had estimated the age of this vessel correctly, they had done this many years before the Immortals sanctioned the last journey that brought the Wellador here.

Only a few lights glowed near the ship's entrance. Tornton used a handheld torch, like those Fajora had seen the Wellador use, powered by solar energy. His was larger and clunkier, with a rusted, crumbling handle and a scuffed solar panel. Its light flickered and wavered as they walked through the narrow corridors. Fajora expected it to go out at any moment, leaving them to feel their way through the dark bowels of the ship.

It continued to cast its narrow beam until they entered a much larger area. Here other lights, like those near the structure's entrance, cast an eerie glow over mammoth machines with control panels that towered over their heads and rolling ladders that gave access to the highest points. Tornton switched off his little light and led them to a corner where Clarise already sat in front of a blinking panel and a flat surface filled with buttons and levers.

"The engineering room," Sebastian murmured. "How can Clarey resist?"

Indeed, Clarise's hands did not lie as quietly in her lap as usual. Her fingers twitched, and to still them, she clasped one hand with the other. Her eyes, also, did not stay still and lowered, but kept lifting to let her gaze roam over the panel in front of her.

How exciting it must be, to children of the Wellador Colony, to see this ship and to dream of its restoration. Did they have anything comparable in the colony? What had happened to the Wellador void ships after they migrated here? Had the Immortals ordered them destroyed? Or were parts of them stored somewhere, rusting like this hulk, but available for study and research?

Dannel Crowner had spoken of Clarise's theories for increasing speed through the void. Just theories, he had insisted. But she must have had more than schematics to work with as she developed those theories. And now Rock Clan had presented her with a vessel that had been in the void, traveling from one world to another, still more or less intact. Unless she was entirely broken, a part of her must long to bring it back to life. Tornton had intimated as much when speaking of Clarise's early days here.

But whatever her inner longings, only her hands and her restless gaze betrayed them today. She had, after all, had two long years to learn to resist the desire. So when Tornton spoke of the need to refigure the fuel cells, she paid no more attention to his instructions, demands, and threats than she had the day before.

"You need to check Brunean's calculations." Tornton spoke in a more respectful tone than Fajora had heard from him before. "He and I have puzzled over them, but we're not sure they're right. Need your bright eyes on them, Clarey."

When she made no answer and refused to look at the electronic device he held, he brought the device over to Sebastian and had one of his men hold it up to him so he could see the calculations glowing on the screen while Tornton went to work with his knife.

"You know these numbers as well as Clarey. So see, you can help yourself today by telling me if there are any mistakes or if these calculations work. I'll stop anytime you tell me about what you see."

Sebastian grimaced and averted his eyes at first, but in a moment his gaze darted to the screen. He stared intently, frowned, glanced up at Tornton, then averted his gaze again. When his blood splattered on the device, the men finally gave up and moved away, leaving Sebastian to hold his arms close to his shirt to try to stop the bleeding. Meanwhile, Clarise remained still, showing no awareness of his suffering.

For Fajora, the excitement of being in this ancient craft wore off as soon as the torture started. The distress of being forced to watch and listen, tied to a stool near one of the huge consoles, without being able to help in any way, was as great as any physical pain. Tornton seemed to understand this, and gave her a leering stare after every round of blows or cuts. She tried to match the courage of the others, blow for blow, cut for cut. If they could hold to their silence and their refusal to cooperate, she could do no less.

The three of them were dull and depressed that evening. Clarise came to clean and anoint Sebastian's cuts and redress Fajora's wounds, which were healing nicely. It would take a moon cycle or two to heal completely, but the two shallowest scratches were pulling together already. The other two appeared raw and weepy, but showed no signs of infection. Clarise nodded with satisfaction as she applied the salve and started wrapping Fajora's thigh with a clean bandage.

She stayed longer than usual. Her reluctance to leave was palpable. Fajora could only imagine what her captors were doing to her at night, and prayed her imagination was in error.

No one seemed to care how long Clarise spent with them that evening. Fajora suspected another ploy to induce the girl to work on the ship's repairs. If Clarise developed a closer relationship with Sebastian and Fajora, she might be more inclined to cooperate to keep them from pain. But Fajora knew the ploy would fail. She read the determination in the girl's eyes. Clarise would not bend. She had already survived the worst they could do to her.

As the three of them sat together, Fajora asked a question that had been burning in her mind throughout the afternoon.

"The calculations he showed you today. Brunean's calculations for resetting the fuel cells. How far off were they?"

Sebastian and Clarise shared a quick, knowing glance before Sebastian answered. "How far off? Not at all. They were exactly right."

"So they could have done the work without any help from either of you?"

"Yes. They are so much closer than they realize to making their bird fly. These men are more intelligent than they let on. It's deceiving, because they smell so bad and they're mostly illiterate, but if they realize what they're actually capable of, look out Dominion."

He lapsed into a morose silence, and Fajora could find nothing cheerful to say to break the dark mood. Her mind was preoccupied with an urgency to stop these men, this clan, but strategies eluded her.

Clarise stayed until the sounds of activity in the settlement dissipated. Fajora hoped the young woman might be allowed to spend the night, but when the cat guards took Sebastian and Fajora to the makeshift latrine that had been dug for them on the edge of the settlement, another came to take Clarise back to her lodging.

The next day, Tornton took Fajora only as far as the entrance to the void ship hangar. A rickety chair waited for her. A guard cat lazed nearby, female and obviously pregnant. She seemed to be enjoying the chance for a slow afternoon in the sun with little physical exertion required. She showed only by her tail's flickering movement that she was alert enough to intervene if Fajora strayed.

"A day in the sun, eh?" Tornton said with a laugh. "You others do as you're told, and help with the work, you can all have a day in the sun tomorrow. Think on it." He gave Clarise and Sebastian a meaningful look before motioning to his men to take them inside.

Fajora squirmed. She shouldn't be out here, enjoying the fresh air, while her friends faced torture. However, she didn't feel guilty enough to ask to be taken inside. She was glad not to hear the blows and see the blood. And a day in the sun was an unexpected gift, one the humans apparently did not comprehend. Sunlight served as a supplemental source of energy for a Light Spinner. Fajora absorbed its energy, so akin to the light she spun, directly through her skin. It enhanced her abilities and had often shored up shortages of food fuel on ordinary missions.

Of course, her situation here was not ordinary, and no amount of sunlight could make up for the recent extreme deficiencies of fuel. But it helped. She closed her eyes, letting herself luxuriate in the sun's warmth and the hopeful thoughts it brought.

She didn't know how long she sat this way, but a scuffling noise brought her back to her senses.

Opening her eyes, Fajora saw the girl who brought her food morning and evening standing nearby. A boy of about the same size accompanied her, and they had large leather sacks slung over their shoulders. For a moment, Fajora entertained a wild hope the sacks contained food, food the children would willingly share with her. But as they stepped closer, the stench struck her, turning her stomach and dashing her hopes. Whatever they carried, she presumed it was not food. If it was, she would not be able to eat it even if they offered it.

The children dropped their sacks and came closer. They stared at her for a while, then the girl reached out and stroked her hair, as she had done before. The boy hesitated longer, but at last he reached out and touched her hand, then looked up at her with expectation clear on his face.

"Robbie wants to see," the girl said.

Fajora drew in her brows, confused, and the boy jumped back.

"To see what?" she asked. Did they want to see her wound? Surely, they had seen claw scratches before. They lived with a clan of warrior cats.

"Light," the girl said. "You. Light Spinner?" She smiled at Fajora, as if to encourage her.

"Ah. Well, it's true, I am a Light Spinner. Under ordinary circumstances, I'd enjoy spinning for you. Making shapes. Soaring birds and waterfalls and other pretty things. I could even take you for a ride, though I doubt you'd enjoy it. But you see," she tapped her bandaged thigh, "I'm wounded. I lost a lot of blood and it made me weak. And the people here don't feed me enough to get my strength back so I can spin light. So I can't, not even a little."

The children stepped back, hanging their heads in dejection. Fajora had a sudden inspiration. This was, after all, the girl who brought her food each day.

She leaned forward and spoke in a near whisper. "If I had more food, if you brought more on my plate, I might be able to spin for you. I would try, at least. What do you say?"

The children lifted their heads and stared at her. A low rumble from nearby brought their attention to the cat guard who lounged nearby. She sat up, ears perked forward, observing them. How much had she heard? Would she demand someone else bring the food, since the girl had been compromised?

The children picked up their sacks and hurried away toward the houses on the west end of the settlement, but before the girl left, Fajora caught a gleam of speculation in her eyes.

She watched the children scamper away, a happy smile tugging at her lips. But, as they disappeared among the houses, she felt the hard edges of the Dark Spinner aura again, like a warning gust of wind before a storm. She stifled a gasp and scanned the area, finding him at once. He stood in the shadow of one of the nearby homes, the gloom surrounding him too deep for her to discern his features. He was tall; she could tell nothing else. She glanced at her guard, who watched her, ears perked forward to catch every sound, searching for the cause of her startled reaction.

A quick calculation of angles in relation to the cat's position convinced Fajora her guard could not see the Dark Spinner. A corner of the house blocked her view.

The Dark Spinner had been careful not to reveal himself to anyone but Fajora. She waited for him to speak, though that would be difficult without being either seen or heard by the guard. If he wanted to be seen, he would probably have already approached. But rather than come forward, he began to spin, a slow, lazy swirl of shadow that made Fajora queasy but kept her riveted, nonetheless.

The cat, alerted by Fajora's focused attention, got to her feet and circled. Fajora watched as her circle took her closer to a place where she would have a view of the Dark Spinner. How would she react when she saw him? Attack? Warn the settlement? Or, perhaps, welcome him?

But he disappeared before the cat moved into position to catch sight of him. The faintest hint of shadow lingered, visible only if one knew to look for it, and then that also dissipated, leaving a still, cold, empty day, despite the burning sun.

18

FAJORA'S TURN

The cat continued to circle Fajora, sniffing. Fajora schooled her expression, not willing to let the cat see her uneasiness. It was the one thing she could control in a situation where enemies on every side, human, feline, and Dark Spinner, all had their own agendas, and where everyone had more agency than she did.

A scream from the void ship hangar checked the cat's investigation. Sebastian, Fajora was sure, but what had happened to him to shatter his determined endurance? Fajora rose out of her chair and turned toward the hangar door. The cat moved toward her, growling. Fajora sat back down, but twisted in the chair to stare at the door.

Sebastian screamed again. Again, Fajora tried to get up and go to him, and again, her guard prevented her, drawing closer and displaying teeth and unsheathed claws. Fajora waited for another sign, her muscles tight and shaking. What had Tornton done to Sebastian? Was he dying?

Her guard pivoted, so she faced away from the hangar, and her growl rumbled loudly in her chest. Following the cat's gaze, Fajora saw Jelok pacing toward them, his tail swishing. He must have been nearby. Perhaps he had been watching Fajora. Had he seen the Dark Spinner?

As he approached, the guard cat backed away, still growling. With the guard out of her way, Fajora tried to get up and scoot into the hangar before Jelok prevented her.

The throbbing of her thigh as she coiled her muscles for a quick dash reminded her of her infirmity. She would not be fast enough. Worse, she might fall and further injure herself. She sank back into her chair, waiting to see what Jelok would do.

He paused a mere three paces from her chair. "My, my. What are those vexing humans doing? How can anyone be expected to sleep with such terrible noise? I must put a stop to it before the kits are roused and their irritable keepers come fussing to me." He paced on toward the door, sniffing at Fajora and the guard as he passed them. He nosed at the hangar door, which was ajar, and disappeared inside.

A tense stillness fell over the settlement. No more screams rent the air. No kits or irritated caregivers left their dens to investigate. Nothing moved anywhere in sight. Fajora's guard didn't even move, but sat watching the hangar with only the tip of her tail twitching.

Finally, Jelok reemerged. He heaved a dramatic sigh as he passed Fajora and spoke in aggrieved tones. "Oh dear, dear, why must I do everything? Seems someone else around here could show a little sense from time to time. Ah well. The burdens of the cat with no position. All these little things fall to him, and he must just persevere."

"What about Sebastian?" Fajora asked his retreating back. "Is he all right?"

Jelok's tail flipped. "All right is such a relative term. He lives. I am sure he has seen better days."

Jelok's voice floated back to her as he continued on his way and disappeared beyond the nearest homes. Fajora rose at once to go into the hangar, and this time, her guard did not try to prevent her. But before she reached the door, it opened and a small procession emerged. One of Tornton's men came first, pulling Clarise along behind him. Next, two more men came out, hovering over Sebastian, who walked between them.

He moved by his own power, walking hunched over his arms. Fajora's legs trembled and she sagged in relief. Then she took a closer look. Sebastian's face was gray and haggard, and he cradled his left arm in his right with deliberate care. The wrist appeared to be swelling.

"Sebastian," Fajora whispered. "What did he do to you?"

He lifted red-rimmed, bleary eyes, but shook his head and stumbled on without answering.

The men herded Fajora back to the house with Sebastian. He huddled in his corner, cradling his injured wrist, and refused to speak. She went to his side and put her arm around his shoulders but didn't try to examine the injury. Even if she had medical knowledge, she had no supplies, so she could do little for him.

Clarise arrived soon, and Fajora gladly turned Sebastian over to her skilled hands. Before Clarise tried to examine the wrist, she gave Sebastian a jar of liquid and pressed it on him until he drained it. Then she sat back on her heels and waited, watching him.

She didn't have to wait long. In a few minutes, he slumped against his corner, not asleep, but groggy and limp. He mumbled when Clarise touched him, and moaned when she pulled his arm away from his body and probed the wrist, but otherwise did not react.

Clarise worked on the wrist for a long time, gently prodding and massaging the bones with unbroken concentration until she had them reset to her satisfaction. Then she applied a poultice, for swelling, Fajora guessed, taking great care not to let the hand or wrist change position as she did so. Finally, she wrapped the wrist, hand, and lower arm, securing everything so nothing would alter the position of the precisely set bones.

The evening meal arrived as Clarise moved over to care for Fajora's thigh. Fajora was pleased to see the same girl who had been bringing the food all along. So far, the cats hadn't become alarmed by Fajora's earlier conversation with the child and decided to replace her. Peeking under the leaf cover on her plate, Fajora saw a much larger portion than she had received at previous meals. She smiled at the girl, who returned a delighted grin.

Then the girl stood tentatively by Sebastian, his plate in her hand.

"Leave it near him," Fajora said, "in case he's hungry when he wakes up. Can you wait until later to pick up the plates?"

The girl nodded and deposited the plate on the ground at Sebastian's side. She did not try to come near Fajora and touch her hair or clothes this time, but gave her one sidelong glance before she skipped out

When Clarise finished rebandaging Fajora's thigh, she set another jar beside Sebastian and made motions indicating he should drink it.

"For pain?" Fajora asked.

Clarise nodded.

"The wrist is broken, isn't it? Is it bad?"

Another nod, slower this time.

"Will he recover? Will he be able to use that hand again?"

It took a moment for Clarise to respond to this question. At last, she gave a hesitant nod, followed by an uncertain shrug.

"Well, his chances are a lot better with you here. How long should he wait before he drinks the pain draught?"

Clarise held up three, then four, fingers.

"Three or four hours? Very well. I'll see to it."

With a satisfied nod, Clarise took up the plate of food the girl had left for her. Fajora joined her, making short work of the large piece of cornbread, the generous pile of greens, and the extra sliver of meat.

Fajora hoped the girl didn't get in trouble for her generous help. But she would encourage the girl to continue, nonetheless. She needed the fuel too much not to.

The next day marked the fifth day of Fajora's captivity. She had been gone from the colony for nine days, a lifetime, it seemed. She awoke to clouds and thunder. The foul weather dampened her spirits and she lay listless, wondering if Fazok was alive. If he died, Trayle could no longer hide Fajora's absence, even if she managed to do so while Fazok lived. Nor would Dannel be able to hold Kinovic off from the truth. And if he had not confirmed whose aura he felt on his visit to Rock Clan, he would know for sure once her absence was disclosed.

Perhaps the Wellador doctors had found the antidote they needed, and Fazok was recovering. But even in the case of such a desirable outcome, he would be weak from his illness, in no condition to deal with the mess Fajora had left him. Kinovic would either press for information or use Fazok's weakness as an excuse to take on more authority. Or both.

It was time she went back. Past time. But she was no closer to a solution, to a plan of escape, than she had been on her first day here.

Tornton and his men herded her and Sebastian through pelting rain and into the void ship hangar. Sebastian was pale and wobbly, still under the influence of Clarise's drug. Fajora supported him more than he supported her, and they made slow progress through the settlement, getting soaked before they reached shelter.

They stopped inside the hangar, near the door, where the four big machines sat. The lights glimmered, swinging in the breeze from the door someone had left open. Several men worked to remove the top from one of the machines.

A guard brought Clarise in and thumped her onto her stool. But after a cursory attempt to force her cooperation, Tornton ignored her to watch his men, with the manual open on the table nearby. Several of them tinkered with the cables and wires inside the open machine. Fajora could see from the flicker of Clarise's eyes she understood what the men were attempting.

A wire began sparking. Gesticulating with both arms, Tornton issued a string of commands, his voice getting louder and harsher as the sparking continued. One of the other men turned to Clarise and asked an urgent question, of which Fajora caught only a few words. They clearly wanted her help to avoid disaster, but she maintained her silence.

Several wires caught the spark from the first, and in a flash of light and a noise of fizzing and popping, the whole machine sputtered and went dark. The odor of burnt wire casings permeated the air. The men stared at the machine, open-mouthed, for a long time. One of them manipulated the levers on the outside panel, while another fussed with the wires inside.

But the machine resisted their efforts, remaining dark and silent. Tornton turned on Clarise and spouted curses at her, followed by blows to her head and stomach. Clarise bore it as usual, with stoic silence, though she fastened her normally downcast gaze on the machine. Once, she turned her head toward Fajora and Sebastian, her expression satisfied despite the pain she endured.

Tornton stopped hitting Clarise, as if he were aware of her reaction. He glanced at Fajora, then laughed, setting her pulse pounding. She knew what was coming even before he spoke.

"It's your fault, Light Spinner. You were supposed to convince this one to cooperate, and you've failed. Can't do nothing much to him now without setting off that awful cat, so I guess it's your turn." He reached for the knife at his back, then hesitated. Instead, he hefted a cylindrical tool another man had dropped when the machine died. Hooks and protrusions studded its length, creating the ideal instrument for tearing into flesh.

He laughed as he approached her. He grabbed her arm, then dropped it as his gaze fell to her thigh. Fajora tried to shrink away, but the ties around her ankles kept her in place, and one of the other men moved up close behind her and held her shoulders. With another laugh, Tornton brought the heavy tool down on Fajora's bandaged thigh.

19

DRISSY

Fajora screamed.

She was at once ashamed of her weakness. Sebastian had also screamed when Tornton shattered his wrist, a justified reaction considering the severity of his injury. But Clarise had endured repeated torture without a sound. What a young woman barely out of girlhood could do, surely a trained agent should be able to match.

Fajora felt a whimper rise in her throat and tried, with only partial success, to suppress it. A stain of blood soaked through the bandage. At least one, and probably more, of her wounds had broken open again.

Feeling silence press down on her, Fajora mastered her pain enough to look up at those gathered around her. The men watched her, their faces intent, curious. Sebastian's face was gray, and he clenched his jaw. He stared straight ahead, giving her an illusion of privacy. Clarise, too, focused on the console in front of her.

Tornton left Fajora's side and went to Clarise. He spoke to her, quietly at first, but more loudly as she gave no response. Through the haze of her pain, Fajora could make no sense of his words, but she knew what he must be saying. The same arguments that had failed thus far continued to fail. She wondered why he did not give up.

He slapped Clarise once, then strode over to Fajora. "You see now what we can do? You tell her to work now, or I'll hurt you even worse than this."

Fajora lifted her head high and stared at him with all the defiance Sebastian had modeled for her. Though she had broken once, she would not break again. She tried to communicate that message to Tornton even as she kept silent.

"Bah!" Tornton turned from Fajora to study Clarise again. "They're all useless. We stole the wrong humans."

One of his men spat. "Must be some of them Wellador would fancy a place on a void ship. Some as would see the good of helping to get her going. Understand the honor and all."

Another man laughed. "We need another raid. Grab more humans as will do what they're told. What you want to do now, boss?"

"Think I'll give them one more chance," Tornton said, hefting his tool-turned-weapon.

All Fajora's stoic determination flew out the door as the tool landed on her bleeding thigh. She screamed again, this time without shame. Her bandages were soaked with blood, and she fought only vaguely against the growing darkness.

Wavering in and out of consciousness, she thought she heard Jelok's voice. But, of course. He kept watch over the settlement. Man-sitting rather than kit-sitting, apparently. He had made them stop torturing Sebastian yesterday, though too late to avoid a serious injury. Would he do as much for her?

"You might want to find a different tactic," he said, his voice cold and dry, but holding a thread of amusement. "I don't think the council will be happy if you damage their prize prisoner, especially after we've taken such pains to get her healed."

"Trying to make them do as they're told," Tornton grumbled. "Groknor said to get a little rough."

"Yes, I remember. And pain does have its uses. But it only goes so far. These subjects have shown it won't move them, so you need to get more creative. Or learn to fix the machines yourselves." Edging toward delirium, Fajora imagined a rumble of laughter.

"Or maybe we need different humans." Tornton's voice took on a note of hope. "Maybe get some when we go to war with Deep Valley Clan, coming up soon."

Now Jelok's laughter was palpable, clearly not a product of Fajora's imagination. "You think any humans you find there will be more cooperative? You're stupider than I thought. Now leave this Light Spinner alone. Have someone take her back to her house."

Fajora could not walk. Two of the men dragged her through the settlement and tossed her through the door of her house. She huddled, breathing raggedly, waiting for the pain to dissipate enough for her to move.

When she could summon the strength, she pulled herself close to her fuzzy bedding hide and pillowed her head on it. She resisted the urge to wrap it around herself, even though she shivered uncontrollably. She didn't want to get it wet and bloody, unfit for use; she didn't expect her captors would provide a replacement.

A little later, she managed to pull herself into a sitting position, leaning against the wall so she could see her leg.

Red shading to rust stained the wrapping. The first rush of bleeding had subsided now. Fajora felt faint with relief, or, more likely, from loss of blood. And from shock and the pain, which hammered her thigh and spread through her lower leg and up into her hip. The reopening of her wound had set her back, but she thought her condition might have been worse on the day she arrived, when the wounds were new and fresh. She would have to wait until Clarise came with supplies and removed the bandages, to be sure.

Her screams, as Tornton brought his tool to bear on her leg, had left a dry scratchiness, as if they had torn through her throat with unsheathed claws. The burning dryness now became a companion to the fire in her leg. She contemplated calling to her guard to have water brought. She saw a gray tail swishing through the gap below the door covering, so she knew the cat lounged within hearing of her voice. But the guards rarely responded to any sound from within the building, and her voice, even when she cleared her throat, did not want to work.

She sat for a long time, trying not to swallow, trying to think of something besides her throat and her leg. Through the haze of her pain, it came to her, again—this was her own fault. If only she had kept track of her pack.

But, no. The fault lay farther back. Pushing through her pain to concentrate, she slowly traced the line of causation back and back, all the way to Jayzam's deathbed. Her vow to finish what he had started. To prove his claim true.

When the Malekem came, just after Jayzam breathed his last, she had begged him to let her return to Kakislane, to complete his mission. Where she had gotten the courage to address one of the Immortals so, she did not now know. Grief must have made her bold. And perhaps the Malekem had recognized this, for he had not reprimanded her, but had spoken to her gravely, almost kindly, and had promised to take her request to Ya-Lohim.

And then, silence. She had waited a while, taking advantage of the gathering of family for the memorial to spend time with her grandchildren. When the family returned to their homes scattered across Luxera, she had become anxious, then impatient.

The service put her to work running courier routes. On a run to the training facility on Midabara, she had again encountered one of the Immortals, this time one of the Lochemeri. Stern and forbidding, the Immortal warrior had listened but made no promises. And again, silence.

She knew enough about the ways of the Immortals to know silence meant Ya-Lohim had not sanctioned her request. That should have ended the matter. But she had made a vow, however ill-considered, and she shut out all else. So, she had worked the system, called in any favors owed her, and a few that weren't, and had at last gotten the coveted reassignment to Kakislane.

Finally, everything seemed to fall into place. Fazok's illness couldn't be called a good thing, but it had gotten her where she needed to be to slip into clan territory. Surely Ya-Lohim blessed her mission, after all.

Self-deception, she knew now. Hubris and close-minded determination. Which meant she could not expect Ya-Lohim to send help. She could not bring herself to even ask. She might plead with him for Sebastian and Clarise, but not for herself. It was up to her to find a way, or to make a way, to get herself out of this fix.

She thought about this for a while, knowing she did not have it quite right. Ya-Lohim was merciful and forgiving. He might come for her and deliver her. But she could not ask.

She could not forgive herself for her willful stupidity, her headlong rush to do what she decided at Jayzam's deathbed she needed to do. She had not thought about the ramifications. She hadn't taken time to rethink the plan once she retreated from her grief. And now she wondered, had she really retreated from her grief, or had she refused to let Jayzam go by holding obstinately to her impulsive vow.

Her determination to complete Jayzam's mission had become more important to her than Clarise and Sebastian, or anyone else she had met along the way. They had all been stick figures in a vague drama she had played out in her mind, over and over again. But now she knew they were real people who suffered and who needed her to find a way out.

Thinking became harder as the fire in her throat burned hotter. Slaking her thirst became her first, her overwhelming priority. To do so, she must maneuver closer to the door and get the guard's attention.

She was working on finding the courage to agitate her leg, when the door covering moved. A head poked in, and the girl who brought her food stared at her, grinned, and wriggled past the door covering. Wonder of wonders, she carried a jar with her. She scooted over to Fajora and offered it, full of cool water. Fajora grabbed it and drank more than half of it in the first draught.

"Thank you." She smiled at the girl, who sidled closer and touched her hair again. Fajora reached out her own hand and touched the girl's hair, a tentative touch at first. A startled expression flashed across the girl's face and she pulled back to stare at Fajora's hand. Then, with a movement as tentative as Fajora's, she took the hand and set it on her own head.

Fajora patted the girl's head and stroked her hair. It felt coarse and dirty, with tangles and mats. She wished for a comb, but the girl seemed oblivious to her own shortcomings. She let her hand fall into her lap and sat, with eyes closed, while Fajora petted her, and, growing bolder, stroked her cheek.

The girl's eyes flew open at this gesture, and when Fajora stilled her hand, the girl grabbed it and rubbed it against her face. She smiled, not her wild grin or the fierce smile she sometimes gave, but something deeper, sweeter, and she crept close to Fajora's side. Fajora put her arm around the small, thin shoulders, and the girl snuggled close.

Fajora felt a strange stirring in her heart. Her own children were long grown, and she seldom saw her grandchildren. She would never have thought this dirty, ignorant little girl could be a substitute for them in any way, and yet, looking down at her, she guessed she needed the love of a parent or grandparent most of all. She saw signs now she had missed before, of the same sort of abuse Clarise suffered. Bruises on her legs and arms. A cut above one eye, mostly covered by the straggly hair, but uncovered when the girl peered up at her. The boniness of her shoulders, evidence the girl didn't get enough to eat.

"What is your name?" Fajora asked.

The girl tilted her face higher, frowning.

"I'm Fajora." She pointed to herself. Then to the girl. "What is your name?"

"Me? Drissy."

"Drissy, I'm very pleased to meet you. You have helped me so much today. I really needed the water, and I thank you."

Drissy smiled, then reached into a deep pocket of her dress and pulled out a leather bag tied with a thong. She opened it and handed it to Fajora. "For you," she whispered. "To make light."

The bag contained an assortment of seeds and small nuts. A treasure trove to Fajora. Hunger asserted itself, but she hesitated to take the gift.

Aware of the cat on the other side of the door cover, Fajora lowered her voice, copying Drissy's whisper. "Don't you need this? Are you hungry?"

Drissy pushed the bag toward Fajora. "No. I feed you and you make light?"

"Not today. They've hurt me again. But with this and the other food you bring me, maybe soon."

"Eat. It's good." Drissy watched her with expectation.

"Thank you, again." Fajora gave the girl a light hug around her shoulders before unwrapping her arm and taking the bag. The pain of her leg had unsettled her stomach, but she needed the food, and she would not disappoint her new friend. She took a few nuts and crunched them in her mouth, savoring the good, earthy flavor.

Drissy watched her for a few minutes, then crawled away, toward the door.

"I have work. Momma waits for me."

Fajora waved toward the door. "Go then. I don't want you to get into trouble. I'll see you later."

Drissy gave her a wide grin and slipped outside.

Sebastian came in a short while later, much earlier than Fajora expected. Pale and shaking, he held his injured wrist carefully in front of him where he would be least likely to bump it against anything. He slumped in his corner with a weary sigh.

"Was it bad after I left?" Fajora asked. "Did they hurt your broken wrist?"

"No. They're afraid of Jelok. I don't trust him at all, but I'm grateful for his interference this time. No one touched me today, but it hardly matters. The damage is done."

"A lot of pain?"

"Yes." He examined her briefly with his eyes, then gave a rueful laugh. "Probably not any more than you. We're quite a pair, aren't we?"

"Yes, we are. You wait. You'll see." Fajora surprised herself with the optimism in her words, and realized Drissy's visit had renewed her hope. At her words, Sebastian lifted his head and his eyes brightened.

Clarise arrived a few minutes later with an armload of medical supplies. She unwound the wrappings on Fajora's thigh and wiped the blood away. Two of the scratches were tender but not bleeding. The other two, the deepest ones, had broken open and bled, but the flow lessened as soon as Clarise applied her salve. The pain eased too, and Fajora relaxed for the first time in hours, as Clarise rewrapped the leg.

Next, Clarise checked Sebastian's wrist, unwrapping it carefully to avoid jostling the bones. Sebastian didn't make a sound, but tears flowed down his cheeks. Clarise cleaned the area and applied a fresh poultice before rebinding the wrist. She offered Sebastian a small portion of her pain-relieving concoction, which he accepted eagerly.

Clarise repacked her supplies but did not leave. Instead, she found a piece of unoccupied wall to lean against, and settled in, as if this was her usual practice. Sebastian, watching her drowsily, smiled tenderly.

Drissy seemed to know Clarise was with them, for when she arrived with the evening meal, she carried three plates. She came at once to

Fajora's side and snuggled close while the three of them ate. She shuffled slowly around to collect the plates when they were empty, her reluctance to leave obvious. She came back to Fajora twice for a pat or hug before slipping out the door.

"What was that about?" Sebastian asked. "You seem to have a new friend."

Fajora told them about Drissy's afternoon visit and offered Sebastian and Clarise the remains of her nut snack. They both declined.

"You need it more than we do," Sebastian told her. "If you regain your ability to spin, it might be the edge we need. If we can come up with a plan. Maybe the girl can help."

"I don't know." Fajora felt a sudden fierce sense of protection for Drissy. She wouldn't agree to any plan that would put the girl in danger. "Drissy might be willing, but I don't know what she could do. She was proud to help me with the food, though. Reminds me of my oldest daughter, once, when she decided to raise a yalveen from an egg she'd found. She wanted to fly more than anything."

"What's a yalveen?" Sebastian's curiosity was mirrored in Clarise's bright gaze.

Fajora settled herself to tell the story, knowing they could all use something to lighten the burden of their current situation.

"Yalveens are huge birds, the size of a young dragon. We ride on them. There's no better way to see Luxera. Unfortunately, what Zizzi thought was a yalveen egg was actually the egg of a spotted ranger—a type of duck. Our neighbors raised the ducks for the eggs. The hatchling impressed on Zizzi and followed her around the yard, but it never grew big enough to ride. It produced a lot of eggs, though, and Zizzi proudly presented her egg concoctions to Jayzam and me every morning."

Fajora chuckled at the memory, then choked on the lump in her throat. Would she ever see sweet Zizzi again? Or Zizzi's children, just as sweet? And what of this little girl, Drissy, growing up in the middle of Rock Clan, without the affection all children needed? What of the other children of the clan? Were they suffering as well? Ruled by the cats, whose culture and ways of showing affection might be very different, perhaps the humans of this clan didn't even know how to show love to their children. They lived in a dark world, a world that embraced the shadows of the Dark Spinners and rejected the light. Someone needed to show them a better way.

It wouldn't be Fajora, however. She needed to get away from the clan, and get Sebastian and Clarise out of here. There were too many responsibilities already unfulfilled, without adding another. She pushed away the wild idea of taking Drissy with her when she finally found a way out. Taking her from her home would only exacerbate the conflict between Rock Clan and other clans or the colony.

At Fajora's continued pensive silence, Sebastian roused himself to tell a story from his own life, a sweet, funny account of how he and Sonja had met. As Fajora leaned forward in interest, she saw Clarise do the same. Clarise's lips parted several times, and Fajora hoped she would speak, but when Sebastian finished the story, she sank back into her passive silence.

Again, an escort, a human woman this time, came to take Clarise back to her lodging when Fajora and Sebastian went out for their last visit to the latrine for the night. Clarise followed the woman without a backward look, her posture one of resignation, acceptance even. Fajora watched her until she lost sight of her in the darkness before responding to the impatient hisses of her guard.

The trip to their makeshift latrine took longer than usual. Fajora hobbled, with Sebastian's help, at a pace that elicited hisses and growls from the two guards who accompanied them. Neither Fajora nor Sebastian minded the slow pace. The night was calm, with a million stars blazing overhead. Fajora, robbed of the ability to spin through the void, let her spirit soar there, nonetheless. She knew the darkness, the illusion of emptiness in a space filled with wonder. She imagined the route home to Luxera, the circuitous turnings to avoid a flaming star and its giant gas satellite, the nebula one could cruise through if one had no urgent schedule to keep or by-pass if travel time was short, the sight of Luxera, shining like a green jewel in the distance with its familiar tug that said home.

An unexpected whoosh of air overhead brought Fajora out of her reverie. Something had passed directly over her. Her guard snarled and paced, frantic, with his tail low and his head tilted toward the sky. Sebastian had disappeared. The other guard had apparently hustled him back to the house already.

Fajora stood, putting her weight on her good leg, and adjusted her clothing, taking her time, watching the sky. This time she saw it coming, a dark shape circling around and dipping straight toward her, an apparitional creature borne up on silent wings. The dimensions of its wingspan suggested the Greater Tufted Owl. The sight gave Fajora a thrill. But it was too close, this creature of the night with beak and talons as alarming as the teeth and claws of the cats.

Her alarm grew as the owl swooped straight down toward her. She had no defense against its attack, could hardly move, let alone run for cover. She lifted her hands to her face, as if to cover it, protect it, but couldn't bring herself to entirely obscure her vision. The owl, at this close range, could do what it wanted with her, no matter what small defensive measures she took.

But the owl, bearing down on her, swooped up at the last second and soared back to its higher circle. As it passed beyond Fajora, her guard leaped into the air, as graceful and lethal as the bird. But, being a creature of the earth, it could not reach the owl's height. The owl, with a powerful sweep of its wings, rose beyond reach.

Growling and spitting, the cat rounded on Fajora, hissing, and herded her back toward the house. His impatience at Fajora's slow pace on the way out was nothing to his impatience now. He nipped at her heels, butted her legs, and growled out commands to hurry.

As soon as Fajora reached the door, the guard left her to confer with his partner, speaking in the language of cats, all hisses, yowls, and growls. A moment later, he hurried away, while the second guard paced in agitation in front of the house and hissed at Fajora until she went in.

She paused halfway through the doorway, listening to the buzz of excitement traveling through the settlement. She heard the murmurs and exclamations of human agitation. She didn't hear the cats, who moved as silently on the ground as the owl did in the air, but she saw shadows passing through the night, heading to one end or the other of the settlement, and even across the river.

Inside, she told Sebastian what had happened.

"An owl here?" His voice betrayed his disbelief. "You must be mistaken."

"I know what I saw. Its wingspan was this wide." She held her arms out to demonstrate. "It flew in silence, as only owls do, and with confidence, even in the dark."

"But owls never come here. They never nest in either Rock or River Clan territory. Not since the days of the great nesting raid, two hundred and more years ago. And if they do fly through, that's all they do, so high they're out of reach. The cats will do anything in their power to kill them."

"Sonja told me they sometimes act as spies for certain of the clans. Could that be why it came?"

"Hmm, yes, maybe." Sebastian's voice turned thoughtful. "They're reported to have a close relationship with several clans." He paused. "Of course, this is all hearsay. We can't confirm any of it. We'd have to talk to the cats or the owls about it, something we can't do. The cats won't talk about it, and we don't know how to talk to the owls. Nothing more than a few phrases, anyway."

Fajora snuggled into her bedding, thinking hard.

"Suppose it is true. Do you have any idea which clans they spy for? Sonja told me, but I can't remember."

"Well, I know Meadow Clan is one. And Sacred Mountain Clan. And a couple of others. Canyons, maybe, or Forest. And Deep Valley. Especially Deep Valley."

"Deep Valley. Yes!"

"What? What do you know?"

"The owl has come to find me. That must be it. Akachi is a Deep Valley Clan cat. He sent it, or convinced his elders to send it. He's alive, and he's coming for me."

Fajora hugged herself, conjuring up a memory of the young cat. The soft bronze-colored fur. The tufted ears. The bounding walk that betrayed his exuberance. She trembled with relief and anticipation. Somehow, he had escaped the attack of the Rock Clan cats and gotten away. That was the only explanation for the owl. Now she must do her part, keeping alert and ready.

20

—·—

FIRST LIGHT

Calm had returned to the settlement by morning, although an underlying tension had fallen over everything. Fajora saw it in the posture of the cats, in the way the normal morning noises were hushed, and in Tornton's curt commands. He scowled when Fajora limped slowly behind Sebastian and finally motioned her away.

"You. You're no use. Stay here today. I'll send a guard down." Tornton addressed the last comment to the night guard. The guard yawned, showing his sharp teeth, and closed his mouth with an irritated snap but didn't argue about the delay in being relieved.

Fajora sat outside near the river all day, soaking up the sun's energy and watching the roaring torrent of a stream, swollen from yesterday's rain. Her guard, the pregnant female again, dozed closer to the house, where she had a view of both Fajora and the path into the center of the settlement. As long as Fajora stayed put, the guard didn't bother her.

Soon after the sun reached its zenith, Drissy appeared, and along with her, the boy, Robbie, who had been with her two days earlier. Drissy came right to Fajora and snuggled close. Robbie stood a few steps away, uncertain. When Fajora motioned him closer, he sat close enough to let her pat his head but not close enough for a hug. He watched her avidly, holding something close to his chest.

"Go on," Drissy told him. "Give it."

Robbie reached out cupped hands. The round globe of a scarlet rib fruit, the blush on its skin a testament to its perfect ripeness, nestled in his hand. Fajora's mouth watered at the sight. But, as with the nuts the day before, she hesitated. These children shouldn't be giving her this food when they were so underfed themselves.

But Robbie held the fruit closer to her, giving it an emphatic shake. "If you eat this, can you make a light?"

"I don't know, but I'll try. Yes?" Fajora stole a glance at the guard cat to make sure she wasn't watching before taking the fruit from the boy.

The children nodded, and watched with intense interest as Fajora bit into the fruit. She closed her eyes and savored its crisp sweetness, with just a hint of tartness. She had been greedy for these fruits during her previous assignment on Kakislane. She had not tasted one since returning. The deprivation of the last few days made this first bite even more delectable.

She opened her eyes to find both children gawking at her, their mouths hanging open, their eyes as round as an owl's. She ate the fruit slowly, savoring each morsel, but careful to leave a few bites, which she urged on the children. They finished the last bit, down to the core, and spent a few more minutes licking their fingers and giggling. Fajora licked her own fingers, which caused the children to giggle even harder.

But when they had settled down again, they came back to her side with solemn expressions.

"You'll make a light, now?" Drissy asked.

"I'll try."

It was time to try this, anyway. If the owl had been looking for her, if Deep Valley Clan had sent it to find her, she needed to know her capabilities. She checked on her guard. The cat lounged with ears perked toward Fajora so she would know if Fajora got up and moved around, but her eyes were closed. If Fajora sheltered any light she managed to produce, the guard wouldn't see it.

Keeping her back to the cat, she reached for light. She felt it as a thin, glowing stream, not the rush she was accustomed to. Weak as it was, it was the most wondrous thing she had ever experienced. Only now, as she touched light, did she realize how encompassed with darkness she had been since becoming a prisoner. It had been a kind of death, but now she had life again, a resurrection out of the shadows. The light wound through her consciousness like a beaten strand of pure silver.

She reached for it and it came at her bidding. Sluggish, weak it was, but it came. She stretched out her left hand, spreading her fingers, and bid the light flow into it. The children gasped. Looking at her hand, Fajora saw it shimmering, with threads of sparkles twining around her fingers.

The beauty of the light brought tears to Fajora's eyes, but she soon tired and knew she must conserve what little energy she had. Reluctantly, she let go of the light and it faded away. The children sighed.

"Do more," Robbie begged, tugging on her sleeve.

"I wish I could. I don't have the strength yet, but if my leg heals and I get plenty of food, I might be able to. For me, food is the fuel for making light. Do you understand fuel?"

Both heads shook. "What does fuel mean?" Drissy asked.

"It burns and creates energy to make things work or go. The big ship in the hangar. You know about that?" Catching their quick nods, Fajora continued. "It needs fuel to fly, something that burns, a gas or a mineral, in a rock maybe, that can be converted to energy? Have you heard your parents talking about needing a fuel source?"

Now the heads nodded emphatically.

"They say they could go if they fixed the propul . . . the ship," Drissy said. "They have lots of stuff to burn."

"My papa helps," Robbie added. "He digs for the big rocks called ore to make the ship go. They make a pile."

"It's the biggest pile you ever saw," Drissy added. "We play on it sometimes, like we're the head of the council, even over the cats. We go up high on the rocks."

"But it's scary, 'cause Chandra fell down it, all the way, and hurt her leg. Papa yelled and made us stay away for a long time." Robbie sat back with a frown, considering.

"Well, everything needs fuel," Fajora told them, "but for people, the fuel is food. And Light Spinners need even more fuel than other people to make the light."

As she finished, she saw both children stiffen as they peered at something behind her. She angled her head enough to see a cat wending its way toward the riverbank. Even in a quick glance, she identified the rakish face with its angled black markings.

She leaned close to the children and whispered, "We don't need to tell Jelok about my light. He might not like me making it. It can be our secret, so he doesn't try to stop me from making it again."

The children had no chance to reply. Their eyes grew large and solemn as Jelok approached. Fajora did not turn to look at him again, but he soon came within her line of vision. He held his tail high and his ears erect, creating a cheerful demeanor. The children, adept at reading cat body language, relaxed and their smiles returned.

"What a lovely sight," he said, his voice almost a purr. "Children playing by the river in the middle of the day when their chores are waiting. What will the parents say?"

The smiles faded, and the children glanced up toward the houses as if expecting to see their mothers coming to scold them.

Jelok laughed, a sound Fajora still couldn't correlate with the rest of her knowledge about cats. "Never fear, dear children." He winked at them. "Your elders will never hear about this from me. I, too, have stolen an afternoon off from time to time. In fact, I might do so today, since I have such agreeable companions available."

He bent down to rub his head against Robbie's leg, then reached up and licked his face. Robbie giggled, and Drissy sidled closer to Jelok, obviously hoping for a lick as well. Jelok obliged, and ruffled her hair playfully with a sheathed paw. Then he sat back on his haunches and swiveled his ears forward, which gave him a more serious expression.

"A little play is one thing. I see no dishonor there. But one must always think of honor, yes, even in play. You must choose your playtime companions with as much care as your working companions. Yes?"

The children gave him slow, tentative nods. Fajora's stomach clenched into an icy knot. She saw, if the children could not, Jelok's intention.

"So let us go into the settlement and find a more fitting playtime activity," he suggested. "Come, I will accompany you. Come now. Honor requires it."

He bumped the children with his nose, first Robbie and then Drissy, pushing them up the bank, away from Fajora. They moved with him, with backward glances at Fajora. She wanted to call them back, to protest, but feared to make matters worse by raising a fuss. Robbie, turning in Fajora's direction, asked loudly, "But why can't we stay and play with her? I like her."

"Oh dear," Jelok said, with a sound like a sigh. "Of course, you would, but she is very deceptive. It is dangerous to get too close to a Light Spinner. She might whisk you away in her wicked light. You would go, in a flash of light, far away from your home here, from the clan and from your parents. To permit such a thing would be a dishonor. And let me tell you what else Light Spinners do."

He nudged the children on up the path and into the center of the settlement as he spoke, his voice becoming more distant, until Fajora no longer heard him. She wondered what else she might do to the children as a wicked Light Spinner.

And what would be the outcome of Jelok's campaign to sully her character? Would Drissy quit bringing her extra food? Would the children avoid her now? If she did see them, would they treat her to fearful glances from a safe distance, instead of giggles and snuggles? And would they learn to fear and hate Light Spinners, and so turn away from any opportunity to move away from the shadow into light?

The sun didn't seem as bright anymore, and the song of the river spoke of grave matters and turbulent times. Fajora could not shake the conviction she had let something precious slip away with her silence in the face of Jelok's slander.

Her somber mood soured even more when she felt the aura of a Dark Spinner on the edge of her consciousness. It grew stronger, and she caught the first tendrils of shadow out of the corner of her eye, as the Dark Spinner coalesced in the deep shade of a nearby tree. She saw his features clearly now, as she had not been able to do when she first spotted him two days ago. Tall, even for a Luxeran, and young, perhaps in his mid-twenties, he was proportioned for both strength and agility. His violet eyes, with their dark, dancing eye flecks, proclaimed his confidence in his superiority. He wore his long hair—a much brighter blue than Fajora's—in a warrior's queue through which he had woven strands of golden thread.

As on his previous visit, he chose a spot out of the line of sight of Fajora's guard, making it clear he wanted only her to see him. This time, he was near enough to make himself heard without attracting the attention of the guard. He pitched his voice to a near whisper, matching the drone of bees in a nearby flowering bush. The singing of the river gave his words additional cover.

"I've been hoping for an opportunity to talk to you."

"Why? Who are you?"

"I am Syjaz. No doubt you've heard of me. Made quite a stir in the service with my defection."

"I'm sorry. Name's vaguely familiar, but I know nothing about you."

Not strictly true. Fazok had mentioned him, counting him among the best of the new agents before his defection. But, unlike the cats, he had no truth-detection capabilities, and she needed to keep him off-balance.

"No?" He frowned. "You must have been out of action for quite a while not to know of me. And I don't know you either. Tell me your name."

"No. Why make it easy for you when you report to your superiors?"

Syjaz laughed, a quiet sound that mimicked the breezes, but heralded, not a quiet summer day, but a menacing storm. "Oh, it will be easy. Your name will matter little when I take you into custody."

"How will you manage that?" Fajora asked, trying to mask her unease. "The cats are competent guards."

"Do you think your guard, heavy with kit as she is, would be faster to protect you than I would be to gather you into my spin?"

"If I give her warning, once you start your spin, yes."

"Well, perhaps." His voice was heavy with doubt. "But it matters little. I will wait until the right time." He leaned casually against his tree. "Did you know the cats are planning to move you in a day or two?"

"Why?"

"Precisely to keep me from doing what I will do despite all their efforts. War is brewing, and when Rock Clan goes on the warpath, this settlement will empty out, except for the kit-sitters. They can't spare too many warriors to guard you. They have a more defensible settlement a half-day's walk from here. They might be able to protect you there, with only a couple of guards." He laughed, louder this time, and Fajora wondered why her guard did not come to investigate. "Trouble is, they must get you there. That will be a trick. Never fear, my dear, you will be on Zukalum soon, meeting my revered lord."

"Zukalum? Where is that?"

She knew of the place, of course—the Dark Spinners' infamous outpost on an asteroid circling a star not far from Luxera. Close enough, though no Light Spinner had identified the exact coordinates, to allow Dark Spinner incursions along the routes between Luxera and the training moons of Ganedena, and between Luxera and Sek-Nar.

Fajora had fended off Dark Spinner attacks along those routes more than once and knew its location as well as any non-Dark Spinner, but she hoped, by feigning ignorance, to trick Syjaz into revealing some new bit of information.

"What? Don't know Zukalum? You have been in a backwater. Zukalum is the most sacred place, where Choshek sits on his throne and gives his decrees. You will be in his presence soon now."

Fajora shivered unaccountably as Syjaz spoke of his dark lord, and the young Dark Spinner laughed.

"Yes, I see you do know. Be expecting me on the trail."

"When I tell the cats about your threat, they'll surely change their plan."

"They will not believe you." He smirked, his self-assurance apparently blinding him to the realities of cat truth-sensing.

Behind her, Fajora's guard yawned loudly, then rumbled in a low growl. Twisting around, Fajora saw the cat pacing toward her. When she turned back to Syjaz, he was spinning. His spin tightened and he shot away as the cat reached Fajora's side and looked around, sniffing.

"I heard voices. Who were you talking to?"

"A Dark Spinner."

"A dark one? Preposterous. Why should I believe you?"

"He didn't want you to see. But you can test me, and then you should take word to your council about his plans."

"What plans?"

"He's going to snatch me when your council moves me to your other settlement."

"How do you know about that?"

"The Dark Spinner told me."

The cat came close and sniffed deeply all over Fajora, head, body, hands, feet, head again. Her test complete, she sat back on her haunches, ears perked forward. Only the tip of her tail moved, twitching in a nervous pattern.

Fajora sat still, waiting, doing nothing to irritate the cat. Hoping she'd said enough to convince the council to change their plan. She needed to be here, in this settlement, not in a more secure place a half-day's journey away, where Akachi could not find her.

The cat sprang to her feet and nosed at Fajora. "Get up. Get inside and stay there."

Fajora complied without complaint even though the warm house smelled bad after the fresh air by the river. The cat left her unguarded and hurried into the settlement. A risky move if Fajora had been healthier, but the cat and Fajora both knew she wouldn't get far if she tried to escape on her own in the middle of the day. It wasn't long before a new guard nosed under the door to check on her. Now she could only wait to discover if she had foiled both Syjaz and Rock Clan and kept the way clear for Deep Valley Clan to rescue her.

21

WEAPONS

In the evening, Drissy brought Fajora a dinner plate piled with the largest portion she had yet received, double that of the first day. Though glad for the extra food, Fajora also felt concern for her young friend.

"Drissy, how are you able to bring so much? Will your mother notice? I don't want you to get into trouble."

Drissy grinned. "Momma thinks it's the phantom taking food. She doesn't know it's me."

"Phantom? What do you mean?"

"Someone is stealing food all over the settlement. I heard today . . . ." Drissy lowered her voice to a conspiratorial whisper. "Some says a dark one is hiding out here and taking food. They be like you. They need lots of food fuel to make their shadows."

Ah. Syjaz had to eat, of course. And no one feasted him now, as the clan did for the regular Dark Spinner visits, because they didn't know he was here. By refusing to show himself and resorting to raids to feed himself, he inadvertently helped Fajora. She smiled. Wouldn't he be livid if he knew?

While the prisoners ate, Drissy again snuggled close to Fajora's side, watching everyone with close attention. Clarise had joined them again. When Sebastian began to talk to her, giving Fajora and Drissy a moment alone, the girl stretched higher toward Fajora's ear to whisper to her.

"Can you really whisk me away from here in your light, like Jelok said?"

Fajora stared at Drissy, her astonishment mixed with desire and frustration. "Not now, dear," she said at last. "I don't have enough strength, and it would cause complications between Rock Clan and the humans and other cat clans on your world." She saw the girl's disappointment and searched for some glimmer of hope to offer her. "But you can go away from here someday, when you're older. Work hard and grow strong first. Then find the other humans and they will take you in."

Drissy's eyes grew large at this new idea. Fajora held onto faith that she did not offer false hope. Dannel, Sonja, and others in the colony would take Drissy in, protect her, and give her a good life if she found her way to them. Getting to them would be the challenge, but looking into the girl's dark eyes, eyes filled with determination, Fajora judged her up to the task.

"I'll go. Where are the humans? What paths do I take?"

"Across neutral territory," Fajora whispered. "Through Deep Valley Clan and then through Meadow Clan. Beyond Meadow Clan is the human colony."

Drissy nodded and sat back to watch Fajora and the others finish their meal. Fajora wondered if she had encouraged what amounted to suicide for her little friend. But she could not leave the girl behind without giving her hope of escape from this den of darkness and abuse.

Sebastian and Clarise watched them now, with curiosity, and for Sebastian's part, with eyes that betrayed his hunger. Much as she needed the food, Fajora felt guilty eating such large helpings while the others had so much less.

"I've had about as much as I can eat at one time," she told Drissy. "Is it all right with you if I share a little? My friends don't spin light, but they also need their strength."

Drissy peeked around Fajora to stare at Sebastian and Clarise in the waning light. She must have sensed kindred spirits, for she rose and walked to them, patting both their heads and stroking their hair, before nodding to Fajora.

"Yes. They are friends." Glancing at the door and lowering her voice, she added, "Tomorrow, I try to bring them more, if Momma doesn't watch too hard. You get strong and go away, and I'll come find you later."

After Drissy left, Clarise took care of Fajora's wounds. The two re-opened gashes wept a faint trickle of blood, but Clarise's salve soon put a stop to the bleeding. Next, she inspected Sebastian's wrist. He bore the examination with only a few suppressed grunts, and she nodded in satisfaction as she rebound the injury.

"You don't have any new cuts or bruises," Fajora noted. "Has Jelok put a stop to the torture?"

Sebastian grimaced. "Apparently. Tornton is spooked, I think, and has found a new tactic. He kept me right by his side all day while he worked on the nav system. He kept talking to me about what he was doing and looking at me for approval or disapproval. It was hard not to give anything away. He may have learned more from me today than during the whole time he tortured me. I tried to control my reactions, but I know I wasn't always successful."

"Does he know enough about navigation to learn from your reactions?"

"He's smarter than he looks, you know. We've noticed that before. If he read well enough to understand the tech manuals, he wouldn't need us at all."

After Clarise left, Fajora and Sebastian put their heads closer together to avoid being overheard by their guard and discussed the possibility of escape, should members of Deep Valley Clan come for them. They needed a plan in place, one they could implement at a moment's notice. But every idea they discussed had some fatal flaw. They couldn't figure out how to get past the guard. The clan had regular patrols roaming the area around the settlement, all endowed with the cats' superior hearing, night-time vision, and keen sense of smell. Not only was Fajora unable to produce a full spin, she could barely limp to the latrine. Her potential adversaries, both feline and human, were all stronger and faster than she was.

"And what about Clarise?" Sebastian asked, his face scrunching with anxiety. "She sleeps in a different part of the settlement and always has a guard. Even if Deep Valley Clan has a plan to get you out, how will we get her, too? I won't go without her."

"I don't want to either, though if I get away and regain my full spinning ability, I might be able to come back and spin her out, now I know more about the settlement." She held up a hand to forestall Sebastian's protest. "I agree we should get her out now, but I don't have any ideas. We'll need to work on it, and sleep on it. Keep alert tomorrow for any opportunity to get a weapon, or get Clarise transferred here to sleep, or whatever else you can think of. I'll do the same. Jelok warned the children off from spending time with me, so I'll have lots of time for thinking."

Fajora spoke on the assumption she would remain at the house again the next day. But when morning came, heralded by the return of storms and heavy rain, Tornton herded her, along with Sebastian, back to the void ship. When she faltered and her speed dipped, one of Tornton's men grabbed her arm and half-dragged her behind Sebastian, making for a painful trek through the settlement.

Clarise was already at the hangar when they arrived. Tornton led them into the ship once more, this time to a work room where piles of equipment lay strewn across several long tables. The men clustered around the largest of the tables and tinkered with the contraptions gathered there. They tied Fajora, Sebastian, and Clarise to stools and left them in a line against one wall.

Fajora stained to get a clear look at the men's work. The equipment they worked on seemed familiar. Focusing on the shape of the items, she identified them as weapons, not dissimilar to those the Wellador Colony's security forces used. These were far larger, appearing clunky and heavy compared to the sleek devices of the Wellador. But they were weapons, nonetheless.

Several of the devices glowed with power. Looking around at the artificial lights and the panels glowing on one of the walls, Fajora realized this entire void ship had power while the rest of the settlement did not. She should have noticed this before, but she had been distracted by other concerns.

Though accustomed to the technology-free lifestyle of Luxera, Fajora had been around the Wellador humans enough to understand and detect power sources. She also understood a little about how the power was transmitted; even if Rock Clan had a power-producing facility else-where, perhaps by the mines where they sourced ore for fuel, they had no infrastructure for getting the power to the ship. Which meant the ship itself must be fuel-ready, capable of converting the ore directly to power.

Rock Clan was closer to lifting into the void than she had imagined. They still had problems with the ship, problems they didn't know how to fix. Their crude attempts to elicit Clarise's cooperation highlighted these deficiencies. But power was not one of their obstacles. And they only needed time and patience to figure out the rest. The question was, how much time?

Every few minutes, Tornton brought one of the devices over to his prisoners and talked about what he was doing, watching their faces for affirmation. It sounded like gibberish to Fajora, who knew nothing about engineering. She started studying Clarise, and especially Sebastian, looking for clues in their expressions to assess Tornton's progress.

What she observed alarmed her. If these weapons were getting as close to operational as she guessed, she and her friends might be fortunate to live out the day.

She thought about the line she, Sebastian, and Clarise made against the wall and swallowed hard. Men with weapons, broken weapons that needed testing, might contemplate using live subjects as target practice, especially if they were trying to convince said subjects to cooperate with them. Even more especially if they were frustrated by the subjects' lack of cooperation. Having witnessed the effects of the Wellador weapons, Fajora knew laser guns dealt a lot more damage in a lot less time than slaps and punches. Doubtless, Sebastian and Clarise knew this as well. Both were pale as they watched the men's progress.

Three men who sat at the table took the weapons apart, tinkered with them, and reassembled them, while their fellows stood around them, looking on and giving advice. Their confidence in handling the devices suggested they had done this before. The reassembled guns gave off a bright glow. The workmen aimed them at a far wall and pushed the trigger levers. All three guns sputtered and emitted weak beams, but none produced a steady light strong enough to reach the wall.

Fajora released the breath she had been holding and let air rush into her lungs in relief. And then tensed up again and strained for a view as the men went back to work. This time they concentrated on one weapon, pulling several others from the pile and mining them for parts. With the replacement parts installed, the weapon gave off a steady hum. Sebastian and Clarise exchanged glances but avoided looking in Fajora's direction.

At last, the men sat back and inspected their work, then handed the refurbished weapon to Tornton. He turned and winked at his line of prisoners. "You see here, what that Deep Valley scum has coming to them? Been working on this special for the war. May get us more help for our project, too."

The men leaned close, intent as Tornton took aim and pressed the trigger. A much steadier stream of light burst from the weapon, blackening a small circle on the metal surface of the far wall. After a moment of shocked silence, the men broke into a confused babble of cheers and exclamations.

The man nearest Tornton reached for the weapon, announcing it was his turn. Another man objected loudly and reached for the weapon. Soon several more hands jostled into the mix and the men began shoving. They bumped Tornton aside, but he did not loosen his grip on the weapon until three men, all reaching for it at the same time, tore it from his grasp and sent it clattering to the floor.

The men jumped back and stared down at it, their babble silenced. Tornton retrieved the weapon and held it up. The trigger mechanism hung loose and useless. The hum had dissipated, and the glow from the power indicator flickered. Tornton spat an oath, glaring around at the men. He pulled out his knife and brandished it at them.

"You're all cat filth. Look what you've done."

"Tren did it, jostling you. It's his fault," someone offered.

"Did no such thing," shouted the one who stood accused. "You're just scrounging for someone to blame. I saw what you did."

Angry denials and accusations erupted from several more of the men. Tornton tried to shout over them, but the men paid no attention to him or his knife. One man picked up a weapon that had failed earlier and pointed it at another man. Tornton reached for it, dropping his knife as he did so. Two more men joined the tussle.

As they struggled for control of the weapon, it emitted a beep and a weak steam of light. Weak, but harmful enough at close range. A man in the middle of the melee threw up his arms with a shrill cry and began to topple.

The other men backed off from him, watching in sudden silence as he crashed to the floor. A patch of his tunic had burned away, exposing his left side a hand's-breadth below his ribs. The stench of scorched flesh filled the air; there was no blood.

The injured man moaned, his hand fumbling for the wound and then falling away. The other men leaned over him, shaking him, calling to him with frantic voices. Tornton barked a command, and two men came and untied Clarise. They yanked her off her stool and pulled her over to the fallen man.

"Fix him up," Tornton said.

Clarise hesitated, then knelt and gently touched the wound. She felt at the man's neck for a pulse. After a moment she pulled back, sitting on her heels. Tornton spoke to her in a low, rough voice. Clarise shook her head. He accompanied his next words with a back-handed slap. Clarise swayed under the blow, but shook her head again.

The men gathered around the fallen one, stirred, muttered, became quiet and stirred again, until Tornton growled out orders. With slow, reluctant movements, the men rose and lifted their fallen comrade, carrying him in a solemn procession toward the exit.

Tornton motioned for one of the men to stay with the prisoners. He grumbled a protest, and even when Tornton repeated his command, the designated guard followed the others down the corridor toward the void ship's exit. The tread of feet echoed from the corridor, then faded, and the three prisoners were alone.

"The guard won't go far," Sebastian murmured. "No chance to escape, I don't imagine, but is there anything we can do to help ourselves before he comes back?"

"Any useful equipment here?" Fajora asked, casting a doubtful eye at the cluttered tables. It all looked like junk to her, but Sebastian and Clarise might have a different perspective.

In answer, Clarise moved to a far table, where a stack of flat, square disks rested, and shuffled through them. She chose one and inserted it into the panel above the table. Her fingers flew over the buttons on the panel, and several lights started blinking.

"She's trying to download old records," Sebastian breathed. "Incredible. If she's successful, we might find out where these people came from. Why they ended up here. How their presence here relates to the history of the Dominion. But it's risky. These old databases will be slow. If Tornton comes back and finds out what she's doing . . . ."

"Do you want her to stop?"

Sebastian closed his eyes and scrunched his face, betraying his struggle. His curiosity—no, more than mere curiosity—his need to know, won out. "No. It's worth the risk. Quick, Clarise, see if there's anything else on any of these tables we can use. A weapon, maybe."

In answer, Clarise picked up an object that lay on the floor near the large worktable. She rose and came to the other two with it, held it up.

Tornton's knife.

"Quick," Sebastian said. "Cut our bindings. We can get away now."

"We have to walk through the entire settlement," Fajora reminded him. "And our guard will be near the ship, if not inside. He or someone else will raise the alarm. And if our ropes are cut, they'll know we have the knife."

"Clarise should hide it until later."

"Hide it where? Where can we get to it if we need it?"

Sebastian hung his head. "Put it back where you found it, Clarey."

She shook her head and approached Fajora. Reaching around, she lifted the back of Fajora's tunic and slid the knife into the waistband of her trousers.

"No," Fajora said, forestalling the young woman. "My tunic's too tight. They'll see the shape of it. Sebastian's is looser."

Clarise pulled the knife away from Fajora. Turning, she lifted Sebastian's tunic and tucked the knife into his waistband, then pulled the tunic back over it. He would have to take care how he moved, so the knife did not cut him, unprotected by a sheath as it was. But he should be able to get it back to the house unseen, unless Tornton decided to beat him and his fist met the hard contours of the blade or handle.

Sebastian blushed bright red as Clarise adjusted his clothing to settle the knife, but Clarise did not show any signs of embarrassment. She stepped back with unselfconscious grace, meeting Fajora's gaze rather than Sebastian's, seeking approval for her actions.

As Fajora nodded, the machine on the far wall made a quick series of beeps. Clarise hurried to remove her disk. Small enough to insert in Fajora's waistband without showing, it was more secure there than it would have been in Sebastian's looser clothing. It lay warm against the small of her back, a reminder of Jayzam's hand, which had often rested in the same spot when he held her.

Dizziness swept through Fajora at the memory, along with a surge of triumph. Here was proof, vindication, demonstrating the truth of all Jayzam had said.

But Jayzam had never mentioned this void ship, or even the hangar. He had not speculated on why there were humans in Rock Clan. His mission had been to find Clarise, to free her, and, failing that, to convince his enclave that Rock Clan held her prisoner with Dark Spinners involved.

The rest—the ship, its distant origins, the human descendants of its first crew, their aspirations to take to the void and make a name for themselves, and the intention of their feline masters to take over Kakislane and advance on the Dominion—had nothing to do with Jayzam's mission. And its repercussions went far beyond what Jayzam had imagined.

What Fajora had learned, was learning, had yet, perhaps, to learn--things the cats of Kakislane already knew—had to do with the Dominion's history, and, perhaps also with the Dominion's future. Fajora was beginning to suspect Sebastian's presence—Sebastian, student of ancient manuscripts rather than Sebastian, astrophysicist—was a message from Ya-Lohim, pointing her to the prophecies she had studied when convenient and then abandoned. With the disk burning at her back, she had become the guardian of both past and future, and she wasn't sure she wanted such responsibility. She just wanted to come through for Jayzam and feel his approbation.

She squirmed and opened her mouth the tell Clarise to take the disk back, to destroy it. Her mind busily offered her a list of plausible reasons why this was necessary. Strong enough reasons to convince both Clarise and Sebastian.

Poised to refuse the tasks she had fallen into, she snapped her mouth shut. She had rushed into clan territory with her own agenda. Ya-Lohim and his Immortals could have stopped her before she ever met Akachi, before she ever crossed that fateful strip of neutral territory, and they had not. She had continued on, and now it was too late to turn back. She had stumbled into something bigger than she wanted or could have imagined, but she was an agent of Light. There were tasks to do here, tasks only she could do. The disk existed now, its warm metal cooling to the temperature of her own body, so she no longer felt it. She would not unmake it.

There was no time, at any rate. Echoing footfalls in the corridor leading to the exit sent Clarise scurrying back to the spot where the man had fallen. She was kneeling exactly as she had been, with her hands clasped in front of her and her head down, when two of the men burst back into the room. They gave the three prisoners a swift appraisal. Nervous laughter burst from their lips when they saw everyone still as they had left them.

For the next several hours these two men kept watch over the three prisoners. They sat Clarise down in a chair near the tables and asked her questions from time to time as they tinkered with the weapons, questions she did not answer. They snarled and growled at her, sounding like the cats, and then returned to their half-hearted work. None of the weapons fired again, despite repeated trials.

Fajora and Sebastian sat and watched, tied to their stools against the wall. Fajora ached from being tied so long, unable to change her position or stretch her muscles. She needed a trip to the latrine, even as thirst plagued her. She was glad when Tornton reappeared.

"Cats going crazy out there," he said in an offhand tone. "How's things in here?"

After a cursory glance at his prisoners, he inspected his men's work, trying each of the weapons and swearing at the results. He cuffed the sides of the men's heads, then reached for his knife. Not finding it in its usual place, he hunted around the tables and on the floor.

"Where's my knife?" he asked, his voice accusing as much as inquiring.

"Haven't seen it," the man nearest Tornton said.

"I left it here, somewhere. Some fool's taken it. Which of you?"

"Not me," the second man said. "What about the prisoners?"

The first man gestured toward Sebastian and Fajora. "Not those two. Been tied up the whole time. What about the girl?"

"What about it, girl?" Tornton moved to where Clarise sat, unmoving. "Hand it over, or you know what I'll do, don't ya? I'll have to look for it myself."

When Clarise neither moved nor displayed any emotion, he pulled her up out of her chair and leaned in close, putting his arms around her to feel her back, from neck to buttocks, taking his time. Finding no knife, he stepped back to examine her front, touching every part of her as he moved down her body. When he reached her waist, he dropped his hands and lifted her skirt.

Fajora averted her eyes. Sebastian made small, mewing noises as he struggled against his bonds, causing them to dig into his arms and ankles. A slow flush spread up his neck and into his face. Fajora surmised, from the compressed lips, the tight jaw, the furrowed brow, that he did not blush from embarrassment. And she understood. The same fury she saw in him heated her own blood and tensed her jaw.

Clarise endured the search without a sound. Fajora knew when Tornton was finished, for he uttered an oath and slapped his victim hard. Fajora turned her eyes back to see Clarise standing passively, showing no awareness of Tornton's invasion. She was used to it, Fajora realized, observing her with a slow twist of nausea.

Fajora held utterly still and silent, praying he would not decide to come and search his other prisoners, wondering what he would do to them, and to Clarise, if he found the knife at Sebastian's back. But he turned on his men rather than on the prisoners. He hovered over them, speaking in a low growl Fajora could not understand. The men's postures became stiff, defensive, their voices as harsh as Tornton's when they answered.

In a sudden motion, taking his victim by surprise, Tornton grabbed the man closest to him by his tunic and hauled him to his feet. His hands felt for a hidden knife before the man could protest and push him away. They tussled for a moment, then broke apart. The other man, watching, stood and held his hands up, motioning for Tornton to come and check him as well.

Tornton spat and waved him away.

"The both of you are useless liars. I'll find wherever you've hidden my knife. Count on it. Meanwhile, make yourself useful and get these prisoners out of here. With Gorbon laid out, won't get no work done anymore today, anyway. Want to see what's got the cats riled, too. Never seen them so worked up."

22

—·—

OWL RECONNAISSANCE

Fajora staggered when the men released her from her stool, and she stumbled down the corridor with tingling feet and hands as blood rushed back into her extremities. As sensation returned, the pain in her thigh intensified, making each step agony as she hobbled through the ship. She clung to railings and to Sebastian's good arm until they emerged from the hangar. Only then did she feel steady enough to stand on her own and take in the activity around her.

A crowd of humans had gathered near one of the larger stone houses, while a couple of cats prowled around its edge. The humans talked in excited, high-pitched voices. The unfortunate Gorbon's home, apparently.

Fajora took note when Tornton grabbed Clarise's arm and tugged her toward a ramshackle lean-to huddled against the next house over from Gorbon's. A rubble of fallen stones collected near the door, and the two windows were mere slits. Bunches of drying herbs hung from the narrow eaves, proclaiming it a healer's residence. As Tornton shoved Clarise inside, one of the prowling cats came and took a position near the door.

Knowing where Clarise slept did Fajora little good, however. The house was in the middle part of the settlement and a long way from the house she and Sebastian shared. In the hurry of a rescue attempt, it would be difficult to get to her.

She forgot about Clarise, however, as she noticed how many cats were dashing about in a high state of agitation. At this time of day, with the sun slanting toward the horizon but true darkness hours away yet, the cats normally emerged from the dens yawning and settled in the sun to clean themselves or grab another nap, not yet ready for socializing or active tasks. It was a sleepy time of day for the felines, except for those who had daytime duties. Even those on daytime patrol or guard duty took things easy in the late afternoon.

But now, cats slunk around every building, and Fajora watched in astonishment as two cats raced to neighboring houses and leaped to the roofs. She looked at Sebastian, hoping for an explanation. He shrugged, then shook his head at her unspoken question.

A shadow overhead, drifting across the settlement, gave Fajora her answer. An owl, its powerful wings creating a gust of air as it passed overhead, scouted the area. It zoomed low over one roof, then banked and lifted, avoiding the roof where a cat waited to leap for it. The cat leaped anyway, stretching, coming within a whisker's length of the wing tip before coming down in a four-pawed landing at the base of the next house.

More cats leaped onto roofs, while some rounded up kits and herded them toward shelter. Others slunk through the settlement, patrolling all parts of it. They spoke in their own feline language, hissing, mewing, and growling. Fajora didn't need to understand the words to sense the fear and the anger permeating the entire clan.

Fajora and Sebastian's human escorts called for their cat guard as they approached their house. The guard tried to usher them inside, but Fajora insisted on a trip to the latrine and refused to go in even when the cat bared his claws and hissed at her, showing his teeth. Her physical needs drove her, and she also wanted closer contact with the owl, a chance to communicate with it somehow.

The man who had brought them to the house laughed as he started back into the settlement. "Go ahead. Take them," he told the cat. "Maybe it's them the birdies want. Let them carry off these two, and your troubles will be over. Might even be fun to watch."

Fajora didn't believe the owl would hurt her. But as she limped to the latrine, she trembled. Her leg throbbed, giving her a good idea of how an owl's talons would feel if they dug into her flesh. The beak didn't bear thinking about.

The relative openness of the latrine area gave Fajora a better view of the skies over the settlement. She saw not one, but three owls soaring overhead. No wonder the cats were agitated. It was also the wrong time of day for the owls to hunt, which made their behavior even more alarming. The large birds made one last circuit of the settlement proper before heading Fajora's way. Four cats streamed from among the houses, following the owls, bounding and leaping as the owls flew low.

All three owls buzzed low over Fajora's head. Though she believed she had nothing to fear, she still ducked down and covered her face. Air beat at her in the wake of the wings as the owls swept past her, gaining height and shrinking as they rose above the cliff edge and sped south.

Fajora stared until the three shapes became indistinct. The cats near her stood staring in the same direction, low growls rumbling in their chests. When the owls vanished into the distance, the cats sniffed with exaggerated disgust and stepped away from the latrine area. They ignored Fajora and Sebastian, leaving them alone with their guard, who hissed at them, making clear his impatience to vacate the area as well.

That evening, Clarise's guard paced outside the door while the young woman worked on Fajora's wounds and checked Sebastian's wrist.

"Take your time," Fajora whispered. "Maybe she'll give up and leave."

But when the bandaging took longer than the cat thought it should, she nosed partway in and stood watching, with her head inside and her haunches outside.

"It is time. You must come now. I have other duties."

"Go about your duties," Fajora said. "Let Clarise stay here with us. One guard can keep watch over all of us."

"Unacceptable." The cat took another half-step in and unsheathed her claws. "You will come now, or you will have more wounds to heal."

Clarise fastened the wrapping and gathered her supplies, while the cat watched with bared teeth. Fajora reached out and gave Clarise's hand a quick squeeze. She was rewarded by a spark in the young woman's eyes and a firming of her lips. Clarise was strong and ready. There was nothing more Fajora could do for now.

Drissy came a little later, carrying two plates. She always knew if Clarise stayed for the evening. Fajora's plate held the largest portion yet, and even Sebastian received a larger serving than usual. Fajora felt new strength pouring through her as she finished. Drissy watched her raptly, and Fajora decided to indulge the girl's desire, since she needed to test her spinning capabilities.

"Watch now," she told Drissy.

The light came more easily, flowing through her, and she let it wrap around her hand and swirl up her arm. Drissy reached for her hand. When she touched warmth but nothing solid, she jumped back, her face flushed with alarm.

Fajora laughed and quenched the light.

"It's all right. It's just light. Energy, not matter."

Drissy shook her head. She didn't understand and wouldn't come close until Sebastian touched Fajora's hand to demonstrate its solidity. Drissy then came for a hug and stroked Fajora's hair, but she did not stay long.

"Momma's scared," she said. "She thinks the owls will get me. But I . . . ." She peered at Fajora. "Does she say right? Will they carry me away and eat me?"

"No. They're not here to capture little girls. I think you're safe. But you'd best get back so your mother doesn't worry."

Drissy nodded. "But why were they here?"

"I think they're looking for someone. But you don't need to tell your Momma, or anyone. Just go let her know you're safe."

Drissy stared at her a moment, her eyes growing larger as her mind worked on what Fajora had said.

"Oh," she said, and threw herself at Fajora for another hug. With many backward glances, she picked up the plates and went to the door. Her lips trembled as she gave Fajora one last look, then she scurried out.

Fajora fought back tears as she listened to Drissy's footfalls fade. Did the girl understand she had to go if she had the opportunity? Or would she feel Fajora had abandoned her? There must be a way to make Drissy understand how much Fajora cared.

"Give me the knife," she mouthed to Sebastian.

"What? What for?" Lowering his voice to a whisper, he added, "We should keep it hidden until we need it."

"I need it. Just for a moment."

Sebastian slipped the knife from under his tunic and handed it to her, keeping a close look out on the door. He watched, wide-eyed, as Fajora pulled her hair over her shoulder, separated a lock, and sawed at it with the knife until it came loose in her hand.

She returned the knife to Sebastian and twisted the lock of hair until she could make a knot at one end. She retrieved the small bag Drissy brought once, full of nuts and seeds. Long since emptied, she had never remembered to return it. She shook the nut and seed debris out of it and nestled the hair into the bag. She laid the bag under her bedding, allowing the top edge to peek out, where Drissy might see it if she came into the house. It was a long chance, but better than nothing.

She patted the bag and whispered, "For Drissy." Would Drissy know it meant, "I love you?" Fajora had no other way to say it.

23

JELOK, KEEPER OF THE SANCTUM

The owls did not show themselves when Fajora and Sebastian visited the latrine again late in the evening. As they walked back, Fajora watched the river. Swollen from the recent heavy rains, it raged and foamed. Fear clenched her stomach into a tight knot. How would Akachi get across if he came for her? It seemed an impassible barrier.

She forced herself to relax as she entered the house, unclenching each muscle in turn. Akachi had displayed so much ingenuity on their trek through River and Rock Clan territories. She must trust him to do so again.

The settlement seemed unnaturally quiet, but several times over the next hour, the cat guarding the door growled or hissed. Listening intently, Fajora thought she heard footfalls and low growls, indicating both humans and cats on the prowl.

Sebastian and Fajora did not talk. Sebastian sat near the door, his head angled to catch the sound of movement outside, and Fajora stood at the window, listening. Finally, in the distance, an owl hooted. The sound sent shivers down Fajora's spine. It spoke of mystery as much as of hope. She believed the owls had been looking for her, but what did she know of the ways of owls? They could as easily have been looking for a kit they could snag, an easy meal.

She shuddered. She would not believe that sort of cannibalism took place, perpetrated by one sentient species on another. She'd like to think she knew more about cats now than she had a handful of days ago, but, in truth, the more she saw, the more of an enigma they became. And whatever small knowledge she had of cats, her knowledge of owls was exponentially smaller.

Yet she clung to hope. And listened. And was rewarded by another distant call. She ignored Sebastian's slight movement as he positioned himself to hear better. She ignored the sound of the guard outside rising and pacing, his deep growl barely audible from this side of the door hanging. She ignored the loud thumping of her own heart and listened with total concentration.

The call came again, and, much closer, an answer. It might be nothing, but instinct and training told Fajora it was a signal. Someone was coming for her, and soon. But the owls had never seen her near her house. They had seen her in the middle of the settlement and near the latrine, but they wouldn't know how to find her now. She needed to respond to their signals with one of her own.

With a rustling of the strange packaging the Wellador used for their food, she pulled her last snacks from her pocket and ripped the wrappings off. She ate with frantic speed, barely chewing, almost choking, while Sebastian stared at her. When she had forced it all down, and it was sticking in her throat, she grabbed the water jug, thankful to find a little liquid in the bottom. As she rinsed her mouth and swallowed, she already felt the extra energy beginning to flow through her.

"I've been saving it," she whispered, by way of explanation to Sebastian. "Like the knife, for when I really need it. Which I hope is now. They need a signal so they can find us."

"What kind of signal?"

Fajora didn't answer, but bent her concentration toward the light in the core of her being. The light swirled around her right hand. This time, she didn't let it tendril up her arm, but held it close, controlling it, letting it grow in density and brightness. Then, with an upward motion of her hand, she released it into the thatch of the roof. It swept through the roof in streaks, sparking and flashing like lightning sweeping across the sky. She let it flow for the count of three, sufficient, she hoped, to get the owls' attention, then closed her hand and pulled the light back into herself. Any more risked attracting the attention of cats and humans.

She and Sebastian stood hushed, waiting for a signal that the owls had seen the light and understood its meaning. The silence outside was complete. Fajora saw, by the light of the moon filtering through the window, the doubt in Sebastian's glance.

Then a shadow blocked the light, coming on silent wings toward the house. Fajora resisted the urge to duck, which had become her automatic response to the approach of this dangerous and magnificent creature. She had the stone walls of the house for protection this time, if she needed protection.

The owl swooped down toward the house. Fajora lost sight of it, but she sensed its presence, much as she felt the auras of Light and Dark Spinners, and she knew the owl roosted above her. Would have known, even if she did not sense its spirit, for the thatch roof rustled and sagged under the bird's weight as it settled.

She motioned Sebastian near so she could whisper and keep her words from the ears of the cat outside, who had, as yet, shown no awareness of the bird on the roof.

"We are marked. Deep Valley Clan will be able to find us when they come. Now we need to find a way to get Clarise here."

He buried his head in his hands for a moment before meeting her gaze. "I've got no ideas. Been musing and mulling all evening. No, longer than that. For days. Since you came, really, but I can't see any way." He closed his eyes. "I won't go without her. If we don't find a way, you go without me. Maybe come back when you can spin us out."

Fajora had suggested this solution before, but now, faced with the possibility of imminent rescue, she didn't like it. She had charged headlong into clan territory for Clarise, even more than for Sebastian. Leaving her now would be to admit defeat, especially knowing Kinovic's dark loyalties. Even if he didn't realize she had been here, even if she hid her infiltration into Rock Clan, he would not make it easy for her to return. And if Fazok did not survive, if Kinovic became head of the enclave, he might make it impossible for her to even stay on Kakislane. If she was going to free Clarise, it must be now.

A glimmer of an idea came to her. It needed thinking over. She moved to her side of the room and sat on her bedding, stretching her bandaged leg out in front of her, sighing with relief to have the weight off it. And the other leg, as well, which had borne more than its share of her weight while she stood at the window. She bent over the good leg, massaging it.

A draft of fresh air brought her head up in time to see the door covering fall back in place behind the body of a cat. In the dim moonlight from the window, the only source of light in the room, she strained to identify this individual. But when he spoke, there could be no mistaking Jelok's voice.

"One would think, from the smell, you still use your den for a latrine. Must I have another talk with your guards about allowing you out?"

"No, Jelok," Fajora answered. "The guards are cooperating as instructed. The smell lingers because we have no way of cleaning the room, and the dampness from the rains makes it worse. A basket of sand and a shovel would work wonders. But I doubt you've come here to talk to us about latrines."

Jelok moved to the wall as far from the old latrine area as possible and sank down into a relaxed position, halfway on his side, his legs stretched out, his tail flopping in an erratic pattern.

"May not your champion come for a visit? To see how you fare?"

"My champion?" Fajora recalled he had been sullying her good character the last time she saw him.

"If not for me, you would be in the hands of the dark ones now," Jelok reminded her. "Or had you forgotten? And where else should I spend an evening when I desire companionship? The humans of Rock Clan are exceedingly poor company, and the cats of Rock Clan do not like me much."

"I'm afraid I will be poor company as well. It's been a rough day and I'm worn out."

"Ah, but that will provide for me a perfect evening. Nothing much will be expected of you. I adore the sound of my own voice, as you know, and never so much as when I have someone else to listen to it. Relax and I will entertain you. Did you hear of the confusion I caused when the dark ones came?"

"No."

He gave his disconcerting chuckle again. "A story in which I win no honor, I admit, but it amused me at the time, and I still find it gratifying."

He launched into a long tale about the misdirection he had handed the Dark Spinners, the cat elders, and the humans during the Dark Spinners' last visit. Fajora tried to follow his story, fearing he would require a response from her. She was amused at how the tables had been turned on the Dark Spinners, usually the masters of deception in any situation.

But she had trouble concentrating. The owl on the roof distracted her, and she wondered if Jelok was aware of its presence. What a disaster it would be if a rescue attempt came while Jelok lingered in the house. And how was she to get Clarise here with a cat in the room? How could she get rid of him without arousing his suspicions?

Jelok's story came to an end. Fajora made a polite comment, which elicited a chuckle from the cat. He watched her with gleaming eyes.

"Perhaps you are interested in the workings of the clan, and how the summer hunt is progressing. I will speak of this, and then perhaps you will be rested enough to tell me something of your people and your world."

Now Fajora tried to listen more closely, interested in the inner workings of the clan with its hierarchy of matrons and elders, its equitable division of duties, and its rituals, developed over the years to ensure the health and well-being of its members. She even picked up a few ideas about how the humans fit into the social structure.

After that, Jelok questioned Fajora. What was her home like? How did her people provide food for themselves? Living with humans as he did, he showed an understanding of the Luxeran farms, with their fields, orchards, and pastures. He had less understanding of the Luxeran social structure, for the humans of Rock Clan organized themselves after the pattern of the cats. He did not understand the farm homestead that sustained a single family, though the villages made more sense to him.

The more questions he asked, the shorter Fajora made her answers. The shorter her answers, the more questions he asked, one coming after another with little time in between. His questions also became more pointed, focusing increasingly on the Luxeran service and the mission of the Light Spinners.

He moved from asking about Luxera to asking about the enclaves, and the Kakislane enclave in particular. Fajora told him little, keeping her answers vague.

"We recognize your reticence," he said in a formal voice. "It is ever so with Light Spinners. We suggest it is because you and your service have no justification for meddling in the affairs of your dark brethren."

"Not true," Fajora retorted. "Ya-Lohim himself has blessed us, and the Immortals have sanctioned our enclaves. We need no further justification, but if you wish to debate theology, I can accommodate you." She hesitated, aware of the late hour and her need to get rid of this visitor as soon as possible. "Some other time, though, when I am less tired."

"You have Ya-Lohim's blessing." Jelok's tone mocked her. "But not the blessing of Choshek, I think."

"Who?" Fajora feigned ignorance, though she knew this name. All agents in the service learned it along with something of its owner's significance, but they were short on details. What better way to fill in her knowledge than from those who followed this Dark Immortal? Syjaz had confirmed Choshek sat on a throne in Zukalum, surely a bleak base from which to rule. Now Jelok brought his name to the fore. What would a cat say of the shadowy leader?

Jelok stirred and rose to his haunches, his movement menacing in the near darkness. Fajora expected him to come near and test her for truthfulness, but he accepted her ignorance, as if he had expected nothing more of her.

"Ah. The truth will out," he said, hissing. "You do not know your enemy. You pride yourself on your mission of righteousness, yet do not know what the youngest cats of Kakislane know. You know only the half-truths your Light Immortals have chosen to tell you, and on this basis, you believe you know truth. But the cats, created to discern truth, know the other side of the argument. All the cats, all the clans, know much of Choshek, though not all give him allegiance. We of Rock Clan will reform them."

A shadow lay over Fajora's spirit and filled the room, which, a moment ago, had been merely dark with the darkness of nighttime. She had wondered if the owl remained on her roof. Now she knew it did, for she felt the same shadow fall over its spirit at the sound of that name. She almost regretted her request for information. She did not want to know more about Choshek, but she needed to understand him, as well as this creature who sat before her, mocking all she believed in. So she pressed forward.

"You're right. I do not know everything the clans know. Enlighten me, please. Tell me of this . . . Choshek?" She shuddered as she made herself pronounce the name.

"Ah. The mind opens, though in truth, not so much as we desire. At least you have the right guide in your search for truth, for I am the keeper of the Sanctum, as was my father before me and his father before him, and back for generations uncounted." Jelok licked his chops and yawned, as if to emphasize how far above her he was, secure in his position.

"What does that mean? I've been wondering. It sounds like an important position, though you claim to have no position in this clan."

"Why, thank you for asking, my dear," he replied, ignoring Fajora's little taunt. "Of course, I must point out how you display your ignorance by doing so. But since you asked . . . ."

He drew himself up taller and arranged his paws at a precise angle in front of him. "Long ago, the Sanctum was a shrine to your Ya-Lohim. Some, who are of a superstitious bent, suggest he condescended to meet individuals face to face there. I cannot attest to the truth of those stories, shaded as they are by the passage of time. I shudder to imagine they are true. Why would anyone want to meet him face to face? But no matter. At some distant time, one of my ancestors liberated the clan from servitude to Ya-Lohim and wrested the shrine away from his followers, toward a more appropriate use. My ancestors, and now myself, have held and kept the Sanctum from that day. Though the elders do not care much for me, they dare not anger me, for I alone have access to Choshek."

Fajora shuddered again at the name, but made herself ask, "And who is Choshek, again?"

"Choshek is the almighty Immortal whom the dark ones serve, and master of all who serve with the dark ones."

"A Dark Immortal?"

"Yes."

"But not almighty. Only Ya-Lohim is almighty."

Jelok chuckled, a decidedly unpleasant sound, Fajora decided. "The mind needs further opening if it is to understand the power of Choshek. You, with your desire for control, are half his already, for he is the advocate of all who want to control their own destiny. You must learn his ways. We will continue this conversation when you are not so tired. I am eager to enlighten you further. Prepare yourself to understand the wisdom of the cats."

Jelok stood, took a step toward the door, then stopped, one paw raised. "I almost forgot. We will have to put off enlightenment for a little. I am afraid the demands of war will intrude on pleasant conversation. I will be leading the clan, as Choshek's representative, and you will be taken to a safe place until victory is assured."

Fajora inhaled, choked, and coughed. Jelok waited, watching her closely. When she calmed, he sniffed, then chuckled. "No doubt that last surprises you. You thought your warning would stop your exodus. And I must say, the council and I are grateful for your warning. We will be on the lookout for this wayward dark one, who thinks to trick us by using stealth to get what we do not willingly give. But we have more than one safe stronghold. He will be watching the wrong path tomorrow when you go to your sanctuary."

"Tomorrow?"

Jelok chuckled again. "Yes, tomorrow. Sleep well now. You have a big day coming up."

Jelok turned from the door and walked the perimeter of the house, sniffing, even as he passed the old latrine. Sniffing especially at Fajora, and only slightly less at Sebastian. Fajora pulled in her aura in the same way she had done to avoid the notice of Kinovic and the other Dark Spinners. It was her best chance to keep Jelok from sensing the conflicting emotions, the hope and the fear, swirling in her mind. The hope especially, and her awareness of the owl sitting on her roof. That, more than anything else, must be kept from him. Perhaps he sensed something already, prompting his careful examination of the house and its inhabitants.

His testing complete, Jelok sat in the middle of the room. The moonlight illuminated his face as he licked his chops, reminding Fajora of a child on Luxera, licking the cream from a pot of honey custard.

The fear that had visited her as he spoke of his dark master and his plans for her suddenly seemed absurd. She might not be in Ya-Lohim's best graces right now, after her willful dash into forbidden territory, but she did not doubt his power. Whatever happened to her, whether she was rescued this night, killed in the attempt, hidden away by the cats, or captured and carried away by Dark Spinners, she believed one of Ya-Lohim's servants would, at some time, force this cat to recognize the limitations of his almighty Choshek. He would come to understand the deceit of the Dark Immortals and their mortal servants.

"Hmm. Well, we shall see," Jelok commented, as if he read Fajora's mind. He gave one last sniff and walked with feline grace from the house.

24

EXTREME MEASURES

Fajora felt a strange lassitude after Jelok left. She listened to his voice without making sense of the words as he spoke to the guard outside. The bird on the roof shifted, and debris sifted down from the thatch at the disturbance, catching in Fajora's throat and prompting a coughing fit.

This brought her mind back to alertness. When her throat had calmed, she motioned Sebastian to her side. He scooted across the floor and leaned his head close to hers.

"Give me the knife," she whispered in his ear.

"What if he comes back?"

"Do you have a way to get Clarise here, now, before our rescuers come?"

"No." He swallowed loudly. "Maybe. I could use the knife on our guard, then go sneak her out. Is that what you were planning?"

"No. The cat would hear you before you could get close enough to stab him. If you could bring yourself to do it. And what makes you think you could get past other patrols and get her back here without being seen? Besides, the Immortals have warned about unnecessary killing."

"How do you define unnecessary?"

"Not for the immediate defense of oneself or one's companions."

He changed position and sighed. "I think I could justify it, to get to Clarise. But you're right. I probably wouldn't make it. I just don't have any other ideas."

"Well, I do. Give me the knife and be prepared to ask the guard to send for Clarise. But put the knife back in its hiding spot first, before you call him. Oh, and I might drop it."

She imagined his stare, though she could barely make out the angle of his head in the dim light. He fumbled with his tunic, reached for her hand, and placed the hilt of the knife in it, careful to keep the sharp edge away from their fingers.

She took the knife in her left hand. For a moment, feeling the weapon's heft, touching the sharp edge of tempered steel, the temptation to do what she had persuaded Sebastian not to do almost overwhelmed her. She changed her hold on the hilt to an underhanded hold, perfect for stabbing a victim who was low to the ground. With a partial spin, she could sneak up on the guard and do away with him. She understood these things better than Sebastian, and knew where to place the blade so the cat would die instantly, without making a sound. This guard had been surlier than most and deserved whatever he got.

Fajora gripped the knife, listening to the rush of blood in her ears. What was she thinking? She believed what she had told Sebastian. The Luxeran service, the Immortals, Ya-Lohim—none of them permitted unnecessary killing. She had taken oaths when she became an agent, and she would not break them now. But she gripped the knife in the stabbing hold for a little longer before she forced herself to loosen her grip.

She had an alternate plan, one that harmed no one but herself, and should, with Ya-Lohim's help, work to bring Clarise back to the house. But she couldn't waste any more time.

She felt for the bandage on her thigh with her right hand. Would a cut work best? No, if the guard came in to investigate, a cut would be suspicious. He would want to know how she had cut herself, since there were no sharp edges or tools in the house. It must be a blow.

But to make it more believable, she would have to appear to have fallen. Maybe she should make the fall real, rather than pretending and trying to make it look authentic. The cat would know if she or Sebastian lied.

"Here, help me up."

She grabbed for Sebastian's arm and pulled herself to her feet. She limped around the room, scuffling and scraping her feet. Make as much noise as possible. Over to the window. Stand a moment as if looking out. Sigh, long, drawn out, loud. Turn and slap a hand against the stone, as if in frustration. Say something, so the cat will hear.

"I don't think it's going to . . . ." *Now*!

She sucked in a deep breath and rammed the hilt of the knife against her wounded leg as hard as she could. Pain shot through her leg. She clamped down hard on her lower lip to stifle her cry. She didn't have to pretend to fall. The leg gave way and she tumbled to the ground. She managed to keep the knife out of the line of her fall by a hair's breadth. She let the cry that had been building escape as she hit the ground.

The warm dampness seeping through her bandage told her the effort had been successful. Sebastian knelt over her, gripping her arm. She needed to tell him something. Remind him to do something. But what?

He touched her shoulder.

"Fajora? Are you all right?" Concern caused his voice to waver.

Good. And now she remembered what he needed to do.

"The knife," she whispered. "Quick. Hide it. Then call for Clarise. I fell. My wound broke open. I need medical attention."

A gurgle of hysterical laughter broke from him, which he quickly stifled. Groping for her arm, he loosened the fingers that gripped the knife hilt and took it from her. A brief rustle of clothing, and he moved toward the door.

As he lifted the hide covering, the guard cat growled, expressing his displeasure at being disturbed. The growl had an edge Fajora recognized despite her limited experience with cats. Nervousness. She'd seen the signs often in junior agents during her years with the service. The different species didn't matter. Anxiety carried the same quivering timbre in any voice.

"Fajora's leg gave out, and she fell." Sebastian's voice was steady, without the undertones of fear the cat exhibited. "Her wounds have broken open, and she's bleeding. She needs medical attention. Can you send for Clarise?"

"What you ask is difficult. The settlement is under alert. You have chosen a bad time for your request."

"A bad time?" Now Sebastian's voice held genuine exasperation. "Do you think medical emergencies wait for a convenient time? How hard can it be, anyway? Clarise isn't needed anywhere else, and if she's here, fixing up Fajora's leg, her guard can help with defense."

Deciding Sebastian could use a little help, Fajora let herself moan. It was a relief to vocalize her pain, and it had the added benefit of bringing the guard to investigate. Fajora tried to lift herself up when he came in, but shooting pain in her thigh forced her to curl in on the agony. The cat approached and sniffed at her, starting with her head. She forgot her pain for a moment as she became keenly aware of those teeth and powerful jaws.

Without commenting on what he sensed, the cat moved his investigation to Fajora's leg. Even Fajora could smell the blood seeping through the bandage and making her fingers sticky when she touched the wrapping. The cat wasted little time checking her wound.

"Very well." He lifted his head and padded toward the door. "I will see if someone can be spared to inform the woman."

They waited a long time. Fajora wondered if she'd made a terrible mistake. Rescuers might come at any minute, Clarise was not here, and

Fajora was not sure she would be able to walk. Certainly, her chances of moving with stealth were slim. And Sebastian would not leave Clarise. Akachi and whatever helpers he had found might put their lives at risk for nothing.

But at last, a hand lifted the door covering, and Clarise stepped in, carrying her water basin and other supplies. She knelt and examined Fajora's leg with her fingers, then lifted questioning eyes to Fajora's face.

"It was necessary," Fajora whispered. "We need you here tonight. Hurry. We need to be ready."

Clarise's gaze lingered on Fajora's face a moment longer, her expression softening, her lips trembling. She pressed her lips together, firming them, and turned her attention to the wounds. She salved and bandaged them with swift, sure movements. The brisk manipulation of the thigh sent waves of pain up and down Fajora's leg and into her hip, but once Clarise finished wrapping the injury, the pain eased off. She might be able to walk, although with a severe limp.

The guard pushed his nose past the door covering. "Finish at once. The woman's escort will return soon."

Clarise had finished, but the cat needed to believe otherwise.

"It's hard in the dark." Fajora gave her voice a hard, bitter twist of complaint. "A little light would help. Could we have a torch or something?"

"No light. Do as you are able in the darkness."

"We don't have a cat's night vision, you know."

"Even so."

"Then we'll need more time. We can't risk infection."

The cat would detect the deception if he came in and tested for truth, but Fajora decided to take the risk. She would do whatever was necessary now to keep Clarise in the house.

The cat responded with a low growl, but he pulled away from the door without giving Fajora a truth check. She groaned a little, and splashed her fingers in the bloody water to convince the cat, with its sensitive hearing, that work continued. Clarise sat back on her heels and looked over her shoulder at the door, then gave a helpless shrug. Sebastian had the knife in his hand again, fingering the blade.

If someone tried to take Clarise away, desperation might lead him to take extreme measures. Fajora reached within herself, testing for light without using energy to create even the tiniest spin. The light responded, weak, but at the ready. She would be able to do something, if she knew what that something should be and when she should do it. In order to avoid wasting her scant energy, she needed another sign.

She stood, wobbling on her bad leg, but kept her balance. Sebastian jumped up and grabbed her elbow, steadying her. She wanted to go outside, to check the surroundings, to see where cats patrolled and to detect any movement that indicated the beginnings of a rescue. She suspected it was past midnight. A rescue attempt, if it happened tonight, needed to come soon, to give them a chance to get away in the dark. And it must come tonight, because tomorrow would be too late. But if she went out now, the cat would know Clarise was done with her work and send her back to her own lodging.

While Fajora wavered with indecision, the distant call of an owl wafted through the air, coming from downriver. Another owl far upriver answered. The guard outside rose to his feet. The rumble in his chest was audible inside the house. A third call came from higher up, somewhere on the south cliff. The downriver owl called again. Debris drifted down from the thatch as the owl on the roof shifted emphatically. Fajora sensed an urgency radiating from it, and it shifted again.

She hesitated an instant longer. What if she misread the signals? What if she misjudged the timing? Then her training took over. Hesitating too long could be fatal. Better too soon than too late.

When two individual owls called from upriver, she hobbled to the door and lifted the covering. The guard gave her a sidelong glance and growled. "Return to your place."

Instead of obeying, she stepped outside and peered around, checking for other cats nearby. She saw none. No moving shadows. No glint of eyes reflecting moonlight. Yowls and hisses came from the upriver end of the settlement as the owls called again. Downriver, all was now silent.

The guard turned full on Fajora and snarled with bared teeth and unsheathed claws. He sank into a crouch, ready to attack. The battle lust glinted in his eyes. His jaws snapped, anticipating the kill. A glint of metal reflecting moonlight caught Fajora's peripheral vision on her left side, and she scented Sebastian. He held the knife in his hand, ready to plunge it into the cat's chest. But despite his willingness and determination, he would fail. He held the knife wrong, and his aim was too high.

With no time to waste, Fajora called on her energy reserves for a burst of spun light, enveloping the cat before he could spring. Holding him immobile in her light, she felt his hate and his desire for blood. With her energy reserves depleted, she didn't know how long she could hold him. The light she created would alert other members of Rock Clan, either feline or human, before long, but she didn't dare release him as long as she had a shred of energy. The moment she did, she would be dead, and along with her, Sebastian and Clarise, who now stood behind her on either side.

A woman appeared in front of her, from downriver. Almost as tall as Fajora, her dark-colored skirt flowing about her legs, she smelled of sand and trees and river water. And something else, a bitter, chemical odor.

The woman leaned close, holding a cloth in one hand, from which the odor emanated. "If you release his muzzle, I can immobilize him," she whispered. "We must hurry. The others are nearby, clearing a safe route from the settlement."

Fajora leaned forward to comply, then stopped as realization hit her. This was not a cat, as she had expected, but a human. And not a Rock Clan human. Scent alone confirmed this. Humans had violated the treaty to come for her.

The woman shifted, impatient at Fajora's astonishment.

"Hurry. We must go at once. Our lives hang in the balance."

25

PREDAWN CONFRONTATION

Fajora tamped down her astonishment and concentrated on her light, easing the cat's muzzle back to physical form. The woman pressed the cloth against its nostrils.

"Release it now."

Fajora withdrew her light so the woman and Sebastian could ease the cat to the ground. The chemicals on the cloth rendered the cat unconscious, and he sank down without a murmur. The woman folded the cloth and tucked it into her belt, then reached into a pouch slung over her shoulder and pulled out a small item that emitted a faint glow. She pressed it against the cat's chest, where it made a small hissing sound.

"That will keep him out for a while. Come, let's go."

She led them downriver, keeping close to the bank. As the house fell behind them, the bird on its roof rose without a sound, drifted over them, and headed upriver, where owl calls and cat vocalizations continued to echo through the canyon.

Sebastian supported Fajora, and she tried to keep up with the woman's brisk pace, though her leg ached and threatened to give out. Clenching her jaw, she tightened the muscles of both legs and her core and forced herself not to think about the pain. She peered about instead, searching for the cats she knew should be patrolling the settlement, expecting at each labored step to be stopped by a growl, a hiss, or the rake of unsheathed claws against exposed skin.

She expected, most of all, to meet Jelok. He would stroll around one of the houses, his demeanor unconcerned, and tell her they had unfinished business—a theological discussion—and how could she leave him? He would chuckle, and then reveal his reinforcements, both cats and humans, who would bundle them back to their prison houses, including this woman who had unwisely attempted a rescue.

But neither Jelok nor any other member of Rock Clan appeared as they hurried through the edge of the settlement along the river. Fajora did not see a cat until they cleared the last house. One waited for them there, crouched down and ready to spring. A warning hovered on her lips, but the woman glanced at the cat without altering her pace or showing any signs of concern.

Looking more closely, Fajora realized the cat was not crouched for attack, but huddled in a heap, too quiet even for a cat. Dead? Or incapacitated by the woman's chemicals?

They moved past the last stone formation and into an area of tilled garden plots. Fajora did not remember this from her arrival at the settlement. She had been unconscious for part of that trip, dragged or carried by her feline and human captors. Despite a dark night with increasing cloud cover, she felt exposed here, but again, no cats or Rock Clan humans accosted them. As they reached the lower edge of the gardens, the clouds parted briefly, and the dim light of a waning moon revealed another huddled form. This time Fajora smelled blood, smelled death, and saw the glint of the moonlight on dark liquid spilled beneath the cat's throat.

Her stomach lurched, and she hurried past as fast as her lame leg allowed. A little farther along, another cat waited for them, this one very much alive, sporting the tufted ears that identified it as a member of Deep Valley Clan.

"Light Spinner, I am pleased to see you," it said in a low rumble.

"Akachi?"

"Indeed."

"I'm pleased to see you as well. I didn't know for the longest time if you lived or . . . ."

"Hush," the woman whispered.

Fajora resisted the urge to kneel and hug Akachi, but when they resumed their trek, he walked beside her and she let her hand trail across his back. He glanced at her, but didn't protest or move away.

They were on the wrong side of the river for the trail Fajora and Akachi had taken coming into the valley, with no way to cross the raging torrent. The river had been quieter when Rock Clan humans brought Fajora to the settlement, but recent rains had turned it into a ferocious monster. Fajora could not imagine how Akachi and his party had gotten across to launch their rescue attempt, and she waited with trepidation to see how they would cross now.

But instead of looking for a ford, the woman led them farther from the river and closer to the north side of the canyon. She adjusted her pace for Fajora only slightly and did not allow stops for rest until they came to a steep trail that scaled the north wall of the canyon.

A female cat from Deep Valley Clan and a human male met them at the trail. No introductions were given, but the man passed a water pouch and produced wafer-like cakes tasting of wheat and honey. The brief rest with food and water rejuvenated Fajora, but she still wondered if she could climb this trail. She recalled her first day back on Kakislane, when she had mentally berated Trayle for using a spin to help her get up the path near the landing site. She would gladly spin up this trail now, but she didn't have enough energy, and the light would draw too much attention, anyway. She must get up the rugged trail the human way, if she could.

The man repacked the food and water, then motioned to Fajora to join him. He matched Fajora's height, rare in a human, with broad shoulders and a comforting strength. His pale face and his roughly braided hair gleamed white even in the dim light. Positioning himself on the side of her bad leg, he put his arm around her waist and pointed toward the top.

With his help, Fajora started up. When the way became too rocky for her weak leg, his arm lifted her and hauled her over the hard places.

At one turn in the path, she glanced down. The tattered clouds allowed a little more moonlight to filter down and illuminate the cliff face, and Fajora saw, to her surprise, they had already completed half the climb. Below her, Sebastian helped Clarise over the stretches too high for her shorter legs. The woman and Akachi brought up the rear. The female cat had disappeared, back toward the settlement.

At the top, another man and four more cats met them. Fajora studied them as well as she could in the darkness. How had three Wellador infiltrated cat territory and not only remained free, but even forged an alliance with a cat clan? Her questions had to wait, however. After another brief rest and a drink, they hurried along, making a sharp turn back to the west and following the north rim of the canyon. They were careful to stay far enough from the edge to avoid a disastrous tumble or a sighting from Rock Clan members down below.

The female cat who had stayed below while they climbed joined them now, and the cats conferred in low growls and mews before spreading out. Three left the group to patrol a wide perimeter, while the other three, including Akachi, padded along within sight of the humans and Fajora.

The path, bare at first, soon became littered with small tufts of grass and gangly, low-spreading shrubs. Fajora struggled to navigate this cluttered terrain with her bad leg, which ached more and more fiercely, but she said nothing as the hours wore away. To give in to weakness now meant putting everyone in danger. They were still in Rock Clan territory, not far from the canyon settlement, and other settlements at undisclosed locations might send out patrols of their own.

Though she knew this, Fajora felt safer the longer they trudged on without meeting Rock Clan warriors. An owl called somewhere ahead of them, and though the haunting sound whispered of danger, it also strengthened the illusion of safety. With owls and cats keeping watch, they were unlikely to be taken by surprise.

Even so, the warning, when it came, left little time to do more than sharpen the senses and coil muscles. No time for changing course or strategizing. At an owl's urgent call, two of the outer patrol cats rushed back to join the group. A moment later, the third patrol appeared like a shadow behind them.

Out of a stand of larger shrubs and small trees, dark, powerful shapes emerged, their outlines sharpening as the sky lightened toward dawn. Their coats, shading to dark gray in the dim light, suggested Rock Clan, as expected. Fajora, straining to see, could not make out any identifying markings. The lead cat's voice, rather than his markings, identified him.

"Fajora, my dear. We are sorry to see you are trying to leave us. We have much to discuss. And I fear you will disappoint the dark ones if I let you go. I planned to introduce you during their next visit. And trying to take the girl from us, too. How unkind of you. She's become a part of the clan, and now you try to rip our family apart? I'm afraid I must insist you return to the settlement at once. We both know you are no match for tooth and claw, nor is your little group a match for my cohort of warriors."

It was so like the conversation she had imagined, lacking only the laughter. Jelok's silken voice purred with a deceptive politeness. But he made his threat clear. What was not clear was his ability to make good on his threat. How many cats did he have with him? How many was he prepared to lose in the struggle to regain control of his prisoners? And how had he anticipated her moves so perfectly?

When she remained silent, and all her group with her, Jelok took two steps forward and sniffed the air. "I sense your fear. Are you too frightened to answer me?"

"Not frightened." As Fajora spoke she realized this was true. "I'm not sure I have anything to say to you. I may not know all the things cats know, but I know things you do not. Taking me back will be more difficult than you anticipate."

With those words, her resolve hardened. She would not go back. She would resist with whatever strength she had and would die here rather than return to her imprisonment.

But even as Fajora spoke, more shadows moved into position behind Jelok. A swift estimate put the Rock Clan numbers at fourteen, at least. Against them stood six cats, five humans, and one wounded Light Spinner. Clarise could not put up much of a fight, Sebastian's shattered wrist seriously handicapped him, and Fajora's light was nearly spent. And they were in the home territory of the Rock Clan cats, who knew every rock and shrub.

Jelok advanced, and the humans spread out. Now Fajora sent out a silent plea for help to Ya-Lohim. Others risked their lives for her; she asked for them, not herself.

Sebastian had his knife in hand, and those who had come with the rescue party pulled small devices from pockets or packs. Fajora had forgotten about the human technology. She should have considered it when figuring the odds. It gave them an advantage, especially if Jelok and the cats of Rock Clan did not know how to compensate.

But perhaps they did. For Jelok and seven or eight of his companions sprang toward the Deep Valley cats rather than toward the humans and Fajora. They engaged with them before the humans could bring their laser weapons to bear. Once two or more cats tangled in snarling combat, the human weapons had as much chance of hitting friend as foe. The

Rock Clans cats who did not engage immediately slunk further into the shadows, again denying the humans a clear shot.

In the center of the melee, Jelok clasped his powerful front legs and paws around Akachi's shoulders and tried to reach his throat with snapping jaws. Akachi squirmed and twisted, raking Jelok's side with his claws, though the resulting scratches had little effect. Jelok refused to be dislodged from his dominant position.

Fajora looked for a way to help Akachi. The humans had supplemented their laser weapons with long knives and fought fiercely, even Sebastian, who fended off a small, sleek cat's claws with awkward thrusts of his blade. He kept himself between the cat and Clarise, putting himself in danger to protect her. Fajora wished for the knife, but he needed it more than she did, and she had no opportunity to appeal to the other humans for additional weapons.

She tested her access to light. It hovered within reach, tenuous, but perhaps enough. She tested her strength and balance, then ran with hobbling steps toward Akachi and Jelok. She thought about light with each step, and a weapon formed, extending from her right hand. She lacked the strength to control a full-length sword, but a dagger proved manageable. A thrill shivered down her spine as the blade shimmered into perfection in her grasp.

But though armed now and hobbling with all the speed she could muster, she moved a little too slowly. While she maneuvered, stepping now forward and now back, looking for a home for her dagger that would deal a blow to her enemy while sparing her friend, Akachi at last pulled free of Jelok's embrace. But as he jerked away, Jelok's claws ripped across his face, slicing through his right eye and across his nose and piercing his left cheek.

Akachi screamed as blood streamed from his face. He turned to protect his head from a second blow and Jelok pounced, pinning him and bringing his jaws down on Akachi's left hind leg.

Fajora heard the thighbone snap as she plunged her blade into Jelok's chest. Jelok lifted his head and, for an instant, stared at her, his claws raking reflexively across her arm. Then the life in his eyes faded away, and he slumped across Akachi.

Fajora pulled her dagger free, but did not let go of her light, despite her weariness. Ignoring the blood seeping from the welts on her arm, she held her blade over Akachi, daring any Rock Clan cat to come near. But five Rock Clan members lay dead in addition to Jelok; the fight had gone out of the rest. One by one, as they realized the fate of their leader, they disengaged and slunk away. Fajora let her light dissipate and sagged to her knees beside Akachi.

One of the Deep Valley cats was dead, a sleek, muscular female in the prime of life. Fajora's breath hitched with sorrow and caught again as the air around the cat shimmered. The entire rescue party became motionless, attention riveted on this one spot. A Malekem hovered over the dead cat. The Immortal took no form mortal eyes could shape and define, its interest being in the dead cat only. It took care for the Deep Valley cat alone, paying no attention to the dead of Rock Clan, which underscored their denial of Ya-Lohim and his Dominion. For a moment the shimmering intensified, then it dissipated.

The cats turned away from their fallen comrade. Her spirit had departed, carried by the Malekem to the Immortal worlds. Their concern must now be with the living.

No one else had serious injuries except Akachi. He lay on the ground, panting and murmuring deep in his chest. When the others drew around him, he lifted his head weakly, his ruined eye staring blankly while the other blinked hard to clear the dripping blood.

"Finish it quickly," he rasped.

26

THE CLAN'S WAY

One of the other cats, a large male with white markings on his face, approached, teeth bared. Fajora stared at him, unbelieving, and reacted just in time. Without worrying about whether she had the strength, she spun light and reformed her dagger, lengthening it so its point met the approaching cat's chest while he was yet an arm's length from Akachi. "What are you doing?"

"Remove your blade," the cat commanded. "You keep me from my duty."

"Your duty? To finish him? No. Why would you do such a thing?"

"It is our way. We must move swiftly to escape Rock Clan territory, and this one will be a burden and endanger all our lives. Better to put him out of his suffering than to leave him to die a slow death, or for Rock Clan to find and torture him. As they will, in retribution for their dead here."

"If you wanted safety, you should never have come for me. Why did you?"

"This one spoke of his honorable duty to preserve the life of one in his care. With his honor at stake, the honor of the entire clan was compromised. Therefore, when he asked, we came."

"Well, this is no different. My honor won't allow me to leave him or let you kill him. It's barbarous." Fajora turned an unrelenting look on the human members of the rescue team. "You have medical supplies in those packs?"

One of the men nodded. He was shorter and slimmer than the man who had helped Fajora up the trail, with a dark, expressive face, in contrast to the bigger man's paleness. He slid the pack from his shoulders.

"Clarise," Fajora called. "Get the supplies from him and come do what you can for Akachi. For my friend."

"There's no time," the woman said.

"We'll make time. I suggest the other cats prowl around and make sure no members of Rock Clan are slinking about. Clarise. We need you now."

Clarise glided forward and reached for the pack.

The man waved her away. "No. I'll do it. You won't understand our instruments."

"I'd prefer Clarise," Fajora said. "You can tell her what to do."

Both Clarise and the man came and knelt beside Akachi. The man pushed Jelok's body aside while Clarise examined the wounds.

Fajora stared at Jelok's body, noting the snarl forever fixed on his muzzle. Without the sound of his silky, cultured voice and his strong, lithe movements to mesmerize her, she perceived his true nature. The idea of talking theology with him had held a certain appeal. Deep down, she had believed she could change his viewpoint if she found the right words. Make him understand the truth about the Dark Immortal he served.

But he wouldn't have listened. She saw that now. And though she shuddered to admit it, she herself was more vulnerable to persuasion than he was. He had been right. She wanted control and often repudiated Ya-Lohim's way, the way of trust and surrender.

Well, she had killed him before he could work on her with his subtle deception. She hadn't planned on it, but he had left her no choice. The moment he tried to kill Akachi, his life was forfeit.

Fajora turned away from the body, putting Jelok out of her mind. She had no worries about the justification for her actions.

Akachi made a feeble attempt to raise his head. His tongue protruded, and he panted but made no other sound. The light of the new day grew stronger, and Fajora could see more than she desired of the deep and dangerous wounds Jelok had dealt before his death.

"Let's start with a sedative with pain blockers," the man said, pushing buttons on a cylindrical instrument and handing it to Clarise. Akachi sighed as the sedative took effect.

The cat with white markings who had been about to end Akachi's life growled, and Fajora waved her dagger at him. He took several steps back and sat on his haunches watching the procedure. Though Fajora struggled to interpret cat expressions, this one radiated his disapproval beyond doubt. She didn't care. Her spin slowed, and her blade sank back toward her hand, but she didn't let it dissipate completely. She glared at the cat, her partial blade thrust forward, before turning her attention back to the medical efforts.

The man removed various instruments and containers from his pack. He handed Clarise another small cylinder with a green glowing tip and pointed at several buttons on one side, murmuring instructions to her. She turned the instrument toward Akachi's eye and let a green ray of light roam back and forth over the bloody injury. The bleeding slowed, then stopped, and Clarise turned the light off.

Another instrument and a cloth swab saturated with chemicals removed the congealing blood, cleaning the wound and preparing it for a salve. Jelok's claw had dug deep into the eye. Fajora doubted even human technology could repair the damage. The man helping Clarise confirmed her fears a moment later.

"It's doubtful he'll recover his vision. We can't do any more for him here. Bandage it and we'll work on the leg."

Fajora averted her eyes, keeping a watch on the rest of the group. Sebastian had moved to Fajora's side, blocking the big male's access to Akachi. Fajora gave him a grateful nod and let her weapon fade away. The taller man and the woman were deep in a heated discussion, of which Fajora caught a word or two, enough to know they were arguing about the logistics of the trail ahead.

This included devising a way to carry Akachi. He would be a burden, increasing the danger of the trek through Rock Clan territory. And Fajora, with her lame leg and her lagging light energy, would be of little help. She had encumbered them with this problem, this extra risk, after they had already risked their lives to rescue her.

Guilt grasped her like a hard fist at her throat, the uncertainty like a knifepoint against her breastbone. There was too much she did not know. About the path ahead. About the relationship between Rock Clan and Deep Valley Clan. About clan customs and what Akachi faced if he survived. She should not have interfered.

But a memory came to her. Akachi, wending his way down the hillside toward her, his brown coat shimmering to bronze. His youthful confidence as he advanced to meet a species he had never encountered before. The formality of that meeting between two people who were to become comrades, and friends. His coat, enchanting her with its changing color. That coat, though caked with blood, still glinted bronze in the light of the risen sun that bathed everything in sudden glory.

Fajora held fiercely to the memory of a friendship's beginning and banished her guilt. She hadn't asked these people to come. Akachi had. For that, she owed him a debt. She owed him more for the gift of his friendship. After her many years on Kakislane, she knew well such a friendship was a rare thing, a gift not lightly given. Not lightly discarded.

After Clarise finished treating and bandaging Akachi's wounds, the man with the medical supplies took care of the scratches on Fajora's arm. While he worked, the rest of the team gathered, including all the cats.

The woman, acting as the leader, handed out more of the wafer cakes and passed around a water canister.

Sebastian took a bite of his wafer, then stared, first at it and then at the other humans.

"Who are you?" he asked. "You're not from the colony. Your food, your clothes, your accents. Especially your technology. All different. Where are you from and what are you doing here?"

Fajora caught her breath. She had assumed these were colony citizens. Had presumed Dannel, becoming concerned about her long absence, had worked out an agreement, a temporary suspension of the treaty, perhaps. But now, examining these people in the bright morning light, she knew Sebastian discerned correctly. She knew the clothing styles of the colonists, their hairstyles, and their way of carrying themselves. These people did not share those characteristics. And beyond such tangible traits, they had a different look about them, a different expression on their faces and in their eyes. A difference not easily defined, but obvious once one looked for it.

"No time now," the woman said. "All will be clear soon."

"We've taken this much time," Sebastian countered. "We'll take a minute or two more for a few answers."

"You, who are in clan territory in violation of treaty, have no right to demand answers."

"Even so." Sebastian folded his arms over his chest, the knife dangling from his good hand. "We've had a rough time lately. I want to know what we're going to isn't worse than what we've come from."

The woman glanced at Sebastian's wrist with a condescending smile. "I hardly think we'll outdo your Rock Clan captors, but very well." The woman's voice was impatient, and she finished packing her supplies as she spoke. "We are of Deep Valley Clan and will take you to our main settlement, if we survive to get beyond Rock Clan. At that time, we will discuss the matter more fully. I will say no more now. You may come or stay here for Rock Clan to find, as you like."

"I'll come." Sebastian stared at the woman as she turned away, his mouth hanging open. Fajora checked her own mouth to make sure she wasn't gawking as openly as he was. Humans as part of Deep Valley Clan? Humans in Rock Clan and humans in Deep Valley Clan. What a tale she'd have for Dannel and Sonja. And Fazok, if he lived. If she dared tell it.

The taller and stronger of the two men donned his pack, and the other man and the woman lifted Akachi onto his shoulders. They secured the young cat on the pack, his back legs and tail draping over one shoulder while his head lolled on the other side, resting on the man's chest.

"Is it all right?" the other man asked.

"Yes. It's not as if I had to carry Chikelu." He inclined his head toward the large male cat with the white markings.

"It would never have been necessary," Chikelu answered. "It should not be necessary now. This young one lacks honor, that he allows this."

"Say not," the shorter man responded. "He asked for a quick finish. By the time we treated him, he was too weak to protest."

"Too weak, and yet we take him to become a burden, something he will not wish."

"Enough!" Fajora's voice sounded harsher than she intended, but she did not try to soften it. "I don't know about your ways, but my way won't let me leave him. Perhaps we should start now, before the risk grows greater."

"You lead, Zuberi," the woman said, "and we'll set our pace to yours."

The big man, Zuberi, after making a slight adjustment to his load, started trudging along the rim of the canyon. Chikelu loped ahead, disappearing in the thickening brush, and two other cats slunk off to the side. The rest of the group ranged behind Zuberi in a ragged line. The man with the medical supplies followed close behind Fajora, where he could reach forward to offer support over the rougher patches along the trail.

Fajora felt surprisingly fit, and she wondered about the food wafers the humans carried. They must be packed with protein and other nutrients, for she felt stronger than she had since she lost her own pack. Her leg ached, but the pace was slower now, due to Zuberi's heavy load, and she had no difficulty keeping up.

They trekked up a gradual incline, and the river fell away to their left side. Wild from the recent rains, it raged through a deep canyon. After a time, Fajora heard a faint roar. It became louder, until it was unmistakably the sound of falling water.

"Rock River Falls," the woman told her when they paused to rest. "Less than a sunprowl ahead now."

The spray rising from the canyon, along with the increasing roar, signaled the nearness of the falls. It permeated the air with a pleasant damp coolness, while prisms of refracted light danced above the canyon rim. A forested outcropping forced a detour away from the canyon, and when the rescue party veered back to its edge, they stood alongside the falls. The sun had already passed its zenith, and the woman announced a longer rest here.

Fajora sat near the canyon's rim, where she could see both the upper river and the roiling, frothing stream it became down below. She watched with growing awe as it tumbled twenty-five meters or more to its lower course, rivaling any of the acclaimed waterfalls on Luxera for beauty and power.

The water surged and swirled as it approached the lip of the falls, deceptively quiet. It flung itself over the edge with graceful abandon, but rebounded with a mighty roar as it hit a boulder-encrusted pool far below. The mist cloud emanating from the fall caught the sunlight and scattered iridescent sparkles through the air.

Fajora felt she could sit and watch all day, drawing peace from the turbulent glory of the falls. But soon, the woman called them back into trekking order.

"I can carry Akachi now," the shorter man offered.

"I could use a break," Zuberi agreed. "But I'll take him back when we're ready to cross. Your legs are not long enough for such a load in the river."

"Agreed."

They started moving again, walking level with the river. It ran through a straight, deep channel, and Fajora watched it in horrified fascination. They expected to cross this raging stream? With the wounded and the weak?

The river widened and shallowed as they went, but it still ran too swiftly for a safe crossing, with an increasing jumble of boulders to create yet more hazards. Even so, the Deep Valley people seemed determined to cross.

"The river shoots out of a deep crevice not too much farther upstream," Zuberi explained. "We couldn't get near, and even if we could, the flow is even faster there than it is here. We'd be almost to Sacred Mountain Clan's territory before we'd find a safer ford. Too far in the wrong direction and too long in Rock Clan's territory. We must cross now."

After a brief rest and another quick snack, they prepared for the attempt. The cats sniffed and hissed with disgust, but Chikelu allowed the woman to tie a rope around his middle, and he stepped without hesitation into the fast-moving water, tail held high and dry. He proved a strong swimmer and made it across without mishap. Unable to untie the rope, he walked twice around a small tree near the river and braced himself. Zuberi tied the other end to a tree on the near side and stepped into the water with Akachi on his shoulders.

The water was waist high on him at first, but about ten paces in, he hit a hole. He went under, and Akachi with him. When he surfaced, he flailed for the rope, now out of reach, and tried to find footing while keeping the wounded youngster on his shoulders. The other man waded in, ready to go to his aid but halted when Zuberi found his footing again.

Having found he couldn't swim while carrying Akachi, he tried going around, downriver from the hole, but he couldn't find firm ground anywhere. Next, he turned upriver, where he might have help from the rope, but in this direction, rocks strewed the river bed. He took a step, and another, then slipped, losing hold of the rope and nearly dumping Akachi into the water. Frantically righting his burden, he turned with a shake of his head and headed back for the river bank.

"I don't know how we're going to get him across," he said as he laid the wounded cat on the grass at the water's edge and sank down beside him, breathing hard.

"We don't have an alternative," the woman said. "It will be dark in a little while, and you can be sure Rock Clan cats will find us if we're still on this side."

"Maybe if Ekene helps me we can manage."

A cat stalked up and nosed Akachi, sniffing and licking him, then turned to the other man, Ekene. "What do you expect for this one's recovery?"

"He'll recover."

"But with impaired sight?"

"Yes."

"And a lame leg, at best?"

"Perhaps."

"And will live on the charity of the clan, being unable to hunt or fight."

"Possibly. Time will tell. He may learn to compensate for his handicaps."

"Unlikely. Our options have narrowed. We no longer have the luxury of carrying a damaged individual from this place. Since Chikelu, on whom the responsibility should rightly fall, is out of reach, our only consideration now is whether you or I will perform the necessary duty."

Ekene lowered his head. "I fear I cannot, after caring for him all day. My honor as a healer will not allow it."

"Then I will do it. It will be my honor and my sorrow." He pawed at Akachi, turning him to expose his neck, and bared his teeth.

27

—·—

ON THE TRAIL

Fajora sat resting, exhausted and dull after the long hours of walking. It took her tired brain a moment to realize what was about to happen.

"No!" she shouted when the cat's preparations brought realization home.

She tried to spring to her feet, but her stiff leg made her movements awkward. Sebastian was faster. In a few swift steps he reached Akachi and interposed his knife between the youngster and the older cat.

The cat hissed. "Do not interfere. This must be done."

"No," Fajora said again, hobbling to Sebastian's side. "Why are we even discussing this again? I thought I made it clear I wouldn't leave him."

Ekene sighed and reached out a hand to stroke Akachi. "I understand how you feel. My shock when the Malekem did not wait for him changed to relief when I realized Akachi would live. I don't want to lose him. But we have no way of getting him across the river. If we're on this side after night falls, Rock Clan will attack. Their honor demands it. And when that happens, they will kill Akachi. Others of our group may die as well. We either kill him now and save ourselves, or let Rock Clan kill him later and take more casualties. He wouldn't want that."

"We can't leave him."

"Then you will have to find a way to get him across. If Zuberi, who is the strongest of us, cannot manage it, no one else can either."

"What if we all help?" Sebastian asked.

"No. Zuberi doesn't like to admit defeat, but the river gets more treacherous closer to the other side. Anyone who slips will get carried away by the river and be over the falls before the rest of us can help. Certain death. I don't think we can get across carrying a wounded and unconscious cat. It will be hard enough without him."

Fajora knelt beside Akachi and ran her hand across his side. The fur was damp from his dunking, but drying fast. She felt its silkiness, felt his breath moving his ribs under her hands. Letting her hand rest there, she surveyed the river.

About two hundred paces wide here, it promised an arduous crossing, even without the dead weight of an unconscious cat on one's shoulders. On the other hand, it would be an easy task for a Light Spinner. If she didn't think too much about it. If she didn't worry about what would happen if she lost her light halfway across. She had only done small things since her capture. But Akachi needed her now. If she faltered mid-river, they might both die, but if she didn't try, he would certainly die, either immediately or within a few hours.

She reached for light. Found it waiting for her, weak but accessible. Pulled herself into a full spin and pulled Akachi into the spin with her. As spun light, he had no actual weight, but such a heavy passenger intertwined in her spin pulled on her energies nonetheless. She had no time to waste if she wanted to get across before her light faltered.

Pulling Akachi closer inside the spin and tightening the spiral of light she had become, Fajora shot across the water. She was aware of the swirling eddies beneath her, but she didn't allow herself to dwell on them, focusing instead on the open space in front of the trees, where Chikelu sat with the rope still around him.

She didn't see with physical eyes while in a spin, but she perceived the cat in a more ephemeral way. He provided a focal point, a haven, and she made for him with her last shred of energy. She knew, as the light faded from her, that she had drained herself again.

But she had brought Akachi safely across the river. He moaned and twitched as he coalesced back to physical form. Humans experienced nausea after a spin. Perhaps cats had the same problem. But that would pass. She sat with her hand on his side, not stroking him, but touching him, to reassure herself as much as him, while the others crossed, swimming with the rope as a guide.

Zuberi came first, with Clarise clinging to his back. Sebastian kept close behind them, sliding his good hand along the rope while stroking weakly with his injured hand, and sometimes forgetting to stroke and reaching out toward Clarise instead when a hard current pulled her about and threatened to tear her away from her helper. The woman and Ekene followed with the cats alongside. The cats swam strongly, but they pulled up onto the bank with sniffs and hisses of disgust and immediately began licking the water out of their fur.

The woman turned at once to Fajora. "Light Spinner, we were not aware you had the capacity, wounded as you are, to carry the young one. Why have you not been helping to carry all along, since bringing him was your wish?"

"I didn't have the strength. You're right about my wound. Blood loss and lack of adequate food for fuel weakened me. What I just did, carrying Akachi across this short distance, drained me. Until I refuel, I have no light."

She held up her hand and attempted to spin. A few sparks shot out from her fingers and fizzled. She tried again, and this time created the merest sputtering at the tips of two fingers. She looked up and shrugged, then sagged, too weary to care what this woman thought.

The woman studied her for a moment. "If you have more food, can you help carry?"

"Perhaps. After a while, once the food has time to reenergize me. How are the supplies? Do you have enough for me to have extra rations?"

"We'll see."

"Sanaa." Zuberi's voice held a warning.

"She won't leave Akachi." Sanaa gave Fajora a glare. "If we refuel you, you're not going to spin away, leaving us here with this wounded cat, are you?"

"Of course not. I'm going to see to Akachi until I'm sure he's safe and home."

"You see, Zuberi? She's not going anywhere. Feed her, unless you want to carry the cat all the way on your shoulders."

Zuberi pulled out supplies and handed wafer cakes and strips of dried meat to Fajora and the humans. Fajora received double portions.

The interplay between Sanaa and Zuberi puzzled her. Had they deliberately held back food, fearing she would spin away and leave them? She worried at this idea while she ate. The meat was unappealing, but she had gotten used to eating it while with Rock Clan, and she didn't hesitate now.

As soon as Zuberi had pulled out the supplies, two of the cats had disappeared. A short time later they returned, each carrying a freshly killed small animal. With a bit of good-humored snarling and batting of sheathed claws, the four cats shared the bloody meat between them. Watching them, Fajora was thankful for her dried strip of meat, seasoned to disguise the intense flavor of flesh, with no blood or other body fluids to deal with. When Zuberi tossed her another strip as he packed things away, she didn't refuse.

"For the trail," he said with a meaningful grin.

The other humans helped him load Akachi back onto his shoulders, and they walked again, heading away from the river, toward the southwest.

They walked until well past nightfall, but when even the cats began to lag, Sanaa, called a halt near a spring. Trees and large boulders provided shelter on three sides.

"We will stop here and sleep for a while. It is defensible, and we need rest." She handed Fajora another wafer. "I suggest you get as much sleep as you can. I expect you to take a turn with Akachi tomorrow."

They laid Akachi in a sheltered spot, and a cat flopped down beside him to guard him. Chikelu delegated another cat for first patrol duty and settled himself on the open side of their camp. Everyone else found places to stretch out and tried to get comfortable on the hard ground.

As the cat on patrol reached the camp's perimeter, her dark, solid shape barely visible in the moonlight, the call of an owl wafted through the night air. She stopped and sat on her haunches, her ears erect and swiveling to catch every sound. The other cats perked their ears forward to listen as well.

Several owls answered the first owl, and the calls came with regularity for several minutes. This was not the evening owling song Fajora had enjoyed with Sonja at Haven Outpost. It sounded more like a conversation. Were the owls communicating among themselves or sending reports to their feline allies? Either way, the cats seemed to understand. When the owl calls ceased, the night scout disappeared without further consultation with her colleagues, and the other three cats settled into their positions and appeared to fall asleep almost at once.

Fajora had trouble getting comfortable until Clarise came and snuggled close to her, for despite the warmth of the day just past, the night was chilly. The young woman's nearness brought fond memories, for Fajora's own daughter loved to snuggle as a child and continued to do so on occasion right up until she left home to be married. Listening to the

Clarise's even breathing, Fajora fell into a deep, dreamless sleep, secure knowing the feline guard and the watchful owls would give the alert if danger approached.

They started again before dawn. Having downed a plentiful breakfast, Fajora felt steady access to light and offered to try transporting Akachi. She enveloped him in light, but kept herself in a partial spin rather than a full spin. Though tricky to maintain, requiring strict focus, this allowed her to keep pace with the group and follow their lead. Translating to a complete spin would require her to either spin very slowly—a greater drain on energy than a faster spin—or go on ahead. But she didn't know where or how far to go. Even if Zuberi and Sanaa had been able to give her precise directions, she no longer trusted her directional senses. They had failed her twice when she first entered clan territory. She couldn't afford such a mistake now, with no food supplies of her own and a heavy passenger.

So, she walked and watched the trail with her physical eyes, but she shimmered and her light cast a veil of brightness over her surroundings. She carried Akachi for two hours before she weakened. During that time, the sedative Ekene had given the young cat the night before began to wear off.

Enveloped in light, Akachi felt no pain, but he gradually came to awareness, and then to panic. Fajora felt the confusion in his aura and tried to reassure him. No words were possible in this form, but she fed him images and wordless encouragement. His confusion changed to understanding, and to wonder.

Fajora regretted the need to hand Akachi off to Zuberi. As soon as she brought Akachi back to physical form, he became distressed and restless with pain.

"He'll have pain and disorientation until his eye heals and he adjusts to his altered vision," Ekene said. He helped Akachi drink and administered another dose of the sedative.

They walked under gathering clouds, and about midmorning, a drenching rain began to fall. Though it was a warm rain, it left everyone soggy and uncomfortable in minutes. The cats shook themselves, and stopped for hurried grooming sessions, licking the water away with frantic speed—a useless gesture, as they were immediately wet again, looking more like bedraggled rodents than elegant, sleek felines.

Everyone was grumpy. Tempers flared over multiple small annoyances, but no one complained aloud. They walked, heads down to keep the rain out of their eyes, enduring what they could not change.

The rain let up after the midday break. Sanaa pushed the group harder as soon as they reached drier ground, but again, no one complained. If the rain hadn't stopped them, it likely had not stopped Rock Clan either. Scouts must surely be scouring the area for them. The longer the rescue party remained in Rock Clan territory, the more vulnerable they became.

About an hour after sunset, they reached another river. Sanaa stood on the bank for a long time, watching the water and listening. Finally, with an exasperated sigh, she ordered a stop for the night.

"We could make the crossing at the gravel ford even in the dark, but that's fifteen kilometers out of the way, on both sides. We'll try crossing here once it's light enough to see."

She had everyone up and ready for the crossing by the time the first glimmer of light crept over the water. Chikelu went first again. As soon as he reached the far side, testing to be sure the current allowed a viable passage for even the weakest swimmer among them, Fajora followed him, spinning Akachi across. The others managed the crossing without incident, though the boulders hidden beneath the fast-moving current battered them and the rough water soaked them.

Sanaa handed out a double portion of the wafer cakes, but she made no other concessions to the weariness everyone, even the cats, betrayed. After a short break, she had them up and trekking again, facing another grueling day. Each time Sanaa allowed a food break, Fajora eyed the packs, which became visibly flatter as the journey progressed. Would they run short of food before they reached safety?

The idea made her weary. She remembered, with a nostalgia bordering on pain, the feasts service trainees indulged in before their first void transit. They ate more in one sitting than she had eaten over the course of many days, food of the highest quality—the signature dishes of the Service chefs.

If Sanaa and Zuberi had any worries about the food supply, they didn't share it with the others. Fajora supposed the cats could share their prey if rations became short. And she would eat the raw meat without complaint. Akachi had taught her that much.

Sanaa kept the cats busy all day, scouting forward, backward, and to either side of the trail. She and Zuberi paused often to consult together. Though not privy to those conversations, when Fajora loitered nearby, she caught Sanaa's "Where are they?" and Zuberi's "tricks under their paws," and surmised they were discussing the whereabouts of the Rock Clan cats. From the frown on Sanaa's face, she gathered the group's leader worried more because they hadn't seen any sign of pursuit than she would have if they'd seen multiple signs. Sanaa expected Rock Clan to attack, but she didn't know when or how.

Toward evening, Zuberi pointed out a large outcropping of rock formations about a three-hour march away. They would climb to that point, where a trail led down out of Rock Clan territory into neutral land. Fajora assured him she would sense any Rock Clan patrols before coalescing, and he sent her spinning up the hill with Akachi. The others followed, aiming to reach her before darkness made walking too dangerous.

No Rock Clan individuals lurked near the rock formation, and Fajora coalesced without incident. She found a place to wait under a large overhanging rock. It provided a little cover and protection on one side. If

Rock Clan cats found her, they couldn't surround her. She could collect Akachi and spin away if she stayed alert and detected their approach in time. If the rest of the group didn't make it this far tonight, she'd have to stay awake and alert all night, but at least, having spun here, she had left no scent trail.

Safe for the moment, she huddled near Akachi, eating the food Zuberi had provided her. Well fueled, she ventured out to look around. Wishing for a cat's sensitive nose to test for pursuers, she stood for a long time studying the area around her sanctuary. She sensed no movement or sound, and at last deemed it safe to climb higher for a better view.

An easy climb took her to the top of the overhang she had been sitting under. From there, she enjoyed a wide view back across the rugged hills and out across a wide, barren valley. Examining the trail she had spun over, she was thankful she had not had to traverse it to get up to this point. The rest of her group would make better time without her and Akachi. Clarise, now their weakest member, had shown surprising agility among the rocky places except when traversing jumbled boulders too high for the reach of her legs.

Turning her gaze out toward the barren valley, she saw cats moving among boulders strewn across the expanse. Fajora's Luxeran vision was sharp; she couldn't see individual markings, but the gray color and the cats' agitated pacing, along with their watchfulness as they scanned the hillsides below and in every direction, identified them as members of Rock Clan.

So, she had discovered the missing cats. Perhaps, having lost the trail at one of the rivers, they had decided this was the more certain strategy. They would force the rescue party to fight their way across neutral territory to Deep Valley Clan carrying a wounded cat, no easy task. She began to understand why the cats dispatched any clan members too badly wounded to travel. Any other choice created too great a hazard for the rest of the clan, as they had already argued.

But though Fajora understood it, she couldn't agree with it. It was too easy. Too convenient. And it took something out of the soul, leaving a comrade behind to die, or worse yet, killing a comrade and leaving the body behind. One's own death was preferable. And that might be what she and the others faced, that possibility made more likely by the burden of a wounded cat.

But they might be doomed whether or not they carried Akachi. Sinking down and stretching out on her stomach, hoping she hadn't already been spotted, Fajora attempted to count the gray cats below. They didn't make it easy; they paced, crossing each other's paths, disappearing and reappearing as they moved close to the rocky trail into their own land or moved out into the middle of the neutral land. By Fajora's best estimate, between fifteen and twenty cats waited below.

Her group of eight or nine who could fight included Sebastian, who was inexperienced and wounded, and Fajora, whose ability to produce a spun weapon was tenuous. They would be greatly challenged to overcome even fifteen of the warrior cats waiting below. The advanced weapons the humans carried might improve their chances, though Rock Clan had already proven they knew of tricks to neutralize that technology. The rescue party's only true hope lay in catching their opponents unawares, unlikely given the cats' alert agitation.

Fajora returned to Akachi's side and sat beside him, letting herself stoke his fur as she watched his shallow breathing.

"I got you into this, little friend," she murmured. "I'm sorry. I've kept you alive this far, but I don't know how we're going to get out of it in one piece now."

28

CROSSING CONTESTED TERRITORY

When Zuberi and Sanaa arrived, sweaty and hungry, at Fajora's resting place, and she told them about the cats waiting below, they showed no surprise. The tension lines in Sanaa's face eased.

"I've been wondering if the cats might be waiting there. Good to know."

"I don't see any way past them."

"We'll figure something out. Wish it wasn't so dark now, but we'll take a look in the morning. Get some sleep. Tomorrow will be a busy day."

Fajora shook her head at the woman's nonchalance, but she lay down to sleep next to Clarise with more assurance. After several days on the trail with Sanaa, she understood and respected the woman's knowledge and ability.

At first light, Sanaa and Zuberi pulled small scanning glasses from their packs and headed up to the top of the overhang to take a look at the valley below. Fajora followed, wondering what they would see with their glasses that she could not with her keen Luxeran vision.

She found them stretched out prone, glasses to eyes, scanning back and forth and murmuring to each other.

"Do you see . . . ?"

"Yes," Sanaa answered Zuberi. "A little to the north, by a lone stand of trees. Four or five."

"Got them. Looks like Chikelu's cohort." He held his glasses steady for a moment, then started scanning again. "Another patrol to the south. Eight. At least. Rufaro's cohort, so there are more than I'm seeing."

"Should we head that way, even though it's longer? Can we get farther south before we go down and show ourselves?"

Zuberi studied the landscape for several more minutes. "There's a ledge not too far below us. Has some trees on the downside that will block their view of us. It'll be a rough climb, but it will put us in a better position when we get to the valley floor. Can't do it carrying a wounded cat, though."

Fajora stiffened, ready to defend Akachi's life yet again. But Zuberi turned and beckoned her. When she scooted up beside him, he didn't suggest leaving Akachi behind. Instead, he shoved his glasses into her hands.

"Look there." He pointed toward the south. "On the hillside across the valley. Deep Valley cats wait there. At least eight of them. Do you see them?"

It took a moment, peering through the strange glasses that magnified everything and shifted the landscape proportions, to find the area he had pointed out. But when she found the right part of the hillside, Fajora also found the cats, bronze-colored with ear tufts, waiting much more calmly than the gray Rock Clan cats in the valley below. They blended in with the rocks and brush around them, not moving, so that one must know where to look before they became visible.

Fajora's heart swelled. Had Akachi mobilized the entire clan to come after her? The gathering of gray cats below seemed less menacing now. The rescue party did not face them alone. But they still had to get Akachi down the hill.

"I see them." Fajora handed the glasses back to Zuberi.

"Good. Do you have enough energy to spin there with Akachi?"

Understanding dawned on Fajora. "I might. Is there anything more to eat?"

He grinned. "Been saving you a choice bit of dried meat."

Fajora felt heat rising into her face. He had noticed her reluctance to eat the meat, the faces she made as she chewed when she thought no one watched.

Sanaa frowned at him. "We'll give you as much as you need to make the crossing."

"How soon do I go?"

"Not yet," Zuberi said. "We need to get down first, ready to head out into the valley. We do not want to give Rock Clan time to pinpoint our warriors and converge on them. The Rock Clan cats will come as soon as they see your light, but we'd rather they remain strung out and not in fighting formation. Our cohort to the north will flank them and work from the rear. So, when we get to the bottom, you fly over and tell the cats it's time. They will create a diversion to allow us to sprint across and join them. Rock Clan won't dare trespass on our territory with so many of our warriors in the area. Not until they are more organized and have all their own warriors on hand, at least."

Fajora thought about this. It seemed like a foolproof plan, except for one thing. "How will I know when it's the right time? I won't be able to see you from here."

"You need a messenger. Come on." Sanaa motioned her down the path.

Mystified, Fajora followed her a little to the south of the overhang where the rest of the group waited. They came to a stand of trees, and Sanaa stopped and tilted her head up.

"Hello, wise one," she called. "We need a messenger. Are you willing?"

"Hoo," came a soft call from a tall fir tree.

A shiver traveled up Fajora's arms and down her spine, as she realized she witnessed, for the first time, a conversation between an owl and a human. Humans in the Wellador Colony had dreamed of this for years, and worked to decipher the owls' language, but had made minimal progress. The owls seemed to have a better tolerance for the cats, or at least for some cats, though shy of humans.

But what if they were only shy of the Wellador humans, with their overwhelming technology, their big shiny buildings, and their loud, fast transports? These Deep Valley humans, who lived with the cats, probably had a much simpler lifestyle, more attuned to nature. This made sense, for if they had a large industrial complex or used extensive technology, more invasive than the small weapons Fajora had seen on this trek, Wellador sensors would have detected them long ago. And Sebastian had not known their location, not until he uncovered the secret cypher in his old documents.

Unless . . . .

But no, what a preposterous idea. If the Wellador leadership knew about the humans here and kept this knowledge a secret from both the Light Spinner enclave and their own population, what else were they keeping secret? Fajora had questions for Dannel if she ever got back to the colony.

But now, the bird was here, honoring its long-standing allegiance to its allies, its round yellow eyes fastened on Sanaa as she spoke. Fajora did not want to diminish this experience by thinking of political intrigues. The owl stood, silent, its talons hooked around its branch, a reminder of what a deadly creature this was. The powerful beak; the soft feathered wings, designed for silent flying; the tufted horns, all gave it a lethal grace.

Sanaa spoke of the plan as Zuberi had outlined it to Fajora. When she paused, the bird made a series of soft hoots, whistles, chitters, and squawks, some long and drawn out, some short and fast. Sanaa cocked her head, listening with great concentration.

"Yes," she said at last. "You have it all. We won't start down until you return."

Without replying, the bird pushed off from its branch and winged silently across the valley. Fajora wondered if the Rock Clan cats below saw it passing over. Given their hatred of the owls, they would become highly agitated. She wished she had a view of them from here and could see how they reacted.

"It is a great imposition to ask her to help us during sunprowl time, when she will be wanting to sleep," Sanaa commented, "but she seems willing enough."

"What will happen now?" Fajora asked.

"We wait. She wishes to consult with her nest brother, who roosts within Deep Valley territory. When she returns, we will start down. She will find a roosting spot where she can watch our progress. When you hear her call, you will spin across."

"How will I know it's her, and I'm not hearing a random owl call?" Fajora felt this plan relied too much on her understanding of things foreign to her.

Sanaa gave a laugh, not quite derisive, but not entirely friendly, either. "There will be no random owl calls today. She will make sure of that in her consultation with her brother." She paused, studying Fajora. "To be clear, though I suppose you're not in a position to know this, there is no such thing as a random owl call. Unlike humans, and to a lesser extent, the cats, owls do not engage in pointless chatter. I don't know how it is with your people. Do not make the mistake of accusing owls of randomness again. Were they to hear you, they would consider it a great insult."

Heat rose up Fajora's neck into her face, and she fought it down. "Thank you for that information," she said with as much grace as she could muster. "I don't have your advantages. I've not had similar opportunities to commune with and understand owls. I will await her call. But can you give me an indication of what the call will sound like, so I don't mistake it for other important communication between herself and her nest brother?"

Sanaa smiled, the first genuine smile Fajora had seen on her face. "You learn fast. Expect a long call followed by three short, fast ones. Like this." Sanaa gave a close approximation of an owl call, quietly, so only Fajora would hear it. "Are you satisfied now?"

"Yes, thank you."

"Good. Let's rejoin the others. Zuberi and I need to eat while we await her return."

Ekene gave Akachi another dose of the sedative and pain medication before the group headed south for the narrow, treacherous path Zuberi had chosen for their descent. Sebastian shot Fajora a nervous smile before he and Clarise followed Sanaa into the brush. He carried his knife tucked into the front of his trouser waistband, within easy reach.

As soon as the group passed beyond her sight, Fajora clambered up to the lookout point to check on the cats below. She saw no sign of the Rock Clan humans—had seen no sign of them since escaping the settlement. She believed the humans planned on taking part in the clan's upcoming incursion against Deep Valley Clan, but this mission to recapture the prisoners and punish the rescuers was another matter. With Jelok dead, the cats, more than the humans, would be concerned with salvaging their injured honor.

Fajora made two more excursions to the look-out rock while she waited, impatient to know what was happening below her. The Rock Clan cats had settled somewhat, though several of them patrolled back and forth across the valley floor. Once she caught a glimpse of the Deep Valley cats across the way. Mostly, they remained hidden. But though she could not see the cats, she remembered where they had been when she found them in Zuberi's glasses. She marked the spot, picking out boulders on the valley floor that followed the correct trajectory and noting how the trees clustered at her destination. She didn't want to make any mistakes as she spun across.

The Deep Valley humans had left her adequate food, and she ate all of it. She felt her strength growing, and with it, her confidence. Her light would be sufficient to carry Akachi across the valley.

Her nerves were taut with listening, and she jumped when the call came, floating up from a hidden spot along the cliff with an eerie, hollow sound. She touched Akachi lightly as she marshaled her resources and reached for light.

"Here we go, young one. Another step toward home."

She scooped him up into her spin and headed at once across the valley, wasting no time and using as little energy as possible. This spin put her at risk of detection from the Welldor Colony and the Luxeran enclave, and she wanted her exposure to be as minimal as possible. In an arc of light, she zoomed across, coming down for a landing in front of the target cluster of trees, and coalescing amid a cohort of cats.

She noticed, as she had not done for several days, the weapons these individuals carried on their bodies. The teeth, the heavy paws armed with razor-sharp claws, the powerful jaws. They made sure she saw their teeth, and they scratched the earth with unsheathed claws.

Two big males and a female, only slightly smaller than the males, came close and sniffed at both her and Akachi.

"I would not have believed the trouble taken for this wounded one, if an owl, wisest and most truthful of creatures, had not brought the word," the female said. "What I don't understand is why."

"I wouldn't leave him behind," Fajora answered, prepared, despite her waning strength, to translate herself and Akachi back into light and flee from this irate cat.

"It is not your place to make demands of Deep Valley Clan. Bardu informed us of his warning to you many days ago. You did not heed the warning. In your disregard for things you do not understand, you have negated any right you might have had to dictate action."

"It doesn't matter. I won't let anyone kill Akachi."

"And you know what is best for him, for his clan?"

"Life is always best." Fajora put the force of her conviction in her voice and tried not to look at Akachi, lying limp and unresponsive, with his ruined eye bandaged to hide the damage. "Enough of this talk," she added, brushing away her doubts. "Your people, along with Rock Clan's human captives, are ready to cross the valley. They need your protection. Four cats and five humans who are more important than this moral argument."

"Four cats? We sent five, besides this young one."

"One fell in a battle with Rock Clan yesterday morning."

The female cat spat. "For this, also, you are responsible. You have much to answer for to Deep Valley Clan."

29

THE RIGHT COORDINATES

A big male cat nudged the female's side. "They come, Rufana. Our help is needed."

Looking out across the valley, Fajora saw the small party that included Sebastian and Clarise spilling onto the valley floor. The entire cohort of cats turned toward the valley, ears pricked forward, tails low. The female, Rufana, hissed to get her cohort's attention.

"We go now. Intercept all Rock Clan cats. No unnecessary killing. This is strictly a retrieval mission."

The cats, ten or twelve by Fajora's quick count, bounded out into the valley. Two human men and two women emerged from among the trees and joined them, carrying laser weapons and long daggers. Another man and woman disengaged themselves from the shadows and ambled toward Fajora. So many humans associated with Deep Valley Clan. Fajora didn't know what to make of it.

The man took up a post where he could watch the skirmish below, but the woman ignored the action and came to sit beside Akachi. Pale of skin with light brown hair and gray eyes, both her appearance and her manner suggested gentleness.

"I'm Lesedi. I'll wait with you here until the others arrive. You are Fajora, right?"

"Yes. And this is . . . ."

"Akachi. Yes, I know. We've been friends since he was a kit. I had the pleasure of teaching him to read."

Fajora sucked in a quick breath. "To read? I didn't think cats . . . ." She let the words trail off. She had made assumptions based on nothing but her own prejudices. Cats were sentient and intelligent. Why shouldn't they read? But it seemed out of character.

Lesedi gave her a knowing smile. "You're right. Most of them don't. Lacking hands and fingers, they never developed writing instruments. But, more important is the way they live, close to their environment, in tune with nature, feeling the rhythms of their world, the patterns and cadences of the lives of their prey. Reading seems unnecessary to them. They have an oral culture for their stories, their history. But sometimes, one of the more curious kits takes an interest, and if they can take lessons without shirking their other duties, the elders allow them to learn. Akachi never had any difficulty keeping up with the training regimen and also studying the ways of his human clanmates."

"Ah, yes." Fajora smiled, remembering. "Top candidate in his denning, I heard."

"Yes. And with insight into the prophecies even we humans who have lived all our lives among the cats missed. Insights about the role the clans will play in future events, when the catalyst comes."

Fajora shook her head. "I'm afraid you're ahead of me. I studied the prophecies in depth as a young agent, and I know about the catalyst, of course, but it's been a long time. I don't remember any mention of the cats of Kakislane."

"Hmm. Not surprising. Off-world scholars have never thought to interpret the writings with cats in mind."

Snarls and yowls, accompanied by human shouts, drew their attention away from their conversation and down to the valley below. The rescue party darted to the south of the Rock Clan cats, and the Deep Valley warriors rushed in to shield them from attack. The gray cats of

Rock Clan attacked with a ferocity born of anger and damaged honor, but they were over-matched. The Deep Valley cohort that had been waiting farther north now harried their flank. Two gray cats went down. One moved feebly; the other lay still. A laser blast from one of the human weapons took down another Rock Clan warrior.

For a few minutes, the battle raged with a chilling wildness and savagery. Shivering, Fajora wrapped her arms around herself and averted her eyes, but the suspense, the need to see how her friends fared, forced her gaze back on them a moment later. The human members of the rescue party kept Sebastian and Clarise on the off side of their group, away from the battle. The cats of the rescue party ran interference, joining Rufaro's cohort several times to tangle with the gray cats.

Sebastian, Clarise, and the humans with them ran flat out, and they quickly reached the rise of the hills leading up into Deep Valley territory. Zuberi grabbed Clarise's arm and hauled her over the first massive boulders, and then slowed, climbing at a moderate pace toward Fajora and Lesedi.

Lesedi rose. "Come. If you have energy to spin, bring Akachi to a higher spot. Though Rock Clan is unlikely to come even this far with our warriors in the area, it will be safer beyond the ridge above."

She pointed to a spot much higher up. With a questioning glance at Fajora, she started to climb. "Will you be able to bring him?" she asked over her shoulder, "or shall I call for Zaire to carry him?" She inclined her head toward the man who had waited with them and now climbed back toward Fajora and Akachi.

"It's almost over," he said as he approached. "We'll regroup above."

"Well?" Lesedi asked.

"I'll carry him." Fajora translated to light, pulling Akachi into the spin with her, and rose to the ridge above.

When Lesedi and Zaire gained the ridge, Zaire picked up Akachi and the three of them continued, hiking down into and along a gully until they reached a broad, open valley, lush with trees and grasses and full of cool evening breezes. Here, Zaire laid Akachi gently down on a bed of soft grass, and they waited again.

It didn't take long for clan members to gather. Chikelu and the other three cats who had been part of the rescue party arrived first. Moments later, the humans came into sight, Sanaa in the lead and Zuberi bringing up the rear. Clarise had her arm through Sebastian's and leaned heavily on him.

Lesedi peered at Clarise as she drew near. With a grave expression and tender gaze, she held out her arms to Clarise.

"Dear girl. What you have suffered. I feel your grief. But you can heal here with us, and we will be your family now, if you wish."

Clarise gave her one startled glance and detached herself from Sebastian, coming into the wide-open arms, the warm embrace without hesitation. She leaned her head on Lesedi's shoulder and sighed, then wrapped her own arms around the older woman. Lesedi stroked her hair. "I know. I know. It's all right now. You're safe."

Sebastian stared, his jaw hanging. He snapped his mouth shut and turned away, a hurt expression flitting across his face. Zaire, standing nearby, observed this by-play and leaned toward him.

"Don't worry. She won't take your friend from you, but give her back to you renewed. She has a gift, one we are all thankful for. Whatever healing your friend needs, healing of head and heart, the empathy of Lesedi will do more for her than years of therapy by one of the famous old psychologists on Exalton, if they ever really existed. Come. The cohorts are heading south. We have a little distance to go yet before we reach our nighttime camp."

Sebastian nodded, but a frown creased his brow and he didn't take his eyes off of Clarise.

More cats arrived, some loping with high spirits, some strutting, tails held high, exulting in their strength and in their victory over the enemy.

A few slunk in, eyes alert, ears pricked forward, as if to warn that the danger had been brushed aside but not banished. After checking in with the cohort leaders, they spread out and worked their way toward the south.

Lesedi and Clarise walked at the front of the excursion. Zaire picked up Akachi, and Fajora and Sebastian followed him down the trail, almost the last of the company. Only a pair of scout cats followed behind them. They had easy walking now and soon reached a wide pleasant place beside a bubbling stream. Here they set patrols and everyone found places to rest for the night.

Fajora kept to the outside of the gathering, watching, curious. Sanaa moved up beside her and handed her one of the wafer cakes. Fajora took it gladly, though it was not enough fuel to restore her depleted access to light, then slaked her thirst at the stream. The water, cold and crisp, tasted of mountain air and sunshine. It buoyed Fajora's spirits and she sought a place to bed down, feeling safer than she had for many days.

That night Clarise snuggled close to Lesedi, leaving Fajora to sleep alone. She lay near Akachi, worried the clan would neglect him in the post-battle bustle. But soon, Ekene came and found a place near him as well. He gave the injured cat more pain medication and sedative and checked his bandages.

"He's doing as well as we can hope," he said in answer to Fajora's unspoken question.

Fajora nodded and tried to sleep. She tossed on her grassy bed until Sebastian came and lay an arm's length away. Sensing his distress over Clarise's abdication pulled Fajora's attention away from herself. Watching him toss, she drifted to sleep.

In the morning, Sanaa gave Fajora one wafer cake for her breakfast. As she turned to move on, Fajora caught and held her gaze.

"Thank you. I, uh, I'll need more than this if you want me to spin Akachi to the settlement."

"No." Sanaa's voice allowed for no argument. "What I have given you is sufficient for your immediate needs. You won't need to spin. There are plenty of us to carry him now, and the terrain is not too difficult."

She moved away before Fajora could respond. Fajora nibbled the wafer, immediately feeling her energy restored enough to walk with the cohorts. However, her thigh hurt, an unrelenting ache, and she longed for the release and power of light.

Sanaa stalked ahead, her back stiff and unrelenting. The other humans moved past, walking with strength and purpose, ignoring Fajora. The cats, if they glanced at her, lifted their heads and gave her brief, imperious stares.

Zaire again carried Akachi, but this time Fajora could not get near enough to keep a close eye on her young friend. She knew Zaire handled the young cat with care, and she had to be satisfied with that. She could do nothing for Akachi except to be alert to any danger, any attempts by one cat or another to do what they perceived to be their duty by him.

Fajora had no trouble keeping up. Their stream joined a rushing river and they walked along its bank. The path meandered with the river but rarely climbed and had been cleared of boulders and other obstructions, providing an easy walking surface. Her injured leg felt stronger at the unhurried pace.

Zuberi and several other men took turns carrying Akachi. Ekene did not take a turn, but kept close to the young cat and checked on him with every stop. This eased Fajora's worry. Ekene had refused to kill Akachi and had confessed a desire to see him recover, as much as possible.

So Fajora left Akachi in Ekene's capable hands and drifted to one side where she could watch the cats, the humans, and the interplay between them. Rufaro and Chikelu were in command and led the cohorts. Sanaa walked near them, and they conferred with her from time to time, showing her a deference that spoke of their respect for her, though her position did not appear to be quite equal to theirs.

Among the other cats and humans, a certain good-humored formality was in play. The humans joked among themselves. The cats listened tolerantly to the banter and batted the humans with unweaponized paws or butted them with their heads as if enjoying the jokes. The cats themselves said little except to discuss the trail, the duties of patrol, or some concern of security.

The last bit before they arrived at the settlement included a long, steep uphill climb. Fajora found this last hill daunting, short on sleep and short on food as she was, and worn down by her recent ongoing ordeal. Marshaling her remaining strength, she shut out the activity around her and concentrated on keeping her feet moving. Though humbled by the limitations she had discovered in herself on this mission, she climbed doggedly, determined not to falter at the end of the journey.

Her legs trembled and her wounds throbbed as she climbed, and it took every shred of willpower to keep going. She knew without testing herself that she did not have the energy to spin up the last section. Sanaa had seen to that. Her behavior suggested a strategy that would keep Fajora underfed and unable to spin away. Fajora would be a prisoner here, as in Rock Clan, though to what end she could not imagine.

She crested the hill and stared down at a broad valley, nestled deep within a protective wall of towering cliffs. Rugged mountains soared beyond the cliffs, breathtaking in their splendor. Two rivers ran through the valley, issuing from two deep canyons. One came from the north and, slowing, ambled along the east side of the valley. Fajora suspected it was the same river they had walked beside earlier in the day. The other rushed from the northwest and hugged the cliffs on the west side of the valley. Farther south, past the settlement, the west river angled over to meet the east, and they joined in a single turbulent channel before disappearing through a narrow notch in the mountains. Vegetation grew in lush patches, mixed with more open, rocky areas.

In the near foreground and again, in the distant reaches, Fajora saw cultivated fields and neat orchards interspersed with several fenced pastures. The settlement itself sprawled in the middle of the valley. Rather than one tight cluster of dens and human houses, as had comprised the Rock Clan settlement, this larger community spread out over a broad area. Four or five distinct denning areas were visible, and as many clusters of houses, a mixture of wood, brick, and stone structures.

All this Fajora saw in her first glance, before an enormous structure built against the cliff wall near the middle of the settlement caught her gaze. Though in much better repair, with a higher, sturdier roof, it bore a striking similarity in size and shape to the hangar that protected Rock Clan's ancient void ship.

Sebastian swooped down on Fajora and grabbed her arm. "Another ship. It has to be." Excitement laced his voice. "And these are the right coordinates. At least, I'm a little turned around, but I think they are. What I crossed over into clan territory to find."

"Explain."

"The lost Wellador ship. These are the coordinates." He hesitated, then added, "I think. If the ship's computers are intact, these people might have the missing documents. The rest of the prophecies. The histories of the last days of the war on Exalton. A record of what happened to the people who landed and got trapped in cat territory."

He grabbed Fajora's other arm, his face turning red, then pale in his excitement. "These people are probably descended from those we couldn't rescue and had to leave behind. We thought they'd died, but no. They must not have. They're here."

30

DEEP VALLEY SETTLEMENT

It took well over an hour to reach the center of the settlement. The downhill climb wore at Fajora's injured leg even more than the uphill climb, and she limped heavily by the time they reached the infirmary, a long, low building near the void ship hangar. Zaire carried Akachi inside, and Ekene motioned Fajora, Sebastian, and Clarise to follow.

The interior was well-lit and pristine. The large, main room held eight beds for humans and four low pallets for cats. At one end, a row of desks faced a wall lined with display screens much like those Fajora had often seen in the Wellador Colony. Lit up with blinking lights and words scrolling across their faces, they created a vivid contrast to Rock Clan's sputtering, outdated technology. While the Rock Clan humans struggled to get their devices back into working condition, Deep Valley Clan's technology appeared to be humming along smoothly.

Doors lined the back wall of the room. Several stood open, revealing private examination or surgical rooms. In their dim recesses, shiny equipment caught the light from the outer room. One room, better lit than the others, revealed shelves of supplies. A woman emerged from this room carrying bandages, jars, and blankets, topped with a flat electronic device that beeped as the woman neared the newcomers.

Zaire laid Akachi on one of the low pallets. Ekene knelt beside him and discussed his case in low tones with another man wearing a loose coat with deep pockets that disgorged all manner of small instruments.

Fajora couldn't hear what they said, and the woman with the bandages prevented her from drawing near to Akachi's pallet to listen. While others tended to Sebastian and Clarise, this woman directed Fajora to sit on one of the beds so the doctor could examine her injuries. Another woman, who wore a loose coat like that of the man treating Akachi, introduced herself as Doctor Tina and the first woman as her assistant, Vi.

The deep scratches on Fajora's leg showed good signs of healing. The doctor retrieved a small, round device from one of her pockets and passed it over the leg. Beeping and humming, it sent a warm pulse into Fajora's thigh, and the deep ache that had plagued her during the last stretch of the trek diminished. Another instrument bathed the wounds in blue light and the redness and ragged edges smoothed away.

Vi gave Fajora a quick appraisal. "I see we won't need these bandages, but it looks like you could use new clothes."

"Yes, please." Fajora gave Vi a rueful smile. Her uniform, so clean and crisp the day she left the colony, was filthy and in tatters. She sniffed, catching a whiff of the rank odor emanating from her equally filthy body—a result of imprisonment with substandard latrines and no chance to wash. "I could use a bath, too, or a dip in the river."

Vi nodded. "Yes, I'm sure washing will feel wonderful. Rock Clan humans aren't known for their hygiene. You'll have facilities in your house. Now, do you prefer skirts or trousers?"

"Trousers, thank you."

Now Vi frowned, assessing her. "With your height, I'm afraid I'll have to raid the men's supplies. I hope you don't mind."

"Not at all."

Vi headed for the supply room. While Fajora waited, two large cats, male and female, entered the infirmary. The sprinkling of white in the fur around their necks, the slight stiffness in their movements, and most of all, the deep wisdom in their eyes proclaimed them to be of advanced age.

Doctor Tina stood when she saw them and inclined her head, a motion just short of a bow. "Patriarch, Matriarch, welcome. I present to you our guest, Agent Fajora of the Light Spinner enclave."

"Welcome, Agent Fajora, Light Spinner," the Patriarch intoned in a formal voice. "I am Obasi, and my counterpart at the head of the female council is Imani. After hearing the reports about you, we have desired to lay eyes on you and know you for ourselves. How fare you? Are you well?"

"Yes, thank you. As well as can be after my ordeal. Your doctor has been treating my wounds, and I trust I will soon be able to clean up and refresh myself."

"A bath, perhaps," the female, Imani said, laughing.

Jelok's laughter had prepared Fajora for the possibility of feline laughter, but his dark nature had turned his laughter into a sound of derision. This was wholly different, full of sly good nature and a delight in everyday humor.

Fajora tried to suppress the heat rising into her face. "Yes, a bath sounds lovely. I've had no opportunity."

"You'll forgive me if I test you now, and do not wait for you to bathe."

"If you can stand it."

Imani nosed forward and sniffed at Fajora. She showed no disgust at Fajora's body odor, but took her time. The Patriarch hurried his testing, and he eased farther back from Fajora when he finished. He and Imani exchanged a long glance.

"We sense an upright character," Obasi said. "We will speak more to you later, but will not now keep you from your bath and rest unless you wish to report anything significant concerning your recent imprisonment and conditions in Rock Clan."

Where to start? There were so many things she could say about Rock Clan, but these things might not be news to Deep Valley Clan, and were not urgent. Only one thing clamored for attention.

"You should know Rock Clan is planning a war against you. I believe they will attack very soon. They are likely on their way even now, spurred on by the death of their spiritual leader, whom I killed. I'm sorry about his death if it stirs up more conflict between the clans. But I didn't know how else to keep him from killing Akachi. As it is, he did damage enough."

"Hmm, yes," the Patriarch murmured, casting a glance toward the pallet where Akachi lay to receive treatment. "Things are always difficult between Deep Valley and Rock Clan. It is not your fault. Do you know how many cats are coming to make war on us?"

"Pretty much the whole clan, I think. Humans too. I don't know numbers."

"I see. Though not unexpected, this is grave news. I must consult with the war leaders." He lifted one paw in farewell and padded out of the infirmary.

Imani lingered a moment longer. "We have not hosted a Light Spinner before. I do not know what your needs are, but Sanaa has been on the trail with you for days, learning your ways. She will see you are provided with what is necessary. I will speak with you again after tomorrow's meeting of the council."

She too, raised a paw a little, then followed Obasi out the door.

"Well, that went well," Doctor Tina said with a broad smile. "They were impressed with you."

"I don't see how they could be, the way I smell," Fajora responded, forcing a smile to hide her displeasure over the results of the interview. Sanaa would not have been her choice for a provider. Though efficient and skilled, she lacked compassion and understanding. She would provide for Fajora in a way that met Sanaa's needs rather than Fajora's.

Vi waited nearby with an array of clothing draped over her arms. She displayed it to Fajora with a gleeful grin that proclaimed her findings to be treasures. As she flourished the last item, a long tunic dyed the same green as Fajora's uniform, Sanaa entered the infirmary. She sauntered over to Akachi's pallet for a quick check, then proceeded to Fajora's station.

"Looks like you're about finished here. I'll take you to your house."

"House? I have a house?"

"Of course. Were you expecting to sleep in the fields?" She sniffed, as if to suggest that might be appropriate.

"I thought I'd spin home tonight, though a good night's sleep would be helpful. But I can bunk anywhere for one night. I don't need my own house."

"Hmm." Sanaa grimaced. "You have a house. The elders consider it necessary since you won't be leaving—at least not until the council has met. Are you ready?"

"No. I need to check on Akachi first."

"Not a good idea. You don't want to distract the doctors. Come now." Sanaa started for the door.

But Fajora refused to follow. Her gaze shifted to the pallet where Ekene, the doctor, and another assistant knelt around Akachi.

"Come," Doctor Tina said. "We'll take a discreet peek."

Ignoring Sanaa's deepening frown, she led Fajora over to the other group. Low growls attested to Akachi's wakefulness even before Fajora got a good view of him. She was thankful to see him moving rather than hanging like limp baggage around someone's neck. He held his head high, but as Fajora drew near, his head shot down, ears pricked forward, and he snapped at something near his paws. Lifting his head, he swallowed and flicked his tongue over his muzzle. As he did so, he saw Fajora and tilted his good eye toward her for a better view.

"It is satisfactory to eat again," he said. "I would have more."

"In a bit," Ekene said. "Let's see how this does first. I pumped you full of sedative during our journey. It will take a while to work its way out of your system, and in the interim, eating too much or too fast might make you nauseous."

"That is *not* satisfactory." Akachi punctuated his dissatisfaction with an enormous yawn that ended on a rumbling growl.

Ekene chuckled. "Fajora is here to check on you. Instead of complaining and feeling sorry for yourself, you should reassure her of your good health, so she can get settled in her house without worrying."

"Ah, yes, Light Spinner." Akachi raised himself taller and perked his ears up, looking alert and formal. "It is because of you I am well. I will talk more with you when these humans allow it."

"I'll come back later," Fajora promised.

She turned with reluctance back to Sanaa, who waited, arms crossed, toe tapping as if to count the seconds Fajora wasted.

Fajora wanted to stay with Akachi, but she followed Sanaa without further protest. The last rays of the sun slanted into the valley, touching the roofs of houses with golden light, while the stone or brick walls fell into shadow. Fajora's house was not far.

A small brick building with a window on each wall and a slate roof, it felt cool inside, but the skin rug in the middle of the floor and the pile of blankets on the bed assured Fajora she'd be warm enough. The main room equaled her Rock Clan's house in size, but she had the whole of it to herself, including the additional luxury of a washroom with running water, a shower stall, and plenty of soap. Two water flasks hanging from hooks near the wash basin ensured she could have a drink whenever she wanted and take water with her when she went out and about.

"You'll want to clean up first thing, I imagine," Sanaa said with a sniff. Sanaa had already bathed, and her fresh soap-and-water scent highlighted Fajora's own filthiness.

"We eat together, those of us who do not have families. The dining building is near the infirmary. Someone will show you in the morning. But it's too late tonight. The kitchen will send food after you've had time to shower. Let them know if you find anything missing in the house."

She left without another word. Fajora wondered, as she stepped into the shower stall and scrubbed away the accumulated grime with a grateful sigh, who would bring her dinner. Would she find another Drissy—someone who regarded her ability to spin light with awe and might be prevailed upon to bring her extra provision? She smiled at the thought of the girl who had loved to stroke her hair and who had begged Fajora to take her away.

This last thought sobered her. What would happen to Drissy, growing up in a clan that did not know how to love her? Would she find her way to a new, better home someday, or had Fajora left her to a life of hopelessness and shadow?

The young man who brought her a plate of food later was clearly no Drissy. He was polite, but not friendly, and the food portions were not nearly large enough. When she asked for more, he raised an eyebrow and smiled, a mere turning up of the corners of his mouth, without warmth.

"This is your allotment. I cannot change it, nor can you. Be content with what has been provided." Like Sanaa, he left without giving her a chance for any additional protests or requests. Sanaa had sent him; he was like her, perhaps even a product of her training. Fajora tried not to judge Deep Valley Clan based on these two. Akachi was much different, of course, as were Lesedi and Zaire, or so it seemed based on her brief acquaintance.

She played with her food, too depressed to eat, though the food tasted wonderful and her stomach growled insistently. Did it matter if she ate at all, if she couldn't eat enough to fuel a spin back to the colony? She had strength to walk, but she didn't imagine she could elude clan patrols without the ability to spin. If the council decided she should stay here, they would track her down and herd her back to her house to become as much a prisoner as she had been in Rock Clan, though with better accommodations.

For the first time, she understood the depression Jayzam had experienced after his injuries, though his had been more profound. So depleted that even ample food, rest, and sunlight did not quickly restore his ability to spin, he went into a decline. In his despair, brought about, not just by the inability to spin, but also by the derision of his colleagues, he gave up and quit eating. Fajora had struggled to hide her impatience from him, an impatience fueled by her fear of losing him.

Nursing these dark memories, Fajora prepared for bed, donning the soft sleeping gown Vi had thoughtfully included in her pile of clothing. She stroked the covers on the bed as she turned them back. A real bed with sheets and blankets, not a fuzzy hide on a dirt floor. She crawled in slowly, savoring the moment, and not even her hunger or her depression could keep her from drifting at once into a deep sleep.

As she dressed in the morning, Fajora decided exhaustion had undoubtedly played a part in her dour mood of the evening before. Well rested, with bright sunshine pouring through her windows, she felt ready to face the challenges ahead of her. Yes, Deep Valley Clan might try to keep her here by keeping her under fueled. And yes, finding the fuel she needed might require creative thinking and even guile.

But she was trained for these challenges. She would face them and find solutions and allies wherever she could.

As a first step, she found the disk Clarise had downloaded on the Rock Clan void ship. She had tossed it into the pile with her filthy clothes last night, but now she retrieved it and hid it under the mattress on her bed. She would keep it there until she found the right use for it.

The same young man who had brought her dinner the night before came again to escort her to breakfast. No more communicative than he had been the evening before, he delivered Fajora to the dining building late, when almost everyone else had finished. However, Sebastian lingered, and as soon as he spied her, he came to sit beside her, keeping her company while she ate her meager breakfast. His wrist had a fresh wrapping, and he held that arm at a more relaxed angle. The lines of pain that had been etched in his face since his injury were gone.

He eyed her small portion with a frown but said nothing. He fidgeted and grinned, as if holding in a great secret, but he restrained himself while Fajora ate, asking her solicitous questions about her accommodations and how her leg fared. Though he appeared genuinely interested in her welfare, he often gazed beyond her, his focus elsewhere. When she left the dining room, he offered to walk back to her house with her.

"Only if you tell me what you're so excited about."

He blushed a deep red. "Am I so obvious? But I can't help it. This is better than anything I ever dreamed. There's a document I've puzzled over for years. It's never made sense, but I knew it would if I could get my hands on the whole thing. We had a fragment in the colony, but they have the entire document here, and last night one of their historians let me have a read-through."

He stopped, overcome by the experience. Fajora stopped beside him and waited for him to recover, catching his excitement.

"Did you get to read the parts the colony is missing?" she prompted when he had stood lost in memories for too long.

"What? Oh, yes. I read the whole thing. And later this morning, I'm getting my own workstation in the void ship—it really is a ship, you know, and still in working order. They could fly it out of here today, if they wanted. It's fully powered, all its computers working and everything. The historian—Dellu is his name—said he'd set me up with a code for access to the old manuscripts. Can you imagine?"

They were walking again, Sebastian with jerky movements as each new thought caused him to slow or even stop at times, and at other times to stride ahead with a burst of energy. Fajora tried to match her speed to his, happy for him, but filled with misgivings and fumbling for a way to put her foreboding into words.

"Will you be able," she started, choosing her words with care, "to get through them before you return home? And after sharing this information with you, will Deep Valley Clan even let you go home? I think they're trying to keep me here, though I can't fathom why. So, I'm wondering about you."

Sebastian gave his head a little shake. "I'm not sure if they'll let me go or not. No one who disappears from the colony ever comes back, and I saw a woman last night I think I saw in the colony a long time ago. I'm not sure, but I have strong suspicions.

"But that's not the right question, is it? I'll have work here to last several lifetimes. To study these manuscripts—and some of them are new. I mean, new to me. We don't have even a fragment in the colonies. And to interpret them based on information I have that no one here has—writings from Exalton that filtered into the colony over the last three hundred years, and new wisdom from the dragons. The question is not if they'll let me go, but if they'll let me stay."

They had reached Fajora's house and stood outside the door, watching as activity picked up in the settlement. Fajora had seen mostly humans since she arrived, but now the cats showed themselves, wandering among the houses, some strolling in apparent aimlessness, but all working their way toward the north end of the valley where a deep depression along the cliff wall created a natural amphitheater.

"The council, I presume." Sebastian watched them, his face intent now, rather than bubbling with his previous excitement. "To discuss what to do with us, I'd guess."

"And the war, too, I imagine." Fajora paused, searching Sebastian's face. "You hope they let you stay? You don't want to go home?"

"No. This is what I've always wanted. Working here, with this database of manuscripts. Though I expected to be working alone, dodging cats and foraging for my food as I tried to bring the old computers back to life. Not this wonder of technology and a welcoming community. I'll stay if they'll let me. Unless . . . ."

"Unless?"

"Oh, nothing. If Clarise wanted to go home, I'd go with her, of course. But I hope she'll want to stay too."

Fajora smiled, envious but pleased by Sebastian's uncomplicated loves and hopes.

"Stay. Study and share your wisdom with all of us. Ya-Lohim knows we need it."

Grinning, he left her alone to watch the last few cats disappearing down into the amphitheater and contemplate, with a bitter twist to her lips, how little control she had over her fate, so much less than she had believed at Sebastian's age.

31

TO GO OR TO STAY?

When the cats were out of sight, Fajora headed to the infirmary to visit the one individual she knew who had even less control than she did. She'd been the one to override Akachi when he asked for a quick finish at the battle site, but the clan's culture, which prompted the request, hadn't offered him workable choices either.

The infirmary was quiet. Doctor Tina sat at a desk along the wall. The wall panel in front of her flashed with scrolling notations. Engrossed in the information on the screen, she looked up and nodded at Fajora, then returned to her work.

Fajora found Akachi awake, bored, and happy for company.

"They have finally fed me as a cat should be fed." He paused to groom himself, as if the mere memory of the food had left him soiled again.

"I wish I could say the same."

"They have not fed you? I do not understand. You appear healthy enough to eat."

"They're feeding me. Enough to keep me alive, but not enough to make a strong spin to take me home."

"Ahh." Akachi seemed to understand and asked no more questions. They fell into companionable silence until Fajora roused herself for a question of her own.

"Didn't you tell me you are on the council? Why aren't you at the meeting? It's happening right now. Someone could have helped you get there."

Akachi lifted his chin, and his ears perked up. "That would dishonor not only me but the entire clan. Only those who can share in the defense of the clan may sit with the council. I am damaged and cannot contribute, so I am not welcome. But," and he drooped as he continued, "I am sorry not to be able to speak for you, for the need to send you home."

"Would one vote make any difference, do you think? Will their decision be close?"

"I do not understand this vote you speak of, but the voice of one cat speaking reason sometimes sways the council. Even one as young as I would receive a fair hearing, once I had won my place. But I cannot do this thing, as I am here, under the care of humans, and have lost the right to speak."

"If Sanaa has anything to do with the decision, it won't be easy for me to get home. She doesn't like me much, and she trusts me even less. She'll want to keep me where she can supervise me."

"Sanaa does not make the decisions. Not here. Only when she is given charge of a mission. She is not feline and will not attend the council, though the humans have already made statements to the elders. She could make recommendations in her statement, but nothing more. But the talk I have overheard suggests some cats share Sanaa's viewpoint." Akachi sighed and his tone became gloomier. "Perhaps neither of us will be where we want."

"But you're home. Don't you want to be here?"

"Yes, but I cannot stay. Blinded and crippled, I cannot fight or hunt. I will be a burden on the clan. Once my leg is strong enough, I will leave the clan and make my way as I can."

"You don't mean that." Fajora jumped to her feet and reached for light, which responded sluggishly, too weak to aid her in exacting justice.

"They will not send me. But they expect me to go. It is our way."

"It's barbarous! Are other clans like this?"

"Yes. It is our way."

"How can that be? How can a species in Ya-Lohim's Dominion decide to kill their own people on the battlefield, or send them out to starve when they can't contribute in the normal way? I never imagined a sentient people could fall this low. Maybe random individuals or small groups, like the Dark Spinners, who have rebelled, or the dark dragons, but not a whole people, a species."

Akachi stretched out his front legs and rested his head on them with a sigh. "My people are not the monsters you make them sound like. My family loves me. They will be sad to see me go. But the clans do not survive if they have to provide for those who cannot contribute. And, except when humans are around, we have no way to take care of a wounded cat on the field, or to carry him home. It is a mercy to kill him, or her, otherwise the enemy will find and mistreat him. He will die either way, but we make it quicker and less painful, surrounded by friends."

Fajora sat back down, deflated. "I don't know. It doesn't feel right. I don't think it's what Ya-Lohim wants. But I'm sorry I interfered. Maybe it would have been better to let Chikelu do his duty, as he called it. Do you wish I had?"

She waited for the answer, trembling. What if she had made a mistake and Akachi blamed her for his current situation?

Akachi lifted his head and looked around, sniffing the air. "No. I am glad to be alive."

Relief flooded through Fajora, making her even shakier than before. She leaned over and hugged a very startled Akachi, a quick, light touch around his neck. Not finding that satisfactory, she allowed herself to put her arms all the way around him in a tight embrace. When she pulled away, she stroked his fur a few times before catching the bemused tolerance in his glance.

"Well," she said, smiling, "you can't blame me for taking advantage while I can. Soon you'll be stronger and I won't dare."

"This touching, have you a name for it?"

"Hugging."

"This hugging is not something that is done. The humans of the clan never attempt it. It is too familiar. But . . . ." Akachi leaned forward to rub his head on her leg. "I find it to be quite nice. You may proceed in the future, when there is cause. But not, please, when anyone is near to see my further decrease in dignity."

Fajora laughed and agreed.

They had no further opportunity for private talk, for at that moment Lesedi came into the infirmary, with Clarise trailing behind. When Doctor Tina saw who had entered, she left her screens and came to greet them.

"Clarise has come for the follow-up you requested," Lesedi told her. "And for a refill of the tonic you gave her."

"Good." Doctor Tina gave Clarise a reassuring smile. "We'll have you back to full health in no time if you follow orders this well. Most of my patients try to squirm out of taking the tonic."

"From what Sebastian has told me, Clarise could concoct your tonics for you, and make them taste better, too." Lesedi's hand on Clarise's shoulder propelled her gently forward.

"Really?" Doctor Tina motioned them toward an exam room. "We'll have to collaborate. I'm always eager to add more natural remedies to my arsenal. Come. Let's have a look at you."

Clarise followed the doctor into the exam room, leaving Lesedi to join Fajora and Akachi.

"How are you doing?" She aimed the question at Akachi, but her eyes included Fajora, welcoming her to respond if she wished. Fajora kept silent, leaving Akachi to answer.

"I do well, thank you. I will try putting weight on my leg before the daylight hours are done."

"And the eye?"

"A little vision, light primarily. Very blurry. It is easier to see from the good eye with the bad one covered. The doctors are devising a patch that will not fall off when I go into the forest."

Lesedi scowled but said nothing more about the matter. "Shall I bring something to read to you to help while away the long hours?"

"Perhaps later. I should like to hear the last of Manu's story. But I will sleep now."

He laid his head down alongside his front legs and closed his eyes, though his ears remained alert. Lesedi offered Fajora a hand up, and Fajora accepted, aware of how awkward her sore leg made her.

"Let's walk. I'll show you around the settlement." Lesedi motioned Fajora toward the door. Akachi didn't move or open his eyes as they walked away, though his ears were alert and Fajora knew he heard every word, every step.

Outside, they met Ekene coming for a shift in the infirmary. Fajora stopped him with a question as he reached for the door latch. "Ekene, tell me truly how Akachi does. To talk to him, you would think he'll be bounding about the forest in a day or two."

Ekene's shoulders slumped. "In truth, he is doing as well as I expected, but not as well as I hoped. We can't do anything for his eye. He won't have much vision on that side. His leg is a matter for debate. The doctors are arguing about whether or not to rebreak it and see if it heals stronger the second time around. He doesn't want them to do it. He'll be able to put weight on it soon, but he'll always limp, and he'll be slow."

"Which will make it even harder for him to hunt."

"Yes. Excuse me. I have work to do." He pulled the latch on the infirmary door and disappeared inside, clearly unwilling to say more about Akachi. Fajora turned in time to see pain flit across Lesedi's face before she hid it behind calm eyes and a resolute mouth.

"Come," Lesedi said. "All will find its right place in time, by Ya-Lohim's will."

Fajora wondered again if she had circumvented Ya-Lohim's will by her determination to prevent Akachi's death. She thought of Akachi's voice, confident, cheerful even, assuring her he was glad to be alive. Small comfort, but it would have to do for now. She nodded at Lesedi and let her lead the way.

The settlement rivaled any town Fajora had seen, complete with homes, storehouses, workshops, eating places, and research facilities.

"The void ship is our most technologically advanced workshop," Lesedi explained, leading Fajora up its entry ramp. "We would have to dismantle it to remove the computers, most of them anyway, and we're not willing to damage the vessel. It may need to fly again someday. Probably will."

Despite Fajora's sour mood, the ship intrigued her. The ship corridors were well lit and shiny, and everything appeared in perfect repair. They popped into a small room where a viewport overlooked the interior of the hangar, with sight lines through the hangar window toward the south end of the compound. Here, an array of computers hummed while their panel lights blinked busily. Sebastian sat before a screen in one corner, so intent on his work he never noticed them enter, never heard their greeting, never knew when they left.

"He's hoping to stay here, you know." Fajora watched Lesedi's face, to read her reaction.

But Lesedi showed no surprise. "Of course. He can contribute greatly to our community, and we have much to offer him in return. He will adjust better than most, since he wants to be here. Clarise, too. She will find ways to contribute and will feel a part of the clan in no time."

"What makes you believe she wants to stay? I'd think she'd want to go home and see her family again. She's so young. She must miss her family."

"Yes, she does, a little. But she's also begun to bond with me, and she'll heal here the way she could not do in the colony where she would face questions, stares, and smothering attention."

"But has she told you she wants to stay here? Has she spoken to you?" Much as Fajora wanted Clarise to talk again, she did not want her first words to be to this woman, who had stolen the girl's heart but had not risked her life, had not risked anything, to free Clarise from her tormentors. She tried to shrug this dishonorable feeling away, but she could not draw a full breath until Lesedi answered.

"No," the other woman admitted, "but I'm sure she will soon. I know she wants to, and only fear of that first word is holding her back. But she'll overcome her fear. She has great strength." Lesedi paused and her gaze caught Fajora's. "I understand her better than you realize, and I understand you as well."

"Do you care to explain?"

"It is a gift."

"So Zaire said. But that means nothing to me. What sort of gift allows you to understand me so well?"

"You ask a personal question. I don't think you realize you are prying, but I'm hoping you'll forgive me if I don't answer."

"No." Fajora heard the belligerence in her voice. She made a half-hearted effort to temper it. "I will press you on this. If you're taking it upon yourself to direct Clarise's future, I need to know what gives you the right. Or at least makes you think you have the right."

"Ah. I see. It is Clarise you are concerned for. Your sense of protection for the girl gives you honor. I will try to answer your questions. Come, let's sit in the shade near the gardens."

Lesedi led Fajora to a bench on the edge of a group of neatly laid-out garden plots. A man and several women worked among the plants beyond earshot of Lesedi and Fajora. A short distance away, a fence marked off pasture land, where the same type of shaggy beasts as those kept by Rock Clan grazed, their occasional lowing creating a pleasant counterpoint to the constant gurgling of the nearest river.

Lesedi swept her arm out to encompass the agrarian scene as she took a seat at one end of the bench. "Our valley provides abundantly for us. Every type of vegetable, fruit, and grain we need for health and enjoyment."

"And the animals? Are those for meat or for dairy products?"

"Both. When our ancestors were stranded here, the cats supplied us with meat, but as the settlement grew, it wasn't enough. The cats have been influenced by our presence as much as we have been changed by living with them. They were once much more spread out and solitary. And we still have other smaller settlements and hunting stations, but the biggest part of the population lives here most of the year. The game in this area can't support this large a population, so we've had to supplement with domesticated animals. What you see here is a small portion of our herd. Several nearby valleys support larger numbers of animals, and we move what we need for immediate use into the local pastures. Some we butcher and some we keep long term for their milk."

She cooed as a fuzzy beast, large with young, pressed up against the fence and lowed at them.

"She's hoping for salt, but I didn't bring any with me."

Fajora watched the animal, remembering the soft hide that had comprised her bedding in Rock Clan. "And Rock Clan follows a similar practice, I assume. I saw creatures like these there."

"Yes, but only since humans came to Deep Valley Clan and provided an example for them. Before that, they lived on what they could grow and what they could convince the cats to share of their kills. They survived, nothing more."

"I imagine. But now, please quit stalling and tell me of your gift."

Lesedi gazed across the valley as she spoke softly. "I am not native to Deep Valley Clan."

"You're from the colony?"

"No. Rock Clan." Lesedi smiled at Fajora's quick intake of breath. "My mother fled with me shortly after my birth, determined not to raise me in that den of darkness. I'm forever grateful to her. I inherited my gift from her."

"But how did she come by this gift of . . . ? What gift is it you have, exactly?"

"Empathy. My grandmother could read minds a little. Just a little. Or so I'm told. My mother and I cannot. We sense someone's emotions, mood, that sort of thing, but on a deep level. My grandmother told my mother we descended from a long line of gifted women."

"Where did these women come from, originally? Because this sounds like one of the gifts of Ara more than anything else."

"My mother says we traveled from Ara, a long time ago."

The idea sent shock coursing through Fajora. She knew something of the Aran gifts. She also knew Ara had never had void travel technology. Had never had, and still did not have advanced technology of any kind.

"How did they get here from Ara? It's impossible."

"No," Lesedi countered. "You've seen the ship they came on. An Exalton ship. I don't know how they ended up on it, but they did. And survived everything Rock Clan could throw at them. Until finally, one of them—my mother—had the courage to try to get away. She taught me all she could about my gift, and I try to use it for good, for healing, with both the humans and the cats here. It's the only way I can repay Deep Valley Clan for taking us in and making us part of the community."

She fell silent, and Fajora, trying to process this amazing information, did not try to respond. After a time, Lesedi said softly, "I can use my gift to help Clarise. I'm sure she's better off here with me than she could possibly be in the colony."

Fajora mulled this statement over. It sounded good. So positive. So generous and compassionate. Lesedi embodied all those characteristics. Nonetheless, it was wrong to separate a young woman from her family and friends at a formative time in her life and to take away her dreams for her future. It had been wrong when Rock Clan kidnapped Clarise, and it remained wrong no matter what kind of benevolent spin Lesedi put on it.

But one look at Lesedi's face convinced Fajora it would do no good to argue about it. Fajora would have to determine Clarise's wishes for herself, and if the young woman wanted to go home, it would be up to her to make it happen. Even more than Fajora's promise to Jayzam, her gratitude and friendship toward Clarise demanded this.

32

—·—

THE OWLING

Lesedi dropped the topic as well. Her gift must have warned her Fajora was not in a receptive mood. She rose from the bench and pointed back toward the settlement buildings.

"Come, we'll get lunch and I'll show you more of my home." She took Fajora to a cluster of tables under the trees near the dining hall. "Wait here. I'll grab plates and we'll eat outside. It's such a pleasant day."

She returned a few minutes later with two plates piled with salads, cheeses, and bread. Fajora's plate held more food than she had eaten at one time since leaving the colony. Lesedi apparently didn't know about Fajora's restricted diet, and Fajora didn't enlighten her. Instead, she ate quickly before someone like Sanaa, who knew more of the situation than Lesedi, could come along and take her bounty from her.

A little later a woman from the dining room removed their empty plates. Fajora detected a shadow of sadness in her eyes. She mentioned it to Lesedi.

"You know of her sadness? You must, with your gift. Have you not been able to help her?"

"That's Brenna. She came to us from the colony a good fifteen years ago. Crossed over by accident while out for a walk after dark. Meadow Clan found her and brought her here. She has a husband and children, but she still pines for her childhood home."

"Why didn't she go back? Why did she stay here?"

"Going back was not allowed. When anyone crosses over from the colonies for any reason, they are brought to us to stay. From all the clans. Except Rock and River, of course."

"Why? Why not send them back? It wouldn't harm anyone, and it would prevent a lot of grief for families whose loved ones disappear and are never heard from again."

"Oh, that is out of the question. There would be no end of violations if they were not penalized. Besides, the colony is so much stronger than we are. If they knew of our settlement here, they would insist on reintegrating us into their society."

"Would that be so bad?" Fajora rose and followed Lesedi as she beckoned her toward the buildings beyond the dining hall. She scrutinized the neat, flourishing, but primitive settlement, remembering the sleek buildings of the colony and their advances in everything from weaponry to medicine.

"Good or bad from a personal perspective is not the issue."

"What is, then?"

"Prophecy. Our place, alongside the cats, in the final struggle against darkness."

Fajora scrunched her forehead in confusion. They refused to let strays from the colony go home because of prophecy? It made no sense. But before Fajora could ask about the specific prophecies in question, Lesedi changed the subject, directing Fajora to the craft houses, where women worked at weaving, pottery making, and other useful occupations. The chance to ask more about the prophecy passed.

"We have replicators, of course," Lesedi said, the pride unmistakable in her tone, "but we've learned to value items with a more personal touch. They fit better into the clan environment and give our people an outlet for their creativity."

Fajora followed her from one part of the settlement to another, making polite remarks when appropriate, but barely listening. There was more going on here than she had at first supposed. She needed to have a long talk with Sebastian and find out what he knew of these prophecies. Despite his excitement at being here, she trusted him to have a less biased viewpoint than clan members like Lesedi, for whom clan pride and honor were involved.

Lesedi finished her tour just in time for the evening meal. The council had disbanded hours earlier, but no one had sought out Fajora to give her an account of what had transpired. Or they had sought but not found her as she roamed throughout the settlement with her guide.

She ate her small dinner with a pretense of resignation, not asking for more. Unless the council had come to a different decision than she expected, she would have to find an alternate way to procure the food she needed. As she ate and then walked back to her house, she observed everything around her. She needed to understand what went on here in order to formulate a plan of escape.

She saw humans going about their work, but few cats. She knew from her time in Rock Clan that early evening was a lazy time of day for the feline population, with many still sleeping. The exception seemed to be the kits. Two groups followed older cats, crouching low and pouncing as they imitated their leaders. The leaders appeared to ignore them, then turned on them, hissing and growling. When this happened, the kits mewed and jumped about, rolling over one another and batting at each other and their leader. A game? A serious training session? Fajora suspected both.

Her house was a cold, lonely, shell, not a home; not a place to come for a relaxing, peaceful evening. She felt the walls closing in on her as soon as she entered. Grabbing a cushion from the pile in one corner, she headed back outside and plopped it on the ground by the front door. It gave her a place to sit and continue to observe the evening routine of the settlement.

Now many clan members walked past her house observing her close-ly, though their scrutiny appeared more curious than hostile. A female cat came close and sniffed at her, but when she greeted the cat with a cheerful "Good evening," the cat bounded away without responding. The humans whispered among themselves but did not approach. A couple of shy smiles were as close as they came to friendliness.

Fajora had become accustomed to interacting with humans during her previous, long tenure with the Kakislane enclave. Colonists and Luxerans had regular contact, including not only business meetings, but shopping and dining in New Skakeet City, attending festivals and celebrations, and even, on occasion, invitations to more intimate social events. Since her return to Kakislane, her interactions with the doctors at the hospital, with Dannel, and with Sonja had felt little different from her interactions with colleagues and friends back on Luxera.

But she realized, watching these people, that interactions with Light Spinners were as novel to them as interactions with the cats were to her. She might look similar to the humans, but there were differences to remind them she was not human. The color of her hair, for one thing. No human had blue hair. It must look odd and alien to them. And the swirling flecks in her eyes. Those took getting used to.

In addition, the uncertainty about what she would do loomed over the settlement, a more compelling barrier to friendship than her ap-pearance. Would Fajora prove to be as hostile and dishonorable as Dark Spinners, with whom they were more familiar? As a Light Spinner rather than a Dark Spinner, would she have abilities they were not prepared for? And she sat openly, right in the heart of their community. These people must know Lesedi had shown her the void ship. She knew their secrets; how could they either befriend her or let her go, with so much uncertainty surrounding both options?

Their concerns were not unfounded. She did intend to share some of what she had learned on this trip. How else could she vindicate Jayzam?

Which was, after all, why she had come here in the first place. Her desire to free Sebastian and Clarise had been motivated by the more personal goal.

How Fajora would share what she knew without revealing too much to Kinovic remained a puzzle. If she could accuse Kinovic of spinning shadow and get him out of the way, Jayzam's vindication would be easier. But she had no evidence, only the sensation of darkness in an aura she was sure was his. She had not seen him to identify him unequivocally. He had not spun shadow in her presence. And she lacked a second witness, necessary for any accusation to stick.

Fajora did not want to give Deep Valley Clan's secrets away. She had that much honor, at least. But she couldn't stay here and integrate into the clan so her knowledge would stay here with her, and, at the same time, shirk her responsibilities in the enclave.

A stir close to the center of the settlement drew her attention, drew everyone's attention. Humans gathered in clusters and gazed in that direction. Cats sat on haunches, ears twitching, or prowled toward the disturbance.

A cat, not quite fully grown, emerged in the dimming light, walking slowly and with a profound limp. Akachi. He had found his legs again, and he came directly toward Fajora. She watched him with affection for a moment before turning her attention to the nearby clan members. The humans whispered, with glances her way. The cats did not speak, but their restless movement, the swiveling of ears, the twitch of tails, betrayed their agitation.

Akachi continued, unwavering, until he reached Fajora's house.

"May I join you here? I would share the owling with you."

"Yes, of course. Please."

Akachi flopped down beside her and began to groom himself. The other clan members watched for a moment before moving away.

Observing Akachi, Fajora grew as restless as the cats. "I wonder if you should be here with me. Your clan does not trust me."

"What have I to lose? I will soon be gone."

"What if they ask you to stay? What if we found a way to change the customs of the clan? You could be jeopardizing that possibility by sitting with me."

"What you suggest will not happen. And you are my friend. Besides, I would make a statement, as I was not allowed to do at the council meeting." Akachi gave his fur two more licks, then paused, as if considering.

"All members of the clan know of the talk at the council today, even those who did not attend. The elders proclaimed your history. How Bardu warned you away and yet you did not leave. How you persisted in infiltrating Rock Clan, a move which could only stir them up. And they know when we met Rock Clan in battle and I sustained a debilitating injury, you prevented the rescue party from following our customs. Most understand that keeping you here is difficult, but letting you go is dangerous. And if the council decides to keep you here, they will have to take you into the clan, despite these transgressions. They know this and they are worried and confused. I wish to announce that despite all these things, I know of your honor."

"You give me too much credit."

Akachi caught her gaze. "Do you say you do not have honor?"

"No, I don't mean that. But what your clan sees as honorable doesn't always agree with what I believe to be honorable. I assure you, I didn't realize how much trouble I was causing."

"If you had realized, would you have gone when Bardu asked you to go?"

"Probably not. I was determined to save Sebastian and Clarise. And I'm glad I did."

"Yes. They are worthy additions to the clan. You have done well in that regard. Some will befriend you because of it. But others will not be swayed."

"When will I hear of the council's decisions?"

"Most likely in the morning. At the time of sunrise. It is considered the best time for bad news."

A retort hovered on Fajora's lips, but she cut it off as the call of an owl floated across the valley.

When it died away, she started again. "It's not right to . . . ."

"Hush," Akachi admonished her. "It is the owling."

Glancing around, Fajora noticed all activity had ceased in the settlement. She could see the figures of people and cats, but they were quiet, listening.

Another owl call came from a different direction. Its tones were haunting, evocative of a wildness beyond even that of the cats. Fajora had heard the owling twice before, once in a small village during her previous assignment on Kakislane, and more recently with Sonja at Haven Outpost.

But she had listened from the outside during those experiences, with a barrier between herself and the owls she did not know how to cross. Now she heard it from within its midst, with a cat, child of the wild just as the owls were, for company. It didn't matter that she didn't understand the words. In some mysterious way, she was a part of the owling now, and it would forever resonate through her soul in a new and thrilling way.

More owls called from every side of the settlement. Fajora shivered and pulled her knees up under her chin, wrapping her arms around her legs with a tight grip. More and more calls came, beautiful and eerie.

A shadow floated above them in the sky. A long, haunting call rang out over the more distant calls as an owl winged over them toward the hunt. The calls in the distance died away, and silence fell over the settlement.

After a few moments, clan members moved about again. Akachi rose to his feet with care, looking as stiff as Fajora felt, but able to maneuver without help.

"Good night, Light Spinner. Sleep well. Prepare yourself for whatever news will come to you in the morning."

33

THE BEST TIME FOR BAD NEWS

At sunrise, clan representatives paid Fajora a visit. Waking after a restless night, she pulled on her clothes in groggy confusion at the loud knocking on her door. She stumbled across the floor and yanked the door open to find a cat and a human standing with formal stiffness in front of her. She recognized Bardu. The imperious tilt of his head had not changed since she saw him that first day when she entered Deep Valley territory by accident, and his powerful build intimidated her as much has it had then.

She did not know the human, an older man with graying hair, though still spry and hearty.

"I am Khari," he said. "And my companion, Bardu, I believe you know."

"Yes."

"The Patriarch and Matriarch of the clan have asked that we bring you to them. They have information, and perhaps wisdom, to impart to you."

"Yes, of course. Lead the way." Fajora stepped out and pulled the door closed behind her.

They led her through the settlement, quiet at this time of day. Few humans were stirring this early, and the cats who were on patrol or hunting had not yet returned. One old woman sat on a mat in front of her house with a steaming cup and a book, and two cats lounged in front of their dens, blinking lazily at the rising sun. These gave Fajora little heed, and no other prying eyes watched her progress through the settlement.

Fajora's guides did not head for any of the dens, but walked past the homes, both human and feline, and through the gardens, past the pastures, and, finally, through a large orchard. The branches of the trees bent low, heavy with glowing, bright red fruits which smelled delicious. Fajora's stomach rumbled, and only Bardu's presence kept her from plucking one and biting into it.

An uncultivated space opened beyond the orchard, and past that grew a mixed woodland of shrubs, small trees, and a large stand of aspens that towered over the other vegetation. The leaves of these tall trees whispered in the light breeze, speaking to Fajora of mystery, of the secrets of this world that she was just beginning to glimpse.

Bardu led the way along the edge of the woodland until they came to a break in the vegetation. Here, a narrow path led into the woods. Turning onto this path, they came presently to a leafy glade. A tiny spring bubbled up on one side, the water trickling into a steam that disappeared among the trees. The edges of the glade were shady and cool, but sunlight, peeking over the tops of the trees as the sun gained height, bathed the center. Fajora felt its warmth on her skin and stood still in delight, soaking in the glade's serene beauty.

Obasi and Imani, the Patriarch and Matriarch of Deep Valley Clan, waited for Fajora near a circle of flat stones. They motioned toward the stones. Khari took a seat and waved Fajora to his side. As she sat, the three cats ranged themselves before her, Obasi and Imani directly in front of her and Bardu to one side.

"Greetings again, Agent Fajora, Light Spinner," Obasi said in formal tones. "We are pleased you came so early to our bidding. We have much to discuss with you."

Fajora stretched her legs in front of her and crossed them at the ankles, a relaxed pose that signaled she would not let them have sole control of the pace and tenor of this meeting. "Yes. The council has come to some conclusions about my presence here and about my plans to leave and return to my home?"

"No."

Fajora pulled her knees up sharply so her feet rested flat on the ground and sat taller. This was unexpected.

Bardu rumbled in his throat, pulling Obasi's attention toward him momentarily.

"No, I am not entirely truthful," Obasi amended. "We have come to a provisional conclusion. Imani and I prefer to send you home. It will be difficult to keep a Light Spinner in our community permanently. Others agreed with this assessment. And our thoughts have great weight within the council. But some are concerned about the repercussions of letting you go, and we cannot adequately answer their concerns until we have gotten to know you. We need to learn the truth of why you came here and your intent, especially knowing you ignored Bardu's early warning to leave clan territory and then bound one of our young, impressionable warriors to your cause."

Fajora stretched her legs back out again. It felt good to stretch her right thigh, which, though healing well, still ached. She heard Akachi's voice distinctly. *I am a fully initiated member of the male council, and I am well qualified.* He would not appreciate being called impressionable. But she didn't want to drag Akachi into any censure she received, so she left him out of her response. "I came here, or at least, into clan territory, to rescue Clarise and Sebastian. It is true Sebastian came into clan territory in violation of the treaty. But Clarise did not, and did not deserve to be stuck here."

Khari turned to stare at her. "If Clarise did not violate the boundary, how did she end up in Rock Clan? You must be mistaken."

"No. It's Rock Clan who violated treaty. They passed through Sacred Mountain Clan and Canyons Clan territories without permission and infiltrated the colony purposely to snatch Clarise. How they knew about her is a mystery, but they definitely targeted her."

Perhaps not such a mystery. Kinovic must have been aware of the colony's rising engineering star. He might well have told Rock Clan about her. But Fajora thought better of bringing him into this discussion.

A deep growl rumbled from Bardu's chest. "This cannot be," he said. "Not even Rock Clan is so dishonorable."

"Do you doubt me? Then test me."

"I will." Bardu paced over to Fajora and sniffed at her, first her hands and face, then randomly about her head, arms, and legs. When he was satisfied, he stepped back to his place and inclined his head toward Obasi and Imani. "She is truthful. We must believe the worst of Rock Clan. But for what purpose did they break honor to procure this young woman? What is her value?"

"Her engineering knowledge, which is unmatched in the colony. They wanted her to fix their void ship. They intend to conquer Kakislane and then carry their ambitions to the rest of the Dominion."

A silence fell over the glade, broken only by the tinkling of the tiny stream. Fajora grew restless, impatient to know more of their decisions about her own status. Imani noticed her fidgeting.

"You must forgive our silence," she said. "What you have said requires much thought. Rock Clan has ever been our adversary, even before humans appeared in their midst. They are a difficult people to deal with, not like the other clans. We assume this is because they listened to the subtle deceits of the dark ones and fell under their sway so long ago. The dark ones continue to plant new ideas among the clan members, requiring that we give each new development careful consideration. This is especially true now, as we face a fresh incursion from Rock Clan and their River Clan allies."

"Will River Clan join the incursion?"

"Yes," Bardu answered. "Even now, their warriors mass along the neutral territory."

"That is one reason," Imani continued, "why we made a provisional agreement concerning your status. We do not have the time to debate the matter adequately with these other clans threatening our borders."

"I understand." Fajora uncrossed and recrossed her legs before asking, "And what is this provisional agreement the council has come to? What do they propose to do with me?" She put emphasis on the word "they," hoping to make it clear she reserved the right to accept or reject their findings.

"You will stay here and live as a clan member until the harvest season has ended. By then we will know you better, and the elders will have time to discuss your character and your future at greater length."

"And how do you propose to keep me here?" She knew the answer, of course, but she wanted to see how they justified her restricted diet.

"We know something of a spinner's fuel needs," Khari answered. "If we restrict your fuel intake, you'll be unable to spin your light, and leaving will become difficult, if not impossible. You will have sufficient food to live, but not to create light. In all other ways, you will have a full and abundant life."

Several retorts sprang to Fajora's mind, but they all gave way to a burst of laughter. Bitter laughter rather than joyful, but laughter nonetheless. The four individuals watching her looked puzzled. Khari frowned, and the cats twitched their tails in agitation.

"This is funny?" Khari asked.

"Yes." Fajora fought for control. "You believe a Light Spinner can have an abundant life without being able to spin? However many more moon cycles that is, I could be beyond recovery by then."

"I don't understand." Imani shifted her stance. "We will feed you enough for physical health."

"No. You won't. You'll feed me enough for physical health in a human. Light Spinners are different. Without the ability to spin light, we cannot survive. But I don't expect you to understand."

"If you suffer," Imani said, her words hesitant, "go to the infirmary. If your condition is beyond the doctors' skill, they will inform us and we will reassess your situation."

As good an offer as she was likely to get. Well, she would be long gone before her health became an issue. She would find a way. But she wouldn't press the point today. She couldn't leave until she did all she could for Akachi, Clarise, and Sebastian.

As if he read her mind, Obasi gave a low rumble, a call to attention. At a nod from Imani, he spoke in a more intimate tone.

"Now that we have made your status clear, we would talk to you about Akachi."

"He intends to go into the wilderness and get on as best he can, to avoid burdening the clan," Fajora said, making no attempt to keep the hostility out of her voice. "He will die a slow death by starvation, unless the invading Rock and River Clan cats find him first. Because it's the clan's way, the way of honor."

Obasi sank down to the ground with a loud, human-sounding sigh. "It has been the clan's way for generations. I am not sure it is the way of honor."

Fajora drew her knees up and leaned forward, interested in this conversation for the first time. "Of course it's not. He's a living soul created by Ya-Lohim, which gives him more value than could ever come from what he can or can't contribute. It can't be right to destroy him because of an injury."

"I am coming to agree with that idea, and so is Imani, but others are not so easy to convince."

Fajora turned to the human beside her. "Khari?"

He smiled. "Most humans in the clan prefer to preserve life whenever possible."

"Bardu?" Fajora turned to the imposing warrior. Based on what she knew of him, she expected him to side with the traditional clan view of honor. His hesitation surprised her.

"I am uncertain," he said at last. "I would agree with you if I knew we were living souls created by Ya-Lohim, but I am not convinced of this truth. It is not something I can test. Honor and the welfare of the clan are all I know beyond a doubt."

"But if you believe in Ya-Lohim, how can you not . . . ."

"But you see," Bardu interrupted, a most unusual informality. "I cannot be certain of Ya-Lohim's existence."

"But the Malekem, who come for the warriors who are killed. Aren't they enough to convince you?"

"Perhaps it would be. I have heard reports of these creatures, but I have never seen one myself. Until I do, I cannot be sure they exist."

"You think your clan members—family, fellow warriors, friends—who have seen the Malekemi come for the dead are lying or crazy."

"Not crazy. Certainly not lying. But perhaps their vision is clouded by grief and by hope that the old teachings are true."

"And you won't believe unless you see?"

"That is correct. But I also will not discount the possibility it is true. And so, I will not stand in the way of our Patriarch's decisions, whatever they may be, concerning young Akachi."

Fajora searched frantically for an answer she could give Bardu to convince him of Ya-Lohim's reality. But she saw the unflinching gaze of the warrior cat and knew only evidence he could see with his own eyes would convince him, something she could not give. At least he would not block the Patriarch from helping Akachi.

"What do you intend for Akachi? Will you insist he stay here and remain part of the clan?"

"Alas, I cannot. First, because the decision is his own as a full member of the council. Also, because I do not have adequate support within the clan. This is something I cannot change by decree, and I can be replaced. Many of the clan cats support the old way, even as they regret that Akachi will leave us and die."

"I don't understand." Fajora got to her feet and paced around the glade, stopping to dip her hand into the clear cool water of the tiny stream. "If there's nothing you can do, why are you discussing this with me? I can't change the clan's collective mind. I don't even have arguments for Bardu, though I know he's wrong."

Imani's voice came to her, low and gentle. "But you might convince Akachi."

Fajora stopped pacing. "Would it matter if I did?"

"Yes. It is expected he will go, but not required."

Fajora took up her pacing again. "He told me he was glad to be alive. So why, if he's not required to go, is he so determined to do so?"

"His father tells him he will dishonor the family if he does otherwise. His father is tied to the old ways, as you well know."

"How could I know that? I don't know who his father is." Seeing the four watching her closely, Fajora stopped again. "Do I know him?"

"His father is Chikelu," Imani said.

"Chikelu!" Fajora dropped to her knees and dangled one hand in the stream. She shuddered. "His own father was ready to tear out his throat. Only my intervention prevented him, and it also angered him. What kind of father is he?"

"A good one, for the most part," Khari said, "but one who believes in the old ways of honor above all. He fears to see his son shamed, to see him hobbling about the settlement, crippled and dependent. Also fears

Akachi's life will be less because of his infirmity. It is a strange kind of love, but it is love, nonetheless."

"And you believe I can convince Akachi to defy his father and stay here?"

"We would like you to try." The Patriarch rose to his feet and started toward the path leading out of the glade. "We have much to do, to plan for the defense of our clan and our territory. We may have need of information about recent Rock Clan activity. Be prepared if one of the warriors approaches you with questions. We trust you will answer them to the best of your ability. In the meanwhile, we will leave you here for a time to consider our request concerning the young one. Khari will wait for you at the edge of the woodland to escort you back to the settlement."

He paced down the path, and Imani and Bardu accompanied him. Khari lingered a moment, giving Fajora a reassuring smile, then followed the others, leaving Fajora alone to think about what she had learned.

She would do as they asked. She would have done so even if they hadn't asked. Now she had more ammunition against any arguments on Akachi's part. The Patriarch and Matriarch wanted him to stay with the clan. To begin a change in the attitudes of the clan toward honor killings. If anyone could start such a change, it would be Akachi.

So Fajora's thoughts turned, not on any decision she needed to make, but on her discovery of a father's willingness to sacrifice his own son for the sake of a horrific idea of honor. The disgust she had felt for Chikelu after the battle with Jelok turned to a loathing so intense it soured her stomach, making her grateful she had not yet eaten breakfast.

34

THE WAY FORWARD

The water from the spring trailed over Fajora's hand as it flowed inexorably along its path into the woods. She spread her hand and made a wall, trying to stop the flow, but the water snuck under and around her hand and continued on its way. She reached beyond the stream for handfuls of fallen leaves to make a dam. For a moment, her leaf pile blocked the water, and it began to pool behind her barrier. But the trickle of the liquid, seeming too small to be significant, pressured the pile of leaves, moving them a little, then a little more. In a tiny rush, the dam broke and the water found its path.

Fajora grabbed a stick and scraped a new trench beside the streambed, trying to divert the water's path. Another small dam closed the old streambed as the new one opened, and the water flowed as Fajora directed it. But a short way beyond her diversion, the water angled over to the old streambed again and sang merrily on its way as it had been doing before she came.

She pounded her fist on the ground beside the spring. She couldn't affect the flow of this tiny stream. What made her suppose she could affect the flow of the events raging around her?

If she confronted Chikelu and called him out for the monster of a father he was, dozens of clan members would come to his defense, and she would be the one ostracized, not him.

If she laid her arguments out to Akachi and he refused to listen to her, she couldn't tie him up and make him stay in the settlement.

If she scouted the entire settlement and knew where the food resources were stored, but could not find a way to access them, she would not escape this place no matter how staunch her determination.

If she managed to return to the colony, ready to bring Kinovic to justice, but could not force him to show his darkness to another witness, a witness willing to put their career and perhaps their life on the line to testify, Kinovic would still run the enclave and Dark Spinners would have free access to Kakislane. Some would remain shadowy figures, like Syjaz. Others would be bolder, making their way to Rock Clan and to the other clans as well, until only pockets of light remained on this world, fighting to keep from being smothered. It would be Exalton all over again, with another world falling into shadow.

And if she couldn't leave Deep Valley Clan, if she couldn't bring Kinovic to justice, if she couldn't take Clarise home, she would never vindicate Jayzam and force the service to give him the accolades he deserved.

As Fajora squeezed her eyes closed and buried her head in her hands, trying to shut out the things she could not control, a shadow fell over her mind. She stiffened. She did not feel the shadow of despair, but a real shadow, the aura of a Dark Spinner. In the next instant she identified Syjaz. He had followed her from Rock Clan. Or, perhaps not, for she had not felt his presence here until now. Perhaps he had been searching for her and only now discovered her location. Either way, she must face him now, and he would try to take her, to engulf her in his shadow and carry her away to Zukalum.

Fajora reached for light. It came, but not with enough strength to make a sword. She might manage some small gesture, but Syjaz would slap it aside with a smirk and sweep her into the embrace of his shadow.

He coalesced on the other side of the glade. Despite the necessity of scavenging for his fuel, he appeared strong and in control.

Fajora stood and stepped across the little stream, as if putting it between herself and Syjaz gave her protection. He glanced around the glade and smiled knowingly. She was alone and at his mercy. She thought through her options, which were few indeed. She could call for Khari. Scream, rather. But Khari could do little against a Dark Spinner once he translated back to shadow form.

At best, Khari could witness her fate so she did not simply vanish, unnoticed, from the realm of light. Little good it would do. If the clan went so far as to send to the enclave for help, they would find Kinovic in charge, and he was in league with Syjaz. Fajora had no doubt he would be delighted to be rid of her. He could report to the service that she had wandered, unauthorized, into clan territory and disappeared. Presumed dead at the claws of the cats.

Syjaz took a step toward her, and another. Fajora opened her mouth to scream. Then blinked as the sunlight grew brighter. Impossibly bright, even for the mid-morning sun. Syjaz stopped and looked around, his eyes narrowing as he tried to find the source of the light. A great pressure accompanied the light, and Fajora struggled to draw a deep breath.

The light shone brightest right above the spring. It grew in brilliance, swelling and separating, until it became two dazzling columns of radiance.

Transfixed, Fajora watched as a Malekem took shape within the nearest column, while the other resolved into the form of a Lochemer. The light around the two figures dimmed, though it did not fade entirely. Robed and weaponless, a messenger, not a warrior, the Malekem nonetheless radiated power and majesty. He regarded Fajora, his gaze piercing. She was on her knees again, though she did not recall moving.

Fajora perceived the Lochemer as a blur observed in quick glances, her attention continually returning to the deep, wise eyes of the Malekem.

Fajora had the impression of short, close-fitting raiment leaving the Lochemer's powerful arms and legs bare. She knew nothing of his face, but discerned that his hair shimmered. The only thing she saw clearly was the huge sword, not a weapon of spun light, but one of a metal that shone brighter than the sun.

The Lochemer ignored her, turning to face Syjaz. "This one is protected today. You may not touch her." He lifted his sword arm, bringing the weapon's point level with the Dark Spinner's throat, though he stood yet ten paces from Syjaz. Fajora heard Syjaz's deep, feral snarl.

"Choshek will avenge this interference," Syjaz spat out. "Wait for him, and tremble."

But as he spoke, he backed away. When the Lochemer took a step toward him, sword still raised, Syjaz translated to shadow and darted away. His aura hovered on the edge of Fajora's awareness a moment longer, and then it, too, disappeared.

The Lochemer followed him, translating to light and spinning away. Only the Malekem remained with Fajora.

"You have suffered many trials, Light Spinner." The Malekem's voice resonated through Fajora's being. "Some of those trials have been of your own making." Fajora huddled low and bowed her head, afraid to look at him as she waited for the next words, words of condemnation. "But you have done well in some regards. You have released Clarise from brutal captivity and you have saved young Akachi's life. These actions are pleasing to Ya-Lohim."

At these words, Fajora found the courage to lift her head and meet the Immortal's eyes again. "I thank your Eminence for these gracious words. I have done that much," she agreed. "But I don't know if I can get Clarise the rest of the way home, and Akachi may yet die, because he cares more for his family's twisted concept of honor than he does for his own life. I don't know how to change these things. Please, I need your wisdom."

The Malekem laughed merrily, his laughter echoing like silver chimes through the glade. "Ah, yes, I see," he said, and though the laughter died away, his voice still carried the sound of silver and light. "Now I understand the Master's instructions. You are not in control. Is that what concerns you? It is a frailty we share. We but serve together."

"What am I to do?"

"You must do whatever comes to hand, whatever your abilities and your temperament have fitted you for. That is all any can do. But I have this word from our master. If you serve well, following the way of justice, you will find a way to make a difference and will be granted the desire of your heart."

Fajora could not slow the mad pounding of her heart and knew her eye flecks must be swirling wildly. She lowered her head to hide her eyes. Her heart's desire! But how? Jayzam was dead two years. Ya-Lohim did not restore the dead to their loved ones. But perhaps vindication for her beloved was closer than she had dared hope. If that was what she most desired.

As if reading her thoughts, the Malekem continued. "I must warn you, however. We are often deceived. The desire of your heart may not be what you assume it is. Do not set your thoughts too much on one thing, or you will lose sight of the work you are to do, the work of justice and mercy. The advancement of the light."

The light that had continued to shimmer faintly around the Malekem grew brighter. His features lost definition, became light to the accompaniment of a rushing as of many waters. Fajora experienced a lessening of pressure, as if a large creature had been sitting on her chest and had now removed itself, allowing her to breathe normally again. She ventured a glance toward the Malekem and found herself alone in the glade.

She sat by the spring, watching the water bubble up and spill over. She tried not to think but to simply absorb into her consciousness the essence of her encounter with the Malekem. Meetings with Immortals, Light or Dark, always shattered a mortal's consciousness, but this had been unlike any other meeting Fajora had experienced. Previous encounters had been chance occurrences, but this time the Malekem had been sent to her, and his attention had been focused solely on her situation. It left her breathless.

But as she tried to absorb the encounter, she found herself pushing back against it as well. The Malekem's instructions had been clear. Give herself to whatever task came to hand. No planning out her own agenda and maneuvering events to achieve her goal.

And what had come to hand?

A request to convince Akachi to stay with the clan. A disk from Rock Clan's void ship that someone should examine—probably Sebastian. The need to discover whether Clarise wanted to go home or stay near Lesedi in Deep Valley Clan. A responsibility to help the war effort with information about Rock Clan, if asked. A Dark Spinner, whom she, as a Luxeran Service agent, must try to apprehend with whatever small power she commanded. Another Dark Spinner running the Kakislane enclave, who must be watched for evidence and brought to justice.

So many things. But one item did not seem to be at hand—a way to vindicate Jayzam. She had set out to do this one thing, but along the way, without her noticing, that agenda had been smothered in other concerns. She found nothing at hand to forward it, and the Malekem had not left her wiggle room to add it in.

You must do whatever comes to hand, whatever your abilities and your temperament have fitted you for.

So, there it was. She either served herself and maneuvered—tried to maneuver—the world around her to fit. Or she gave up her own agenda and served Ya-Lohim by doing whatever he brought to hand.

The water flowing from the spring had worked on her alternate channel, filling it with silt and closing it. Now the water flowed down its original streambed with a tiny, gurgling song. If Fajora came back tomorrow, she would find no sign of her attempt to alter the course of the stream.

She patted the silty alternate channel, filling it in a little more. The stream flowed beautifully in its original course. She did not need to alter it or control it in any way.

"Light Spinner? Fajora?"

Khari's voice jerked her attention away from the stream. He stood at the entrance to the glade, his brow wrinkled with concern.

"You've been alone here so long, I thought I'd better check on you. Are you well?"

His expression, his tone, his words gave no indication he had seen or heard anything unusual, though Fajora thought the light of the Immortals must have illuminated the entire settlement. But perhaps their light, their presence had been only for her benefit, for her protection and instruction.

She got up with one last fond glance at the stream. "I'm sorry. I lost track of time. We've missed breakfast, and it's my fault. I hope you're not too hungry."

He smiled as she joined him, and they walked along the short path through the woods toward the pastures and the settlement beyond. "I brought a little something along, knowing I might be here for a while. With some to spare." He held out a bread roll stuffed with meat and cheese. "Already breaking the rules, I guess, but you were roused early and have had a busy morning. I doubt you'll spin away on just this for fuel."

He did, indeed, break the rules, as the dining room would have given her only half this much food. She accepted it gratefully, her rumbling stomach anticipating the feast. They laughed, and she consumed the offering without delay. As they walked through the orchard, Khari plucked two of the fragrant red fruits and handed one to Fajora. "Might as well finish breakfast properly."

And Fajora reflected that a Drissy could appear in any form when least expected. Fajora ate the sweet, energy-laden fruit and tossed the pit into the long grass at the edge of the pasture with a laugh. This time, her laughter held an unmistakable note of merriment.

35

— · —

INTERPRETING PROPHECY

When Khari left Fajora outside her house, she went straight to the infirmary. Time to get started on those things that came to hand.

But when she entered the building and looked toward Akachi's pallet, hoping for a welcome, she saw Chikelu sitting beside his son, his back to the door. The two were deep in conversation. Fajora's muscles twitched and she glanced toward the door and escape but then forced herself to take several steps toward the pair, trying to catch Akachi's attention.

Finally, the young cat's good eye flicked toward her. His shifting gaze alerted Chikelu to her presence. He turned to see what had caught Akachi's attention, and when he saw Fajora, his posture stiffened and he raised his nose, giving him an imperious demeanor. A low rumbled issued from his chest.

"You have no business here," he said. "Your presence dishonors my clan and my family. Please leave now, or I will be required to take stringent measures."

Akachi's ears perked forward, but he didn't glance at Fajora again, staring instead at a point somewhere on the wall beyond his father's head. He made it clear he would not contradict his father, even if he wished to. Fajora scurried back and yanked the door open. With one last glance at Akachi, she fled, ran to her house, and shut herself in. She leaned against the wall, taking in deep gulps of breath and clenching and unclenching her hands.

When she had calmed a little, she got a drink of water and washed her face. She had tried. Chikelu held his son to the old way of honor with tooth and claw and fatherly authority. She could have done nothing more. But until Akachi left the settlement, she wouldn't give up. She would merely wait for a more opportune moment.

So, what next?

She remembered the Rock Clan disk, hidden under her mattress. Retrieving it, she went out again, this time heading for the void ship hangar.

The center of the settlement bustled with activity, even more than on the previous day. The hurried pace and the solemn, determined faces suggested duties outside the normal routine. Humans moved supplies, prepared packs, and loaded and wheeled cartloads of food toward the north end of town, where a series of caves served as emergency shelters.

One workshop near the hangar hummed with exceptional busyness. Humans, from children nearly grown to aged adults, checked in with a clerk at one entrance and exited another door with metal devices of various shapes and sizes in their hands.

Weapons, Fajora realized with a shudder. The entire settlement armed itself. Some of these people would go into the wilderness to meet the enemy while others stayed behind to defend the settlement itself. And what would her role be? If she was here when Rock Clan attacked, she needed to help, as everyone else would do. She considered Rock Clan her foe as much as anyone's. For now, no one paid attention to her, intent on their own assignments.

She wondered if anyone would prevent her from entering the void ship. But she went up the ramp and entered without being challenged. She roamed through the pristine metal corridors, getting more confused with each step. Now she would have welcomed even an unfriendly face to give her directions, but the corridors remained empty.

At last, and only by accident, she found the little room where Sebastian had taken sanctuary. He sat hunched over his work station, but he didn't seem upset by the interruption. Keeping the disk hidden for the moment, Fajora took advantage of his good mood to pose the question she had been wrestling with.

"Why are these humans worried about rejoining the colony? They seem to think that would mess with prophecy."

Sebastian stared past her, his brows drawn together in thought then turned to his console and tapped rapidly on it. He held a hand up to stop her as she started to talk again, then pointed to words scrolling across his screen.

"This might be the one they're referring to. Look here." He ran a finger over a line of words. "It mentions the clans rising into the void to go to the aid of the catalyst. 'They will go as one people,' it says. And here, 'Those who have lived as one for generations will be the first to answer the call, and it will be unto them a great honor.' I've known of this text for a long time. Some experts think it refers to the tribes in the Arabah on Exalton, which are sometimes referred to as clans, but I've always wondered if it meant the cat clans."

"Couldn't it also refer to the clans and the colony? They've shared this world for three hundred years and counting."

"That's possible. Another text refers to them as aliens who have become brothers and sisters."

"Semantics. Could still refer to the colony and the clans. Though it is this clan, and not the colony, that has a ship capable of rising into the void."

Sebastian gave her a startled look, and his expression closed.

Fajora pressed him, convinced he kept something from her. "Is that why it has to refer to Deep Valley and not the colony?"

"Maybe. I suppose," he said, weighing his words, "with the colony's technological knowledge, they might have void flight capability when the time comes. But they have documents here the colony doesn't have, so they have more basis for their theories. I already know, after the short time I've been here, they believe unconditionally they will go as a mixed clan into their ship to answer when the catalyst needs them. Until that day comes, they are determined to keep themselves separate, to make sure the colony doesn't absorb them and destroy their destiny. They believe that would negate all the prophecy, in which case, the dark mortals and their Dark Immortal masters win."

Sebastian turned back to studying his manuscript. Fajora watched him, fingering the disk in her tunic pocket. She felt an illogical reluctance to give it up, but if this wasn't an opportunity that had come to her hand, what else was it?

"Sebastian?" He squinted up at her, something in her tone catching his attention. "Here's another idea. What if this prophecy refers to Rock Clan? Humans and cats have lived together there for longer than here in Deep Valley Clan. And they have a ship. They'll probably get it working someday, if no one interferes."

Sebastian wrinkled his nose, making plain his distaste at this idea. "I suppose they could interpret it that way. But I'm not sure they qualify as one people. The humans and cats barely tolerate one another. They don't like each other or work together the way the people here in Deep Valley do."

"I see your point. But they might believe it refers to them if they know the prophecies at all. Though I don't see them caring too much about the catalyst. As long as they're aligned with Dark Spinners and Dark Immortals, they're more likely to try to destroy the catalyst rather than come to his aid." She brought the disk out of her pocket and held it out to him. "Let's see if this offers any insight."

He stared at the disk a moment. "The disk Clarise made on Rock Clan's ship." He seized it.

Fajora let go of it with reluctance. "I want it back. I want to take it to the colony when I leave."

"Yes." He paused midway in pushing his chair back. "Sonja should see this. I'll have to go to another station to one of the few slots that may be capable of reading this old disk. Come on."

He led her to another room, where the sleek machinery and massive wall screens were interspersed with several pieces of equipment that looked old enough to have come from Rock Clan's ship.

Sebastian grinned. "I can guess what you're thinking. And you're right. Refugees from Rock Clan brought bits and pieces with them. I suspect Deep Valley has executed a raid or two, as well, based on what Dellu tells me."

He slid the disk into a slot roughly the same size. The old machine buzzed, and the sleek machines whirred in response. Pages of documents flashed across one of the screens. Sebastian tapped the console below, and the flood of information slowed.

"It's ships' logs," he said in a husky voice. "Some data is more than 600 years old. Three ships went out from Exalton. Explorers. Look at this entry. They made it all the way to Ara."

"Ara," Fajora murmured. "So Lesedi was right."

"What?" But Sebastian didn't wait for an answer. His eyes scanned the documents, his excitement palpable. "The Exaltons got into trouble on Ara. Tried to take over a region in the north part of the world, and the Arans fought back."

"The Arans didn't have technology. Still don't. How could they fend off lasers?"

"I don't know, but they seem to have driven the invaders away. The Exaltons took off in a hurry. Took prisoners with them." He paused. "Did you say something about Lesedi?"

"Yes. She claims to be of Aran descent. It's how she comes by her gift."

"Makes sense." Sebastian's mouth drew into a thin line, and Fajora guessed he thought about Clarise.

Sebastian tapped rapidly, and the flow of information sped up while more of the modern machines whirred into action.

"I'm making copies of this disk so I can study it later at my own station and you can take a better disk to Sonja. She won't have anything capable of reading this old Rock Clan disk. This world is tangled up with the rest of the Dominion in ways we never guessed. And with the prophecies. We need to study this information from all angles, here and in the colony. I hope you make it back. Sonja needs this information."

As she left the hangar later and headed to lunch, Fajora realized something else had been given into her hands. She was now a courier, perhaps one of her most important tasks. Because, as Sebastian had said, the tangled interrelationships of Kakislane with the rest of the Dominion loomed larger than anyone had guessed, with the possibility of far-reaching repercussions. She needed to start paying more attention to the prophecies herself, after all these years of ignoring them.

She noticed later, as she wandered around the settlement again, how often the clan's artistic designs reflected their belief in an interstellar mission. Intertwined amongst designs based on the natural world and a mix of human, feline, and owlish figures, were representations of the void ship, no longer in its hangar, but swooping into a place of stars and moons, its back end shooting a spray that appeared to represent sparks.

Though she hadn't noticed it before, she now saw this design, sometimes portrayed realistically, sometimes stylized, on pottery, weavings, woodcarving, and basketry. It showed up in clothing and on doorposts, and a scaled-down version had even been scratched into rocks by the entrances to some of the cats' dens. The clan indoctrinated its members with this idea from infancy. No wonder they believed it so adamantly and guarded their autonomy with such singlemindedness.

Fajora could not ignore the idea they might be right. Even Sebastian, after his extensive study, didn't know. And she had only dabbled in prophetic studies. She mustn't jump to conclusions because their idea was inconvenient to her own agenda. If the clan understood their destiny correctly, she was bound to do all in her power to protect them.

Had Jayzam made this same choice ahead of her? Had this same knowledge prompted his silence? If he had told all he knew, the colony, perhaps the Luxeran Service as well, would have investigated, leaving the treaty in shambles and clan life in upheaval. Enmity between species, held at bay for three hundred years, would have erupted, throwing this world into chaos. She felt her agenda to vindicate Jayzam slipping farther away and let it go with little more than a deep sigh.

At dinner Fajora found the void ship design on her empty plate and studied it, her mind whirling as she waited for her food allotment. It wasn't until Clarise's slim hand touched hers and traced the design with one finger that she became aware of Clarise and Sebastian taking seats on either side of her. Fajora greeted them with a welcoming smile. Clarise answered her greeting with a small smile, the first Fajora had ever seen from her. Sebastian's gaze followed Clarise's finger as it traced out the void ship design on the plate, and he grinned.

"See what I told you?" he said. "It's the same prophecy again."

Which she didn't need him to tell her. Especially since he continued talking without offering any new information on the topic. She was glad when their dinner arrived, interrupting his flow of chatter.

Fajora's portion was less than half the size Sebastian and Clarise each received. They stared at Fajora's plate until Sebastian burst out, "What in all the after-burners! Is someone angry with you? Did you offend the kitchen staff or something? Why is that all they gave you?"

"The council is trying to keep me here until they decide if I'm trustworthy or not. They know the best way to do that is to keep me too low on fuel to spin," Fajora explained.

Understanding widened Sebastian's eyes. "I heard something about that, but I didn't believe it. What a rotten thing."

"Yes, I agree."

What more could either of them say? Fajora ate slowly in order to savor her friends' companionship. In the end, the other two, even with their larger portions, finished before her. They left as soon as they finished.

"We're going to hunt up an herb Clarise wants for a medicine," Sebastian said by way of apology. "I don't know much about it, but the database suggests growing conditions are right down at the south end of the settlement. I promised Clarise we'd go look before it gets too dark."

"Go, then. And thank you for joining me."

Sebastian answered with a grin, and the two of them scurried away.

Leaning back, Fajora's gaze snagged on an orange, leathery fruit left behind on Sebastian's chair. Fajora didn't know its name, but she had eaten a half portion the day before and knew it tasted wonderful as well as being a great source of energy.

She pounced on the fruit, securing it in a pocket, before glancing at Clarise's chair. Here, an even greater offering awaited—a bread roll pulled open and stuffed with a slice of Clarise's meat and a generous slather of sauteed vegetables. Though unlikely, Sebastian could have dropped the fruit onto his chair by accident. Fajora had no doubt Clarise's stuffed bread, neatly positioned so as not to spill its contents, had been left on purpose.

Whispering a blessing on her friends, Fajora grabbed the bread and placed it carefully in her second pocket. Holding her hand over the lump it created and hoping to avoid notice, she hurried back to her house and closed the door. She also closed the shutters, and then, free from watching eyes, she withdrew the food and devoured it.

She had not found a single Drissy here in Deep Valley Clan, but a whole string of them. Different people, who, not knowing about each other, inadvertently provided her with a portion of the fuel she needed.

She tested her light, managing a spin that encompassed her hand and flickered up her arm into her torso. But it was weak. Trying to force a complete, sustained spin at this energy level was more likely to cause a permanent depletion than to end in a successful spin home.

She was grateful to her friends. But at the rate she progressed, Fazok would be dead and Kinovic in complete control of the enclave, if he wasn't already, by the time she got home. Clarise would be firmly under Lesedi's influence, unwilling to go home, and Fajora, herself, would be in disgrace.

36

THE WAY OF HONOR

Fajora's discouragement did not yet lead her into despair. The time of the owling approached, and she looked forward to sharing it with Akachi again, unless Chikelu had found a way to prevent him from joining her.

She grabbed a cushion and went outside, where she found the young cat waiting for her. He butted her leg in greeting as she settled near him. As they exchanged pleasantries, Fajora tried to assess Akachi's mood. He was subdued, but she didn't know if his quiet mood sprang from depression or if he merely adhered to a cat's formality and dislike of idle chit-chat. Either way, she might never have a better chance to talk to him without Chikelu's interference.

"Akachi, I must speak with you." She deliberately adopted a formal tone to emphasize the importance of her words.

"You may speak."

"It is always wise to consider custom and honor in light of Ya-Lohim's will."

"Yes. I see the wisdom in your words."

"When Ya-Lohim creates a thing of beauty, it is dishonorable to destroy it even when custom suggests otherwise."

"Yes, Light Spinner. That is truth."

"And this truth is an important reason for you to remain here in the settlement and help change old customs that destroy what Ya-Lohim has created."

"Ah." Akachi's tail twitched, as he considered Fajora's argument.

"Light Spinner," he said at last. "Would you not say to honor and obey one's parents is also pleasing to Ya-Lohim?"

"Yes, Akachi."

"So you will understand why I cannot stay. My father wishes me to honor the old ways, and I would dishonor him to do otherwise."

"Even if the Patriarch and Matriarch of the clan wish you to stay? Surely their opinions carry weight as well."

Fajora sat still, forcing herself not to add arguments while Akachi considered her words.

"Their opinion carries weight, of course," he said finally, "but I do not believe it supersedes the honor due a parent. Please speak no more on this matter. I wish to enjoy the owling with you without contention between us."

He turned to reposition his injured leg, giving Fajora a sidelong glance as he did so. She responded with a tiny nod, admitting defeat for the moment. She would have until tomorrow's owling to come up with more arguments.

After the owling, Akachi bid her goodnight and returned to the infirmary. Though he walked with greater confidence, his limp remained as prominent as on the previous day. Fajora shuddered, watching him. How long before he walked out of the settlement and disappeared into the wild? And what were his chances of survival once he lost the support of his clan and had to hunt half-blind and with a debilitating limp?

The following day, the bustle of war preparations increased. Humans joined the cats in scouting, in order to cover more territory. They carried food for a day or two, but other humans carried heavier packs as they set out. Lesedi, with whom Fajora ate breakfast, explained these were messengers going to solicit help from Deep Valley Clan's allies, Forest Clan and Meadow Clan.

"I think Forest Clan will come," Fajora said. "At least, I met a Forest cat who gave that impression."

"Both clans are pledged to come. It is not a matter of honoring agreements. It is a matter of finding them to call them to action."

"Will that be difficult?"

"Yes, perhaps. These clans have no human members and so do not gather permanently in a settlement as we do. They go where the prey is, in small groups or even alone. Only the mothers with kits stay in one place for a longer time period, but they cannot leave their young to answer our summons or to help locate available warriors."

"Perhaps I could help. Given enough fuel for a sustained spin, I can cover a lot of territory faster than even the swiftest cat." Fajora cast a suggestive glance toward her empty plate.

Lesedi shook her head, her smile amused. "And if you found a group of hunting Forest Clan cats, do you think they would respond to your call? "

"They can test me for truthfulness, even as your cats do."

"Even so, they would not come. The call must be made formally, by an established member of the clan and with the prescribed formulas."

"But that's crazy. Your safety, perhaps even your clan's existence, hangs in the balance, and you worry about rituals?"

"It is our way."

They walked out of the dining building to a buzz of excitement coming from the south end of the settlement. A group of cats emerged from around the houses a moment later, with other cats and humans hovering nearby or trailing behind. Fajora recognized several scouts who had left to patrol the border soon after she had arrived in the settlement. They clustered around a large female who walked with a slow, weaving step. As she approached, she turned her head toward Fajora, revealing a series of deep scratches, starting on the right side of her head, where her ear hung in a mangled mess, and traveling across her shoulder and down her side.

It was a wonder the cat had come so far, but this patrol had not included humans who could carry her, even if any had been willing. If she had not been able to make it to the settlement by her own power, the cats would have ended her life—the way of the clan.

Now she stopped and swayed. She appeared to be at the end of her strength. The short distance to the infirmary stretched impossibly before her, but none of the humans hovering around moved forward to help her. Lesedi made strangled noises in her throat, but she made no move to offer help either. Perhaps the cat would be insulted if someone offered help. Or perhaps—there must be a way.

Fajora stepped toward the cat, not rushing as she wanted to do, but with an attitude of respect.

"Brave warrior." She made a half-bow toward the wounded cat. "I see your sacrifice. It brings honor to your clan. You will bring honor to me as well if you allow me to carry you to the infirmary." She knelt in front of the cat and held out her hand but did not touch her.

The cat leaned forward to sniff at the hand and sighed. "You may." Her voice was faint, and she swayed again.

Fajora placed a hand on the cat's good side to steady her, then stepped to that side and got her arms under the cat, front and back, and lifted her. She was solid muscle and very heavy. Fajora staggered under the weight. She heard the cat's labored breathing and the small mew, too faint to carry beyond Fajora's hearing. She must not drop this cat, or the damage to her body and to her pride would be greater than if Fajora had not tried at all.

A man stepped forward as if to help, but Fajora held him off with a shake of her head. Though her light was weak, she felt it at the ready, and she let it travel through her arms and into the cat. She ignored the murmurs around her as the light sparkled and spun, concentrating on adjusting the light to absorb the burden of the cat's weight.

When she had her balance, as much as possible with the thin light that was all she could manage, she started slowly toward the infirmary. A blessing she had such a short distance to traverse. Lesedi walked alongside, her presence lending Fajora strength of will. Someone else dashed ahead and opened the infirmary door. She focused her eyes on the pallet next to Akachi's and headed for it without looking to the right or to the left.

But when she reached the pallet, she could not lower the cat to her resting place, even with the help of light. One of the doctors came to the rescue, grimacing, but not hesitating to touch her light and try to get a grip on her passenger. Fajora pulled her light back slowly and the doctor lowered the cat.

Fajora trembled from head to toe as she stepped back from the pallet. She looked for Akachi, wanting to reassure herself of his wellbeing after the shock of this new and devasting injury. His pallet was empty. Her stomach clenched.

A hand touched her arm. "Akachi's in the exam room with Doctor Tina. Just routine. Come out of the way." Vi steered her toward the supply room.

"I've never seen a cat come so far and not be able to make it to the infirmary," Vi said softly, turning to watch the bustle around the wounded individual. "When she faltered, no one knew what to do. The idea of being carried is anathema to a cat. You saved her life." She paused, giving Fajora a speculative look. "You may have given the clan a new idea to think about."

"I hope so. But I'm a bloody mess, now."

"Come in here." Vi drew her into the supply room and closed the door, shutting out the hubbub of the treatment room. "Let's find something for you to change into. And a snack. If I understand your physiology, your use of light has weakened you. Not good, with a war coming on." If only everyone showed such wisdom.

For the rest of the day, people watched Fajora, and even smiled at her, the first time she had felt such friendliness aimed toward her. But as they cast their eyes toward the infirmary, their smiles faded and they hurried about the business of preparing the settlement for war.

They tried to put Fajora to work. First an older woman found her and took her to the weaving room. Here a group of young girls sorted woven blankets into piles to be taken to the emergency shelter or sent with the humans who were joining the patrols. The woman explained the routines of the weaving room as she handed Fajora blankets to add to one pile or another.

"You need to find suitable work while you stay with us. Perhaps you will have a talent for weaving."

Fajora didn't think so, but she stayed, helping pile the blankets and carry them to the shelter. This gave her an opportunity to visit the shelter and assess it as a source of supplemental food. She hoped, with all the bustle of preparation, the shelter would be open, easy for her to enter. Her stomach rumbled as she recalled the cartloads of food that clan members had transported to this area.

Three deep caves comprised the shelter. Gates with iron bars secured the openings, and a contingent of humans and cats patrolled the area in front of the caves. Syjaz, who had not lost the ability to translate fully to shadow, would have easy access here. As spun shadow, he could slip through the bars without being noticed. However, Fajora must obtain enough food to fuel a full spin before the stored food became accessible to her.

Deflated, she slipped away from the blanket crew to do more reconnaissance in the central part of the settlement.

This proved more difficult than she expected. Clan members kept intercepting her and showing her places to help: the laundries, where workers washed and folded bandages; a small building where machines regulated the plumbing throughout the settlement and controlled emergency systems; and even the children's classroom, where the teacher pressed Fajora for a lesson in interstellar travel to keep the youngsters' minds off the impending conflict. This last opportunity tempted Fajora, but she managed to extract herself by suggesting a winter lesson, when more of the stars would be visible.

Late in the morning, they took her to the void ship and asked her to duplicate and catalog manuscripts for safekeeping. Ignoring the computer station assigned to her, which she didn't know how to use, she wandered through the ship until she found Sebastian. He showed her how to do the work at the station next to his and the two of them spent the shift discussing the finer points of the dragon commentaries. The pile of duplicate disks to be hidden in a secret location grew, but Fajora fidgeted and finally quit altogether. Though important, the work kept her from an even more vital task.

In the afternoon, Zuberi found her, took her to a small, fenced-off area, and handed her a long knife. "Everyone will need to be able to defend themselves if any Rock or River Clan cats get past the patrols and into the settlement. Our records show Light Spinner agents are skilled fighters, so this should come naturally to you."

"If you provide adequate fuel, I can use the weapon I've been training with for years. If you're going to keep me in the middle of your war zone, you should take advantage of my full capabilities."

He offered no response but a scowl as he pushed her into the middle of the practice area. He showed her how to hold the knife and demonstrated several moves for blocking attacks from the agile cats. Fajora cooperated, her curiosity compelling her to accept the knife and test this man's skill as they moved into a practice bout.

She equaled him in height, but he carried more bulk, more muscle. At first, she felt at a disadvantage because of her stiff leg, but as they circled, testing each other, her muscles warmed and the stiffness in her thigh eased. Their fighting styles differed, but his skill nearly matched hers. Their practice duel drew a small crowd of onlookers, most of whom cheered for her opponent and groaned and booed when she disarmed him.

Zuberi scowled and made her return the knife to the armory when they were done.

"I'll be hard-pressed to defend myself with my weapon locked away here," she commented.

"You haven't earned the right to carry a weapon, except in an emergency," he responded. "You may go now. Someone will open the armory in case of attack."

Fajora suppressed an irritated retort. Who would have time to open the armory in the middle of an attack, and how many cats would block access to her weapon as the attack unfolded? But she understood the clan's reluctance to arm her.

They wanted her skill but they didn't trust her. Probably a wise attitude. When Zuberi turned his back to straighten the selection of long knives, Fajora swiped a short knife with a slim sheath from a bin by the door and slid it into her boot. She intended to practice with it later in the privacy of her own house.

That evening, Akachi again refused to listen to any talk of staying in the settlement in defiance of his father's wishes, but he sat with Fajora for a long time after the owling. He said little, but he nuzzled her leg once, which she took as an invitation to stroke his fur. Darkness hid the compromise to his dignity from passers-by, and Fajora took full advantage of the opportunity.

But at last he shrugged her hand away and rose. "It has been a great pleasure to know you, Light Spinner. I cherish the wondrous memory of spinning with you on the trail. May you go with Ya-Lohim, and may he grant you all you desire."

He turned and limped away in the direction of the infirmary, leaving Fajora sputtering, too astonished to make the proper reply. She stared after him until his form disappeared into the darkness.

"Go with Ya-Lohim," she whispered. Then, more loudly, "Wait a minute. That sounded too much like goodbye. What's he up to?"

Akachi had chosen not to allow further treatment on his leg, since every procedure the medical staff suggested was as likely to damage the leg further as to improve it. And the doctors didn't know what else to do for his eye. He had no more reason to stay at the infirmary. Which could only mean . . . .

"No. It can't be. I need more time. I didn't give him all the arguments. I didn't say the most important thing. Akachi, wait."

Fajora jumped to her feet and scurried to the infirmary, leaving the cushion in the dust by her door. The interior of the infirmary was dimly lit, the main room deserted. Akachi's pallet, made up with a clean blanket and with a fresh bowl of water nearby, was empty.

"Hello? Is someone here?" Urgency lent a loud shrillness to Fajora's voice and brought hurried footsteps from the storage room. Ekene appeared at the door, data pad in hand.

"Fajora. What is it? Are you sick? Or injured?"

"Akachi, where is he?"

"He went out for the owling." Ekene glanced at Akachi's empty pallet. "He isn't back yet. But I thought he was with you."

"He left me a few minutes ago with a very formal farewell blessing. It took me a moment to process it, and by then he was gone."

"Hmm. Come to think of it, he spoke quite formally with me when he left as well." Ekene pressed his mouth into a grim line. "He must have decided not to stay in the settlement any longer. We've exhausted our medical options. I was trying to find a place for him to fit into clan life and contribute."

"And did you? Find a place for him?"

"No. Not yet."

"Then he's gone. Can we go look for him?"

Ekene closed his eyes briefly. "No. Not at night. Only the cats could hope to find him now, but they won't help us. This is what they expected him to do. They will find the action honorable and would not dream of taking Akachi's honor from him. Or of crossing Chikelu."

"Oh, honor! I'm starting to hate that word. All it's good for is to get him killed."

Fajora's hands balled into fists. Letting go of discipline, she marched to the wall and slammed first one fist and then the other into it. Pain exploded in both hands, but she welcomed it.

"Watch it." Ekene took her hands and massaged them, testing for damage. "You start breaking bones and you'll have even more problems than you do now." He finished his examination and patted her hands before releasing them. "Now, go home. Get some sleep. Maybe he'll change his mind when he gets hungry and show back up tomorrow. It's too soon to worry."

But Fajora knew it was late to begin worrying. She should have worried sooner and tried harder to talk Akachi into a new way of thinking. She should have told him how she felt, how it would devastate her if he died. But she had let him go, not paying enough attention, not believing in his determination.

She tested her access to light. With the extra food Sebastian and Clarise had slipped to her again today, her light continued to strengthen, but not enough, yet, to translate to a full spin. And without access to light, she couldn't leave the settlement tonight. She was as likely to meet a Rock or River Clan cat and fall into their claws as she was to find and rescue Akachi.

She spent hours pacing the confines of her house, unwilling to lie down and try to sleep. She practiced with the small knife, experimenting with different holds for the greatest defense against teeth and claws, but her growing proficiency gave her no satisfaction.

As her eyes drooped and she finally thought about resting for a while, Fajora felt Syjaz's dark aura again, hard and sharp and much too near. He hovered somewhere on the north edge of the settlement. He stopped along the base of the cliff, probably raiding the shelter for food.

He lingered a while before his aura moved again. His new trajectory took him to the vicinity of the void ship hangar, where he lingered again. After a while, his aura dissipated, but Fajora did not relax for a long time.

Deep Valley wanted to keep their ship and their technology a secret from the colony and from the Luxeran Service. But if Fajora's senses told true, Syjaz now knew those secrets, and he posed a far greater threat than the colony.

37

REQUESTS AND DEMANDS

Fajora spent more time pacing than sleeping that night. In the morning, Akachi remained missing. No one had seen him after he left Fajora. And as Ekene had predicted, no cat showed any interest in searching for the youngster. "He has accepted the way of honor, as he should," clan members responded to Fajora's inquiries. "It is not your place to question this honorable action," she heard several times when she pressed the issue.

Sebastian voiced his sympathy emphatically when he met Fajora at the breakfast table. Clarise took her arm and leaned close to whisper, "I'm so sorry."

Fajora caught her breath. Those were the first words she had heard Clarise utter. A piece of her rejoiced, even in her grief and anger over losing Akachi. But Sebastian and Clarise could do nothing to help find Akachi and bring him back, nor could Fajora be sure the clan would accept him now if he did come back.

Fajora left the dining hall more uncertain of what to do next than she had been since she arrived in the settlement. The Malekem had said to do whatever task came to hand, but she saw only a blank in front of her. She wanted to hunt for Akachi, but to what purpose? She wanted to work on procuring fuel, but she found every possibility blocked. And she no longer felt Syjaz's aura anywhere near the settlement, so she could not take her frustration out on him.

She sauntered toward her house, stopping several times to watch the activity around her, searching for inspiration. The human children walked toward the school building, playing along the way or loitering to watch the hurried preparations of the adults. Several kits tumbled over one another, wrestling and batting soft paws at each other. Others followed their parents toward the dens for their daytime sleep. A group of cats and humans entered the south end of the settlement, looking weary after a long patrol. The humans headed for the arsenal to check and recharge their weapons. The cats headed toward one of the larger dens where Fajora knew the cohort leaders received scouting reports. Everyone kept busy except her.

But when she arrived at her house, she found Ekene and Lesedi waiting for her, with Clarise hovering in Lesedi's shadow. Lesedi's face bore a hint of a frown, anxious but not unfriendly. Ekene clenched his jaw tight, and his usually placid face also wore a frown.

"Will you walk with us?" Lesedi asked. "Some things must be discussed."

They followed the path Fajora had walked with Bardu and Khari a couple of days earlier, to the north edge of the settlement, through the gardens and orchards, and toward the woodland beyond.

"The glade?" Fajora glanced back and forth between her silent companions. "What is this about? You wanted to talk to me about something?"

"Not yet," Ekene answered. "Not us."

His answer, cryptic though it was, prepared Fajora to find Obasi and Imani waiting for them in the glade near the stone seats.

The three humans and Fajora settled themselves on the damp, rugged stones. The cats circled them, sniffing and testing them. When they were satisfied, they found places for themselves among the stones, but sat silent for a while, as if uncertain how to begin.

"Thank you for coming, Light Spinner," Obasi said at last. "We must make this brief. The reports of the scouts are troubling. I fear Rock Clan will be upon us soon and we will go to meet them within our own territory. But the presence of enemy warriors in our land makes other matters urgent as well, which is why we called you here before we meet with the war leaders and take a brief rest."

"What matters would you discuss with me?"

"We regret," Imani answered, "you were unable to convince young Akachi to stay in the settlement."

"He hardly allowed me to bring up the subject, and he made his determination clear. I intended to keep trying. I didn't realize how soon he planned to go until it was too late."

"Ah, yes." Imani's tail flicked and she reached down to give her paw a couple of reassuring licks. "Chikelu has great influence with his son. And Ekene, I fear, had not found a place for him yet where he could contribute with honor."

"There is little a cat in his condition can do," Ekene said. "But if I'd had more time, I'm sure I would have come up with something."

"Perhaps there is another solution," Obasi said, "if the Light Spinner is willing to help."

This brought Fajora up straight. "Of course I'm willing. I'll do whatever I can for Akachi."

"Unfortunately, this solution must be pursued quietly. The council's decisions cannot be openly altered. Whatever we do in defiance of their decision must be done before clan members have a chance to object and stop us."

Fajora pondered this. "I don't understand. Did the council make a ruling about Akachi? Or, no. It's not a ruling about Akachi you're worried about. It's the ruling about me. You want me to leave the settlement and go after Akachi."

"You're the only one who can help him now," Lesedi said softly.

"I do not see how. Even if I could spin into the wilderness and had the good fortune to find him, he won't come back with me. He does not wish to shame his father."

"He won't come back as he is," Lesedi agreed. "But if his eye was healed?"

"Something that's beyond the skills of the clan physicians, I understand."

"Yes," Ekene intervened. "But I have always believed the colony outdoes us in medical expertise. Since I've had a chance to question Sebastian, I'm sure of it. Clarise can confirm that."

Clarise nodded.

Fajora let her breath out slowly, trying not to show her excitement. "You want me to find Akachi and take him to the colony doctors?"

"Yes."

"Will he go? It would be frightening for him."

Ekene smiled. "He has a great fondness for you. We feel he would go, but only with you."

"And how am I to accomplish this? I require sufficient high-energy food to fuel a full spin and detailed information on how to find Akachi. Will you provide these things?"

Obasi lifted a front paw, a restless motion. "I can take care of the second requirement. I have many duties to fulfill today and need my rest, so we will wait until after nightfall. Akachi will be denned somewhere during the hot hours and hard to find until he comes out to hunt. If he comes out to hunt. Either way, we will have more chance of finding him tonight. I will be with a patrol, but I will break away from them, and we will track him together. We believe he went south, and there are certain areas where the prey is small, which are better hunting grounds for one such as Akachi. Look for me three moonprowls after sundown. Here are directions on where to meet me."

He scratched a rough map in the dust with an unsheathed claw, explaining the terrain and describing landmarks that would lead her to the meeting spot, including a tree with a thick covering of moss and a rock shaped like the head of a spring deer.

"And do I need to worry about patrols intercepting me and trying to stop me?" Fajora asked, studying the crude map and memorizing each part as the Patriarch spoke of it.

"Most of the patrols will be closer to our borders. We are expecting the incursion to begin any time and are keeping close watch on those places where our enemy has the best access. A greater danger than tangling with our own patrols is intercepting invading members of Rock Clan. They make it farther into our territory every night before our patrols find them and chase them out. If I smell any Rock Clan cats, I will do my best to draw them away from you while you continue to search for Akachi. It should be easy, for I am old and sometimes move clumsily through the wilds, an irresistible target." He made a chuffing sound, very like Jelok's laughter.

Fajora caught herself responding with a smile and quickly forced a more sober expression. "What if we can't find Akachi?"

Obasi sobered as well. "That will not be well. If he is not successful in the hunt, he will weaken and easily become a victim of Rock Clan invaders. Each day will lessen his chances, and I may not be able to help you another night."

"Hmm. What about the food?"

Now the cats looked away. Fajora turned toward the humans. Ekene and Lesedi had also averted their eyes. Only Clarise met her gaze, her lips pulled into a troubled pucker.

"The cats do not keep the kind of food you need," Imani said presently. "And we cannot give orders to the human custodians without drawing attention to our plans and alerting those who oppose us. We cannot help you."

"Ekene? Lesedi?"

They looked at Fajora now, and what she read in their gazes did not please her.

"I don't have access to the storage facilities," Ekene said. "If we had human patients at the infirmary, we might have food on hand, but we have nothing now."

"Lesedi?"

"No. I don't have access either. I sometimes teach the children, but even their snacks are provided by the kitchen staff and not kept in the schoolroom."

"But I thought you had special training," Ekene added. "Don't you know how to break into places and get what you need? In the old stories, Light Spinning agents always turned to light and slipped under doors, or through windows. In one story, they even went through a solid wall."

"Yes, of course I can do that." Fajora let a little sarcasm filter into her voice. "I have done it, fully fueled. But if I were fully fueled now, enough to produce the kind of thermal energy needed to go through a wall, I wouldn't need to break into the food storage to get fuel, now would I?"

A flush crept up Ekene's neck and into his face, and Fajora immediately regretted belittling him. He had supported her in the past, and she had expected to take care of the fuel problem for herself anyway.

"I'll do what I can," she said, giving Ekene an apologetic smile. "I'll have to find a way. You're very trusting of each other around here, so who knows? Maybe the doors to the storerooms aren't even locked."

"You bring honor to your people," Obasi said. "And now I must ask one more thing of you."

Oh, great! From no tasks to too many.

"What is it?"

"We do not know the colony's ways or values, and our people do not trust them. The humans here have lived among us a long time and understand our ways, but the humans of the colony always try to take advantage or exert control. When you return to them with Akachi, you must be careful what you say, not only concerning what you have learned about us but also about the human colony and the ship in Rock Clan territory."

"They are in league with Dark Spinners." Fajora twirled her hand, imitating tendrils of shadow. "It's my mission, the mission of all Light Spinner agents, to root out the Dark Spinners wherever they have influence. I can't ignore it. I can't let them do whatever they want. What if they fix their ship and take off into the void for other worlds? They could do a lot of harm."

Lesedi broke in, speaking urgently. "You must understand. It is not your duty, or the duty of the colony, to keep watch over them or keep them from making mischief. It is our duty, one we took on three hundred years ago, when the first humans joined Deep Valley Clan and discovered the Rock Clan humans. *We* will make sure they do not take their ship into the void. *We* will keep them from harming the other clans, and even from harming the colony. You have your mission, yes, but Rock Clan is ours. You must leave it to us."

"We'll see. I make no absolute promise. And I wonder, regarding your own ship, your own technology—why did you show them to me if you want to keep them such a secret?"

"Imani decided I should. She told me to explain it all to you. We believed if I convinced you of the importance of who we are and what we are working toward, you would want to protect our privacy. You had already guessed so much, anyway. You needed to understand why you can't tell anyone."

"Yes." Obasi got to his feet, his tail swishing in agitation. "Only one circumstance releases you from that stricture. If we are overcome by Rock and River Clans in the coming conflict, you must tell the colony. Then they must stop Rock Clan. But I do not believe we will falter. Deep

Valley Clan warriors are strong and valiant, and we have stalwart allies. We will prevail."

"And what of the humans, like Clarise, who become Rock Clan's victims? Will you take care of them also? What of the humans of Rock Clan who do not want to be there and are also victims? What of Drissy, my little friend, who helped me and begged me to take her with me? Will you intervene to save her, as you did not do for Clarise?"

Silence fell over the little glade. Obasi sank back down into a crouch and wrapped his tail close around his body.

Imani answered in a low voice. "This Drissy, she will find us when she is ready."

"Yes," Lesedi broke in. "We can't remove her from her mother, but we will keep a watch for her. We have had others, my mother and I among them, and Drissy will not be the last. We will be able to help her. All she needs to do is make the first move. From what these others have told me, she will come soon. As for Clarise . . . ."

"We beg the forgiveness of young Clarise," Imani said. "We were remiss, and the honor of our entire clan suffers because of it."

Fajora wanted push Imani to say or do more. A simple apology seemed far too little too late. But these clan members had made concessions today, and she wouldn't say anything to jeopardize Obasi's willingness to help her find Akachi. So she bit back the quick retort. Clarise was safe now, and that would have to suffice.

A light hiss sounded from the entrance to the glade, drawing everyone's attention. A young cat, even younger than Akachi stood there, tail lowered in a submissive attitude.

"What is it, Mosi?" Obasi asked.

"Pardon, Patriarch." The young cat spoke quickly, as if he had memorized his message and wanted to relay it before he forgot. "A scout has returned with an ambassador from Forest Clan. They will join us in battle if they can gather their members in time. He wishes to speak with you."

Obasi made a quiet mewing sound. "Thank you. You have done well. Please tell the ambassador I will join him in a short time. I am grateful he is here."

"Yes, Patriarch." The youngster scampered away.

"Good news, I guess," Fajora commented. "So you now have pressing business to attend to, and I have a pantry to raid. Is there anything else?"

She gathered from the reaction of the cats, from their unwillingness to look her in the eye, that they had more to say. "Well, what is it?

"Only this," Imani said. "Our humans have the old prophecies intact, but young Sebastian informs us new writings are expected from his faraway world, which the humans came from in the old days. He has heard rumors of further prophetic words being smuggled out of that world. These writings might now be with the creatures he calls dragons. We must have all the prophecies if we are to interpret them correctly. So, when they become available to the colonists, you will see they are delivered to Sebastian. Get word to Meadow Clan and they will help you contact us."

Fajora stared at Imani until the sound of her silence became deafening. Suddenly weary and angry, she felt sharply out of place here. She longed to go home and bury her head in Jayzam's shoulder and forget clan wars and prophecies and supercilious cats who felt authorized to dictate and control her life. She may have transgressed by infiltrating clan territory, but she had been through a lot, and this was too much.

She stood, startling the rest of the circle. "I would like to believe you don't understand what you are asking, but I think you do. Either way, I can tell you this isn't how it works. If you assume you have the right to make demands of me and of the colony, you are wrong. You make an issue of what I can and cannot reveal to the colony, to my enclave. You want no information to flow out of this territory, but you expect whatever information you desire to flow into it. But no. You have Sebastian. You have his knowledge. You'll have to be content with that. If you want more information in the future, you'll have to find a way to work with the colony to get it."

She narrowed her eyes and let her gaze pass over each individual before her. She only softened her gaze for Clarise, who had made no demands. No one spoke or tried to stop her when she strode from the glade.

Later, sitting in her house and staring at the walls, trying to plan, she asked herself what she would have done on the day she snuck out of the colony outpost, if she had known all that would transpire and the kind of mission she would ultimately find herself in. Would she have come?

When the answer came, a resounding *yes,* she turned her mind to serious planning.

38

CLARISE HELPS

Fajora's previous explorations paid off now, for she knew which building housed the main food storage facility. She had observed workers carrying various foodstuffs from the facility, including the types of food she needed: high-energy nuts and grains, honey, and dense fruits and vegetables. She hoped to get her hands on some of the wafer cakes the rescue team had carried, which had provided a higher source of energy than anything else she had eaten while with the clan. She suspected they were products of the high-tech replicators, designed to provide extra energy in a compact form for long journeys.

After a long day of waiting, she sat in front of her house for the owling as she had done every evening since she arrived in the valley. She missed Akachi with an ache so intense she almost went inside and closed the door to shut out the song. Instead, to honor him, she remained in her place and let the music of the owls wash over her like balm, grasping the moment of peace, as if taking a deep breath before plunging into an icy river.

When the owling died away and the owls had moved off for the nightly hunt, Fajora went back inside and took advantage of the shower spigot in her washroom, washing with plain water and avoiding the scented soap supplied for her use. The strong scent of the soap would be too vivid a signal for any cats hunting for her.

She had no gear, so her preparations were complete. She sat in her dark house and waited, working through the mental exercises all agents used to keep calm before a mission. Out of practice, she struggled to keep her focus.

When a check out the window assured her the settlement had quieted for the night, she slipped out her door and started toward the central compound. She kept to the shadows, and when she reached the supply building door, she stood motionless for a long time, watching the houses and open spaces in front of her for any sign of movement. Finally convinced no one loitered nearby who might see her, she reached out with one hand and tried the latch.

It sprang open, and the door gave. Fajora took one more careful look around the front of the building and hurried inside, closing the door behind her. A single blue light gleamed on a console at the far side of the entryway. An alarm?

She hesitated. But boldness, not hesitation, made for successful missions. She touched the latch on the inner door. The silence continued. She turned the knob. Still no shrill alarm, though she tensed, ready to dash through the outer door at the first sound. She pushed the door open and the blue light winked, but the silence held. Based on her experiences with the Wellador Colony's technology, including their sophisticated sensors, she guessed the light indicated a similar sensor with the ability to record movement. But, understanding a little about the bucolic nature of the settlement, she assumed no one would see the recording until she was long gone.

Metal plating lined the inner room, interspersed with metal doors, each containing a screen on its upper panel. The screens glowed with a dim grey light. Fajora touched one, and the light brightened as a flow of words passed down one side. Leaning close, she read a list of the food-stuffs and other supplies stored behind that door. And, at the bottom of the screen, one word—*Password*—with a blinking blank space beside it.

She touched other screens with the same result. She tried the door handles. Not one budged. She could spend all night trying to guess the password without success. Shaking her head and breathing hard, trying to calm the pounding of her heart, she stood in front of the door with the supplies she most wanted and contemplated her options.

Humans must store supplies in other places. Families in shared homes did not always eat in the communal dining room. They must have food storage. She knew which houses sheltered the families, but breaking into one of them without rousing anyone would be difficult and risky, even if she could be sure they had what she needed. The orchard presented another possibility, but she would have to eat a lot of fruit to derive sufficient energy, and it would be hard to transport.

She had to find a way to get behind one of these doors. Creating thermal energy hot enough to pass through metal took tremendous amounts of fuel. But perhaps a light sword would penetrate, if she had the energy to create one and hold it steady. She hated to destroy the door, but she had run out less destructive options.

She reached for light. It came at once, tingling through her arm and hand, but not as strong and steady as she had hoped. She let her favorite sword hilt form in her hands. So far, good enough. Then she extended the blade. It thickened and spun, if not exactly fast, at least at an adequate speed, but the farther she extended it, the thinner and slower it spun.

With an exclamation, she let it dissipate, knowing she did not have the strength to cut through even a much thinner, lighter-weight substance than the metal she faced now. She took a step toward the outer door, thinking of the fruit in the orchard. She didn't really have time to visit the orchard, but what other option did she have?

Try to guess the passwords, perhaps. Not knowing what else to do, she tapped on the screen of her chosen door and thought about keywords a Deep Valley Clan member might choose.

Void Ship. No.

Prophecy. No.

Honor. Still no.

Clan Honor. Not that either.

Deep Valley Honor. Again, no.

"Fajora?" A soft voice broke Fajora's concentration.

She whirled around, her hand curled and ready for her sword, though she waited to reach for light. In the darkness, she could not see who had discovered her. She didn't recognize the voice, but heard no threat in its tones. And whoever it was, they spoke her name as if they knew her.

"Who's there?"

"Clarise." The voice was still soft, hesitant.

"Clarise?" Fajora's voice hitched on her surprise. "What are you doing here?"

"Helping." Her voice gained strength and confidence.

"Thank you, but what can you do?"

A shadow moved toward Fajora, resolving into the familiar form of Clarise as the young woman drew near enough for the weak light of the panel to illuminate her face. Clarise raised her hand to the panel, then peered closely at Fajora.

"This one?"

"Yes."

Fajora held her breath as Clarise tapped in a series of letters, numbers, and symbols. They didn't make a recognizable word or have any obvious sense about them. Fajora would never have guessed them if she had tried all night. But as Clarise finished, the panel pinged and the door handle buzzed. Clarise grabbed the handle and turned it. As the door slid open, a light sprang on in the storage room beyond.

"Ya-Lohim's blessings," Fajora breathed, grinning at Clarise as she entered the room.

Woven bags hung on a peg near the door. Fajora grabbed one and headed for the rows of shelves lining the room. She found the wafer cakes and shoved a pile of them into her bag. Bags of nuts went in next, and several blocks of wax that encased honey. She hesitated at the shelf piled with jerked meat, but finally tossed in a large handful of neatly wrapped sticks. She didn't like them, but she remembered how much energy similar meat products had supplied on the trail. This room held no fresh produce, but she found packets of dried fruit of several varieties. She topped off the bag with as many of these as fit comfortably while allowing the bag to close.

The bag was fitted with shoulder straps so it could be worn as a pack. Slinging it over one shoulder, she turned back to Clarise, who stood in the doorway to make sure it didn't close and shut them either in or out.

"How did you know?" Fajora asked slipping past her into the outer room. "That I stood here wishing for help? And how did you get the password?"

"I've been watching for you. Nearby. I saw you come."

Fajora had taken such care on her approach. But Clarise had spent two years cultivating the ability to be still. It would have been easy for her to watch from the shadows without moving a muscle, undetectable to even the most discerning eye.

"And the password?"

"I helped with clean-up this evening. I offered to put extra supplies away, and they gave me the passwords without a second thought. I memorized them all. I didn't know which ones you would need."

"You'd make a good agent, Clarise. If you were a Light Spinner, I'd sponsor you at the training academy. But you're human, so I don't know how I can repay you for this. What can I do?"

Clarise clutched her sleeve and her lips trembled. "Take me home."

Fajora grabbed Clarise's arms to calm the sudden shaking in her own hands. Her vision blurred briefly and she knew her eyes flecks swirled with uncontrolled giddiness. But when she looked Clarise in the eyes, the girl didn't flinch.

"Are you sure?" Her voice shook and she steadied it. "Lesedi believes you should stay here where she can help you deal with your trauma."

"No. Lesedi has helped me. But I want my mother."

"Ah, Clarise." Fajora pulled the young woman into a tight hug. "I'll do everything I can to get you home. But you'll have to wait a little, please. I have to find Akachi first. Before it's too late."

"Yes. I know. But," Clarise's voice faltered, "come back for me, please."

"Yes. I promise. No matter what happens, I'll take you home."

"Thank you." Clarise's arms tightened around Fajora.

"No. Thank you. With your help tonight, you may have saved my life, and Akachi's too." Fajora's voice was husky.

"But you saved mine first." Clarise pulled away and smiled, before slipping away through the doors and out into the nighttime shadows.

Fajora wiped her eyes, trying to clear vision that kept blurring. She stepped out, pulling doors closed behind her, one after another. She studied the shadows even more carefully than she had before entry, but if anyone watched her, they were as careful and still as Clarise had been. As swiftly as she dared, Fajora made her way back to her house.

She had her hand on the latch when a shadow detached itself from the far corner and approached. She felt the tingle of adrenaline and instinctively reached for light.

"Fajora?"

She relaxed, recognizing Sebastian's voice.

"Yes. What is it?"

"I hear you're leaving."

"How did you . . . ?"

"Never mind. I have ways. I want you to take these to Sonja." He pushed several hard, flat objects into her free hand. "Disks. The manuscripts the colony is missing. She'll need them." He hesitated, then continued in a shaky voice. "Are you taking Clarise with you?"

"Has she spoken to you?"

"No. But I know what she wants."

"She asked to go home. I can't take her while I hunt for Akachi, but I promised to come back for her. You could come too."

His pause stretched longer this time. "No. I need to stay here, for a while at least. I have things to learn from these people. Important things. I'll try to come later. Tell Clarise."

"Tell her yourself. You'll have time before I come back."

"Yes. Maybe."

As suddenly as he had appeared, he disappeared, melting into the shadows of the houses. Fajora peered around, wondering who else would appear out of the darkness. But if anyone idled nearby, she didn't see them. She pulled on the door latch and let herself in before anyone else could stop her.

39

—·—

WILDERNESS CONFRONTATION

With the door fastened securely, Fajora sorted through her plunder, organized it, and repacked what she didn't intend to eat right away. After removing four wafer cakes, a package of nuts, and a package of dried fruit, she hid the packed bag behind the bed, out of the way in case someone paid her an unexpected late-night visit. A filled water flask, packed in her bag beside the food, rounded out her supplies. With everything ready, she turned out the light and sat in the dark, eating her way through her selected food.

Her highly strung metabolism felt a surge by the time she munched halfway through the second cake. By the time she started on the nuts, she tingled with energy. She felt normal for the first time since she'd lost her pack, but she didn't try to spin yet. She kept eating until she had consumed her whole pile of food, then went to the bag and pulled out another cake, and, after a moment's hesitation, a meat stick.

She disposed of the wrappings from her feast before she allowed herself to test her light. She didn't need the test. She felt the energy soaring through her. But she wanted confirmation, and it was such a pleasure to spin. She took her time, savoring the sensation of turning from physical substance into light, spinning in a tightly controlled spiral, impatient to soar through the night.

She coalesced after a short trial. She had more than enough fuel to get home now, but she had a task to perform first and hoped to arrive in the colony with a passenger or two. She must save her energy until she needed it, not play with it merely for the joy of the experience.

She sat down to wait, hoping her sense of time did not betray her tonight. As she waited, she became aware of a Luxeran aura nearby. Nebulous at first, it grew stronger and she recognized Syjaz. She stood, ready to rush out and find him now that she had the power to confront him. Then she sat again, slowly, reigning in her impulses with great effort. She must not let anything interfere with her primary task at hand—finding Akachi.

Syjaz's timing posed a dangerous liability. She could not have him following her on the hunt. She would have to elude him, or find some other way to keep him out of the game. A couple of ideas came to mind, but she dismissed them, at least for now. Syjaz's aura drifted through the settlement with random, jumpy progress, furtive and tense. He might not be aware of her as he focused his attention on spying out the settlement.

She pulled her awareness in, as she had done during the Dark Spinner visit in Rock Clan. As time passed and Syjaz's aura lingered, it became difficult for Fajora to banish her awareness of passing time. If she didn't leave soon, she might miss Obasi and, without his help, be unable to find Akachi. But she forced herself to remain still and closed, with only a sliver of her awareness reaching out to test for the Dark Spinner's aura.

At last, she felt the distance between herself and the dark aura grow, until she no longer sensed it at all. Only then did she snug her food pack onto her back and leave her house, moving quietly and keeping to the shadows. She walked rather than spinning. The bright light of her spinning would be visible to any member of the clan who prowled about and a beacon to Syjaz if he remained within sensing range. She held herself ready, light almost sparking from her fingertips, prepared to get away or defend herself, if necessary. But she kept the light tightly leashed until she reached the south edge of the settlement's fields and orchards.

South of the cultivated land, the valley narrowed to a deep canyon through which the river sluiced with increasing speed. Rocky paths climbed out of the canyon on either side. The cats would have no trouble traversing these paths in the dark, and even the humans would find them navigable, provided they were familiar enough with them to anticipate twists and jutting rocks.

For Fajora, they presented too much risk in the dark. An injury could end her search before it began. She must resort to her natural ability, which she had honed into a weapon the way the teeth and claws and night vision of the cats were weapons. Translating into light, she skimmed the surface of the water, following the river down the canyon.

Fajora coalesced back to her physical form as soon as she had navigated the canyon and reached more manageable terrain. The temptation to keep spinning, to dart through the wilderness until she reached the colony, grew stronger the longer she held to the light. But she would not find Akachi in that mode. Though she perceived many things while spinning light, one small cat in the wilderness created too inconspicuous a target. If he had companions, she might have tried it, for a group traveling together presented a larger sphere of movement. But she might zoom right over the solo cat and never know she had missed him.

So, with reluctance, Fajora resumed her physical shape and scanned for landmarks, keeping the rough map Obasi had drawn for her clear in her mind. The rock formation shaped like the head of a deer stood out in the light of the waning moon, ahead and to the left. At least, she hoped it was the correct rock. She did not have the cats' experience with deer, but her limited knowledge gave her enough confidence to proceed.

A huge tree covered thickly with moss, which she found by accident when she braced herself against it to avoid a fall, reassured her. Another landmark, identified after an additional fifty paces, bolstered her confidence. She had come to the right area. Now she must wait in the dark, hoping Obasi found her, since she had no idea which way to go next.

While she waited, Fajora pulled a wafer cake out of her bag, making a quick snack to top off her energy levels. As she swallowed the last bite, a warning hiss set her limbs tingling, prepared for flight or conflict.

A moment later, Obasi stalked out from a thick stand of trees and greeted her. "Light Spinner. You should have been here sooner. I feared you were not coming."

"A Dark Spinner visited the settlement. To elude him, I had to wait."

Obasi uttered a low growl, and, as her eyes adjusted to the dim light, Fajora saw his tail swishing back and forth in low, strong sweeps.

"Come then," he said, giving her a quick sniff before nudging her hand. "I have found Akachi's trail. It is old, probably from last night, but he left enough scent for me to follow. We must find him before invaders arrive."

"Is Forest Clan coming?"

"They will come. I do not know when. We must be ready with what we have. I must finish this and return to my patrol. No more talk."

Fajora followed in the night lit only by a crescent moon, obscured as often as not by drifting clouds. She tried to suppress memories of a similar nighttime trek with Akachi, not so long ago. At least Obasi did not lead her into any rivers, though they walked alongside one for a while.

When they left the river, Obasi picked up the pace, moving so fast across rugged terrain Fajora had difficulty following him. When he finally paused to wait for her, she asked, "Why are we going so fast? Is someone following us?"

"Not yet, but many cats are moving about this region. They have left their scent as a signal for me to find, and they are not of Deep Valley Clan. They might find our trail at any time. And Akachi's trail is now clear, his scent left within the last few moonprowls. I am anxious to find him before Rock Clan finds us. I forgot you would not be able to catch his scent and follow the trail as easily as I. We will slow a little, but you must come as fast as you are able."

Fajora pushed herself, holding light at the ready to help her if she stumbled. Obasi set a brutal pace and only remembered occasionally to slow down and give her a brief break. She worried her heavy breathing would give them away to any nearby cats. What if Rock Clan had discovered them and followed from behind while Obasi's nose worked only on the path ahead?

She tried not to think about the possibility that they would not find Akachi. Or worse, that Rock Clan would find him first and kill him before Fajora could rescue him. His slow, broken body stood no chance against cats on the warpath. She blinked away the vision of Akachi's dead body splayed across the middle of their trail somewhere ahead.

When Obasi stopped abruptly, Fajora crashed into him, uttering an exclamation, as if crying out at her loss before it was confirmed.

"Hush," Obasi whispered. "Rock Clan cats. Nearby."

Fajora froze while Obasi nosed around the area, first in a tight circle, then in a widening arc. When he returned to her side and sat on his haunches, she leaned close to whisper, "Akachi? Have they found him?"

"They are close. But they will be more interested in a warrior on the prowl than in a wounded young cat. I will lead them toward my patrol, which is not far away. You find Akachi."

"How? Where is he? How close?"

"Follow this line of trees until you come to a rocky area with deep ravines. I believe he is somewhere there."

Letting a continuous growl rumble out from his chest, Obasi slunk into the trees and disappeared. Fajora watched him go with a sinking in her stomach. He had the advantage, being in his own territory, but if he encountered too large a group of Rock Clan cats, his advantage would disintegrate.

But Fajora could not follow him, and she wouldn't let him put himself in danger for nothing. She started along the trees, listening as she went and watching every moving shadow. A noise a little way ahead made her jump, until she recognized the call of an owl. Perhaps a random call? But Sanaa had assured her owls never made random calls. A warning, then, or a call to attract her attention?

She continued toward the ravines, treading softly, trying not to announce her presence to any Rock Clan cats with unnecessary noise. When she reached the first ravine, she hesitated. Should she walk along the top edge and peer down, or walk into the ravine and scan both the floor and the edges? Walking on top would make her more visible to enemy eyes, but on the bottom, she would be more vulnerable to attack, for no cat would have difficulty jumping on her from above.

Checking to make sure she held light at the ready, Fajora opted for the lower path. She walked slowly, scanning the ravine floor and its upper edges, but a cat's voice floating to her from above her head still made her jump.

"Light Spinner, why are you here? Are you lost?"

She shifted in the direction of the voice, though she could not see the cat. "Akachi, is it you?"

"Yes, Light Spinner. Who else would it be?"

"A patrol, perhaps."

"No, it is only I, alone and out of the way of any patrols."

"Not so far out of the way, actually. Obasi is even now leading Rock Clan cats toward his patrol."

"Why is he alone? That is dangerous with enemy cats on the prowl. He should not have left his designated group."

"He helped me hunt for you, but he left to lead them away from us."

"Ah. It is a ploy?"

"Yes."

"Why?"

"He and the Matriarch don't believe Ya-Lohim wants me to remain with the clan."

Akachi thought this over. "That is good," he said finally. "But why does he wish for you to find me?"

Fajora took a deep breath and sent a silent plea to Ya-Lohim. "He wishes me to take you to the colony with me."

Another pause. "Why?"

"We hope their doctors can restore your sight and heal your leg." She heard a slight hiss and rushed on. "We don't know if it's possible, but I'm sure they'd be willing to try. But only if you're willing to let them."

"And I'd live in the colony?" His voice was plaintive, like a kit's tiny meow.

"The Patriarch and Matriarch believe the clan will accept you back if your vision allows you to contribute to the clan as before."

A slight scuffling sound and a murmur, almost a growl, helped Fajora find Akachi in the dim light. He crouched on a rock ledge about ten paces from her and a little higher than her reach. Concentrating, she picked out the gleam of his eye. He made no additional sound, nor did he move again. Fajora waited until her legs ached from standing still and her neck developed a crick from staring up at him.

"Akachi? What do you say? Will you come to the colony?"

"These doctors. Do you know them?"

"Yes. Some of them. A little. Enough to trust them."

"And will you stay with me?"

"Yes. I'll do my best. If the humans and my own people will let me. Yes. I'll make sure they let me."

Another long silence ensued. Fajora tried to be patient. Such a huge decision would make her hesitate, even though she was familiar with the colony and its doctors. How much more world-shattering it would seem for Akachi.

She wanted to sit. A flat rock under Akachi's ledge offered a suitable spot, but she hesitated to cause any distraction or put pressure on Akachi by showing signs of impatience.

She turned her face away from the inviting rock, determined to remain still as long as possible. Making only the slightest movement, she rose up to stretch her calves, feeling an ache in her thigh as she did so and marveling at the medical technology of the Deep Valley Clan humans. They weren't as advanced as the colony, but they could still do amazing things. Her wounds, which would have taken two moon cycles to heal under the ministrations of Luxeran medicine, were only a slight irritation after Doctor Tina's treatments.

Easing back onto her heels with a grateful sigh, she hunched her shoulders to work on the crick in her neck. As she settled back into her quiet stance, sudden movement from the ledge startled her, drawing her attention upwards again.

Akachi lumbered to his feet, his ears twitching. The sound of his snuffling sounded loud in the stillness, but his voice came in a hushed whisper.

"Light Spinner. I scent cats nearby. Several at least, and only one is of Deep Valley Clan."

A shiver tingled down Fajora's spine and into her legs as she instinctively reached for light. Holding herself ready to create a sword or surge into a full spin, she rotated, searching the shadows and listening. A yowl broke the silence, followed by hisses, barely audible.

"It is the Patriarch." Akachi sank back down into an awkward crouch. "We must help him. I cannot run, so it will be your task to get us there."

"How? Oh. You want me to spin?"

"Yes. And carry me as you did on the return from Rock Clan."

Fajora embraced light gladly. Well-fueled, she had no difficulty absorbing Akachi into her spin. His sharp ears had honed in on Obasi's location, and, though the spin muted their senses, Fajora understood Akachi as he directed her to a stand of trees close to Obasi.

She coalesced around ten meters away from the Patriarch. Akachi wobbled as he reformed and snuffed loud and hard for the space of about twenty heartbeats, but he gave no further concession to the nausea that often beset non-Luxerans after a spin. With one last, loud huff, he set off toward the ruckus beyond the trees.

They found Obasi in a clearing, surrounded by intruders. His quick movements and unsheathed claws held them off for the moment, but he faced six gray cats. They kneaded the ground in front of them and kicked up soil with their back claws, spoiling for a fight and losing patience.

Fajora recognized the markings on several of them. One she identified as the guard outside her house in the Rock Clan settlement on the night of her rescue. Akachi's growl alerted the intruders, and several of them paced to one side and then around. In a moment the six cats surrounded Fajora, Akachi, and Obasi in a slowly tightening circle.

Akachi and the Patriarch assumed a defensive position, flank to flank, facing toward the Rock Clan cats at slight angles from each other. Fajora drew near Akachi on his other side and readied her light. Her fingers tingled with the beginnings of her sword hilt, but she didn't push it any farther yet. If this confrontation ended in violence, almost a certainty, she didn't want to be the one to provoke it.

One of the Rock Clan cats eased ahead of the others and sat on his haunches, nose in the air. He had one white paw and white markings across his shoulders. This cat had wanted to give her to Dark Spinners. A name hovered on the edge of Fajora's mind. Groknor, friend of the dark ones. Fajora shifted her eyes, searching for Syjaz, and reached out for his aura. But the only Luxeran aura she felt was her own.

While the other cats held positions around a loose circle, Groknor paced in a tighter circle. Obasi and Akachi held their position, turning their heads and swiveling their ears to keep track of Groknor, but Fajora moved to the flank, turning as Groknor circled around. He stopped at the back of his circle and sat, studying her with unblinking eyes.

"So, the one who killed Jelok thinks to resist yet again. Do you not know that once you belong to Rock Clan, you forever belong to Rock Clan? You will return with us now, and we will punish you for leaving, as you deserve. When we have taken all but your life from you, we will give you to the dark ones. You cannot prevent this. I have other warriors besides these five, and the humans are with us as well."

"I can prevent it. When you captured me, I was weak. But no more."

"You think you are strong. But you are only one, while we are six of the best warriors of Rock Clan, and others wait in the forest. With you is an old cat and a cripple. They will die first, and then we will go. After we find the woman and man who also left us. They are ours as well."

"No. They are not."

At Groknor's menacing growl, Fajora let her sword form, watching until it reached full length, and lowering it so its tip hovered a few hands' breadths away from the cat's chest. Groknor did not move, but the rumbling in his throat and chest increased. The other cats growled and snarled now, as well. The movement of sound alerted her when several of these cats rose and began to prowl. She tracked the sound but kept her gaze fastened on Groknor.

The sword had a satisfying heft, and after days of inaction, Fajora wanted to plunge into the fight. She knew better, however, with these odds. She would be foolish to engage in a fight she could not win. If she must fight tonight, she should pick her place and find additional allies, if possible.

The window for getting away narrowed. Fajora needed time to translate to light, and she preferred to do it without a cat leaping for her throat. And she must give no warning about what she planned to do.

She braced herself. Groknor stood, then crouched with his tail low and swishing. It must be now or not at all.

Letting her sword dissipate, Fajora flung herself into a full spin, pulling Akachi and Obasi into the swirling light as she rose from the ground. The last thing she saw with her physical eyes was Groknor's mighty leap as he tried to prevent her escape.

She soared over the trees until they were well away, then searched for a safe place to land. The two cats made a heavy load and drained her energies. If she carried them too long and then tried to fight, she would be too weak to face her enemies.

She considered spinning clear of cat territory. The protection of the colony's superior technology beckoned enticingly. She could leave Akachi in the colonists' care and return Obasi to the clan to rejoin his patrol. Neither Obasi nor Akachi would be pleased with her for carrying them away with a battle brewing. But Akachi had no business fighting, no matter how willing his spirit.

Fajora hesitated, uncertain. She hovered, a pillar of spinning light that cast illumination over the narrow end of a long valley thick with trees. A herd of shaggy domestic animals, pressed together to form a dark mass, stampeded toward the valley's north end in frantic confusion. In a clearing at the valley's midpoint, shapes scattered to find cover beneath the trees—cats and humans who had seen her light.

She moved closer, hovering, letting go of enough light to reform her face. Blinking hard, she peered down at the figures. Deep Valley Clan or Rock Clan? With color washed out by the dark, and size difficult to determine in the shifting shadows, she couldn't be sure. Then she sighted a cat's head in profile and saw the outline of the ears, not rounded like a Rock Clan cat's ears, but tufted.

She landed in the clearing and coalesced, dumping her passengers on the ground unceremoniously and rotating as she tried to get her bearings. At her feet, Akachi wobbled and hung his head, unable to counteract the queasiness brought on from spinning, while Obasi crouched to one side, heaving and gasping. Until they regained their wits, she must protect them. But on the ground in her solid form, she faced a distinct disadvantage without the night vision, keen sense of smell, and acute hearing of the cats.

She formed a sword and held it high, allowing it to brighten her face. Its light flared in the dark space under the trees, outshining tenfold the gray opalescence creeping in from the eastern horizon, herald to the dawn.

"Fajora," she called. "Light Spinner. With a warning. Rock Clan is nearby. At least six individuals. Likely more."

"Where?" Fajora recognized Zaire as he stepped out of his hiding place, a laser weapon in his hand.

His question gave Fajora pause. She wasn't sure where the encounter with Groknor and his band had taken place. She looked to her companions. Obasi continued emptying his stomach, but Akachi stiffened his stance and lifted his head.

"Akachi. Where did we meet Groknor and his warriors?"

"Above the river, near the turkey run, with Matriarch rock behind us."

"That's too close to the settlement," Zaire said.

A cat moved forward. Fajora recognized Bardu. "You must warn them," he said. "No one else can get there fast enough."

"They want me. If they follow me . . . ." Fajora tightened the spin on her sword, reluctant to quit the field of impending battle.

"At least our people will be warned. And take Akachi with you."

"I'm staying here to . . . ." The snarls of surrounding cats cut off Akachi's protest.

"Too late. You need me here." Fajora rotated, trying to glimpse the cats, to determine which were Deep Valley and which were intruders. In the valley, the black of night continued to recede and the light strengthened, warming from gray to gilt rose as the sun reached for the horizon.

In this light, she detected many restless shapes but could not yet see them clearly.

Then the Deep Valley cats and humans pulled closer together, and Fajora made a swift count—twelve cats and five humans, besides Obasi, Akachi, and herself. But the shifting shadows beyond Deep Valley's perimeter suggested Rock Clan's numbers were much greater. As the light grew stronger, she detected brown coats among the gray. River Clan had joined Rock Clan in the invasion.

40

MANUEVERING

"Bardu," Zaire whispered urgently, but a whoosh of wings cut off his next words. An owl skimmed over their heads and landed on a low branch of the nearest tree, drawing all eyes.

The owl made a series of low, intense calls, then raised itself from its branch with a mighty downbeat of wings, and with powerful, silent strokes, flew back over their heads and disappeared.

"Bardu," Zaire said again, "we are nearly surrounded. Only the south end of the valley is clear, for now."

"Call the owl back," Bardu commanded. "We must have help."

Zaire raised his voice and sent a series of hoots and screeches echoing among the trees and soaring to the sky. Then he looked at Bardu and shrugged. "It may be too far away already. Prepare for battle with what we have. Even Akachi must fight."

"Light Spinner, stay where you are, and use your sword upon any enemy that tries to break for the valley outlet." Bardu didn't wait for a reply, but began issuing a string of commands in the hissing, snarling, mewing cat language.

An overhead swoosh interrupted him. And another. Two owls soared over their heads and landed on a pair of trees to Fajora's left. Bardu stopped giving orders to his cat warriors long enough to spit out a command to Zaire before turning back to the cats.

Zaire hurried to the owls' trees and took up an urgent conversation with them, speaking their own language with a proficiency that mesmerized Fajora. She strained to hear, though she knew she wouldn't understand.

Bardu, moving nearer to Fajora's position as he continued to issue orders, blocked out most of the Zaire's conversation. She turned away, disappointed. Then the sense of Syjaz's dark aura swept over her like a dark owl descending, driving all other concerns from her mind.

Not now. The odds already fell in Rock Clan's favor. Fajora couldn't afford to divide her attention. She glanced back toward the end of the valley. She had her bearings now and drew a quick mental picture of the terrain. This valley funneled south to the river, opening out again on its banks not far below the flume that carried the river out of the settlement canyon.

Any enemy cats who got past her had a clear path to the settlement, unless clan members guarded the rocky paths down into the canyon. But those narrow paths allowed for only one or two defenders at a time. If attackers overcame them before the patrols raised the alarm, they could take the settlement by surprise.

Fajora's protest when Bardu wanted to send her back, driven by her desire to fight more than by wisdom or a desire for the good of the clan, seemed foolish now. She should go without delay.

But as she started to translate, Syjaz's aura grew stronger, though she could not identify his exact location.

"Show yourself," she muttered. "Let's get this over with. I have other things to do."

As she spoke, she rotated, her sword poised in front of her. She caught glimpses of Deep Valley cats moving among nearby trees. She saw Zaire lean over to speak to Akachi at his side as he adjusted controls on his laser weapon. The two of them withdrew into the trees, concealing themselves from Fajora's view.

Good. Zaire could protect Akachi. She glimpsed the other Deep Valley humans, positioned in spots where they could employ their weapons from cover. All the Deep Valley cats were hidden from her brief glances now, but she saw the blurs of gray and brown coats as she turned. Rock Clan and River Clan cats—too many of them.

Ignoring them, she reached out, searching for Syjaz. She couldn't get a fix on him until he coalesced. And for now, he chose to hover somewhere nearby as spun shadow, foiling her attempts to find him. Instead, Tornton walked into the clearing, the first invader to show himself openly. Bardu and Fajora, the only two of Deep Valley Clan who remained in the open, watched him approach. When he finally stopped, he was close enough for Fajora to smell him. He carried one of the bulky weapons he had been working so hard to repair in one hand, and a new knife, longer than the one with which he had tortured Sebastian, in his other hand. Fajora's stomach soured and she reached down to sooth the thigh that suddenly throbbed.

His eyes followed her movement, and he grinned. When she moved her hand away from her leg, his grin widened.

"Good to see you, Light Spinner. You probably didn't expect me today."

Fajora remained silent.

He laughed, a harsh sound, but his laughter cut off on a strangled note as Sanaa stepped out from the trees at Fajora's right.

"That's right," Sanaa said, her voice amused. "You've seen me before in your own settlement. Just before you took a nice nap. Apparently slept all night. At least, I don't remember seeing you when Jelok tried to keep us from taking your prisoners. You'd better go home. You're out of your class." She gave her weapon a casual wave.

Tornton glanced down with a frown at his own heavy, rust-pocked device. Then he relaxed and his grin flashed out again. "Don't be so sure, missy. You might find yourself in my camp come night. Have us a little party. I've got help you ain't seen yet. More'n match for this sickly, weak Light Spinner."

The dark aura Fajora had been trying to pinpoint localized, as if at Tornton's command. To Tornton's right, a swirling shadow swooped down, touched the ground, and took on solid form. Syjaz's costume showed the strain of his clandestine living. A dirty rent marred one orange sleeve, and a leather thong held his hair from his face in place of the golden threads he had sported on their last encounter.

But the dark flecks in his violet eyes still danced in a confident pattern, and the tilt of his chin still proclaimed his disdain for those he looked down upon. His lips curved in a supercilious smile, beautiful despite the scorn it manifested. He held a sword spun of shadows in a negligent grasp.

He stared at Fajora, ignoring everyone else. "We meet again, Light Spinner. Are you ready for your trip to Zukalum? Rock Clan and I have come to an agreement. I help them and they give you to me. Everyone wins."

Fajora's training, which had failed her so often since she left the colony, now snapped into place, leaving her calm, with a clarity that allowed her to take measure of everyone within view and taught her what to say, what questions to ask, what information she must glean.

"What kind of help have they asked for?"

"I'm to retrieve some stolen items."

"What items? Stolen by whom?"

He laughed, a sound of dark mirth. "Deep Valley Clan is the thief. The whole clan collaborated in their own dishonor, and Rock Clan will make sure they pay the price. Can't you guess the items they want back? Members of their clan, or so they claim. The question is, should I go get the other strays or secure you first?"

He looked around the clearing. "I'm tempted to deal with you first. But I'd have to find a way to secure you. If it were only you, I'd take you straight to Zukalum. But then I'd miss my chance to carry off Sebastian and sweet young Clarise. I promised a fair price for you, and I always pay my debts. Perhaps I'll let the cats and their human cronies here take care of you while I attend to the other business."

"Which might be more difficult than you imagine."

He laughed again. "Oh, I don't know. It looks like a short, ugly contest coming up. My colleagues can handle it. Isn't that right, my good man?"

He grinned at Tornton, who grinned back. "Yes. We'll take them. No trouble." He shook his weapon, and it beeped while the light on its top blinked erratically.

Having moved in as shadow, Syjaz must be even more aware than Fajora of the positions and numbers of the opposing clan members. But he could not see the owls flying in on silent wings to rest in the trees behind him. Tilting her chin to match the angle of his, Fajora rotated slowly, scanning the treetops at her back, and the underbrush as well. She detected no movement in the sky or the upper canopies of the forest behind her, but at ground level, dark shadows, blacker than any Rock Clan cat, caught her eye, moving into position near the lower end of the valley.

When her rotation brought her back to face Syjaz and Tornton again, she found they had moved several steps closer, and a dozen gray and brown cats slunk forward behind them. Beside her, Bardu growled, a growl that started in his chest and burst from deep in his throat. He unsheathed his claws and tore into the ground in front of him.

But when he glanced at Fajora, she gave him a minute shake of her head. She wasn't done with Syjaz. She needed more information from him. Bardu snarled but held back.

"I'm surprised you didn't take Sebastian and Clarise when you were in the Deep Valley settlement the other night. It would have been so much easier."

Sanaa, standing at ease nearby, started and straightened. Bardu stopped clawing the ground and turned to sniff at Fajora. Even Tornton stiffened.

Syjaz retained his relaxed posture and twirled his shadow sword lazily. "I always wait for the right time. I had other business that evening. You might guess what it was."

"And have you told your colleague, Kinovic, the secrets you learned?"

Movement among the trees told Fajora other members of Deep Valley Clan had heard this and understood its meaning.

"Secrets?" Tornton blurted. "What secrets? Dark one, are you holding out on us? We had an agreement."

Syjaz flicked his sword in Tornton's direction, and the man jumped back. Syjaz laughed. Fajora shuddered at that sound. Even Jelok's laughter had been preferable.

"Our agreement didn't involve information," Syjaz told Tornton. "You want to know what they're hiding, gather your own information, if you're not too stupid or lazy to do so. Have to earn it. You'll get nothing from me until my superiors have considered my intelligence and determined how much to share."

He ignored Tornton's spluttering protest and spoke again to Fajora. "It's got nothing to do with Kinovic, either. He's insignificant, a mere sycophant. Information about a technological artifact of this importance is for Choshek's people only, those who understand the prophecies. They will know what to do about it. These clans have no idea what's coming."

Fajora bit back a smile. No point in letting him see her pleasure. In his arrogance, his certainty of victory, he had revealed everything she needed to know. He had found Deep Valley Clan's void ship, as she had already guessed. He seemed to understand it had prophetic significance. He should have taken his findings immediately to other Dark Spinners. Kinovic, certainly, if he didn't want to leave Kakislane just yet. His bosses on Zukalum would have been better, but Fajora knew he hadn't had time to go there.

Apparently, Syjaz didn't imagine any danger to himself or his information. He expected to succeed in every venture and return to Zukalum victorious, carrying a Light Spinner prisoner, without sharing the glory with any other Dark Spinners assigned to Kakislane, including Kinovic.

Nor did he show any awareness of the potential to escalate this clan conflict by sharing his information with his Rock Clan allies. Rock Clan's greed would spur them on to appropriate Deep Valley Clan's technology by any means if they knew of it. Deep Valley Clan would never know peace again. But Syjaz made the same mistake Dark Spinners had been making for centuries—using other sentient beings when it suited them but not respecting them enough to study and understand them.

Fajora had the information she needed now. If she waited, Syjaz might realize the advantages of sharing information with his allies, making damage control so much more difficult. She had to stop him now, but taking him prisoner and keeping him in light stasis was too much for one person. She knew of only one other way to stop him.

She must kill him.

She braced herself, and her stiff leg reminded her of another option. If she wounded him badly enough to incapacitate him, Deep Valley Clan could hold him until she found more help. She preferred this plan, if she could manage it.

Fajora held her sword in the same negligent way Syjaz had held his a few minutes ago, lulling him. The Rock and River Clan cats in the clearing crouched, tails flicking, preparing to attack. Beside Fajora, Bardu snarled and yowled, a call to action every member of his clan, feline and human, understood.

As a frenzy of snarling, twisting bodies and flashes of laser light erupted around Fajora, she lunged at Syjaz, bringing her sword into attack position and tightening its spin as she moved. Caught off guard, he responded, off balance and wide-eyed but fast enough to block her first thrust. She pressed her attack, pushing him back a step at a time.

In her peripheral vision, she saw a gray blur leap in her direction. Without lessening the speed of her sword thrusts, she let her body translate toward light. A partial spin allowed her to continue her attack and yet soften the blow of the Rock Clan cat at her heels. A flash of laser light caught the cat in the shoulder, throwing it to the ground. A snarl warned of another cat behind her, and she caught a glimpse of tufted ears and an eyepatch as Akachi pounced on the fallen cat. How had he gotten here so fast on his crippled leg?

But she had no more time to wonder. The Rock Clan cat's wounds did not incapacitate him. He responded to Akachi's attack with a swipe of a weaponized paw. The two cats rolled away, spitting, scratching, and attempting to bite.

Yowls erupted all around her as the dam of restraint burst. Grey, brown, and bronze bodies joined the fray, leaping, twisting, scrabbling, and rolling. Black cats, the stealthy denizens of Forest Clan, slunk in for lightning assaults, wounding and disorienting their targets, confirmation of Fajora's earlier sighting. Yowls of frustration resounded as cats lunged back at the aggressors, only to find them gone.

All this Fajora saw in a blur of speed and sound as she exchanged blow after blow with Syjaz. The dull thud of the shadow sword was echoed by a bell-like note as her light sword sang. Despite the sudden fury of the battle, the cats managed to stay clear of Fajora and Syjaz. A thin stream of light buzzed through the air beside Fajora as the Deep Valley humans brought their laser weapons to bear again and again. Circling Syjaz, Fajora saw the first Rock Clan human fall.

Fajora and Syjaz struck blow for blow, thrust, block, and counterthrust, evenly matched. Taller and stronger, he should have had the advantage. But Fajora's feet moved faster, bringing her close for a thrust and moving her back again, keeping her body beyond the reach of his counterthrust. Her sword swung into each blow a split second faster than his. He struggled to keep up, enabling her to push him back.

She didn't touch him, didn't draw blood. Nonetheless, she moved him, step by step, closer to pair of trees whose massive trunks blocked the way behind him. Soon she would force him to quit playing defense and go on the attack. Attackers, especially attackers without the experience of long years in the field, made mistakes. She had trained young agents for a time, and she knew all the mistakes. She was ready for Syjaz.

He glanced back, stumbling and swinging his sword with two-handed blocks, then jumped back over a tree root, turned, and fled.

Fajora sprang after him. But before he had gone more than three steps, his form vanished in a swirl of shadow.

Fajora stopped, leaning over and breathing heavily, gathering her wits. Why had he spun away? Even in their short sparring match, she had sensed his skill. Combined with his superior strength, it should have compensated for his lack of experience. He was too sure of his own superiority to give up so quickly. Which meant he wasn't running away from her, but hurrying to do something else.

Fajora straightened. The melee swirled about her, frightening in its ferocity. Owls swooped in silent attacks. Cats snarled as they scratched and bit, or screamed as another cat's claws found purchase in their flesh. Some cats lay still, and several tried to drag their mangled bodies out of the way of the fight. She couldn't see Akachi. Her heart thumped harder as she searched to no avail.

Bardu and Obasi, fighting rump to rump and moving as one, held off four opponents. Other cats, even a pair of Forest Clan cats, used similar tactics, though other black cats employed the strike-and-withdraw tactic. The humans had resorted to their long knives, the air being too full of wings and talons to use their lasers. An owl, flying low, raked talons across the back of one of Bardu's Rock Clan opponents. When the gray cat raised a startled face to the bird, a swipe of Bardu's claws across its throat finished the cat. Blood spurted from its neck as it sank to the ground.

Very good, but where was Akachi? Fajora needed to follow Syjaz, but she wanted to ensure Akachi's safety first. She stumbled out of the way of a roiling group of cats, finding her way to the shelter of two intertwined trees. She would have to venture into the woods to find her young friend, but which way?

While she hesitated, a group of three Deep Valley cats charged into the middle of the fight. Chikelu led them. He bore no scratches or other wounds, but his sides heaved with exertion. Making a quick survey of the battle, his gaze landed on Bardu and he bounded toward him, followed by his companions. His powerful front paw batted one of the gray cats to the ground, and his teeth clamped on its throat an instant later. His head came up smeared with blood.

While his companions dispatched the other two gray cats in the tangle, Chikelu spoke in hurried growls and yowls to Bardu and Obasi. Abandoning her search for Akachi, Fajora ran across the clearing, dodging rolling cats and grappling humans. She passed Tornton as he brought his heavy laser weapon up in both blood-soaked hands. An alarm went off in the corner of Fajora's mind, but her focus on the conference of the leaders distracted her.

Chikelu, Bardu, and Obasi swung around at her approached.

"Light Spinner, the settlement is under attack," Obasi said as Fajora skidded to a stop. "A group of six Rock Clan cats breached the security measures on the path down to the canyon, and River Clan cats wait above to join the attack."

Fajora shuddered. She realized she had not seen Groknor in this battle. She should have fought him when they met earlier, despite the bad odds.

"You must go at once," Bardu added, command in his voice. "No arguments this time."

Syjaz must be there by now, as well, but Fajora did not tell the cats this. Without waiting to hear more, she reached for light. As it swirled around her, she saw a flash of laser fire. Following its trajectory with the last of her true sight, she saw Zaire clutch his side and fall to the ground. At the source of the laser light, two black cats sprang at Tornton, tearing out his throat as the laser gun fell from his hands.

41

—·—

FOILING SYJAZ

Fajora sped to the settlement, a short spin, and coalesced in front of the infirmary. A frenzy of activity greeted her. A group of adults shepherded kits and children toward the shelter of the caves on the north side of the settlement, while others rushed to the armory to retrieve weapons and headed toward the canyon trails at the south end of the valley.

Fajora met Ekene as she jerked open the infirmary door. He carried a small pack and wore a long knife on one side of his belt and a laser weapon on the other side. The wrongness of his appearance struck Fajora. He healed. He did not take life. But, like everyone else, he roused to protect his home.

"Fajora! I didn't know you were still here."

"I wasn't. I came from another valley, over there." She waved her hand in the general direction. "We battle Rock Clan there, but their warriors have also breached the guard on the southern entrance to this valley. Rock Clan and River Clan are on their way. I came to give warning." She glanced at his weapons. "But you know already."

"Yes. We're mustering everyone to meet them and drive them away. We could use your help. Get a weapon from the armory."

"Don't need one." Fajora let the beginnings of her sword form.

Ekene's eyes widened and he grinned. "Good. Come with me. You can join my cohort." He strode away, heading south.

"No. Wait."

Ekene stopped. "What is it? We've got to hurry."

"A Dark Spinner headed this way. I've got to find him."

"Too late. He's been and left. Took your friends with him."

"Clarise? Sebastian?"

"Yes. We'll hunt for them after we block this attack. There's no time now."

"You go. I've got to find them. Any idea which way he took them?"

"Up." Ekene lifted his eyes to the sky, then pointed to the mountains forming the west side of the valley. "Went that way, but I don't know how far. Probably gone by now. Are you coming?"

"He won't leave Kakislane until he gets me. I have a chance to catch him if I go now. I'll see you later. Be well."

Fajora translated to light and shot up out of the valley. She landed high on the side of the mountain and coalesced, reaching out, searching for a sense of Syjaz's aura. She felt it on the edge of her awareness but could not localize it.

A haunting call floated through the lower branches of the trees. An owl clutched a branch not far beyond Fajora. Her eyes met its gaze, the contact sending a jolt of connection through her. She knew it wanted something of her.

It preened its feathers with its beak. Raising its head, it launched from its branch and drifted toward her, its immense wingspan breathtaking at such close range. Instinctively, she raised her hands to protect her face as the owl swooped at her head. Its wingtips brushed her hair as it glided beyond her.

It came to rest on a branch behind Fajora. She twisted around to find it watching her, its expression unreadable. After a moment, it left its perch and circled, swooping low and again brushing Fajora's hair with a wingtip. Again, it found a perch, in the same direction but a little beyond the tree it had lighted on before.

Fajora regarded it with growing attentiveness. It hooted and whistled softly, a long series of vocalizations. What was it trying to tell her? Straining for understanding, she walked toward it, her gaze never wavering. One more time, it took off and circled, brushed past her, and headed farther along in the same direction. Fajora strained to see it, nearly camouflaged by the branches of intervening trees.

She understood now. She stepped closer to its tree. It watched until she was close, then circled again. This time it thumped the back of her head as it passed, and it did not land. Though quickly gone from sight, its call carried back to her. She translated to light and followed, as swift and silent as the bird.

On the far side of the mountain, she caught up to the owl in a tree at the edge of a clearing. The valley where the battle between the clans still raged lay not far below them. She chose a sturdy branch in a tree near the owl's and partially coalesced to take stock of her surroundings.

Below her in the clearing, six River Clan cats paced back and forth. Clarise and Sebastian sat with their backs to a large tree, tied with ropes and under the care of a Rock Clan human. Fajora recognized the man as one of Tornton's underlings. He stood beside Clarise, clutching a knife, but he paid little attention to his prisoners. He focused instead on the cats—River Clan cats and not his own clanmates. He watched every move they made, and his knife hand followed their movements with jerky gestures. The knife matched the one Clarise and Sebastian had stolen from Tornton. Likely it was the same, taken from Sebastian when Syjaz delivered him to Rock Clan.

Fajora glanced at her owl guide. She coveted its help in rescuing her friends, but she didn't have a way to communicate her intentions. Though the owl might comprehend Standard, speaking aloud would betray her presence to the cats below. So, she watched the cats carefully and tried to plan a solo rescue.

As she surveyed the scene before her, another owl glided in and landed in a tree near the prisoners. Fajora's owl hooted, and the other owl answered. The River Clan cats reacted by bunching in groups beneath both owls' trees, hissing, snarling, and trying to jump up toward the owls. They did not try to climb the trees. They must have known the owls would be gone before they reached them.

Jumping made no sense, either, but they jumped anyway. The owls conversed a little longer. Fajora listened, so caught up in the sound, she hardly realized she had completely coalesced and clung to her branch with a precarious hold.

She shifted to get a better grip, though she could easily embrace her light again if she started to fall. Having her eyes and ears fully functional allowed her to make a more detailed survey of the area's features. A boulder near Clarise and Sebastian offered a place for them to hide if she managed to release them from their bonds. A closely spaced row of trees along that side of the clearing provided further protection.

A shadow moving within the forest downslope from the clearing caught her eye. It was black as night and moved with a stealth even beyond most cats' capabilities. Two more shadows joined the first. Ah. A better view, as one slunk through an open place between vegetation. A long tail tipped in white confirmed the identification. Forest Clan cats.

Something else paced among the trees as well. A shape with brighter fur, tawny in color, and too large to be a member of any of the warring clans. The Forest cats she trusted. But who was this other cat, if cat it was, who moved with power toward the clearing, not trying to hide, as if knowing that was impossible?

It stepped into the clearing, its dark-rimmed eyes and white muzzle accentuating the sculpted leanness of its face. It was almost as large as a Big Leaf Clan cat, its long body heavy and powerful, its paws half again as large as a Deep Valley cat's. As the black tip of its tawny tail cleared the underbrush, it screamed, a chilling sound that fell to a snarl, deepened to a growl, and rose again to a high-pitched warning.

A chill ran down Fajora's spine, and she felt the blood drain from her face. Sebastian and Clarise struggled frantically against their bonds, their faces ashen. The vocalization of the tawny cat intermingled with the growls of the River Clan cats as they paced or crouched, tails lashing behind them. The Forest Clan cats remained hidden.

Fajora, though shaken by this new arrival, felt the glimmer of a plan form in her mind. This tawny cat, a precise match for the image of a Meadow Clan cat she had seen in the colony, seemed bent on confrontation, and the River Clan cats responded in kind. This might provide the distraction she needed to swoop down and release her friends. Surely this big cat, the three Forest Clan cats, and the two owls were equal to six River Clan cats. Fajora could focus on incapacitating the human guard and freeing Clarise and Sebastian.

She resumed a partial spin and prepared, watching the Meadow Clan cat closely. A River cat pranced forward, growling a challenge. The tawny cat swatted at the River cat, sparring, testing, and suddenly raking the River cat's shoulder. The River cat yelped and leaped back, and the Meadow cat advanced.

Fajora waited for all the cats to commit fully to the fight. She held light loosely, ready to complete her spin and zoom down to Clarise and Sebastian as soon as she had a clear path.

Then, unexpectedly, a dark aura slammed into her awareness. Tendrils of shadow slithered down from the tree beside Clarise, and Syjaz took on physical form, knocking the human guard off his feet in the process.

The tawny cat stopped its advance, though it did not back away. The injured River cat slunk behind its comrades and licked at its bleeding shoulder, but the other River cats paced in an agitated pattern just beyond the Meadow cat's reach.

Syjaz watched the cats for a moment, then laughed. "What a bunch of pretties you all are. I would love to stay and watch you tear each other's throats out, but I have other work to do."

He formed a shadow dagger and leaned toward Clarise. Fajora's heart jumped and she stifled a shout. She hovered, frozen, her ears buzzing with the sudden rush of blood. She knew she could not move fast enough to keep Syjaz from driving the dagger into Clarise's flesh.

In the next instant, Syjaz sliced through the ropes that bound the prisoners, freeing them. Sebastian jumped to his feet, wobbling at the sudden change of position. Waving his injured arm in a wild quest for balance, he grabbed Clarise with his other hand and tugged her away from the Dark Spinner. But a River Clan cat blocked his escape. Sebastian and Clarise stopped short, swaying and clutching at the tree trunk for support.

Syjaz reached out and stroked Clarise's hair. "Don't try running, my sweet. I have a much easier way to get you where you're going. A short spin back to Rock Clan settlement, and I can claim my own prize." He swirled into shadow, leaning toward the pair to engulf them in his spin.

No! Fajora's cry vibrated in her mind as she flung herself into a full spin and zoomed toward the Dark Spinner. She collided with him in a shower of intertwining light and shadow, knocking them both from their spins. They became flesh again, and their feet tangled as they struggled for firm footing.

"Light spawn!" Syjaz spat out, trying to regain his balance and, at the same time, form a shadow sword. Fajora's own attempt to form a weapon fizzled as she rammed into him. His nascent sword dissolved into wisps of shadow, and they grappled for control, arms around each other. Tripped up by an exposed root, they toppled to the ground, rolling as each struggled to free an arm. Sword arm or off arm—it didn't matter to Fajora. Either could hold an effective weapon at this close range. But each time she rolled on top of Syjaz and tried to free a hand, he heaved her onto her back again.

His strength outmatched Fajora's, and her conditioning had suffered from her recent imprisonment and injury. At swordplay she might match him indefinitely, but this contest of strength had her at a disadvantage. As she struggled to regain a position of power, she felt the brush of fur and heard a warning snarl. Black fur flashed before her eyes, and then bronze.

Bronze?

Even with Syjaz grappling at her, Fajora risked a glance around. The clearing seethed with cats and the air buzzed with laser blasts. Either more combatants had entered the war, or the battle from the valley below had moved up the side of the mountain. Fajora had no time to discern which.

She squirmed as Syjaz pinned her with his weight and a dagger formed in his free hand. His face distorted in a snarl of hate and the lust for a kill.

Her own hand came free, but his dagger already swirled toward its finished shape. She would not be able to form her own in time to counter his. So much for fancy Luxeran battle techniques. She chortled, startling him, as she balled her fist and punched him on the underside of his chin.

His head snapped back. She threw him off and jumped to her feet. She reached for light one more time, but a pair of twisting, snarling cats bumped her from behind. A claw caught the back of her leg near the top of her boot, and the sudden searing pain knocked the connection with light from her mind.

Bending over, she instinctively searched for the scratch with her fingers and felt blood as Syjaz stumbled toward her. He shook his head, his eye flecks spinning wildly, dizzily. Disoriented, he would be slow to spin a shadow weapon. But instead of attempting to form a blade, he charged at her, fast, his arms outstretched. As he groped toward her, he let his hands shift toward shadow, threatening to envelop her.

Fajora's fingers, still exploring the bloody scratch on her leg, felt something hard inside the edge of her boot. Confusion changed to recognition. Her hand grasped the smooth handle of the knife she had secreted there and yanked the blade from its sheath as she straightened to meet her enemy's charge.

Syjaz's dark, swirling hands found her neck and tightened. Fajora managed one strangled gasp for air before the shadow shut off her breath. Her body and Syjaz's still held solid form, though tendrils of shadow began to curl around both. She had but an instant to act, one last chance before she was lost.

In a smooth, desperate motion, she brought the little knife up to meet Syjaz's chest. Her hand, already bloodied, felt the hot rush of his life pour over it as he screamed.

For a moment they stood frozen, connected by the blade of good, human-forged steel. She twisted the hilt, let her hand slide to its end, and pushed. The tendrils of shadow dissipated as he fell away from her. His hand reached for the blade, his lips mouthing silent words of shock or cursing, or perhaps of pleading to his dark lord. He writhed as he hit the ground, but Fajora's aim had been true, directing the knife straight into his heart. He took one last rasping breath and lay still.

42

AKACHI'S VALOR

An odd, hollow ringing filled Fajora's ears, and a cold mist shuddered through her as the life seeped out of Syjaz. She regarded him with a detached sorrow. She'd had no choice. But he was Luxeran. Deceived by the master deceiver, but of her people nonetheless, born to spin light. And he had been beautiful. Fajora had glimpsed his beauty even in his shadowed state, saw traces of it still in his lifeless body. She waited, watching for the Malechem she knew would not come, but at last turned away.

Around her, the battle raged, its energy ferocious and terrifying, but the combatants avoided Fajora with uncanny awareness. She tried to make sense of the conflict, to see patterns in the clumps of struggling warriors and the bodies strewn across the ground. She saw Chikelu and Bardu, relatively undamaged and clearly dominating their foes. She saw Obasi huddled in a silent heap. And she saw a great many River Clan cats and a smaller number of Rock Clan cats bleeding or bled out.

She saw not one, but four large tawny Meadow Clan cats, fighting in pairs and dealing out unrelenting punishment, while the black wraiths that were Forest Clan warriors streaked in for a strike and out again, leaving devastation in their wakes. Sebastion stood over the Rock Clan man who had guarded him and Clarise, the knife in his hand dripping blood, while Clarise crouched behind the boulder near him. Two owls swooped toward a Rock Clan cat, the first one knocking it over with its talons while the second, following, tore a piece of flesh from its side with its beak.

Then she saw Akachi.

How had he gotten here through the rough terrain between this clearing and the valley floor? It must have been a slow, torturous climb for him, dragging his wounded leg behind him. But here he was, fighting awkwardly, bleeding from a handful of minor scratches, but alive and holding his own.

Fajora drew in a deep breath. It felt like the first breath she had drawn in a great while. She noticed a burning in her throat and reached for her water flask. It remained where she had placed it the night before, snugged inside her pack, which was still on her back. With the battle raging all around her, she pulled off the pack, found the flask, and took a drink. Refreshed, she rummaged for wafer cakes. They were crumbling from the battering her pack had taken, but still full of high-energy nutrition. She ate two of them with a growing sense of joy and lightness.

Her enemy lay dead. Akachi stood, alive.

The largest of the Meadow Clan cats swiped a claw across the head of a River Clan cat, sending it spinning across the clearing. The big cat's scream pierced the air, loud even over the snarls and screeches of the tangling warriors. It sent a shudder of shock through the invading troops. The River Clan cats, and then some from Rock Clan, disengaged and slunk into the forest. The heat of the battle seeped away. Some of the allied warriors gave chase to the Rock and River cats, while others stopped to rest and groom their blood-crusted fur. Only a few isolated battles continued at the edges of the clearing.

Under the first line of trees, their movement shadowed, half hidden, Akachi and Groknor faced each other. Fajora had expected Groknor to be ambushing the settlement, but here he was, showing no inclination to abandon the fight. His snarls held the sound of contempt rather than alarm. Much larger than Akachi and without any visible injuries, he had a clear advantage. Akachi scrambled, stumbling, to dodge the swipe of Groknor's claws, but he would not back down.

Fajora shrugged back into her pack and let a sword form in her hands. She ran toward the pair, dodging fallen bodies. Bardu and Chikelu dashed toward the fighting pair from a different angle, and the biggest Meadow Clan cat bounded ahead of them, snarling and screaming.

Groknor saw them coming. He backed a step and checked the terrain behind him, where he had a clear path of escape. But he refused to give up his prey. He had time for one last lunge at the wounded young cat, and he took it. Akachi collapsed in front of him, and Fajora's heart froze. But as Groknor pounced for the kill, Akachi rolled and his left front paw, claws fully extended, shot up to rake across Groknor's exposed throat above him.

The bigger cat collapsed in a spray of blood, burying Akachi. Fajora skidded to a halt beside them, but the Meadow Clan cat was already sinking its teeth into the base of Groknor's skull and dragging him off Akachi.

Akachi lay still for a moment, then lifted his head. "Is he dead?"

"Yes." The Meadow Clan cat sat on its haunches and scrutinized Akachi as the young cat rose stiffly to his feet, his wounded leg held above the ground, as if it pained him too much to put weight on it. The big, tawny cat turned to Chikelu and Bardu. "But why is this maimed individual among the warriors? He has no place in battle. This is not our way."

The sounds of battle died out in the clearing. Those cats still on their feet paced toward Akachi and the tawny cat, sniffing, listening, questing to see if a new fight was brewing.

Chikelu stalked toward the bigger cat, tail swishing, showing no sign of submission. "It is our way that any who can contribute must do so. This cat has proven his valor today, and I will not hear his honor or the honor of his clan questioned."

The Meadow Clan cat regarded Chikelu for a moment, then reached forward and sniffed at Akachi's face. "Yes. He is valorous, indeed. It shall be as you say. Now come. The enemy must not be allowed to linger and hide, but must be harried back to their own territory."

"Some must go," Bardu replied, "but most must return to the settlement to ensure its safety."

"I thought Groknor led that attack," Fajora said, drawing attention to herself for the first time. "Perhaps the attack on the settlement has already been repulsed."

Bardu considered. "Perhaps. But we must not assume."

He turned to his warriors and began issuing orders in the language of the cats. Soon most of the cats and all the human warriors streamed out of the clearing, some heading north to push the enemy out of Deep Valley Clan territory, and others heading south toward a pass leading over the mountain and down into the settlement valley.

The big Meadow Clan cat lingered, studying Fajora. "Lasei, Meadow Clan," he said at last.

Fajora inclined her head. "Fajora. Light Spinner agent."

Lasei's eyes flicked toward the spot where Syjaz lay and back to Fajora's face. He stepped close to sniff at Fajora. She held herself motionless, banishing fear with a stiff determination. Satisfied, Lasei stepped back and regarded her a moment longer with unblinking eyes.

"You have done your duty with honor today," he said. "Be well, Light Spinner." He turned and vanished into the wilderness, leaving Fajora tingling with released anxiety and exhilaration.

Akachi limped to Fajora's side and nuzzled her hand. She rubbed his head, and her chest expanded with a deep, heartfelt sigh. Akachi regarded her with his one good eye, while the other eye remained partially hidden by the torn and peeling eye patch. One ear was ragged and bleeding, and he had a mat of blood on his left side. Groknor's blood, Fajora assumed.

"Light Spinner, your leg bleeds. Are you well?"

"I am well, Akachi. And you?"

"Yes. Well."

"But not all are so."

They surveyed the carnage around them. Light shimmered down in multiple columns as the Malekemi came to collect the spirits of Ya-Lo-him's faithful. They hovered over the dead of Deep Valley Clan and their allies, and on several of the Rock and River Clan cats, proving that some individuals of those clans had given allegiance to the Creator despite their dark environment.

Two Forest cats and one Deep Valley cat remained in the clearing. They inspected the fallen, checking for life. If they found a living cat, they dispatched that individual with cold efficiency, whether it be friend or foe. If they felt remorse in their task, they gave no sign.

Fajora's stomach twisted, and she turned away. Besides the three clean-up cats, only Fajora, Sebastian, Clarise, and Akachi remained in the clearing.

Fajora knelt beside Akachi. "Well, my friend, I don't remember you ever answering my question."

"What question, Light Spinner?"

"Will you go to the colony with me and see what their doctors can do for you?"

Akachi's good eye caught Fajora's gaze and held it. "Do you think it wise?"

"Yes. I think so. I don't know for sure." She wouldn't deceive him with a level of certainty she didn't feel, as if deceit would work with a cat anyway.

"Then I will go. What of these two? Do they go with us, to their homes?"

Fajora peered up at Sebastian and Clarise. "Well?"

"Yes." Clarise's answer came swift and sure. "I want to see my mother and father. I want to be home."

"Sebastian?"

His answer came much more slowly. "I want to be home, it's true. Especially to be close to Clarise." He reached out to touch her hand, and she smiled at him, encouraging him. "But I came into clan territory, at risk of my life, because I have work to do here. I'm not ready to give up on it." He stared intently at Clarise. "You do understand, don't you?"

"Yes. Come home when you can."

"I'll find a way, when I've done what I came to do." He looked back at Fajora. "I'll stay." He peered around the battleground and at the tall mountain behind them. "I guess I'll have to walk back to the settlement."

Fajora slipped out of her pack and pulled food from it, which she shared around. She even gave one of her meat sticks to Akachi. It wasn't the sort of food a cat usually considered, but if she could eat raw meat, he could give processed meat a try. He sniffed at it, then chewed and swallowed greedily, a sign of his deep hunger.

"We'll hunt in a bit," she promised him. "When we get away from here." To Sebastian she added, "Once I'm fueled up, I'll take you to the pass and get you started down to the settlement. It will shorten your hike. Do you have your knife, in case you run into more fighting?"

"No. I dropped it after I . . . ." His face flushed with sudden emotion.

"You did what you had to do," Fajora said. "But a warrior never abandons his weapon. Find it and clean it on the grass. If we find a stream, you can clean it better."

"I'm a scholar, not a warrior. And I killed in anger. I don't think I'll kill again, even if it means my own life."

"That man, all the men of Rock Clan, brought the battle to us, even before we escaped. There's no shame in what you did. Get your knife. You may not care if you defend yourself, but you might wish to defend someone you love."

Sebastian's flush faded and he nodded, a slow, understanding nod. He retrieved the knife from near the body of his victim and cleaned it on a patch of grass.

"I'm ready now."

"We're all ready," Fajora replied. "Ready to face whatever the next task is that comes to hand."

43

RETURN TO THE COLONY

Fajora found the pass without difficulty and dropped Sebastian along the steep path leading down to the settlement. She waited with him until his dizziness from the spin had abated and he found his climbing legs. As she reached for light again, she heard voices approaching. Her alarm dissolved when Bardu appeared on the path at the head of a line of cats and humans, the war band heading down to secure the settlement. She pulled Clarise and Akachi back into her spin, certain Sebastian would be safe with his clan members.

She planned to head for the western edges of Deep Valley territory, where she could help Akachi hunt, but the memory of a friend hit with laser light and slumping to the ground altered her trajectory. She swooped down into the valley where battle had first commenced and coalesced at the south end in a thick stand of trees, where she instructed Clarise and Akachi to remain hidden.

Many dead lay strewn here, more than on the battleground above. Tornton lay in a sprawl, his torn, blood-soaked body blasted by lasers from two angles, his rusted weapon thrown to one side. Not far away, Fajora spotted Zaire's body, stretched out where he had fallen. Someone had attempted to staunch the flow of blood with a band of cloth, which was bound tightly around his torso. Blood had soaked through the bandage leaving a wide stain, turning dark around the edges as it dried.

She had hoped Zaire had been taken to the settlement for treatment. Was he dead, that he had been left behind? She bit her lip to keep back the tears. The figure of a woman sat beside him, head in hands. A grief-stricken lover? And if so, who? Not Lesedi. Of that Fajora was certain.

She approached and the woman raised her head, reaching for the laser weapon at her side in the same movement.

"Sanaa?"

Sanaa scrambled to her feet and waved her weapon. "Keep away. What are you doing here?"

"I came to check on Zaire. How is he? Is he . . . ?"

"Dead? Not yet. But he soon will be. What do you care, anyway? You'll soon be back in the colony, betraying us and all we stand for. What does one Deep Valley life matter to you?"

"It matters. Let me examine him."

"You're not a doctor. Leave him be."

"If he had immediate medical care, would he have a chance?"

Sanaa waved her weapon again and started to speak, then pursed her lips. Her shoulders slumped.

"Sanaa? Is there any hope for him?"

"I don't know. It doesn't matter. I can't carry him home and there's no one to help me. Everyone else is defending the settlement. I should be fighting with them, but I couldn't leave him. If I try to move him, he'll die before I get to the end of the valley. And I don't know how I'm going to tell Lesedi about this."

"Sanaa. Let me see. I can get him to the doctors if there's a chance."

"You?" Sanaa gave a derisive laugh. "You're so weak you can't crawl out of a hole when someone pushes you in. I made sure of that. So how do you expect to get a heavy warrior all the way to the settlement? Besides, he'll die no matter which of us is carrying him."

"No, he won't. I'm fully fueled now and can carry him in light stasis. If he's alive when I gather him up, he'll be alive when I put him down in the infirmary."

"Light stasis?" Sanaa stepped aside and motioned for Fajora to approach. "You can do that?"

Fajora knelt to examine Zaire, easing aside the bandage just enough to assess the injury. The laser had torn into his side, leaving a ragged, burned wound. The heat of the laser had cauterized part of the wound, but the weapon used had been weak, leaving the rest of the wound open and bleeding. A stronger laser would have killed him outright, but the weaker beam left him alive to bleed out. Even now, it might be too late.

"Clarise and Akachi are nearby, in the woods," she told Sanaa. "Protect them. I'll be back, but if anything happens to them in the meantime, I'll hold you responsible."

"You are giving me orders?" Sanaa's voice took on a spark of vibrancy.

"Just do it. I'll be back."

She gathered Zaire into her light and zoomed up over the trees, reflecting on the ample locational data she was providing the colony's sensors and any spinners in the enclave who happened to be paying attention. It couldn't be helped, and they were unlikely to come for her before she returned to the colony of her own volition.

Her arrival at the Deep Valley clinic caused little stir in the settlement. She saw no sign of enemy cats within the housing area, and little civilian activity. Anyone not on the battlefront hid in the emergency shelter. But Deep Valley cats and heavily armed humans patrolled the perimeter. They sighted her, identified her, and moved on, leaving her with the tricky task of getting the door to the infirmary open on her own without losing enough of her spin to release Zaire from stasis. She released only her hand from the spin and managed a hard push to fling the door open.

In contrast to the quiet on the paths outside, an air of chaos reigned inside the infirmary. The room teamed with medical personnel, flying from one bed or pallet to another, all hands busy with wounds and bandages. But when the door flew open to admit Fajora, everyone stopped, mid-step, mid-sentence to stare at her.

She released enough light to free her voice and say, "Zaire."

Doctor Tina ran to one side of her and a white-faced Lesedi to the other. They stared in growing horror as Fajora released Zaire from stasis enough for them to see his wound. As soon as Doctor Tina understood the injury, she sent her aide scrambling for more helpers to get a surgical room ready.

Fajora reinforced her stasis light and held Zaire cocooned in it until Doctor Tina had her team assembled. They brought in a floating cart, much like those used in the Wellador hospitals, and Fajora arranged the wounded man on it. She released him from stasis only when the medical staff assured her they were ready for him, and then she gave him over to the doctors and sagged with weary relief.

Lesedi gave Zaire one hurried touch with gentle fingers before the door to the surgery room closed. While Vi treated Fajora's lower leg wound, which was neither deep nor dangerous, Lesedi brought her food and plied her with questions about the battle. Other members of the clan, human and feline, crowded close to hear her answers.

"Bardu will tell you the rest of the pertinent details," Fajora said finally, more wearied with the telling than with the battle and the spinning of a wounded passenger. "I must go back now. I promised Clarise and Akachi."

This last brought a smile to Lesedi's face. She put her arms around Fajora and whispered in her ear, a message for her alone and not for the ears of those who gathered around. "Give them my love and tell them I said to go to the colony and find healing."

Vi finished her ministrations with a blue light treatment. "This should keep you from having a scar. If you do scar, have one of the colony doctors work on it."

Fajora spun away then, glad to escape the vicinity of so many wounded. She found Bardu and several other Deep Valley Clan members with Sanaa when she returned to the valley where she had left Clarise and Akachi.

"Is the settlement secure?" Fajora asked Bardu.

"Yes. And Zaire?"

"In surgery. The doctors will do their best to save him."

"It is well. I am pleased the Malekemi have not needed to come for him. Not yet, anyway."

Fajora arched her eyebrows at him. "The Malekemi? I thought you didn't believe in the Immortals."

"I believe what I see with my own eyes. I saw the Malekemi, bathed in light, come for my comrades today. They are in the Immortal lands now."

"I'm glad you didn't have to help them on their way." Fajora thought of the cats up above, finishing off the wounded. Some checked the fallen here as well, but Bardu's muzzle was clean. He did not join in that duty.

"As am I," he said.

Fajora studied him, surprised.

Bardu lifted his chin, his dark eyes unblinking. "My clan is my family, Light Spinner. I care for them more than you can fathom. We follow our way as a duty that is best for the clan and for the individuals in it, not out of a desire to kill our friends. We prefer to restore our comrades when possible, because we care for them. This especially holds true now, as we need all our warriors. We have dealt Rock Clan a blow and will have peace for a short space, but they will not give up."

Bardu paused to survey the carnage on the battlefield. He lifted one paw and groomed it briefly, but when Akachi limped across his field of vision, he lowered his paw and gave Fajora a steady look. "I am glad you saved young Akachi. He has acquitted himself well today, despite his blinded eye and lame leg. If he comes back to us after his visit to the doctors of the colony, he will be welcomed home."

Akachi and Clarise, shadowed by Sanaa, wandered among the fallen. Fajora joined them as Akachi stopped beside the body of a female cat.

"The sister of my mother," he said.

"I'm sorry."

"She died with honor. But she will be missed among my family. My mother will grieve her littermate."

"All the more reason for you to get your eye fixed so you can go home and comfort your mother."

Akachi put his head down and licked his paw, avoiding Fajora's gaze. He lifted his head and gave his chest a couple of thoughtful licks. Finally, his gaze met hers. "Let us go. We shall see what they can do. I will have an adventure like no one else in my clan ever has."

Fajora scooped him and Clarise into a spin. They didn't go far at first. She stopped at the edge of Deep Valley Clan, scanning the area from above first to make sure no Rock Clan cats lurked nearby. Then, they hunted.

Akachi found his prey by scent and stalked it with little trouble. His vision and his lame leg betrayed him when he pounced, however, and Fajora had to help. She would not deprive him of the kill, but she turned to spinning light and herded the Rothfur straight into his path.

She turned away once he had a firm hold on his quarry and let him do his bloody work unobserved. Leaving him alone, she sat quietly with Clarise, sharing a snack, for half of a sunprowl, by her uncertain calculation. When they returned to Akachi, he had reduced his Rothfur to a pile of bones and busied himself with his washing up. He glanced up at her.

"The Rothfur tasted good." He paused to lick his paw, then added, "I was hungry."

Fajora knew this was his way of thanking her for her assistance without compromising his dignity, and she was content.

When he was clean to his satisfaction, Fajora pulled her passengers into a spin again, and this time they made the short journey to the Wellador Colony. They coalesced on top of the Council Rock near Haven Outpost. Dusk deepened toward night, and if anyone had seen Fajora's light and guessed a Light Spinner had arrived, they would not be able to see the passengers she brought with her.

Fajora and Akachi had agreed it would be better if as few people as possible knew about his presence here. So Fajora left him hunkered down with Clarise in the near dark and walked to the outpost. The climb down the stair-stepped path to the meadow below the Council Rock seemed easy, even in the dark. The harder part of her walk came when she had to find the right people to alert in the outpost without attracting anyone else's attention.

She went first to the guest quarters and knocked on the door to the apartment assigned to Sonja Benjamin. Fajora had been gone so long, she couldn't be sure Sonja even remained at the outpost. If Sonja had finished going through Sebastian's things, she might have returned to her work in New Skakeet City. If a stranger answered the door, how would Fajora account for her presence?

But no one answered, either friend or stranger. On a whim, Fajora tried the door to her own apartment, pleased when it responded to her touch. She slid it open to reveal her few belongings stacked neatly where she had left them. Dannel and Sonja had not given up on her. This encouraged her, but it didn't help her decide where to look for help next.

She decided to try the clinic but changed her mind as she passed the building where Sebastian's apartment was located. She slipped inside. Perhaps she'd find Sonja here, working late. She heard voices coming from the lounge beyond her line of vision, and she turned to light, staying high against the ceiling as she passed through.

"Did you see a flash?" someone asked.

"The lights are flickering," someone else answered. "Keep an eye on it and call maintenance if it happens again."

Sebastian's apartment was at the end of a dimly lit hall, beyond the view of those in the lounge. Fajora let her light fade and rang the buzzer. After a brief wait, she heard footsteps, and the door slid open. Sonja stood motionless before her, a hand-held information device in one hand and a sheaf of papers in the other. Her little dog, Bessie, crowded at her feet yapping.

Sonja stared at Fajora so long Fajora grew worried. Didn't Sonja recognize her? Was something wrong or odd about her appearance? She was suddenly aware of the blood on her clothing and her disheveled condition. She must appear to Sonja to be an apparition from the dead. Or from the horrors of the war zone on Exalton, a part of the Wellador communal memory.

Well, she did come from a war zone. She had done battle, with no sleep for more hours than she could count, and her legs threatened to give out on her. She grabbed the doorframe, wishing Sonja would give her a chair before she fell. Wondering why Sonja didn't say something. And not knowing what to say to break the silence.

44

AKACHI'S PRECONDITION

Fajora cleared her throat, and Sonja started.

"Fajora?" Her voice squeaked. She dropped her device and grabbed Fajora's arm, pulling her into the apartment. "I can't believe it. I thought I'd never see you again. Is Sebastian with you?" She peered out the door with an eager expression.

"No. I'm afraid he isn't."

"Is he coming? Did you find him?"

What to say? Until this moment, Fajora hadn't decided how much she would tell the Wellador colonists. She had killed to preserve Deep Valley's secrets, but she hadn't ruled out the possibility of entrusting those secrets to her friends here. But now, words stuck in her throat. The secrets were not hers to share. Not yet, anyway. That might change if she decided to hand over Sebastian's disks, but she needed time to think it over and take the measure of conditions in the colony.

But Sonja waited, expectant, and she had to say something.

"He's not coming back, Sonja. Not now."

Sonja's face fell. "But he's not dead? Is he? Did the cats do something to him? They didn't . . . eat him, did they?"

Fajora couldn't help but smile. "No. They didn't eat him. I'm pretty sure the cats don't do that. And he isn't . . . ." But how to even tell her he lived without revealing too much? "I'm sorry. I can't tell you. Or even explain why. You'll have to trust me on this, at least until I get everything sorted."

Sonja stood still, staring at her for what seemed an eternity but must have been only a minute or two. She gave a slow nod and her whole body slumped. "I wish you had better news, but I'm glad you're back. Trayle's had a hard time keeping Kinovic from coming down here. Dannel had to lay down the rules pretty sternly, from what I understand. And none of us knew if you were dead or alive. I've imagined the worst for days and dreamed about your half-eaten face at night. Did you see any cats?"

"Yes. I've brought one with me."

Sonja's eyes widened and her hand went to her mouth. The sheaf of papers fluttered to the floor as her other hand grabbed the doorframe. She stepped into the hall and peered around. When no cat materialized, she started down the hall toward the lounge area.

"No, Sonja, wait." Fajora beckoned her back. "Not here, in this building. He's at the Council Rock. I didn't want to attract too much attention. He needs a doctor, but not just any doctor. Could we get the doctor who saw Fazok to come down to the outpost? Or is he already here?"

"You mean Jarrod Pellar? Or Silviann, maybe?"

"Jerrod. That's it."

"He's usually here, but he went up to check on Agent Fazok. I can call him."

"Fazok is alive?" Relief sent a rush of adrenaline through Fajora's veins and she grabbed a nearby chair for support. "Is he well?"

"No. I'm afraid I'm the one with bad news now. They finally identified the poison, but there's no known antidote. They've tried everything they know, and they've kept him alive, but he's in a lot of pain. The only way to give him relief is to sedate him, so he sleeps a lot."

"When he's awake, is he . . . lucid?"

"Oh yes. He spends time every day dictating instructions for the enclave, and Trayle reads to him a lot. Since you came down here, supposedly to help with the prophecy documents, he's been asking for the old writings." She smiled. "Trayle is getting interested too."

Fajora laughed. That flighty jokester interested in the old prophetic writings? It seemed a stretch too far. But she saw no sign of teasing in Sonja's demeanor. Just delight in making a convert.

"So, I can see him, once Akachi is taken care of? But what do we do about getting him the help he needs? How do we get the doctor here without letting anyone at the hospital, and Kinovic most of all, know what's going on?"

"That's easy. I have Doctor Pellar's number. I'll call him on his direct line."

"And you'd better tell him to bring Dannel with him. I have someone else with me he'll want to see. Needs to, in fact, to figure out what to do with her, how to get her home."

"Someone else?" Sonja's eyes widened again. "Ohhh. Let me guess. You didn't find Clarise Howard? After two years?"

"Yes. She's on the rock with Akachi. But don't tell anyone. Not yet, anyway. Not until Dannel comes. Promise me."

"Oh yes. Let me call Doctor Pellar and Dannel now."

While Sonja closed the door and retrieved her device from among the scattered papers on the floor, Fajora sank into a chair and surveyed the room, taking in the maps and notes—so many more notes now than when she left—and tried to make sense of them. She half-listened to Sonja's excited voice as she explained the situation to Doctor Pellar. Sonja mentioned Dannel's name several times, along with Trayle's and Fazok's, but Fajora made no effort to follow the conversation. Her perceptions became increasingly hazy as the surreal nature of her situation dawned on her.

She was at an outpost of the human colony, which lived under strict treaty rules with the cats of Kakislane, rules that nearly forbade and certainly curtailed any interaction among the two species. And she had brought a cat here for medical treatment.

It had seemed natural, logical, when Obasi suggested it. But now it seemed preposterous. And how would the humans view it? Would they suggest the cat go back where it belonged? Or complain to the cats about treaty violations? Perhaps even treat this as an opportunity to wrestle concessions from the cats?

Later, settling in a sheltered spot on the Council Rock, with Clarise and Akachi pressed close to Fajora on either side, the cat raised the same question.

"What will the humans want in return for this medical treatment you have promised me?"

"I don't know." Akachi deserved her complete honesty, and not only because of his ability to sense her truthfulness or lack thereof. She had come to care too much for him to deceive him, even to make things easier for him. They would find out what the humans wanted when Doctor Pellar and Dannel arrived by private transport in a few hours. Sonja had gone to wait for the two men at the transport landing pad, too excited to try to sleep or even to stay indoors.

"You can ask them any questions you want, once they arrive," Fajora told Akachi. "If they don't answer to your satisfaction, I'll take you home. Just let me know. And don't answer any of their questions if you think you shouldn't."

"That is well. I will follow your advice. You must promise to stay close so I can get away if I need to."

"I promise."

Akachi pressed closer and made no protest when Fajora stroked the soft fur on his head and back. He also allowed Clarise to stroke him a little. There was no one else to witness the insult to his dignity, but Fajora sensed the young cat also needed the physical touch and the reassurance it brought. Slowly, as she stroked, he relaxed against her and a deep, contented rumble emanated from his chest. When she moved her hand to her lap, Akachi nudged it with his nose until she started stroking again.

In the darkest time of night, with dawn several hours away, Fajora heard voices and the sound of feet on the rough stairway leading up to the top of Council Rock. She prodded Clarise and Akachi, who snuggled together, asleep. They came instantly to alertness.

They saw the artificial torch first, as Sonja crested the top of the rock, followed closely by Jerrod Pellar and Dannel Crowner. Fajora shifted to her knees to greet Doctor Pellar, who quickly knelt as well, bringing him close to Akachi's level.

"I'm Jerrod. And you are Akachi?"

"Yes."

"I understand you have an injured eye and a lame leg. May I take you down to my medical clinic and have a look at them?"

"Perhaps." Akachi's cool tone elicited a glance between Jerrod and Dannel.

"You have reservations? You are worried, perhaps, about what I will do to you."

"I would like to know the cost to myself and to my people before we proceed. What concessions will you seek in exchange for this service. In what way must I betray my people in order to see with this eye again?"

Jerrod sat back on his heels and flashed a grin up at Dannel. "Well. It appears you have your wits about you. Or Agent Fajora has been coaching you."

"I do not need coaching. However, the Light Spinner did assure me I could ask any questions I wanted and need not answer any I do not want to answer."

Jerrod's grin widened. "What do you say, Dannel? This cat wants to know about concessions and betrayal. What do you know about that?"

Dannel's voice floated down from his superior height, soft and serious, with no hint of the laughter evident in Jerrod's voice. "This cat is wise. Let me assure you, Akachi, we don't expect any concessions. Always good to get everything out in the open, though. I agree with you. Can't be too careful, can we? But we want to help. We're invaders on your world, in a way. Don't get a chance too often to pay your people back for letting us live here in peace and have reasonable lives. More than our own people granted us, back on the home world. So, you say or don't say anything you want, and we'll do whatever we can to fix you up. How about it?"

Akachi got up and paced around Dannel and Jerrod, sniffing at them. Dannel squatted low so Akachi could reach his face. Otherwise, both men held perfectly still, though their eyes glinted as they followed Akachi's every movement. When Akachi was satisfied, he came back to Fajora's side and sat on his haunches.

"These men are truthful. I will go with them to see what their superior medicine can do."

"Excellent," Dannel said. "And here is someone else I must greet and welcome home." He held his hand out to Clarise to help her up, pulling her into a warm, gentle embrace. "I've thought of you often over the past two years, but I had no way to get to you. I'm so grateful Agent Fajora found you and brought you home. Come. Once we get Akachi settled at the clinic, we'll talk and contact your parents."

Tears rained down Clarise's face as Dannel released her. In the torchlight Fajora thought she saw suspicious moisture around Dannel's eyes as well. He took Clarise's hand and led her toward the stairs.

"Will you walk, or will Agent Fajora spin you down?" Jerrod asked Akachi as he also rose and started for the stairway.

"I will walk." Akachi pressed ahead of the doctor, his limping gate almost graceful in the dark. Fajora held her breath as he disappeared over the edge of the cliff, fearing his impaired vision or lame leg would cause a fall on the steep path. But she heard nothing beyond the crunching of all their feet.

Fajora spun to the bottom to keep out of the way of the others. She waited anxiously to see if Akachi would make it down alone, ready to spin to his rescue if he floundered. But a few moments later, Akachi stepped down onto flat ground, tail held high, well ahead of Jerrod. Dannel gave Akachi a bemused glance before leading the way back to the compound.

"Jerrod has called several assistants," he said as they neared the medical clinic. "We've closed the clinic and given the rest of the staff the day off. Sonja can take care of any necessary lab work for us. We'll keep this as quiet as possible, at least for now."

"Good. Thank you," Fajora answered.

Akachi said nothing, but he watched closely, especially as they entered the clinic, where lights flickered on automatically and doors whooshed open on approach.

A female medic met them and led Clarise away down the hall while Jerrod led the rest of the group into a sleek room with towers and metal boxes and shiny wall panels, all bright with blinking lights and glowing text. Jerrod Pellar gave Akachi's eye a quick but thorough examination. Akachi stood under scanning devices, hooked up to other devices by wires and sensors. Quivering but otherwise motionless, he kept his good eye fixed on Fajora.

Fajora's admiration for him increased. She had been around the human medicine for years while serving on Kakislane. While she trusted the human doctors and had even consulted them herself, she abhorred the machines, the wires, the tubes, and especially the low hum they emitted, like the hum of deadly biting insects at night near the Marsh Lakes on Luxera. Akachi, whose experience with human medicine was the substantially less invasive medicine of the Deep Valley Clan doctors, bore the examination without moving or making a sound.

When he finished the exam, Jerrod announced he would try to repair the eye with Akachi's permission. "It will require artificial implants to replace the damaged tissue, but we can model those on the other eye. It's a new technique, still experimental, but I think it will work. I can't promise anything, but, well?" Jerrod shrugged. "What do you have to lose?"

Akachi leaned forward to sniff at Jerrod's hand. Fajora knew he tested for truthfulness, but Jerrod apparently took the gesture for a sign of acceptance.

"Good," he said. "And we'll work on that leg while you're under anesthesia. We should be able to give you better movement, maybe close to normal. No more hobbling around if I have anything to do with it."

A low rumble emanated from Akachi's chest. He gave his fur several licks before turning to consult Fajora. "Why does this man assume he may do as he pleases? It is I who have been hobbling, as he says, and I beat him down the trail to this place."

"Yes, you did." Fajora kept her voice calm, hoping to soothe Akachi's ruffled pride. "He assumes too much, but he is a skilled doctor. It would be a shame not to let him help you."

Akachi needed more time to consider this. Jerrod and the staff stood still, their faces tense, while they waited.

"Very well," Akachi agreed. "You may try. But if the trial is not successful, you must follow the way of the clans."

"The way of the clans?" Jerrod frowned in confusion. "I don't understand."

"It is the way of the clans to relieve a warrior of his life when he is injured beyond repair. This keeps him from becoming a burden and restores his honor. My clan would have performed this duty, but this Light Spinner prevented it. Now you will perform this duty if your treatment fails."

Jerrod's face, Dannel's face, the faces of all the medical staff reflected Fajora's horror at this demand.

"You mean kill you?" Jerrod whispered. "I can't. I've sworn to protect life at all costs."

Akachi regarded him a moment, then lifted his chin. "Very well. I will leave now. Light Spinner, you must take me from this place with your spinning, as you promised."

Tears pooled in the corners of Fajora's eyes. If she took Akachi back to the forests and hills of Deep Valley Clan, he faced a slow death from starvation.

But as he sat, surrounded by gawking humans, holding himself tall and proud, Fajora understood him as she had not fully done before. Intelligent and articulate, his formal speech giving him a veneer of civilization, he was, at heart, wild and free and full of dignity. He could not live as a cripple, needing to be helped and waited on, any more than she could live without spinning light.

Her hands sparked light as she stepped toward the examination table.

"Wait." Jerrod wiped his hand across his eyes and down his chin, then dropped it to his side. "I agree to whatever you ask if you'll let me try to fix your eye and your leg."

Everyone in the room stared at him. Dannel shifted his stance and reached a hand toward the doctor. "Jerrod, what are you doing?"

"Trust me on this, Dannel, please."

Dannel studied him, then nodded. "All right. What do you say, Akachi?"

Akachi leaned forward to sniff at Jerrod again, then leaned back, satisfied. "It is well. You may begin when you are ready."

Fajora waited with Akachi while Jerrod called in a medical engineer to fashion implants to his specifications and started other preparations. As soon as Akachi and Fajora were alone, Akachi began a thorough cleaning of his coat, from his ears down to his toes, which he worked on with a rigor that amused Fajora even as it made her long for a wash herself. When he finished, he smelled fresh and his fur glowed. He settled in a relaxed position, calmed by his grooming, and closed his eyes, though his ears remained upright and alert.

Fajora waited until the implants had been formed and the operating room prepared. She watched, stiff and short of breath, as they put Akachi to sleep for the surgery. She swallowed hard against the memory of Akachi, sedated and limp on the trail out of Rock Clan territory, when his pain was intense and his recovery uncertain. *This will help him. This is necessary. This is how he survives.* The words, repeated over and over in her mind, kept Fajora still until Akachi lost consciousness and Jerrod motioned for her to leave.

She fled to her own apartment in the guest house, where she showered, dressed in a clean uniform, and grabbed a quick snack of honey wafers and fruit. Refreshed, she hurried back to the medical clinic to wait for the doctors to finish and give her their report. She arrived to find Dannel pacing outside the surgery room, his hands clasped behind him. He gave Fajora a wan smile.

"Jerrod asked me to trust him, but he may have gotten himself in over his head this time."

Dannel's nervousness did nothing to allay Fajora's own fears. Though she dreaded the coming interview, she welcomed the distraction when Dannel motioned her across the hall to the lounge.

"Let's talk about your adventures while we wait, shall we? Keep our minds off the surgery."

She followed him into the lounge, wondering how to satisfy his curiosity without telling what she knew of Rock Clan and Deep Valley Clan. Wondering, as well, what Clarise had already told him.

45

QUESTIONS AND ANSWERS

"What shall I get you?" Dannel asked, heading for the cooking console and control panels against one wall. "I'm guessing, because I know something of Light Spinners, that you would like something to eat."

"Yes, please. I had a snack, but it wasn't anywhere near enough."

"It never is." He smiled. "I'm known for my omelets. Care to give one a try?"

"Of course." The fame of his omelets had reached the enclave, but Fajora had never had a chance to sample them. Her stomach growled, and Dannel laughed as he ordered up eggs, cheese, and other ingredients.

"It's all in the freshness of the ingredients, you know." He smacked an egg against the edge of the console and emptied the bright, yoke yellow contents into a bowl with a flourish. "Also the wrist motion as you swirl the eggs in the pan. I'll show you the secret, if you promise not to share it with anyone else."

He kept up a stream of chatter as he laid out a row of pans and prepared not one, but three omelets bursting with cheese and vegetables. Two he piled on a plate for Fajora. The third he dished up for himself. By the time he set them on the table in front of Fajora, her mouth watered and she felt at ease with Dannel.

He waited patiently, not asking any questions until she was well into the second omelet and had slowed down, near repletion and savoring the last delicious bites. It wasn't fair of him to soften her up with food before he questioned her. She would have to be sharp now, not to give in and tell him everything she knew.

"So, you've been to Deep Valley Clan, have you?"

Fajora lifted startled eyes to Dannel's face, forgetting to hide her reaction. "What makes you think that?"

"It stands to reason. I suppose you could have found a wounded Deep Valley cat wandering around in the wilderness, but I'm guessing not."

"How do you know Akachi's clan?"

"It's my business to know. I've studied the cat clans all my life. Especially since I got into politics. How can I govern my colony if I don't know the societies we share this planet with? Share uneasily, I might add. I know Deep Valley when I see it. Akachi is young, and Jerrod says he received his injuries recently. Expertly treated, too, with laser technology, which I know you don't have access to but I suspect Deep Valley does. Residue of sedatives and other drugs in his bloodstream, though wearing off now, which sets the timeframe of his injury to well after you headed out. And the fur around his eyepatch contained a residue of a poultice Jerrod recognized as one Clarise developed several years ago. Do I need to go on?"

"Have you talked to Clarise about this?"

"No. After we called her parents, I had someone take her to a guest apartment to get cleaned up and rested so she's ready to greet them. She's probably sleeping now."

"Her parents. Are they . . . ? Will they be coming down or will they wait for her to go home?"

"They won't wait. I sent my personal transport for them. They'll be here by the time she wakes up."

"Good. She's waited long enough."

"Yes. I'll debrief her after the reunion. But now, Deep Valley Clan. Your adventures."

Fajora sent a quick plea to Ya-Lohim for wisdom. In her exhaustion, she could easily say too much. Dannel had already gleaned a stunning amount of information during a short examination and had drawn astute conclusions. Fajora suspected, feared, he knew even more than he revealed.

"You're right. I've been to Deep Valley Clan."

"And found Clarise there as well, with enough of her wits about her to treat a wounded cat, along with freedom of movement to do so. Am I too far off if I guess Deep Valley's guest list included our astrophysicist, Sebastian? Includes him yet, perhaps?"

Fajora said nothing this time. Tried to keep her facial muscles from twitching and giving anything away. Steadied her emotional profile to keep her eye flecks neutral. But there was no way to deceive Dannel.

"Your silence gives you away. If you don't want me to know things, you should learn to tell a convincing lie. Tell me you never saw him. Or you found him lying in a ravine, half eaten by cats, or by owls, or by some wild, nonsentient creature. With your silence, you simply tell me you don't want to confirm that I'm right."

Fajora shook her head. "Why do you even need to talk to me?"

"Because you tell me things, you see, by your non-answers as well as by your answers. Things I could only guess at otherwise. Good guesses, perhaps, but still guesses. I know a little about Deep Valley Clan. Scans and sensors and things, you know. They give us a peek on occasion. But only a peek. I'm sure you could tell me a thing or two if you had a mind to. For instance, what Clarise has been doing all this time. And why Sebastian stayed when you came home. Sensors can't tell me that, no?"

Again, Fajora remained silent, fingering the disks she had secreted in her tunic pocket. The disks of prophecy manuscripts Sebastian had given her, and the disk with information from Rock Clan's void ship. Should she hand them over? Sebastian had wanted her to, but she heard Lesedi's voice in her head, telling her Rock Clan's void aspirations were Deep Valley Clan's responsibility. Not the colony's. And Obasi's voice—poor, dead Obasi—warning her only to give information about Rock Clan if Deep Valley Clan lost the war.

Well, they had won. The first battle, anyway. She dropped the clunky Rock Clan disk but continued to finger the slim Deep Valley disks. Sebastian had asked her to give them to Sonja, not Dannel. He might need to know eventually. But not yet. She let the disks drop back to the bottom of her pocket.

Dannel had confirmed, at least through inference, the suspicions she had entertained half-heartedly. He knew humans lived in Deep Valley Clan. The medical treatment Akachi had received from them did not surprise him. But Fajora would not give him the satisfaction of her eye-witness confirmation.

He sighed. "Ah well. Knowing a thing or two about Deep Valley, I can make pretty good guesses about why you won't talk. If we could talk openly, you and I, about what we know, we would fashion quite a tale. But you distrust too many people here in the colony. Know a few myself I don't trust. And some people in the enclave . . . ." Dannel coughed apologetically. "One in particular I can't trust, so there we are."

Fajora smiled. "I think I know who you mean. I don't trust him either. And he's bound to be looking for me soon, with questions I can't answer."

"Been looking already. It's challenged our wits, devising ways to keep him away from here. I laid down the law, but in the end, if a Light Spinner decides to go somewhere, it's pretty hard to stop him. Or her."

He grinned as he rose and gathered the empty plates. "Need another omelet? Or shall I bring out the butterscotch mousse? I whipped up a batch while you waited with the cat, and I have two servings chilling in the cooler."

"In that case, how can I refuse?"

Fajora had never heard of either butterscotch or a mousse, but the omelets had been so delicious she was ready to try anything Dannel offered her. He set before her a beautiful dish with an enticing, buttery smell, but even those attributes could not prepare her for the creamy, sweet sensation on her tongue as she took the first bite. She was pretty sure she would tell Dannel anything he wanted to know if he asked her while she reveled in this dessert.

But he asked her nothing, appearing content to enjoy the treat with her, making this a moment to remember. He didn't speak again until the dishes were empty, by which time she recovered some of her reticence.

"Now, you've admitted you visited Deep Valley Clan. Not much point in denying it with Akachi in Jerrod's care over in the next room, after all. But what about Rock Clan and River Clan? If I had to guess—which I seem to be doing a lot here—I'd say Akachi got those nasty wounds tangling with one of those clans. They're both known to be rivals of Deep Valley. Do you mind clearing up which was the culprit in this case?"

Fajora said nothing as she eased the empty mousse dish away from her.

"I see. You do mind. So the next question is, why? We know those two clans are welcoming to Dark Spinners, but I can't imagine why you want to hide that kind of activity from me. I infer some other complication with one or both clans, yes?" He worked his spoon in his empty mousse dish, getting the last bit of creamy goodness, before pressing her again. "We won't interfere with your friends in Deep Valley Clan. But it seems it can only help them if we know what to keep an eye out for in these other clans. Don't you agree?" Dannel's gaze caught and held her, unrelenting now.

She faced him honestly. "I understand how it would seem that way from your perspective, but some things, things between the clans, are simply none of your business."

It was blunt. Maybe too blunt. Dannel regarded her without responding for a long time, his fingers drumming on the table as he considered her words. Fajora closed her eyes to hide eye flecks she knew were swirling chaotically. No need to make him queasy as well as angry.

She was so tired she almost fell asleep where she sat, and memories rushed through her mind in jumbled bits, as if she dreamed a series of disconnected dreams. One image stood out, and her eyes flew open. She could share this with Dannel, a peace offering of sorts.

"I can tell you one thing. Dark Spinners came to clan territory while I was there. I killed one of them. I don't know if Kinovic will hear of it. For various reasons, I can't share this information with him, or with anyone at the enclave. But if he does find out, if he starts asking questions, I thought you should know."

"Hmm." Dannel shoved his dish away. "Our sensors picked up Dark Spinners, or something similar, several times. The first occasion appeared to be in Rock Clan. Can you confirm that?"

So. He foiled every attempt to withhold information from him. Each time she gave him something she deemed harmless, he paired it with knowledge he already had, and his conclusions were startlingly on target. He had her on his territory, eating his delicious food, and he appeared to believe that gave him the right to gather as much information as he could from her.

Fajora would do the same, in his position, but she did not work for him and she held high ranking in the enclave. She decided she could ask a few questions of her own.

She caught his gaze, ignored his question, and asked, "Why is it you don't trust Kinovic? He is, after all, a senior agent of the enclave and in good standing."

Dannel burst out in a short laugh. "My dear, you also don't trust him. You've admitted as much yourself. Why do you wonder that I don't?"

"I have my own reasons for my mistrust. I would like to know what yours are."

Dannel's grin faded and he spoke in a serious tone again. "Fair enough. You've given me answers to my questions, even if reluctantly. So I'll answer yours. For starters, Kinovic always seems to be angry, and I don't know any reason for it. Gives me a bad feeling, and I take emotional reactions seriously. Also, he's always poking his nose in where it doesn't belong. We have agreements with the enclave on the information we will share with each other. But he's always probing. Trying to get a great deal more from us than we are bound to share. At the same time, he has, to my mind, an incomprehensible aversion to sharing what the agreement demands from his side. For one thing, he seldom gives a hint about Dark Spinner activity, even when we know he knows about a visitation. Can't figure the reason for his reluctance, though Jerrod has raised one idea, which I must say I hate to entertain."

"And that idea is?"

"Ah. Yes, you would ask. Fair again. Confirm for me that the Dark Spinner activity took place in Rock Clan, as, I might point out, Kinovic should have done, and I'll tell you Jerrod's idea."

Dannel was wily, but they were beginning to understand one another. If Fajora ran the enclave, the two groups might work well together.

"Yes," she admitted. "You are correct. Four or five days after I left the colony, a group of between six and eight Dark Spinners visited Rock Clan. I felt their auras but did not see them, nor was I privy in any way to their business. They departed after a scant day. One Dark Spinner lingered after the others left. Eventually he forced me to kill him. I hadn't met him before, but we've both heard of him, from Fazok."

"The rogue Light Spinner agent? Salez or Sytaz or . . . ?

"Syjaz."

"Right. That's it. So he's dead? Won't have to worry about tracking him anymore, then."

"No. I'm sorry I had to kill him, but he didn't leave me a choice." An image of Syjaz as she had first seen him, hair braided with gold, eye flecks dancing, intruded on Fajora's thoughts. She brushed it aside. In the end, Syjaz had become little more than a wisp of a shadow. Meanwhile, a very real, solid, dependable human sat across from her, someone with whom she could work and build trust. "That's all I can tell you. But I offer you this. If, in the future, Kinovic is the head of the enclave, which is, unfortunately, likely if Fazok doesn't recover, let me know if he refuses to meet the requirements of our agreement."

"And what will you do about his noncompliance?"

"I will do my best to provide you with the information you need, though doing so without his interference will be tricky. And I will document his noncompliance. Too many infractions of that sort could see his commission rescinded." Dannel started to speak, but Fajora held up a hand to forestall him. "Don't put too much hope in that. I suspect he will be documenting similar grievances against me. It will be a race to see who has the evidence to get rid of the other first. And the advantage will be on his side, due to some previous circumstances."

Dannel got up and carried the dirty dishes to the disposal slot. He brought a cloth and wiped the table, then returned to the cooking console and tidied it as well. When he returned to the table, his manner became easy, affable, as if their conversation had been one of light, non-consequential chatter between friends.

"You've had a busy day. How long since you've slept?"

"Two days. No, probably longer."

He whistled. "Should have told me. I wouldn't have kept you so long. Go to your quarters and get some sleep. I'll have someone call you when Akachi starts waking up."

"Yes, I'd like that. But first, keep your side of our bargain."

"What bargain?" He gave her a half smile, which told her he knew.

"Jerrod's idea about why Kinovic doesn't share information on Dark Spinners."

"Hmm, yes. Well, I thought it would be obvious. Jerrod thinks Kinovic is a Dark Spinner."

"Interesting." Fajora's lack of reaction pleased her. She had half-expected this.

"And should I tell him to put that idea to rest?"

"Oh, no, not yet. You understand it takes two eyewitnesses to a shadow spinning before the Luxeran justice system will entertain such an accusation. But Kinovic's behavior does warrant a certain level of scrutiny. A sense of readiness, you might call it. And there is no requirement for those witnesses to be Luxeran."

Dannel grinned and stretched expansively. "I'm happy to hear you confirm that. And I know whom to speak with, now, if any of my people witness such an event. But he's safely up north, for today at least. And I intend to keep it that way as long as the cat is here."

"Thank you. I think I'll grab my nap now." Fajora stood and started for the door, but as she reached it, she remembered one last thing, another peace offering for Dannel. "Lieutenant Governor?"

"Actually, it's Governor now. Dario's resignation became effective two days ago." Dannel grinned.

"Congratulations."

"Thank you. You have something else?"

"Yes. A suggestion. The cats are wary of the colony. I don't see a lot of options for changing that. Akachi might be a start. But I know of one other thing. Just a possibility."

"Yes?" Dannel leaned toward her, his avid interest clear in his expression and voice.

"If the cats—if Deep Valley Clan cats in particular—approach you with a request for information about new prophecies, be ready to work with them. If you have contacts on Luxera or any other worlds—someone you can reach through the service's courier system, I suggest you mine them for any mention of new prophecies leaking out of Exalton. Get your hands on whatever you can, and have trustworthy people in place to deal with the cats."

"New prophecies, you say?" Dannel's expression held a strange mixture of curiosity, wonder, and caution.

Now it was Fajora's turn for guesses, though she based hers on Dannel's reaction and on intuition more than on any prior knowledge. "New prophecies. Which you already have, don't you?"

"Let my silence be my answer, as yours has been so often today." Dannel's voice betrayed his laughter.

"So be it," Fajora said, with laughter in her voice as well. "I'm off to sleep."

Fajora's eyes refused to focus, and her mind kept drifting. Anything else she and Dannel needed to discuss could wait until she was sharp enough to combat his verbal acuity. After he debriefed Clarise, he might have more questions for her. She had no idea what Clarise would choose to reveal about her two-year ordeal.

Fajora walked to her apartment with numb mind and weary steps and fell onto the bed without undressing. Even her worry about Akachi did not keep her from falling asleep as soon as she snuggled into the pillow. She slept without dreaming until the door buzzer, ringing repeatedly, roused her.

46

HUNTING

Fajora heard Sonja's voice calling to her as she stumbled toward the door, which slid open at her touch.

"Fajora, you must come. Akachi's awake, and he's tearing up the recovery room. He won't settle down." Sonja's voice squeaked, on the edge of panic.

Fajora found her boots and shoved her feet into them as she hurried to follow Sonja to the medical clinic. Silence greeted them as they entered, but as they drew near the surgery area, they heard a crash followed by a frantic female voice and the lower voice of a human male. Sonja broke into a run, and Fajora followed, keeping pace with her. Dannel met them as they rounded the last corner and followed them.

Drawing closer, they heard hisses, snarls, and growls mixed with the sounds of human voices. Akachi, very much awake, voiced his displeasure emphatically.

Sonja and Fajora skidded to a halt in the recovery room doorway as an instrument tray crashed to the floor with the tinkling sound of shattering glass. Two instrument towers lay on their sides on the floor as well. A low growl drew Fajora's gaze up, almost to the ceiling, where Akachi huddled in an open cupboard, well above the reach of the human medical staff. He crouched low, with all four legs tucked neatly under him, a position Fajora had not seen since his fight with Jelok. His ease in this position gave her hope.

"Akachi! What are you doing up there?"

"These medical humans wanted to put more drugs in me, but I do not know them. I do not know how to trust them."

"I understand. Their ways are sometimes strange to me, too."

"You said you would stay with me."

"I had to sleep. I thought they would call me before you woke up."

"He shook off the sedative sooner than expected," Jerrod interjected. "One minute he slept soundly, and the next he jumped up and started climbing all over the equipment. I wanted to give him something to calm him, but he wasn't having it."

Fajora smiled, more amused by the mess than distressed. "I can't say I blame him. How about his eye?"

"The procedure went well, I think." Jerrod grimaced. "I won't know for sure until I take a look. We can test the eye if he'll come down here and stand still. After that, it needs to stay covered and he needs to stay *quiet* for at least another day. His leg looks better, but it's fragile. Two or three days of rest would be better."

"That would not be good," Akachi said from his high perch. "I am hungry. I need to hunt."

"We'll bring you food," Jerrod promised. "Just come down so we can check your eye."

Akachi peered down at the group, his gaze landing last on Fajora, where it remained. "Light Spinner?"

"Come down, Akachi. It will be all right. I, for one, want to know if you have vision in your injured eye. Don't you?"

Akachi hesitated a moment longer. "Yes," he said finally. "But you must stay here."

He jumped easily down to the bed where a nest of blankets had been made for him, now in disarray. To Fajora, the movement was a miracle.

Akachi sat on his haunches watching Jerrod, who approached slowly, trying not to make any sudden movements. Akachi's ears twitched and the tip of his tail bent up, flickering back and forth.

"Do not worry," he told Jerrod. "I will not bite unless you do something foolish."

The blood drained from Jerrod's face, but he kept coming until he was near enough to touch Akachi. The rest of the staff, including Sonja, pressed themselves against walls or pieces of equipment, as far from the cat as they could get. The only one in the room besides Fajora who appeared at ease was Dannel. He stood in a relaxed stance to Fajora's left side, an amused quirk lifting the corners of his mouth. He showed no sign of nervousness.

Jerrod eased the patch off Akachi's eye and stood back while the cat blinked hard against the sudden bright light. After a tense silence, Jerrod shifted his feet and leaned forward, curiosity apparently overcoming fear.

"Well? What do you see?"

Akachi's gaze roamed the room. "I see silly humans who are afraid of one not yet full-grown cat. It makes me wonder about the courage and honor of humans."

Fajora smiled.

"Light Spinner, why do you smile?"

"You make me smile, Akachi. You are indomitable."

"I do not know that word, but I think you mean to compliment me."

"I do indeed."

"Very well." He looked at Jerrod. "Is there more to this checking you wanted to do?"

"Yes." Jerrod turned to an instrument tray and selected an instrument with a laser light on one end. "First, I'll use this scanner to check the implant connections. Then I'll shine this light in your eye, so I can make sure everything is moving correctly and healing has begun. It will be bright but will not harm you in any way."

"Proceed."

When Jerrod was satisfied, he stepped back and contemplated Akachi with a puzzled look on his face.

"What is it, doctor?" Fajora asked.

"I'm pleased with my findings so far, but I may have to devise a new test. I usually check vision with a reading test, but . . . I don't normally have a cat for a patient. I'm not sure what else to use."

"You may proceed with your test," Akachi said, lifting his head to give it an arrogant tilt.

"I don't understand." Jerrod turned to Fajora for an explanation.

"Akachi can read. Use your usual test, as he suggests." The humans' gasps and wide eyes made Fajora feel as smug as Akachi looked. Even Dannel looked stunned.

Jerrod recovered first. "Very well. Sonja, you and Paul lift the equipment tower and make sure it has power." As the two assistants complied, Jerrod typed into his handheld device. Soon a screen appeared on the restored tower and a series of letters and words blinked on.

The words and phrases were simple, designed to test vision rather than comprehension. Akachi read them flawlessly, even though Jerrod covered the uninjured eye. When the screen went blank, he took in the wide grins on the humans' faces and yawned, showing his teeth and his disdain all in one gesture. Fajora suppressed her own grin, not wishing to insult Akachi's dignity.

"I am hungry," he said. "I will hunt now."

"No," Jerrod said, no longer showing fear as he replaced the patch over Akachi's eye. "You won't. We've sent for food. It should arrive momentarily."

As he spoke, a female assistant entered, pushing a cart with several covered dishes. Each one contained a different kind of meat. She set them in front of Akachi and removed the covers, eyeing the cat nervously.

Akachi sniffed at the dishes, one after another, until he had checked all of them.

"I cannot eat this."

"Why not?" The woman with the food cart backed up two steps, her eyes watching the cat carefully. "It's perfectly good."

"It's not fresh."

"Yes, it is. I replicated the chicken and the pork just now. The beef is from our stores, delivered only yesterday from the ranches."

"It doesn't smell fresh. I will hunt."

"We've been over this already." Jerrod stepped in front of the cart and leaned over the dishes, smelling each one. "You can't go running around and jumping on animals until your eye has time to heal. To say nothing of the leg. You'll have to eat this or wait until your eye has recovered."

Everyone in the room leaned in, silent, waiting for Akachi's decision. Fajora could never have predicted his next demand.

"Light Spinner. This medical man says I cannot hunt until my eye is better, but I am hungry. You will hunt for me."

So Fajora found herself in the forest northwest of the outpost, spinning back and forth through the trees, trying to drive a large hare into a jumble of rocks, where it would not be able to get away from her. In the form of spinning light, she should have had a distinct advantage over the hare, but her inexperience and distaste for the task made her erratic. Twice, already, the hare had escaped her. She would not lose it a third time.

When at last she had the hare cornered, rump against the rock jumble, paws and nose quivering with terror, Fajora felt safe to resume her solid form. She approached the hare and grabbed it by its long ears, while the animal shrieked so loudly, she feared the sound carried all the way to the outpost. She was tempted to drop the creature and cover her ears, but if she did so, she would have to start over again or face Akachi without the fresh kill he demanded.

She held on to the creature by sheer force of will and reached for the knife at her waist. Dannel had given it to her with a bemused expression on his face.

"All you have to do," he had said, "is hold the animal still and slit its throat. The knife is sharp, so you should have no trouble. Drain the blood before you put it in your bag, or you'll be a bloody mess before you get back."

But no, she wouldn't be a bloody mess if she couldn't bring herself to slit the throat. She had killed sentient cats and Dark Spinners, but she wavered now, unable to kill this non-sentient creature to feed a friend. Her hand trembled as she brought the knife into position for the fatal strike, and the hare screamed again. She didn't know how long she stood, her hand shaking, the hare screaming, but suddenly, she didn't have the hare anymore.

Something swooped past her on the wing and tore the hare from her grasp. It landed with a quiet thud about ten paces from her, and an owl examined her with round yellow eyes. The hare was silent; blood poured from its torn throat.

"I guess you deserve it more than I do, since you're the one with the skill and courage to kill it. But what am I going to tell Akachi?"

The owl uttered a series of hoots, barks, and whistles, shook the animal, and stepped away.

"What? I don't understand." Fajora tried to read some clue to the owl's words in its body language.

The owl spoke again, then made clicking sounds that to Fajora's untrained ears sounded too much like disgust. It flew at her, too swift and unexpected for her to duck or guard her face. But the owl didn't touch her. Instead, it tugged at the bag that hung from her shoulder. After a moment of confusion, followed by disbelief, understanding dawned.

"You want me to put it in the bag and take it back to Akachi?"

The owl hooted softly.

"All right. Thank you. I could never have done this myself. I'll be sure to tell Akachi what you've done for him."

The owl hooted one more time before launching itself into the air and disappearing among the trees. Fajora had the sense of being watched as she lifted the dead hare by its ears and dropped it into the bag. She didn't mind.

Back in the clinic, she had the staff spread a disposable covering on the floor before she emptied her bag in front of Akachi.

"I'm not the right person to hunt for you," she told him as he tore the skin from the flesh. "I cornered the hare without trouble, but I couldn't kill it."

"I'd say you did a pretty good job," Dannel said. He and Jerrod were the only ones in the room, having sent the rest of the staff about their duties to give Akachi a little privacy.

Akachi paused in his bloody work to peer up at the men. "No, she didn't. This is owl kill. I trust you thanked the owl properly, Light Spinner."

The expressions on the two men's faces made all the trouble and anguish Fajora had experienced during her solo hunt worthwhile. What a delight to know these two powerful men were as captivated as she by the majesty and mystery of the owls.

47

GOODBYE

Two days later, Jerrod announced Akachi's eye had recovered enough for him to be released from the prison of his recovery room.

"I need to devise a test to see how the eyes work together in an active situation. I've tried pulling objects around the room and enticing Akachi to pounce, but he lifts his nose in disdain and refuses to cooperate."

"Can you blame him?" Dannel asked. "I would find it beneath my dignity. How much more so a cat, whose honor and dignity are always of the utmost importance."

"But I still need a test."

"Let him go hunting," Fajora suggested. "I'm getting tired of doing it, and the owl has its own needs to attend to. He'll have to do it eventually, anyway, to survive."

The four of them headed to the forest a few hours later. Fajora found the walk long and tedious, for she had always spun before. But the men labored through the high grass of the meadow without complaining, and Akachi loped ahead with boundless energy.

As they walked, Fajora asked Jerrod the question that had nagged at her since the day of Akachi's surgery. "Would you have followed the way of the clan as you promised if your treatment was unsuccessful?"

Dannel drew close to hear the answer. Jerrod walked a good twenty paces before he stopped and turned to his companions.

"Yes," he said, his voice low and solemn. "I promised. If I had been deceptive, Akachi would have known and would not have allowed the surgery."

"And what about your medical oath?" Dannel asked. "You set yourself up to be foresworn no matter what you did."

"No. I just had to make sure I didn't fail. I've never been more motivated in the operating room, let me assure you."

Dannel laughed and slapped Jerrod on the shoulder. "I don't know why I doubted you, my friend."

Akachi sniffed out a hare and began stalking as soon as they entered the forest. The men found a comfortable spot to wait, while Fajora translated to light and followed Akachi's progress unobtrusively, not wanting to interfere with the hunt but anxious to see how he fared.

He had no trouble tracking the hare, but he missed when he pounced, and the hare bounded away, fright giving it speed. Undaunted, Akachi picked up the trail with his sensitive nose and started again. This time, he missed by only a tiny margin.

Again, he showed no sign of discouragement but patiently stalked his prey until it was within reach again. This time, he took more time, observing the hare, creeping up ever so carefully, and when he finally pounced, he did not miss. Akachi cut short the hare's squeal as he skillfully dispatched his catch and tore it open.

Fajora waited until he finished eating to coalesce a few paces away from him. He began to wash himself, ignoring Fajora until he was reasonably clean.

"Light Spinner," he said at last, between work on his toes. "It is time for me to go home."

"I know, Akachi. I'm glad you're healed, but I'll miss you."

"Perhaps you will need to come to my lands to kill another Dark Spinner. I would be glad to see you then."

"Perhaps. But I have a Dark Spinner closer to home to catch first."

"Good hunting, then, Light Spinner. Let us go tell the humans I am leaving."

Dannel and Jerrod congratulated Akachi on his successful hunt. They invited him to stay longer, and Jerrod made him promise to return to the clinic if he had any difficulties with the repaired eye. They walked back to the outpost at a leisurely pace. Not even Akachi seemed in a hurry to say goodbye.

As they walked, a twisting of spun light zoomed over them, looped around, and zoomed back to coalesce in front of them. Trayle emerged from the light in a rush, her natural grace lost in her agitation.

"I am sooo glad to see you," she said to Fajora as soon as her lips formed. "He's on his way here, swearing he'll find out where you are. That he'll turn the place upside down until someone tells him the truth. I tried to stop him. Fazok ordered him to stay away, but I think he's coming anyway."

"Who?" Fajora's mind, still on the hunt and on the coming goodbye, only slowly processed Trayle's presence, let alone her words.

"Agent Kinovic, of course. Who else would I rush down here in a panic because of? But you're here, so it will work out. But why didn't anyone tell me she was back?" Trayle directed this last complaint to Dannel.

He patted her shoulder. "I'm sorry, my dear. We've been so preoccupied by the cat, it completely slipped my mind."

"The cat?"

Trayle noticed Akachi for the first time as the cat stalked up to stand at Fajora's side. She slid to her knees and held out a hand to him.

"Oh. You're so beautiful. I never dreamed. Are you going to eat me?"

Akachi growled, and everyone else laughed.

"You would not taste good," Akachi said. "And I would not want to answer to the elders for such a breach of honor. Besides, I would not desire to harm someone who is a friend of this Light Spinner." He rubbed his head against Fajora's hand, but his voice held a clear question.

"Yes," Fajora assured him. "Trayle is a friend. But Trayle, you shouldn't be here when Kinovic arrives. He can't know you've been here to warn us."

"Yes, ma'am." Trayle began to translate back to light even as she continued to speak. "But please be careful. He's been getting angrier and angrier over the past few days."

"Good."

A grin broke over Trayle's face. "I see. Yes, I'm going now. Cat, whatever your name is, I'm glad you're not interested in eating me, and I'm glad I got to meet you."

She finished translation and disappeared in a flash, leaving Dannel, Jarrod, and Fajora staring blankly at each other.

"One thing I know," Jerrod said after a moment. "Akachi should not be here when Kinovic arrives."

"No," Fajora agreed. "I planned to spin him home, but I don't know if I should leave now."

"The morning report from the sensor room detected possible Dark Spinner activity in Forest Clan territory," Dannel said. "Indications are low, but since we have our own resident Light Spinner, perhaps we should be sure. It won't take more than an hour or so for an experienced Light Spinner to make a survey and report back. Will save us from bothering the enclave for a fully agented expedition, if it's not warranted." He paused, his eyes on Akachi, his expression shifting from cynicism to wonder. "If you happen to pass beyond the edge of Forest Clan by mistake and make a stop in Deep Valley Clan, who's to be the wiser?"

"Kinovic will be furious that we took matters into our own hands." Fajora reached for light as she spoke. "He might put me on report, but I don't think he can do much else. I haven't been here long enough to build up a list of infractions. Akachi, are you ready to go? I'll take you home."

She landed below the canyon that sluiced the river out of the Deep Valley settlement. She could have carried Akachi to the top of the bluff, of course, but she wanted to watch him bound ahead of her, bursting with energy, as they climbed the trail to the top. To see him move like that, restored to his youthful vigor and enthusiasm, was her heart's desire.

The thought made her stop. The Malekem had told true. Things had turned out much different than she had planned. But she had followed his advice and put her hand to the tasks as they came to her, and now she received her reward. Her heart expanded with joy.

From the bluff, they had a view of the Deep Valley Clan settlement. Figures moved, tiny in the distance, toward the homes and community buildings. Almost dinnertime, time for the clan to gather. Rock Clan cats would return to the war path once they recovered from their recent defeat, but for now, peace lay over the valley.

In her imagination, Fajora followed her friends and acquaintances through their evening routine. In the void ship, Sebastian cleared his work station and prepared to join the other unattached humans in their communal dinner. Cats formed hunting parties and patrols, ready to head out for the night's work. Owls woke from their day's slumber and also prepared for the hunt. If Fajora waited, she might hear the owling before she bid Akachi farewell. She longed to share that with him one last time.

Akachi sniffed the air, testing it for scents. "Light Spinner, a patrol approaches. I do not think you should be here when they find me."

"No. And I must get back soon to uphold the story Dannel has prepared for Kinovic."

"This Kinovic. He is like a cat so concerned with his own honor he ignores the greatest good of his clan?"

"No. Not like that. Kinovic has no honor. He is dark and dangerous."

"You must be careful. I should not like to hear he has eaten you."

And Kinovic would do exactly that, in his own shadowy way, if he could devour Fajora without revealing his own loyalties.

"I will be careful, Akachi. Greet my friends in Deep Valley for me."

"I will."

They stood, at a loss for anything more to say. The next word should be goodbye, but Akachi seemed as reluctant as Fajora to say it. Akachi growled, stepped forward, and rubbed his cheek against Fajora's hand. She knelt and put her arms around him, sliding her hands through his fur, reveling in its softness.

"There's no one here to see this affront to your dignity, after all," she said.

Without another word, without waiting for his answer, she translated to light and headed back to the colony.

48

THESIS AND ANTITHESIS

Fajora sat in her office late into the evening working on personnel reports and deciding on staff assignments in preparation for the arrival of the next training class. Her new office, recently Kinovic's office. But also, her old office from an earlier time, before she left two years ago, before Jayzam made his fateful solo excursion into clan territory. Fazok's books, all but a treasured few he had taken to give to his children, lined the walls of the office.

Fajora worked on Fazok's desk of honey-colored wood, lovingly crafted by a human from the colony more than one hundred years ago. Kinovic had a new desk, sleek and modern. He had ordered it from the city as soon as the courier brought confirmation of his appointment as head of the enclave.

A shadow blocked the light shining through Fajora's window, and the door opened to admit Kinovic. So like him to enter without knocking. He took it as his right to do as he pleased, and her duty to put up with it. She caught a glimpse of his countenance and shuddered, at the same time suppressing a smile of triumph. Kinovic scowled, his face distorted by the angry, brooding expression that was becoming habitual. But today, his lips twisted in a more venomous snarl than usual. He seethed over something that hadn't gone his way. Fajora guessed what it was.

"I assume Fazok got off without any problems," she said by way of greeting. "The couriers who are spinning him home appeared careful and capable. He should arrive on Luxera in good shape, with energy to greet his family."

"He won't last long. Good decision, to get out of our way before the end, so we don't have to deal with getting a corpse back to Luxera." Kinovic's eye flecks swirled in a manner Fajora could only describe as gleeful. Even as she noticed this, they changed, swirling faster in the regimented pattern of consuming anger.

"He'll have time for goodbyes, at least. His family will be grateful." Fajora kept her voice gentle and carefully controlled her own eye flecks. In this game she played with Kinovic, she might do everything else right, but her eye flecks could give away her true intentions. Controlling them required extreme effort, an effort that involved keeping a tight rein on her thoughts and emotions.

"Good for him." Kinovic stepped closer to the desk, towering over Fajora. "But I didn't come here to talk about Fazok. He's no longer our concern. I want to know why none of the junior agents I requested to aide me tomorrow are available. How can they be unavailable when the head of the enclave requests them? They should drop any other assignments and put themselves at my disposal."

"Have a seat, sir, and I'll check into it." Fajora motioned toward one of the chairs arranged opposite her desk. "Let's see. Whom did you request? Oh, yes. I have that memo here, on one of these piles."

She took her time shuffling through several piles of paper, though she knew exactly where the memo in question was. Kinovic waited, holding himself perfectly still, and Fajora imagined the struggle he must be having not to burst loose and start spinning shadow. She glanced out the window, wondering where her backup was. She must work this just right. She didn't want to push Kinovic over the edge, only to find she didn't have the second witness. And she would be in grave danger with a Dark Spinner as powerful as Kinovic if he tried to envelop her in his shadow before she could counteract his action with spun light.

Nonetheless, she let his anger smolder while she crafted her response. She finally allowed herself to take hold of the memo and scan it with her eyes.

"Oh yes. I see. Agents Leajast, Croztell, and Britza. I'm sorry to say Agent Britza is ill. Possibly something she ate. Paltoz is treating her and has confined her to quarters in case it turns out to be something contagious. Your other two requests, Leajast and Croztell, are serving detention due to some difficulty adhering to one of your latest rules. I know you don't want to go soft on enforcing your directives. You'd end up with chaos. No one wants that, so I made sure I punished them according to protocol. I'll release them if you wish. I'm sure they'll be happy to give up cleaning out latrines. But it sets a bad precedent if they get away with their infractions without consequences."

Kinovic scowled. "We have a deplorable lack of disciplined junior agents who follow rules. I'm tempted to send the whole batch back to Luxera and request more experienced agents."

"I don't expect you can. Experienced agents are spread thin already, and the enclaves must do their part in training the juniors. We're no different. But that's why I've assigned extra agents to the incoming training class. The better we get them trained ahead of time, the less we'll have to do once they're commissioned. I've got a rigorous schedule planned for the trainees."

Kinovic's scowl deepened. "How many of our regular agents are involved?"

"Everyone but the core administrative staff. Of course, we'll pull them if there's a Dark Spinner crisis, but otherwise, I think we need to leave them in place."

Kinovic's hand came down on the desk, causing writing instruments to jump and the bowl of sweets at one corner to rattle. "Just get rid of them. I don't have time to coddle a bunch of trainees."

"We can't. Part of our charter demands we do our share of the off-world training. Besides, we'll have a chance to inspect them, in case any are capable candidates we should request for assignment here."

Kinovic's face brightened at this idea, and Fajora's heart missed a beat as she recognized her mistake. While she evaluated students for agent potential, Kinovic would be considering which ones had a leaning toward the shadow. New agents were so vulnerable to the subtle ideas the respected head of an enclave planted in their heads. Some would fall for his deception unless she managed to create a buffer between him and them. She made a mental note to add more activities to the trainees' schedule—keep them so busy Kinovic had no chance at them.

"Don't think I don't know what you're doing." Kinovic lowered his voice, adding an undercurrent of threat.

Fajora started. Were her thought processes so obvious? She schooled her emotions, charging her eye flecks to behave themselves.

"Sir?"

"You undermine me at any opportunity. Whatever I ask for, you do the opposite. You seem to think this enclave is yours. That you can win the junior agents' loyalties and thereby ensure your position. You put on your innocent face so boldly. And you have Dannel and his vile colony in the palm of your hand, covering for you at every turn. But I know." The snarl returned to his voice, and Fajora made a swift scan of her office, trying to reassure herself she was in the enclave and not back in that hideous house in Rock Clan with its denizens full of hate and abuse.

"I know you weren't innocently studying prophecy at Haven outpost while the humans treated Fazok for his mysterious illness. The two of you seized the opportunity to do secret work behind my back. Grooming the clans for some wild scheme. I have it on good authority you killed a Dark Spinner during that time, in clan territory, and without authorization."

Kinovic's voice became more heated as he spoke. Tendrils of shadow swirled around his hand as it lay on the armrest of the chair.

"What authority?" As she spoke, Fajora closed her eyes for an instant to clear her vision, and when she opened them, she saw nothing suspicious. Had she imagined it? She didn't think so. Kinovic's frustration edged him closer to losing control.

"That's none of your business." He might hint, but he wasn't giving away how much he knew about Fajora's recent mission to free Clarise and Sebastian. Not yet. But among Dark Spinners known for their subtleties, Kinovic lacked the finesse of a master deceiver. He faltered under the pressure of pretending to be something he was not. Fajora must keep pressing now.

"It is my business if you are accusing me of misconduct. Reveal your source or desist in these accusations, sir."

"I won't be manipulated by. . ."

The door flew open and Trayle flounced in, then stopped, bringing her hand to her mouth.

"I'm so sorry, sir, ma'am. I didn't realize you had someone here, I mean, I didn't know the head was . . . . Oh, I'm making a mess of this, aren't I?"

"Did you need something, Agent Trayle?" Fajora fought to keep her voice neutral and avoid revealing her relief. If Kinovic gave in to the shadow, Fajora needed Trayle here to witness it. But it might have been better if she had waited a minute or two. Kinovic's jaw was clenched and his eye flecks swirled in murderous patterns, but the darkness that had begun to creep over his visage had cleared.

"May I borrow a book from Fazok's library?" Trayle glanced toward the bookshelves lining the room. "And I had a message, or something, for the head. I could tell him, now he's here and I'm here. I just have to remember."

"Get your book and get out." Kinovic spoke in clipped tones.

"Yes sir. But I'll think of that other thing in a minute. I'm sure of it."

Trayle went to the other side of the room and withdrew a book from one of the shelves, appearing to have an intense interest in it, though she angled herself so Kinovic remained in her peripheral vision. Kinovic watched her with a scowl for a moment before turning his attention back to Fajora. He stood, placing his hands on her desk and resting his weight on them as he leaned toward her.

"As I said, I know exactly what you're doing." He kept his voice low to avoid being overheard. He didn't know how sharp Trayle's hearing was. "I'm keeping records of everything you say and do. Soon, I'll have enough to request your removal from Kakislane. Then none of this will matter. Dannel Crowner will lose his lackey, and the enclave will be mine."

What could Fajora say to this? The dark antithesis to her thesis of light, Kinovic would do everything in his power to limit her days on Kakislane. And he had considerable power. She could only avoid a reassignment by giving him as little fuel as possible and hoping he accidentally revealed the shadow in his being in the presence of witnesses. So, she said nothing.

Trayle was not so reticent, but as usual, she responded in a way Fajora could never have predicted. She closed her book with a bang and pushed it into its spot with exaggerated movements, ensuring she had the attention of both Fajora and Kinovic. Then she pranced the few steps across the floor to Kinovic's side.

"It doesn't have the information I wanted. I'll get it later if I decide I need it. But the good news is, I remember what that thing was, about the head, about Agent Kinovic. Sir, I found out something interesting about you." She reached a hand toward Kinovic. She brushed his sleeve with the tips of her fingers, and he shrank away as if she rubbed him forcefully with a contaminant. "Oh, don't worry." Her voice brightened, unabashed. "It's a good thing. I found out your birthday is in two days. Can you imagine?" She turned to Fajora with a baffled headshake. "He hasn't said a word, not to anyone, as far as I can tell. How are we supposed to celebrate when he keeps mum about this?

"But everything's arranged now. You're going to have a birthday to remember, sir. Just you wait." She hesitated, her eyes growing large. "Oh, I forgot. We wanted to surprise you. But no matter." She shrugged and her grin flashed out. "You'll never guess all the arrangements, so those will be a surprise." And she giggled, the most disconcerting, un-agent-like sound Fajora had ever heard from her lips.

Kinovic's mouth had drawn into a hard line as Trayle prattled, and his eyes smoldered. Fajora watched him for the smoky tendrils of spinning shadow, ready if Trayle finally pushed him over the edge. But he pulled himself together and straightened, giving Trayle a venomous glare.

"Stop this foolishness." His voice held a hard warning. "I neither need nor want a birthday celebration. And what classified records have you been sneaking into, that you even know this?"

Trayle's grin never faltered, despite his harsh reprimand. "Oh, nothing classified, sir. There's a list—everyone's birthdays and such. Didn't you know?"

Her voice trailed away as Kinovic stomped out of the office, slamming the door behind him so hard the building shook. Trayle's shoulders relaxed and she scooted onto the corner of Fajora's desk. Sitting on one's superior officer's desk constituted a terrible breach of protocol, but Fajora was learning to let these things slide when she and Trayle were alone.

"Where'd you get such an idea? Kinovic's birthday?"

"But it really is his birthday, day after tomorrow. As close as we can get, anyway, accounting for time and date differences between here and Luxera. And we've got the party all planned. He'll be the toast of the enclave."

"He'll hate it."

Trayle's grin became wicked. "I'm counting on it."

Fajora smiled despite herself, then frowned. "I guess it will be an irritant he can't do anything about but fume privately. But be careful, pushing this hard. He's a dangerous man."

"I know." Trayle's grin faded and her eye flecks marched in a somber cadence. "I didn't sign up to be safe. None of us did. We're fighting Dark Spinners. That's the mission. I doubt he's any more dangerous than the DS other agents fight on Sek-Nar or Merdoma. I won't let up now. I'm certain if I push hard, he'll break. He's close already."

"Yes. It's time to be extra careful. Keep pushing him, but make sure our contingencies are in place. Always a back-up or two. For protection and to make sure we have the witnesses we need when he does break. I'm not sure what we'll see when he's finally had enough."

"I am." Trayle jumped down from her perch and walked to the door, a bounce in her step. With her hand on the latch, she turned her grin on Fajora one more time. "When everyone, including him, least expects it, he's going to get angry and lose control. And then we'll see some dark spinning." She drew out the last two words with a flourish. "I've always wanted to see spun shadow. Been waiting for a chance to take down a Dark Spinner. It's time I did what I trained for. Need the splash. Not just me. All of us."

She jerked the door open and disappeared out into the slanted evening sunshine. Fresh air poured into the office along with the sound of birdsong. In the distance, an owl called. Fajora rose and stepped outside to listen. The call came again, from the west side of the compound, beyond the cottages.

She pulled her door closed and headed toward that side of the enclave. She might catch a glimpse of the owl if she hurried.

A young male agent rose from a bench in front of her office and followed at a discreet distance. She resisted telling him to leave her alone. They all needed to take these precautions, those who had secretly signed on to expose Kinovic. Fajora needed to adhere to them most of all, for she would be his first target, and any action he took against her would provide the best chance to get the evidence they needed.

She found the owl a short time later. It sat on a high branch in a tree behind her own cottage and peered at her with round yellow eyes. A series of vocalizations suggested an attempt to communicate with her.

"I don't understand you," she called softly. "If I'd stayed with the cats, I might have learned your language, but I am needed here. If you see my friends in Deep Valley Clan, carry my greeting, please."

The owl gave a few final hoots before launching itself from into the evening sky. It was time to hunt. It carried whatever it knew from this place without revealing it to her.

She surmised it knew many astonishing things. Useful things, perhaps, and surely wondrous things. The cats, too, knew things she had never imagined. She had been too much like Kinovic, smug in her own understanding of the world. But her eyes had been opened. To the things she did not know as much as to what she knew.

One thing she did know. Or maybe two. First, she would seek Ya-Lohim's light, even when she wasn't sure what else she should do. Thinking of light, she reached for it and let it spark in her fingers and travel up her arms. She savored its warmth and the rightness it engendered in her soul. She called up additional light, spinning it, playing with it, until she almost entirely translated from physical solidity to pure light. With a sigh of contentment, she let it dissipate, secure in the knowledge of the light, confident in her ability to access it when she needed it.

And the second thing she knew? Her work here no longer centered on Jayzam and vindication. It centered now on the colony and the clans and the nestings, and on all the individuals within these groups. As long as the service allowed her to stay here on Kakislane, her task at hand was to protect the lives and the cultures here with all her resources.

She committed herself to this, in part, because of her love for the life on this world. But, just as much, she made this commitment because the

Dominion needed these people—the human scholars and technologists and administrators, the clans of cats with their secret knowledge and sense of destiny, the owls with their deep mystery and beauty and the talents she had not yet discovered. When the darkest days came, as the prophecies promised, everyone would be needed, and it might be what the cats of Kakislane knew that made the greatest difference in bringing light to a dark and troubled world.

Darkness descended rapidly now. Fajora turned to walk to her cottage, finding the path by instinct in the low light. She paused and turned for a moment toward the center of the enclave, looking down to the administrative complex, reduced to dim shapes in the growing dark. She didn't need light to know how the complex appeared, nestled in a hollow, surrounded by the residential buildings on higher ground.

On her first day back on Kakislane, she had imagined it as a self-satisfied entity, smug and arrogant, a place that made her vaguely uneasy. But now she knew the young agents that lived and worked here, Light Spinners offering her their lives to help dislodge and destroy the shadows and evil that had taken root in enclave soil. She knew them, and she knew this place was vibrant with their belief, their dedication.

Above all, it was a battleground. The enemy was strong and subtle, but Fajora had recently come from another battleground and tasted victory. She was confident victory would be hers again, soon.

As Fajora turned away from the enclave center and headed for her cottage door, a dim shape detached itself from the shadow of a neighboring cottage, and her young attendant drew near. "Are you all right, ma'am?"

"Yes, Joxas. I'm heading in for the night. You may do the same."

"Thank you, ma'am. But excuse me, ma'am. Were you talking to that owl?"

"Yes, Joxas. I was."

"And was it . . . ? Did I imagine it, or was it talking to you?"

"Yes. Unfortunately, I didn't understand what it said. Its language is a mystery to me."

After a serene pause, Joxas answered. "It doesn't matter, does it? The owl knows."

"The owl knows," Fajora repeated softly. "And the cats know."

Their knowledge remained a mystery for today, for next week, perhaps for years, as they waited, laboring in secret with the patience of wild ones for the day of revelation. Then they would rise above the violence, darkness, and deceit of their world, and their greatness and honor would be known not only on Kakislane but beyond, in the realm of the stars and throughout the Dominion. Fajora might be here, or she might be long gone, but she would have done her part to protect this world and its secret knowledge.

Fajora hummed as she prepared for bed. She had a quick snack while she read a passage from the prophecies, and she gave her hair a good brushing before turning back the bedding. She switched off all the lamps but the one beside her bed, and she crawled in and plumped the pillow. With the last lamp finally out, she lay in the dark remembering.

But instead of pursuing fond memories of her courting days with Jayzam, or of the times when her children snuggled around her or played on the hillsides of the farm on Luxera, the memories that came to her now were of a young man bent over his viewscreen while he scribbled notes about obscure and exciting ideas, and of a young woman offering healing while her own body was wracked with pain. And the last memory, as she drifted into sleep, was of her hand running through the soft fur, bronzed in the sun, of a cat who, of all the amazing, unimaginable things, could read and counted himself her friend.

THE END

AUTHOR'S NOTE

If you're wondering about—

Yes, I know. I've left some things hanging at the end of *What the Cats of Kakislane Know*. You may be wondering if Fajora will ever unmask Kinovic and how their conflict will end. But that is the subject of another tale.

I first uncovered the conflict between Fajora and Kinovic as I was writing a duology about a Light Spinner trainee named Zovala. The duology follows Zovala and Keyar (the same Keyar you may have met in *Tendrils of Shadow)* in a Dominion-wide chase as they pursue a Dark Spinner named Vorkan. Vorkan has a scheme to disrupt the prophecies and shatter any hope that Light will triumph over shadow. Zovala and Keyar follow him to Sek-Nar, where the white dragon, Aknar, shares her wisdom with Zovala.

Aknar sends Zovala to Kakislane, where she meets Dannel, Sonja, and Fajora, and must deal with the deceptive practices of enclave Head Agent Kinovic. But will she be able to unmask him and send him off to Yellaz prison, or will he be one more complication in her quest to foil Vorkan?

While I was writing the first draft of the duology, I became interested in Fajora and decided to explore her story. That exploration led to *What the Cats of Kakislane Know,* but I couldn't resolve the Fajora/Kinovic conflict, because I knew that was part of the duology. So have patience, my friends. The first book of the duology should be out in late 2024, and your questions will be answered.

If you are curious about the timeframe of my Seven World Dominion history and how *What the Cats of Kakislane Know* fits in with my other stories. I've anticipated that curiosity. I am developing a timeline which I will include in future books but will also upload to my website as soon as it is ready. Then I will be able to update it as the saga develops.

I have not forgotten about Sebastian and Drissy, whom I've left behind in cat territory. I have more to share with you about their stories. To receive updates on when the duology and other stories will be available, as well as when the timeline is ready, sign up for my monthly newsletter at my website: www.eileenrhickman.com.

I hope you enjoyed reading *What the Cats of Kakislane Know* as much as I enjoyed writing it. I hope you take the time to learn more about the real owls and large cats of our world that inspired the owls and cats in my story. They aren't exactly the same—I took a lot of creative license—but they are magnificent and mysterious creatures. The more I learn, the more fascinated I become, and I think you will too. You might start with *What An Owl Knows* by Jennifer Ackerman or *Path of the Puma* by Jim Williams. I highly recommend both books, and there are many others you can try.

The important thing is to always keep reading,

Eileen

AKNOWLEDGEMENTS

To my family and friends, and especially to my children and my ever-supportive husband, thank you for your constant encouragement on this journey to bring the cat clans to the world. To my friends in the Colorado Springs chapter of ACFW—you constantly point the way along the writing path. Having friends who understand this journey has been invaluable. Thank you.

A huge thank you to my Beta Readers, Alan Pfaff, Brittany Thiel, and Janice Addis-Weber. First you encouraged me. Then you found all this story's flaws and plot holes and helped it find its shape. I'm not sure what it would have been without you, but I know it would not have been as good. I give it to the world with confidence because of your careful reading and honest feedback.

A heartfelt thanks to the wonderful, creative professionals who have contributed to the book. Annie Douglass Lima, your editing was invaluable. Your knowledge and hard work helped me take this manuscript from messy to something a lot closer to polished, and I'm grateful to you And to Jenneth Dyke—thank you for another fabulous cover design.

And finally, to my Creator and Lord, thank you for the gift of story, and for giving me grace, strength, and skill to tell the particular stories you have favored me with.

IF YOU ENJOYED THIS BOOK--

If you enjoyed *What the Cats of Kakislane Know*, please consider leaving a review at your favorite retail platform. It will help others find and enjoy this story. Thank you.

You may also enjoy Eileen's novella, *At the Boundary Between Daylight and Shadow*. Find it at your favorite on-line retailer or ask your local brick and mortar bookstore to order it for you. As a bonus, the book includes the short story, *Tendrils of Shadow*.

To get updates on new stories in the Seven World Dominion, sign up for Eileen's monthly newsletter at www.eileenrhickman.com. As a thankyou gift, you'll receive the free story, *Dragon Light*, which introduces you to the first world in the Dominion, Sek-Nar.

While you're at the website, check out the Seven World Dominion page to learn more about some of the worlds in the Dominion, including Fajora's world, Kakislane.

ABOUT EILEEN R HICKMAN

Eileen's favorite books are Fantasy or Science Fiction, so it was natural for her to start writing tales that bridge the divide between the two genres—a lot of Fantasy elements with a Science Fiction vibe. Her stories take place in her Seven World Dominion, and she delights in discovering new things about this many-faceted cosmos.

When she isn't writing and world-building, she's reading, making music, watching Star Trek, or traveling the world with camera in hand. She lives with her husband on the Colorado Front Range.

The foundation for her storytelling, and for everything else she does, is her faith in God. A committed Christ follower, she seeks to honor him in all she does and in every story she tells.

www.ingramcontent.com/pod-product-compliance
Lightning Source LLC
Chambersburg PA
CBHW031237310726
48971CB00004B/1058